W9-BEH-726

Once Upon a Nervous Breakdown

PATRICK SANCHEZ

KENSINGTON BOOKS
http://www.kensingtonbooks.com

KENSINGTON BOOKS are published by

Kensington Publishing Corp.
850 Third Avenue
New York, NY 10022

Copyright © 2007 by William Patrick Sanchez

All rights reserved. No part of this book may be reproduced in any form or by any means without the prior written consent of the Publisher, excepting brief quotes used in reviews.

All Kensington titles, imprints and distributed lines are available at special quantity discounts for bulk purchases for sales promotion, premiums, fund-raising, educational or institutional use.

Special book excerpts or customized printings can also be created to fit specific needs. For details, write or phone the office of the Kensington Special Sales Manager, Kensington Publishing Corp., 850 Third Avenue, New York, NY 10022. Attn. Special Sales Department. Phone: 1-800-221-2647.

Kensington and the K logo Reg. U.S. Pat. & TM Off.

ISBN-13: 978-0-7582-1002-9
ISBN-10: 0-7582-1002-7

First Kensington Trade Paperback Printing: August 2007
10 9 8 7 6 5 4 3 2 1

Printed in the United States of America

Once Upon a Nervous Breakdown

Praise for the Novels of Patrick Sanchez!

ONCE UPON A NERVOUS BREAKDOWN

"*Once Upon a Nervous Breakdown* is absorbing and fun, with characters as distinctive and realistic as they come. Patrick Sanchez has written a phenomenal story that will not only make you laugh out loud, but also touch the deepest parts of your heart and soul. Don't miss the chance to root for Jen, a woman boldly balancing the world (or at least her mother, her son, her friends, and a gay ex-husband) . . . and searching for the happiness—and the sanity—she truly deserves."
—Kelley St. John, author of *Real Women Don't Wear Size 2*

"*Once Upon a Nervous Breakdown* reels you in with a vivid picture of thirty-something life—fun, frenzied, and feverishly juggling love, family, friends, and career. Patrick Sanchez is a great storyteller who, once again, has created a world of witty, smart, and identifiable women who jump off the page."   —Frederick Smith, author of *Right Side of the Wrong Bed*

"*Once Upon a Nervous Breakdown* illuminates the sometimes humorous and sometimes challenging daily struggles of the every-woman. Patrick Sanchez pays a positive tribute to today's thirtysomething working moms in his latest literary touchdown."
—Johnny Diaz, author of *Boston Boys Club*

"This 'Nervous Breakdown' is actually an uplifting breakthrough for anyone who reads it! The first page alone will make you clench your heart in agony, yet giggle at the same time. Patrick has a magical way of making every character adorably flawed, yet genuine to the bone. What I love the most is that this story sheds a comical and sentimental light on moms, daughters, dads, divorcees, the gay community, and those crazy-ass, over-the-top friends and family members we all have in our lives. I've been a fan of Patrick's books from the start, and *Once Upon a Nervous Breakdown*, by far, is my favorite. It's not too heavy, not too fluffy—it's skillfully balanced in the 'just-right' center. Yes, a five-hankie/triple-giggle page turner indeed!!!
—Kathy Cano Murillo, syndicated columnist and author of *Crafty Chica's Art de La Soul*

"Did a man actually write this novel? Patrick Sanchez has an amazing ability to get inside the head of women. His female characters are so real—they feel just like my friends . . . except much more interesting. *Once Upon a Nervous Breakdown* is wickedly entertaining. It'll have you saying about the main character, Jennifer Costas: 'What? No she didn't!'"
—Cindy Rodriguez, *Denver Post* columnist

"By turns bittersweet, insightful and naughtily funny, *Once Upon a Nervous Breakdown* perfectly captures one woman's struggle as she tries to cope with the highs and lows of life as a daughter, mother, ex-wife, friend, and career woman. Patrick Sanchez's keen eye for detail and ear for dialogue made me sniffle, laugh, and blush page after page."
—Margo Candela, author of *Underneath It All*

**Please turn the page for more outstanding praise
for the novels of Patrick Sanchez!**

TIGHT

"A frank comedy of manners that exposes both the highs and lows of the modern quest for youth and beauty." —*Kirkus Reviews*

"In his delightfully catty, fast-paced new novel *Tight*, Patrick Sanchez explores our culture's obsession with cosmetic surgery, and proves without a doubt that he is the top male writer in the American chick-lit genre—and one of the best writers in the genre, period. With zippy prose and fabulous dialogue, Patrick tells the stories of realistic, endearingly flawed characters. A wonderful read! I loved it."
—Alisa Valdes Rodriguez, *New York Times* bestselling author of *Playing with Boys*

THE WAY IT IS

"A witty tale about single women searching for friendship, unconditional love and the perfect dessert." —*Booklist*

"Lots of drama and truly hilarious moments make this a fast, enjoyable read that readers will devour!" —*Romantic Times*

GIRLFRIENDS

"Clearly taking his cue from Candace Bushnell and Helen Fielding, Sanchez's style is light and entertaining." —*Publishers Weekly*

"Grab your girlfriends and read *Girlfriends*. Who knows what will happen!" —Rita Mae Brown, *New York Times* bestselling author

"If Armistead Maupin and Terry McMillan collaborated on a novel, *Girlfriends* would be the result . . . It is a fast, funny and surprisingly moving romp through the urban singles scene . . . Patrick Sanchez has written a wildly entertaining first novel."
—Todd D. Brown, author of *Entries from a Hot Pink Notebook*

"Straight girls, gay girls and all the people who muck up their lives! What a great thrill ride of a book for all the girls—immensely readable—you'll pass this one around."
—Suzanne Westenhoefer, HBO comedy star and author of *Nothing in My Closet But My Clothes*

"*Valley of the Dolls* meets *Bridget Jones* via *Three Coins in the Fountain!*"
—Michael Musto, *The Village Voice*

an online love affair with some other woman came to mind. But after he and Andrew were asleep, curiosity got the best of me, and I snuck downstairs and checked the history feature in Microsoft Explorer. To my surprise, Mario had been visiting a host of travel sites, most of them related to vacations in Hawaii. Hawaii!!!

Then, a few days later, I couldn't help myself and snooped through his briefcase while he was in the bathroom. I opened a manila folder and saw a printed copy of an e-mail confirmation for plane tickets to the South Pacific. Mario never takes long in the bathroom, so I didn't have a chance to look the document over thoroughly and, maybe a part of me really didn't want to know any more. Even though I knew about the trip, I thought it might be nice for at least the details to still be a surprise.

After I collect Andrew from daycare and drop him off at the house of one of his playmates, I drive the rest of the way home with visions of Mario and me lying on sun-drenched beaches, Mai tais in hand, and palm trees swaying in the distance. I think of the new clothes I'll have to buy, arrangements that I need to make to stop the mail and see that the plants are watered, and I guess I'm also wondering if I have to find a sitter for Andrew. I'm not sure if Mario has planned to make this a family vacation or more of a second honeymoon. Normally, I could leave Andrew with my mother. She used to be the most reliable sitter in the world. She adores Andrew, but since my father died a few months ago, she hasn't been herself, and I'm not sure I feel comfortable leaving Andrew in her care for an extended period. She turned seventy-three two months ago, and up until my father's passing, she was the picture of health. But, since he died, she's developed diabetes and Dr. Miller says her heart is showing signs of weakness. She's also been forgetful and tired and even more cranky than usual.

It's been a hard year for all of us with my father passing, and me being left to look after my mother alone. I have a brother, but he lives in Florida with his wife and two kids and could barely be bothered to fly in for Daddy's funeral. I rarely hear from him and neither does my mother. With all the family and work stress that has been idling around, I think a tropical vaca-

Prologue

I'm so excited. I've just had this feeling that something big is about to happen—a feeling that was confirmed when my husband, Mario, phoned this morning and asked if I could arrange for our son, Andrew, to be out of the house this evening, so we could be alone to talk. Apparently, he has something "very important" to tell me. I know that he wants his news to be a surprise, but unbeknownst to him, I'm already aware of what he plans to tell me.

A couple hours after the phone call, on my lunch break, I went to Victoria's Secret to find something seductive to wear to bed tonight, after Mario tells me about the surprise. I tried on a few different things—I wanted something revealing that would make me look sexy but, at the same time, not draw attention to the few extra pounds I haven't been able to drop since I became a mother. I ended up buying a lavender silk nightie that I plan to don after Mario tells me about the trip.

Things have been a little tense between Mario and me for a few months. I've been so busy at work, and Mario has been sort of distant, and maybe a little depressed. I broached the subject with him a few weeks ago, and he assured me that nothing was wrong. We talked a bit more about how we needed to make an effort to spend time together and maybe rekindle our romance. Little did I know, Mario would take our discussion to heart.

A week ago, I stepped into the den while Mario was working on the computer, and he quickly closed his Web browser, obviously not wanting me to see what he was viewing on the Internet. It concerned me a bit, especially considering how distant he has been lately—everything from an addiction to Internet porn to

tion is just what Mario and I need, and I'm about to burst with anticipation when I come through the door of our home, a four bedroom colonial a few miles outside Washington, D.C., in Alexandria, Virginia. Mario is sitting on the sofa, anxiously awaiting my arrival.

"Hi," I say, eager to pretend to be totally surprised about the trip and to hear the details about it.

"Hey," he replies as I sit down on the sofa next to him.

"So. You have news?" I literally cannot get the eager smile off my face. I can already smell the suntan lotion and taste the piña coladas I plan to drink out of many a coconut.

"Yes . . . yeah . . . I do." He looks nervous and sort of apprehensive.

"So?" I look at him with wide eyes, like a little girl on Christmas morning.

"I don't know how to say this, so I guess I should just come out with it."

"Okay."

He looks down at the floor and is quiet for a moment.

"Oh, tell me already!"

"Jennifer," he says to me, before pausing for a moment. "I'm gay."

1

I'm lying in bed, staring at the clock radio as an old Mariah Carey song wails from the speaker. I want to hit the snooze button so bad, but I know I can't. If I'm not out of bed within five minutes, it will throw my whole schedule off for the day. With the radio blaring, I let my eyes shut for just a second or two before summoning all my willpower and pop them open again. I fold the covers over, sit up in bed, and put my feet on the floor.

It's January 2, and, I must say, I'm grateful to have the holidays over and done with. Not that I'm a Grinch or anything, but December is such a busy month—the shopping and the cooking and the gift wrapping and the social obligations just exhaust me, and waiting for Mario to arrive before Andrew can open his presents on Christmas morning just reminds me that we're a broken family. But I guess it's all worth it when I see Andrew's face light up when he opens his presents.

I'm particularly tired this morning. I stayed up late last night taking down the Christmas tree and our other decorations and hauling them up to the attic. Life is so busy these days, I knew if I didn't get the decorations down last night, it may well be spring before I get around to it.

"Get off the bed, Jennifer," I say to myself. "Once you're in the shower, the hardest part of starting the day will be over."

The air in the house is cool and dry as I step into my slippers and scurry across the hardwood floor toward the bathroom. I shut the bathroom door behind me, rest my hands on the sink, and take a look in the mirror. I wish there was some way I could make all the mirrors in my house disappear until I've had a shower, done my hair and put some makeup on. I don't know when the exact day was that it happened, but sometime, a year or two ago, I started looking really haggard when I first get out of bed. I've got bed head, and sleep lines on my face, and the area under my eyes is swollen and puffy. I'll be thirty-six next month. Should a nearly-thirty-six-year-old woman really look this hard first thing in the morning? What happened to the days when I could get out of bed and still look presentable? In college, I stayed up half the night, sometimes studying . . . sometimes partying, and the next day I'd sling my hair up in a ponytail, throw on a pair of sweats, and head to class. Now I hate to leave the house without at least a little concealer on my face, so I don't scare any little children.

When I get out of the shower, I wrap a towel around me and open the door. I listen for a moment to make sure I don't hear anything that would lead me to believe that Andrew is up. On weekdays, he usually sleeps until I jostle him awake, but every now and then he gets up before me, and being the independent five-year-old that he is, he has a tendency to get into all sorts of trouble when he's not supervised.

I blow-dry the front of my hair (the back will have to dry on the way to work) and brush my teeth. "Much better," I say to my reflection once my hair is under control and I have some makeup on. After I get dressed, I sneak past Andrew's room, so I can start the coffeemaker and maybe have about five minutes of alone time before I wake him up.

"Crap," I say out loud when I see the dirty dishes still in the sink from last night. I was too tired to be bothered with them before going to bed. I start the coffeemaker, and, while that's going, I rinse the dishes in the sink and place them in the dishwasher. When the coffee's ready, I pour myself a cup, take it into the family room, and try to enjoy what may be the only "me time" I get all day. I sip the warm coffee and stare out the back window and watch a squirrel scurry by. *God, even the squirrels are in a hurry,* I think to myself as I take a breath and lift myself off the sofa.

I head back upstairs and softly step inside Andrew's room. I watch him sleep for a moment or two. I love to watch him sleep . . . to see him so peaceful and relaxed.

"Time to get up, Sport," I say and jiggle his shoulder.

He slowly opens his eyes, looks at me, and then closes them again.

"Up, up, let's start the day." I start to pull the covers off him, but he grabs them and tries to keep them over himself.

"No. I'm too sleepy."

"Come on, big guy. I'll make you some hot chocolate, and we'll turn *Jimmy Neutron* on the TV in the kitchen."

"Grandma's hot chocolate?" he asks, now a bit more receptive to getting out of bed.

"No. Swiss Miss," I say much to his dismay. My mother makes this killer Colombian hot chocolate with whole milk and solid pieces of chocolate, but there's no time for all that this morning.

"Do we have marshmallows?"

I laugh. "I'm not sure."

"I'm not getting up unless we have marshmallows."

"Ah . . . *yeah*, you are." My tone is starting to change a bit to show him I mean business.

He gives me a cross look and sits up in bed. "Can we stay home today, Mommy?"

"I wish we could, sweetheart . . . more than you know." I look at him in his soft cotton Spiderman pajamas and give him a big hug like he's a plush snuggle bunny. I can understand him wanting to stay home. He has an awfully long day for a five-year-old. He goes to all-day kindergarten and then attends the after school program until I can pick him up at six. "Go downstairs and get yourself a bowl of cereal, and I'll be down in a minute," I say before I let go.

As he wanders out of the bedroom with his hair sticking up, I open up his closet and take out a pair of his navy blue uniform pants, a long sleeve white dress shirt, and a blue sweater, which make up his uniform for St. Paul's Elementary School, where he attends kindergarten. I lay the items on the bed with some dark socks and a pair of Batman underwear.

I'm about to grab his school shoes from the closet floor when, suddenly, I think I smell smoke. I walk into the hallway, and I can see smoke wafting up the stairs.

"Oh, my God!" I run down the steps toward the kitchen as the smoke detector begins to sound. When I make it to the kitchen, I see Andrew throwing a glass of water over the flaming stove.

"Move back, Andrew! Move back!" I say and run past him to the pantry. I grab the fire extinguisher and point it toward the stove, but when I press the lever nothing happens.

"Shit! Shit!" I turn the canister to read the directions, flames rising higher on the stove.

"Stop, hop, and roll," Andrew yells at me. "That's what they taught us in school . . . stop, hop, and roll!"

I glance over the directions and see something about removing a pin from the handle, which I do. Then I aim it again, press the lever, and a spray of white mist comes out of the hose and douses the flames in just a few seconds.

When the fire's out, and I've turned off the stove, I look at Andrew quivering in the corner of the kitchen. I walk over to him, get on my knees and shake him by the shoulders. "What were you doing?! What happened?!"

"I was trying to make the hot chocolate," he says, tears coming to his eyes.

"I've told you to never touch the stove . . . *never* touch the stove."

"I'm sorry, Mommy," he says. "I tried to put the fire out before you got mad."

"I'm not mad." I'm making a conscious effort to sound calm,

which is hard with the smoke detector still going off in the background. "I'm glad you're safe, but don't ever touch the stove again. Do you understand me?"

"Yes."

I give him a hug. "I mean it, Andrew. This could have really been a lot worse than it was."

"Okay," he says back to me. He's obviously learned his lesson, and he looks so frightened that I don't have the heart to lecture him anymore. "Go upstairs and put your clothes on while I let some fresh air in here."

I open the window in the kitchen, reset the smoke detector, and then survey the damage to the stove. Thankfully, aside from the mess made by the fire extinguisher, the only damage seems to be to the oil-laden frying pan Andrew was going to use to make hot chocolate. I grab the handle of the pan with a pot rag and toss it in the trash can. I guess I now have to add "buy a frying pan" to my to-do list. As I start wiping up the mess, I have one of those guilt moments: What was I thinking, leaving a greasy frying pan on the stove? What if I hadn't gotten down here when I did? What if Andrew had gotten too close to the flames and his pajama sleeve caught on fire or . . . I start to tremble at the thoughts coming into my head.

"Will we get to stay home today now . . . because of the fire?" Andrew asks, interrupting my thoughts as he comes back into the kitchen with his sweater on backwards.

I let out a quick laugh. "No, Andrew. I'm afraid not." I bend down and reach for the bottom of his sweater. "Arms up." Andrew lifts his arms up, and I pull the sweater over his head. "What have I told you about the tags in your shirts?"

"That they should always be in the back."

"That's right," I say and pull the sweater back over his head and help him get his arms into it. Then I run a comb under the faucet and try to tame his hair. "Go get your coat, sweetie. We need to get moving," I say, pulling the window down, but not closing it entirely. I'll have to leave it slightly open to let the rest of the smoke escape while we're gone and just hope that no bur-glars will be running around the neighborhood looking for slightly ajar windows.

As Andrew scurries off to get his jacket, I give the stove one last look to make sure all the knobs are turned to off and that no little cinders are left from the fire. I'll have to really clean up the mess when I get home. I just don't have time right now. By the time I drop Andrew off at school, I'm already going to be late for work. I had wanted to stop by the dry cleaner this morn-ing as well, but I guess I'll have to put that off until tomorrow.

"All right, I'm ready," Andrew says with a defeated tone in his voice. I think he wants to stay home today even more than I do.

I can't help but smile at him as I grab my own coat.

"What's funny?" he asks, noticing my grin.

"Nothing."

"No. Why are you laughing?"

"I'm not laughing. I was just smiling because you're such a cutie . . . a cutie who'd better not touch the stove anymore," I say as I open the front door. "And Andrew, it's stop, *drop,* and roll, not stop, *hop,* and roll."

"Oh, yeah," he responds as we make our way out the door and into the freezing January air.

We're about halfway to school when Andrew pipes up. "Mommy, you forgot to feed me breakfast."

"Oh, you're right." With all the excitement this morning, I forgot that Andrew didn't get his morning cereal. Then, as I'm thinking about what a horrible mother I am for sending my child off to school with no breakfast, we see the McDonald's we pass every morning coming up on the right. I realize that it's probably not a coincidence that Andrew mentioned me forget-ting his breakfast just as we are about to pass McDonald's.

"Maybe we can stop at McDonald's," he suggests as if this idea just occurred to him. I bet the little stinker consciously de-cided not to remind me about his cereal before we left the house. He loves McDonald's and knows that the only time I'll take him there is when I'm in a big rush.

"All right," I say and turn to look at him, telling him with my eyes that I know he tricked me into this. I want to laugh again as I watch him get the look on his face that he conjures up when he wants to appear innocent.

"You play me like a fiddle, you little scoundrel," I say with a grin as we pull up to the drive-through window.

2

"I'm putting my foot down, Mario," I say into the phone. "I'm not bringing Andrew with me to the show."

"I think he'll get a kick out of it."

"I don't care. I'm glad that you're comfortable with yourself and all this, Mario. But I just don't think Andrew is at an age at which he needs to see his father in a wig wearing my old Oscar de la Renta beaded evening gown."

"I'll make sure he knows it's just for fun . . . just something I do once a year to raise money for charity."

It's not like Mario is a full-blown drag queen or anything (at least not to my knowledge). He and some friends are just planning on donning women's clothes and lip-syncing to Jennifer Lopez and Christina Aguilera to raise money for Food and Friends, the Whitman Walker Clinic, or some other charitable organization, but still, it's hard enough for *me* to see him like that—I used to be married to him, for Christ's sake. I don't think it's a vision that our five-year-old son needs of his father at this point in his life.

"I'll think about it."

"All right," Mario says. The tone in his voice tells me that he knows I didn't mean it, which I didn't—I have thought about it . . . for about two seconds, and the answer is a big fat no. "I'll be by to get him for the weekend tomorrow. Is six o'clock okay?"

"Yeah. That should be fine. I'll have him ready to go." And, as I hear myself speak, I have that same haunting vision that loves to swirl around in my head—the vision of Andrew walking out the front door with his backpack to spend the weekend with Mario. At least I don't cry immediately after he leaves anymore. Mario and I split up almost two years ago, and, since then, Andrew spends every other weekend with him. The first time I had to send Andrew off for a weekend stay with his father, I managed to hold it together until he left the house, but as soon as Andrew was out of sight, I broke down sobbing. I wasn't so much sad that Andrew was going to be gone for a weekend. I knew it was only for two days and, quite honestly, I could have used a child-free weekend. It was more that, at that moment, it really hit me that my son was now from a broken home and would be one of those kids who's juggled between two parents. My heart sank as I stood at the door, watching Andrew, with his *SpongeBob SquarePants* suitcase, walk to the car with Mario. He looked like he should have been cast in one of those *Kramer vs Kramer*-type movies—it was a heart-breaking moment.

I hate that everything is so complicated for Andrew now. I hate that he will have to say "they're divorced," when other kids ask about his parents; I hate that he'll never have another Christmas when he wakes up in the same house with both his parents; I hate that he may end up with stepparents and half brothers or half sisters at some point. I never wanted it to be this way for him . . . I never wanted it to be this way for me.

Mario and I say good-bye, and, as I hang up the phone, I think about when we first met. It was more than ten years ago. I was twenty-four and just starting out in the workforce, and Mario was a junior at George Washington University. We were both volunteers for Crisis Link, a crisis and referral hotline for the D.C. metro area. I volunteered with the hotline because I felt like I was too self-absorbed at the time—like I was just focusing on me and my career and putting money in the bank—so I started looking for a way to give back to the community. Mario, on the other hand, was a college psychology major who thought a stint at a crisis hotline would look good on his grad school applications.

The hotline had a very intensive training process. We had to go to class a couple nights a week for three weeks and do all sorts of telephonic role plays. On the second night of training, Mario and I were paired to do a role play. I had to pretend to be a caller who was distraught over the death of her dog, and Mario was the crisis-listener. I went into full acting mode and got very emotional as I talked about losing my pooch and how hard it was going to be to carry on without him. Mario responded like a pro, using all the "reflective listening" skills we had learned in training. "Reflective listening" essentially means you regurgitate whatever the caller is saying and spit it back at them. I would say "I'm so angry . . . I'm angry at God for taking my dog from me. I just can't go on." And Mario would respond with, "I'm hearing that you're angry. You're feeling that you're even angry with God . . . that you feel that you can't carry on." That's all we were allowed to do at the hotline. We could never actually offer insight or advice. We could only try to interpret the feelings the callers were espousing and offer our interpretation back to them.

Even though Mario was really only telling me the same things I was telling him, he had this kindness and understanding in his voice. He seemed so nice, and it didn't hurt that he was young and cute with wavy brown hair and deep brown eyes. As we went through the role play I could see the other women in our small group looking at him, thinking about how sweet and good-looking he was, probably jealous that I was the one who actually got to be paired with him for the exercise.

When the role play was over, Mario smiled at me, we went back to our chairs, and I didn't really give him much thought. He was a few years younger than me and still in college, so, despite my attraction to him, he didn't really seem like a "tential." Tential (short for "potential") was a word my girlfriends and I came up with for guys who we were not only attracted to, but were also potential dating or husband candidates. Of course, we always saw men whom we found appealing, but one of a number of things could keep them from being tentials—maybe they were absolutely gorgeous but didn't have a decent job or any career ambition, or maybe they were really nice but very unattractive. Tentials were guys who were the whole package—guys that had everything we wanted in a man—needless to say, we didn't come across too many of them.

I have to say, it was quite a surprise, when, one day at work I got a call from Mario. He'd gotten my number off the volunteer phone list. He sounded just as nice (and cute, if people can sound cute over the phone) when he asked me out, and, even though I hadn't really thought of him as someone I would date, I immediately said yes.

We went to T.G.I. Friday's for our first date. I remember it like it was yesterday. I had the shrimp scampi, he had a New York strip, and we shared some sort of chocolate dessert. He made me laugh as we talked about some of the people in our training class at the hotline and how weird some of them were or how oddly some of them dressed. Maybe his love of gossip and critiquing people should have raised a flag or two about his sexual orientation, but the thought never crossed my mind. Gay people just were not on my radar back then—there wasn't as much gay stuff in the news or gay characters on television in the early nineties like there is now. As far as I knew, at that point in my life, I had never even really known a gay person.

Even though I liked Mario and found him attractive, I was leaning toward making our first date our last (and I often wonder how life would have turned out if I actually had). I think I had decided that he was too young for me. Even though he was only three years my junior (I was twenty-four, he was twenty-one), we were in two different phases of life. He was still in college with almost two years left to go, and I was already pushing my way through corporate America.

It was a nice spring evening when we left the restaurant, and I still remember him asking me if I'd like to take a walk around the mall. Thinking that maybe we should just call it a night, I replied, "I don't think so. I'm one of the few girls who actually hates shopping."

He laughed. "No, not the *shopping* mall," he said. "The Mall, downtown. You know, the National Mall . . . the monuments and stuff."

There was something about the way he looked when he laughed at me, a gleam in his eyes maybe, that made me change my mind about ending the date.

"That might be nice," I replied and off we went toward the city.

I grew up only about fifty miles outside D.C., in Fredericksburg, Virginia, but aside from the occasional grade school field trip, I'd never really taken an interest in the museums and monuments in the city. Accordingly, my first date with Mario was also my first time to the Jefferson Memorial. Who would have thought that a staid old monument could be romantic? But on a balmy September night, sitting on marble pillars as we looked out on the Tidal Basin, there was something in the air. We sat there and talked for hours and got to know each other. When he offered his jacket to me as the air started to chill, that's when I began to think this could really be the start of something. By the time he leaned in and kissed me, I was hooked. Who would have guessed that years later, I'd be on the phone talking to him about a drag show in which he planned to perform.

3

It's nine o'clock, and I've just gotten Andrew tucked into bed. I'd like to sit on the sofa and watch a couple of the shows I've TiVo'd over the past few days . . . maybe catch up on some *Oprah* episodes or see what's happening on *The Young and the Restless*, but I'm just too tired. I don't know why I bother recording shows at all. I never get around to watching them.

I'm about to go upstairs and get into bed myself, but I have to do one thing first—call my mother. Before my father died, we only talked about once a week, but, since he passed away, I've been calling her every night to check in on her. I usually call her much earlier in the evening, but the day got away from me. I pick up the portable phone from the counter and dial her number. It rings a few times before she picks up.

"I'm not dead," she says in lieu of "hello."

"Good to know." She swears the only reason I call her every night is to make sure she isn't dead (which isn't *completely* untrue). "How was your day, Mom?"

"It was fine," she replies, her thick Colombian accent coming through loud and clear. She's been in the U.S. for more than forty years now and, although her English grammar is perfect, she will never lose her accent. "Not much to report when you're stuck in the house all day. Lifetime moved my shows around again. They replaced *The Golden Girls* with that show about the homosexual and the Jewess."

"There must have been something else to watch. You have more than a hundred channels."

Thanks to diabetes, Mom's eyesight isn't good enough to drive anymore; accordingly, she spends a lot of time alone in the house, so I had digital cable installed for her a few months ago. This is the first time in her seventy-five years that she's had cable TV. She has a plethora of channels to choose from, but, aside from watching *The Golden Girls* on Lifetime, she rarely strays from her staples of soap operas ("my stories" she calls them), Colombian telenovelas, and game shows that she's been regularly watching for the last few years.

"It's all garbage. One hundred channels of garbage. If I see that little Paris Hilton–hussy one more time I'm going to throw a brick through the TV screen."

I laugh. "What about the Discovery Channel? They have a lot of programs I'll bet you'd like."

"What channel is that?"

"I'm not sure offhand. If you turn to channel two it will tell you."

"Is that the channel where the schedule constantly rolls on the screen? It goes way too fast for my poor vision."

"Yeah. I don't know why they make it go so fast," I lie. I was actually just wondering why it went so painstakingly slow the other day when I wanted to know what was on channel 61, and I turned the TV on just as channel 62 rolled to the top of the screen.

"Are you coming by tomorrow?" Every day, she asks if I'm 'coming by tomorrow.' I generally go over there twice a week, on Saturday mornings and on Wednesdays after work. On Saturdays, we run errands to the grocery store and the bank and the mall. Then, on Wednesdays, I usually drive out there for an hour or so, chat for a while, and maybe go over some bills or other paperwork that has come in the mail. I feel like I should go by more often, but she lives a good hour away from me (and that's if traffic is moving), I've got Andrew to look after and a full-time job, and there are only so many hours in the day.

"No, not tomorrow. I'll be by on Saturday. Do you need me to pick up anything for you before I come?"

"No. I don't need much. I'm doing okay." She says this, but when I arrive, she'll insist that she's out of all sorts of necessities and will want me to drive her all over town to get laundry detergent, or new sheets for the bed, or some new product she saw on TV and just has to have. She doesn't like me to pick up things for her before I come over, so she tells me she has everything she needs when we're on the phone and then changes her story when I get there. She only gets out of the house a few days a week, so she likes to have all sorts of places for me to take her when we go on our outings. I know it's hard for her to be dependent on other people for her transportation needs. She lives in the outlying suburbs where there is little public transportation available, so, aside from a couple of her friends who stop by now and then, it's pretty much up to me to be her chauffeur.

I hated to take away her driving privileges, and I felt like some sort of evil stepmother doing it, but I had no choice. By the time she'd had fender-bender number four, I told her I wanted to take a ride with her. Up to that point, since my father passed away, I had always driven when Mom and I went somewhere together, so it had been quite some time since I'd been a passenger in her car. We went on a simple outing to the mall, and, during the brief half-hour excursion, I was absolutely horrified by what I experienced. She went straight through a stop sign as if it wasn't even there, came just shy of rear ending most of the cars she stopped behind, and, at one point, she almost killed both of us when she turned into the mall parking lot just as another car was racing down the opposite side of the highway. Her vision was clearly not good enough to drive, and she seemed to have a general sense of oblivion to everything that was happening around her on the road.

After a long and heated discussion, I confiscated Mom's car keys and later arranged for her car to be sold. She was furious at me for weeks afterward even though I'm certain she knew it was the necessary thing to do. She hated to give up her freedom as much as I hated becoming her personal limo service, but unfortunately, we both had no choice in the matter.

Her dependence on me to get around is just one of the reasons I've broached the subject of her moving to a retirement home where she could have more transportation options and a lot more social interaction, but you would have thought I was suggesting she slice off her finger from the reaction I got. I think she has a hard time separating *retirement* home from *nursing* home. I wasn't talking about a nursing home or even an assisted-living facility—I meant a building where she would have her own apartment and live independently, but also be able to dine in a community dining room, attend socials and workshops, and have assistance when and if she needs it. But she wanted nothing to do with any of it. And I can certainly understand her wanting to stay in her home of thirty years, but I know she's lonely, and I only have so much time that I can spend with her.

"Okay. Well, I just wanted to check in with you before bed. Call me if you need anything, and I'll see you on Saturday."

"Okay. See you then."

We end our call, and, for a moment, I stand in the kitchen and can't help but think of a more pleasant time when Mom was independent and healthy, and we could talk about more than what's on television or which one of her prescriptions is troubling her. Our conversations used to be much more interesting, although many of them were more arguments than conversations. Mom and I have always had a different way of thinking about things. I think a lot of our differences stem from her being born and raised in Colombia and me being born and raised in America. My parents left Colombia in the nineteen-sixties, but they, my mother in particular, didn't leave their Colombian way of seeing the world behind. Most of the conflicts between Mom and I are rooted in her ideas about how a proper girl should behave. I wasn't allowed to go on dates until I was sixteen years old, and, when I did, my mother fully expected me to have a chaperone. A chaperone didn't necessarily have to be an adult, but Mom was convinced that it wasn't proper for me to go on a date with a boy without at least one of my girlfriends along as well. On the hottest days, when even the nuns at my Catholic school allowed us to do away with our uniforms and wear shorts, my mother forbade it. She didn't believe in me moving out of the house until I was married, and the idea of premarital sex was so far out of the realm of possibility that it wasn't even discussed. But I was an American teenager, and I refused to adhere to what I considered her "absurd" rules—rules I thought to be particularly ridiculous and unfair because none of them applied to my older brother, Tom. He was allowed to go on dates without a chaperone, wear shorts to school, and my parents had no problems with him moving out of the house whenever he wanted. My parents hadn't quite caught on to the American idea of raising sons in the same manner as daughters. I was always held to stricter rules in all areas except one: my education. While my parents valued education for both my brother and me, they clearly placed more emphasis on Tom's academic success. It was almost troublesome to them that I excelled at school, and Tom squeaked by with mediocre grades—girls were supposed to marry intelligent men, not necessarily be intelligent ourselves.

Doing well in school wasn't the only way that I perplexed my parents. At first, I quietly rebelled against their rules. I'd wear shorts under my skirt, and then just take the skirt off when I got to school on hot days, or I'd lie and say that a friend was accompanying me on a date to meet their chaperone requirement. But, by the time I was sixteen, I basically said to hell with it, and openly defied them. At some point, I just decided that their rules were unfair and silly, and I was no longer going to patronize them. My father was aloof and didn't pay that much attention to my rebellion, but Mom didn't cave quite so easily. She had a fit the first time a date picked me up at the house without a third party along to supervise us. She actually cried (something she was able to do on cue) as I was leaving the house, which I'm sure she did more to make me feel guilty than because she was sad. She'd try to ground me if I stayed out past my ridiculously early curfew, but I'd just ignore the grounding as well. And to this day, I have no regrets about how I behaved. In retrospect, I was a pretty well-behaved daughter. I did well in school, I never did drugs, I rarely drank before I was of age, and I was in college when I lost my virginity. My mother's restrictions really were ridiculous, and I would have had virtually no life at all if I hadn't disobeyed them.

"You don't respect me." I can still hear those words coming out of my mother's mouth over and over again.

"I do respect you, Mom," I'd always reply. "It's your crazy rules that I don't respect."

"We never had these problems with your brother."

"That's because Tom's allowed to do whatever he wants."

At some time during the conversation Mom would always say, "I never should have given you such an American name," as if my name was at the root of our problems. With my brother, my parents went with a traditional Latino name and called him Tomás. But when I was born, they had been in the country for almost five years, and my mother decided she wanted me to have an American name. And, at the time I was born, it seemed that everyone was naming their baby girls Jennifer. In fact, Mom saw an article in the newspaper that mentioned that Jennifer was the most popular baby name for girls the year I was born. And, right then, she decided I was going to have the most popular American name. Of course, she didn't think of the fact that there would always be at least four or five other Jennifers in every one of my classes from grade school to high school to college, which really became a pain in the ass, but that's another story.

"My name has nothing to do with anything," I'd always say.

"Marta. We should have gone with Marta." This was my mother's warped sense of reality. I think she honestly believed that if she had given me a more traditional Colombian name, that I would have been more submissive and obedient.

Even today, when she's annoyed with me, which isn't a rare occurrence, she still brings up the whole name thing. But now it just makes me laugh and actually makes me long for a time when her believing that a name had any impact on my behavior was the only way she confused fantasy with reality.

4

"Did you buy stuff to make cookies for the bake sale?" Andrew asks me as we come through the front door of the house.

"I sure did." I'm hoping that Andrew won't be upset that I just bought the refrigerated dough that you break off, plop on a cookie sheet, and throw in the oven. His school is having a bake sale to raise money for something—I have no idea what. Andrew came home with a notice about it a week ago, but I was too tired to read it thoroughly. I only scanned it quickly enough to realize that I'd have to come up with something resembling home-baked goods.

"Why don't you go in the bathroom and wash your hands while I put the rest of the groceries away, and then we'll make the cookies."

"Okay," he says and heads toward the steps while I unpack the groceries and set the cookie dough on the counter.

"I'm ready to make cookies," Andrew says a few minutes later, and I turn around and see that he's grabbed my apron from the hall closet. "Can I wear this? I wore an apron when we made cookies over at Betsy's." Betsy is a playmate of Andrew's. She's a year older than him and lives a few houses down from us. Betsy's mother doesn't have a job, and whenever Andrew goes over there, he comes back with stories of extravagant craft-making and cooking projects that make me feel like a slug.

"I think it's too big for you, sweetie." I pull a stool up to the counter. "Hop up."

Andrew climbs up on the stool and looks at me suspiciously as I open the wrapper around the dough and pull it out. "Now, you get to pull the little pieces of dough apart and put them on the cookie sheet." I'm trying my best to sound like it's really more of a process than it actually is.

"This isn't cookie making," he says and looks at me for a response.

"Sure it is," I lie. "We can watch them bake up in the oven." *We can watch them bake up in the oven?* Surely I can do better than that.

"I don't want to watch the dumb oven. When we made cookies at Betsy's, we used flour and sugar and stirred it all up with a big spoon."

I want to say, "Yes, but those are called stay-at-home-mommy cookies. We're making mommy-is-so-tired-she-could-drop-to-the-floor-right-now cookies." Instead, I offer, "I'm sure you did, but these are so much better." I lie again, and he sees right through me.

"They are not! You're making them 'cause they're easier."

Busted! "I'm sorry, sweetie. Mommy's very tired from a long day, and I didn't know exactly what we needed from the store to make cookies from scratch, so I figured we'd make the best of it with the pre-made dough. No one will know the difference. I promise."

"Make 'em yourself." Andrew gives his nose a crinkle, hops off the bar stool, and leaves the room.

"Andrew, you get back here! You don't talk to Mommy like that," I call behind him. He ignores me, and I'm too tired to pursue him, so I finish putting the lumps of dough on the cookie sheet, click on the oven, and put the whole thing inside.

While the cookies are baking, I find Andrew sitting on his little chair facing the television, which is turned off. I walk over in front of him. He's sitting with his arms crossed and a disdainful expression on his face. Kids learn how to be dramatic so early in life.

"I'm sorry we didn't get to make cookies the way you wanted to. I'll try to plan better next time, but tonight, this was the best I could do."

He turns his eyes up toward me, but not his head.

"What do you say we make a big batch of popcorn . . . and not the microwave kind. We'll use the popper, and then we can watch one of your movies."

Immediately his eyes widen and a little smile comes over his face. "Okay," he says, and we are about to walk back into the kitchen when the doorbell rings.

"Who could that be at this hour?" Andrew says, sounding very adult. I'm sure he heard someone on TV say the same thing.

"Let's go see."

We walk toward the foyer, and I look out the peephole when we reach the door. I see a small black woman, and, although I can't make out her facial features through the peephole, I'd know her hair anywhere. I quickly open the door.

"Desma! What are you doing here?" I'm sure I'm smiling as wide as the Cheshire Cat. I love Desma . . . even if only in limited quantities. Desma and I were roommates in college, but I haven't seen her in years. Last I heard she was running around New York City taking photographs of homeless people and trying to get her pictures showcased in art galleries throughout the city.

"Jen, honey, I'm in town for the protest." I love the way she says "honey," all long and drawn out . . . huhhhhney.

I'd ask what protest she's talking about, but I don't want Desma to know I'm unaware of whatever protest is going on in the city at the moment. When you live in the D.C. area, you pretty much get immune to protests and marches and demonstrations. It seems like there's one every weekend tying up traffic and causing a ruckus. One week it's gay rights, then it's anti-gay rights . . . then it's the Million Man March, then it's the Million Mom March. And after every demonstration everyone argues about how many people actually attended each event. The organizers will say eight hundred thousand people participated while the park service will say it was more like one hundred thousand—like it matters . . . as if some bigot in Mississippi is going to change his stance on gay rights or women's issues or whatever because of the number of people who showed up to some demonstration in a city miles and miles away.

It's embarrassing how out of touch I am with regard to current events, but who has time to watch the news? Besides, it wouldn't surprise me if Desma doesn't know what the protest is for either. She goes to so many of these things, she probably can't keep track of them herself. If there's a demonstration going on, you don't have to tell Desma what it's for, just tell her what time to be there.

"Oh . . . for the protest. Good . . . good," I say. "Well, get in here." I swear her unruly curls almost brush against each side of the door frame as she steps into the house. She's only about five feet two inches tall, but, let me tell you, she's a five-foot-two powerhouse. I pity anyone who tries to rail against her.

You wouldn't know it from looking at her, with her wild tangle of black curls and the worn looking jean jacket she's sporting, but Desma comes from money. Her father was actually a delegate or a senator in the state government in New Jersey where she's from, but she's been on the outs with him for years. Her father is a Republican, and, to Desma, an African American Republican is like a Jewish Nazi.

"Oh, my God!" she shrieks with her trademark big smile and squats down to Andrew's level. "Is this little Andrew? Oh, who am I kidding? Of course this is little Andrew. Come here and give Aunt Desma a hug."

Andrew just stands there and looks at her. I think he's afraid of her. Desma is a lot for a young child to take in at once. She's just plain loud—the way she speaks, you'd think she assumes the whole world has a hearing impairment.

"He's shy," I say as Andrew continues to look at her like a deer caught in the headlights.

Since Andrew isn't going to come to her, Desma decides to go to him. When she reaches him, she gives him a big hug, and I swear Andrew wants to take off running.

"My God, how you've grown. You were just a wee baby when I saw you last."

"Yeah. I think that's the last time I heard from you," I say with a grin, chiding her for being out of touch for so long. Although I guess it's not really just *her* fault. I haven't exactly moved mountains to try to get in touch with her either, but at least I'm stationary—Desma knows where to find *me*. Trying to locate Desma at any given moment is like trying to find a natural body part on Victoria Beckham.

"Jen, honey," she says. "Do you think I can stay here for a little while? I've got the protest this weekend, and then I thought I might hang around town and take some photos . . . see if anything inspires me." That's Desma for you. She goes straight to the punch. Most people would make a lot of small talk before asking if they can crash at your place for a few days—God I hope it *is* only for a few days—but not Desma. She isn't one for beating around the bush.

"Of course," I say, and I can feel my neck tightening as the words fall from my lips. Like I said, I love Desma . . . I do, but she can also be a royal pain in the ass. When she said she might hang around town for a few days, it could very well mean that she wants to stay for a few days, but it could also mean that she will be sleeping in my guest room for months. She's a nomad, always going from one place to the next, and staying in some places much longer than others. But I guess it would be nice to have an adult around the house to talk to about something other than *The Suite Life of Zack and Cody.*

"Oh, thank you, Jen! I have all my stuff out in the car." "All her stuff" generally amounts to a backpack with a few articles of clothing and some underground newsletters about the government being out to get us all. "We'll have so much fun. We'll catch up, and stay up late, and I'll help you take care of Andrew."

I can see the look in Andrew's eyes. *The crazy black lady is staying?*

"Sure," I say and almost start to lose my apprehension. Desma has a way about her. You're forced to like her because of her big smiles and her outgoing demeanor, but I've known her for a long time, so I'm not as easily taken in by her bravado. She has a way of getting people to agree to anything with her charm. And she really does have good intentions. It's just that she's so scattered and goofy, when it comes time to deliver on her promises, she's moved on to some other initiative in which she'll probably lose interest in a few weeks.

"I'll be right back. Let me grab my things from the car."

Andrew and I watch Desma walk out the door, and I give his shoulder a squeeze.

"So, Desma is going to stay with us for a little while. You'll like her. She's fun," I say, and it *is* true. Desma is fun, but Desma is a lot of other things . . . some of them good . . . some of them, well . . . not so good.

5

"Hi, Mom. How are you doing?" I ask as I come through the front door of her house.

"I'm doing okay," she says. I'm sure this story will change over the course of the afternoon, and I'll hear about her arthritis acting up, or how she's convinced the Koreans next door are kidnapping the cats in the neighborhood and cooking them up for dinner. "I thought you were going to be here at eleven," she adds, disappointment in her voice.

"It's ten after."

"I need to go to the bank, and it closes at noon on Saturdays, you know."

"We have plenty of time. The bank is ten minutes away. Why don't you grab your coat, and we'll get moving."

"I don't think we're going to make it," she says and lifts her coat off the sofa.

"Sure we will."

I walk out of the house ahead of her and make my way to the car. As I open the car door, I look back and see that she is still descending the three steps in front of the house. I sometimes forget how slow she moves these days and have to remind myself to cut my stride by more than half so she can keep up with me.

When she finally makes it to the car and gets inside, we go through the whole seat belt issue. She grew up in a generation that never used seat belts, and, although she's finally stopped moaning and groaning when I insist that she put it on, for some reason, she still has a terrible time getting it around herself and clicked into place. First, she feels all over God's creation on the right side of the seat trying to find the end of the belt, and, when she finally does, she pulls it around her like it's attached to a fifty-pound weight. Then she starts jabbing it around trying to find the holder. The whole process seems to take forever, but I always resist the urge the grab it from her and click it into place myself. I don't want to embarrass her or make her feel helpless, so I usually play with the radio or go ahead and start to pull out of the driveway while she gets herself situated.

"That damn cat is back," she says, when she finally gets the seat belt in place and sees an orange tabby approach her front steps.

"How long has it been coming around?"

"I don't know. He seems to be out front every time I open the door. I just can't get him to go away."

"You're not feeding him, are you?" I ask.

"Jennifer, I *have* to feed him. I can't let him starve."

I laugh and start to back out of the driveway.

"Oh my," she says a few minutes after we get on the road. "They're going to close, Jennifer. Then I won't be able to deposit my check until next week."

"We have plenty of time. Just relax. If you'd just let them direct deposit the check, you wouldn't have to worry about making it to the bank at all." Mom still gets my father's pension check (and her Social Security check) in the mail, and we take it to the bank once a month and deposit it. I know there is no point in me even suggesting that she have the check directly deposited into her account. We've been over it enough times, and she's always getting letters from my dad's company asking her to switch to direct deposit, but she won't hear of it. She's been getting a hard-copy check in the mail for years, and that's the way it's going to continue.

One time I actually did show up too late to get to the bank on time, and I foolishly suggested we use the ATM to deposit her check—you would have thought I had suggested that she give the check to aliens and ask them to drop it by the bank on their way back to Mars. She wouldn't even *have* an ATM card if the bank hadn't sent it to her, and I hadn't insisted that she keep it just in case there was an emergency, and she needed cash when the bank was closed. After I convinced her not to cut it up into a zillion pieces and throw it away, she taped it to the floor underneath the big rug in the living room so "no robbers would be able to find it and clean out the account." I explained that the card has a daily withdrawal limit, and that she wouldn't be liable for any money taken if the card were stolen and all that good stuff, but it wasn't enough to ease her mind.

"So after the bank, what else is on the agenda for today?"

"I'd like to go to the grocery store . . . and to the mall to get some new sheets and then to the hair parlor to get my hair set. And then we need to stop by the CVS, so I can pick up a box of candy to take to Dot for her birthday." We go to CVS every week to pick up a box of one of those quasi-gift-wrapped boxes of chocolates for Mom to give as a gift to someone. She swears by them. "Who doesn't like chocolate, and it's already wrapped up nice and pretty," she says before adding, "And you can't beat the price."

I'd suggest that she buy three or four of them at a time, so we don't have to keep going back to CVS, but I know she'd make up some excuse about how they'd go stale or something. Mom likes to stretch out our Saturday afternoon outings with as many stops as possible, so I'm sure a weekly pit stop at CVS will remain on the itinerary.

"So then I guess we need to stop by Dot's, so I can give her the chocolates and wish her a happy birthday. I haven't seen her in months." She pauses for a moment before starting again. "She was quite the athlete in high school. Remember how she always wanted to play baseball with the boys and finally ended up starting the first girls' softball team at our school? You remember that, Clara, don't you?" she says to me with a distant look on her face.

"Hello! Earth to Mother," I say, with an awkward laugh. "Clara is your sister, Mom. I'm your *daughter*. You went to school in Colombia. And you've only known Dot for a few years."

She gets a look of recognition in her eyes. "Oh, yes," she says. "I was spacey there for a moment."

We're both quiet for a second or two, and there's an uncomfortable feeling in the air. "That's okay. I get spacey myself all the time."

"Huh . . . really?" she asks.

"Sure. I even call Andrew by the wrong name sometimes," I lie. I do my share of spacey things, but to my knowledge, I haven't called Andrew by the wrong name.

Mom looks out the window and then eyes the clock on the dash. "Jennifer, it's almost eleven-thirty. We may as well forget the bank. We're not going to make it in time. I'll deposit the check next week."

"Oh, dear God!" I say, raising my voice. "It's eleven twenty-five." I take a breath, remind myself to be patient, and soften my tone. "The bank is *five* minutes up the road. Barring some unforeseen natural disaster, we'll make it there by noon." I don't get her vision issues sometimes. She's always commenting on how bad her eyesight is, yet she can see the tiny little digital time display on my dashboard. And she certainly sees well enough to tell me how fat I've gotten or that my hair is all wrong.

"Well, you know how bad traffic can be on Saturday afternoons."

"Would you just chill? I promise you, we'll make it in time."

I don't know what's going on with her lately, but Mom's perception of reality seems to be getting worse by the day. Her concern about getting to the bank on time is just one example of how she inappropriately obsesses over things. A couple of weeks ago she called me at two in the morning because she woke up and was worried about a check I had written for her when we were paying her bills. She thought I'd put the wrong date on it, and it took me several minutes to convince her that the bank would honor the check, and, even if they didn't, it was no big deal—the electric company was not going to shut off her power because she wrote one bad check. She worries about anything and everything these days. If she isn't afraid the grocery store is going to be out of eggs by the time we get there, she's worried that we won't be able to find a parking space at the mall, or that her favorite beautician won't be at the salon when she gets there even though she's made an appointment. It drives me crazy.

We walk into the bank, a full half hour before closing time and get in line behind two other customers and wait for a couple of minutes. When we reach the front of the line, the next available teller calls us to her station, but Mom motions for the person behind us to go on ahead. Mom insists on waiting to be served by Tina, a pretty young girl who Mom swears is the only competent teller in the whole bank. It helps that Tina is patient and always has a few kind words for Mom and asks her how she's doing.

"*Buenos días, Señora Costas,*" Tina says to Mom. Tina's a white girl from South Carolina, but apparently she's taking Spanish lessons through the county, and likes to practice her Spanish, which is probably better than mine, with Mom.

"*Hola,*" Mom says back to her with a smile. "*Cómo está?*"

"*Soy muy ocupado.*"

"*Estoy muy ocupada.*" Mom corrects her. It's nice to know it's not just me Mom criticizes.

"*Estoy muy ocupada,*" Tina repeats back to her. "*Y usted?*"

"*Muy bien,*" Mom says.

I think Tina's voiced most of the Spanish she knows, so she switches back to English. "Just making this deposit?" she asks, taking the check and the deposit slip from Mom.

"Yes. That's all for today . . . won't be getting my Social Security check until next week," Mom responds. "This is my daughter, Jennifer. She doesn't speak Spanish . . . never interested her," Mom adds, taking a jab at me. And, I guess she's mostly right—my Spanish is negligible at best. Everyone is surprised to learn that I'm not fluent when they hear that both of my parents are from Colombia. But, one thing so many people don't understand is that immigrant parents do not *teach* their native language to their children. Their children just happen to learn it because it's what's spoken in their home. And, for the most part, my parents had stopped speaking Spanish in our home by the time I was born. When they came to the U.S., my father, who had gone to a language institute in Bogotá, spoke reasonably proficient English, but my mother spoke next to none. Although she enrolled in English classes shortly after they got here, she rarely tried to practice it, and my father was smart enough to realize that if he didn't force her to speak English, she'd never really learn it. So, he refused to converse with her in Spanish. He demanded that she speak English to him. I believe this decision is the only reason my mother speaks fluent English now. She's so stubborn, and, if she had not been forced, I doubt she would have ever made an honest effort to learn a new language. I'm not sure that my father had intended that his insistence that they speak only English while Mom was learning the language would become a habit. But, nonetheless, by the time I was born, aside from the occasional get together with relatives, my parents were speaking English full time. Accordingly, I rarely heard Spanish growing up, and most of my knowledge of the language comes from the courses I took in high school and college.

"Oh, I've met Jennifer before," Tina says. We've probably met a few hundred times. I bring Mom to the bank almost once a week. I don't know why Mom introduces me to her all the time.

"How are you?" she asks me.

"Just fine, thanks."

Tina does her thing with Mom's check, clicks a few keys on her computer, and hands her a printed receipt. "You two have a good day."

"We will," I respond, and I guess that isn't a complete lie. There are certainly worse ways to spend a day than driving your mother all over the place. Honestly, I wouldn't mind doing it so much if I had more free time. It's just that there are about fifty other things I need to get done. I have to do my own grocery shopping and get my own hair cut. Andrew needs some new uniform pants for school, and I can't remember the last time I ran the vacuum over the carpet at home. I've also got some work I took home from the office to finish up before a meeting on Monday, and I know I'll be too tired to tackle it by the time I get home today. If only there were more hours in the day, or I had an endless supply of energy. But then I guess I could reason that if only my father hadn't died . . . or if only Mom's eyesight and reflexes were still good enough for her to drive . . . if only I won the lottery . . . if only life were perfect. Since none of the above have happened or are likely to happen, I guess I don't have much choice but to do the best I can.

"So, where to next?" I ask Mom, trying to make my voice sound upbeat. I don't want to sound like I'm being put out. I'm not sure if I'm adding the cheerful tone in my voice so I can convince Mom that I don't feel imposed upon by running all these errands with her, or if I'm just trying to convince myself that I don't feel imposed upon by running all these errands with her.

6

As I turn onto my street, I'm looking forward to a quiet evening at home. Andrew's at Mario's apartment for the weekend, so I figure I'll get some of my paperwork from the office done for an hour or two and then just lounge in front of the television until bedtime. I'm loving the idea of an evening with almost nothing to do when I spot Desma's whoopty of a car, which occasionally serves as her home, parked in front of the house. It's a Ford Escort with mismatched fenders that should have been put out to pasture about ten years ago. I'd forgotten that she might be there. There's no such thing as a quiet anything when Desma is around.

"Hello," I say to Desma when I come into the house, trying to hide the fact that I really wish I could have the place to myself.

"Hey," she says, looking up from some papers she's reading. "Did you know that, according to Greenpeace, more than eighty-seven human cultures have been wiped out in Brazil? And, over the next ten years, we could lose thousands of species of plants and animals due to the deforestation of the Amazon?"

"Ah . . . no . . . well, maybe I heard something about it on the news."

"My God, Jennifer! What are we going to do?" she asks with

urgency, like I'm supposed to hop a plane to South America and chain myself to a tree in the rain forest right this minute.

"I don't know about you, but I'm going to tackle some paperwork, take a hot bath, and then set up camp in front of the television for the evening."

"Television?" Desma says, wrinkling up her nose. "You can't spend the night in front of the squawk box."

"Ah . . . yeah, I can."

"Watching TV is a total waste of time."

"And that's a problem how?"

"You shouldn't even have a television in the house. Before you know it, Andrew will become yet another TV-addicted consumer of material things."

I want to tell her that I'd sooner give up my left arm than my built-in babysitter (a.k.a. my television). If I didn't have *Phil of the Future* and *Dora the Explorer* to occasionally occupy Andrew, I'd never get anything accomplished. "I don't let him watch that much TV," I say, and I'm not sure if I'm lying or not. *That much* is a relative term.

"You should try getting him interested in reading. I have a friend in New York who owns a socially conscious bookstore. I can ask him to send some books. He has some great titles for kids. There's one about a lamb who refuses to be sheared and saves his friends from becoming lamb chops. And there's one about a vegetarian dragon and another about a young girl who discovers that her two turkey friends are going to be killed for Thanksgiving dinner and ultimately becomes a vegetarian. There's another one called *Princess Smarty Pants,* about a princess who doesn't want to get married—she wants to stay a Ms. and live happily ever after. And there's one about—"

"Sure. That would be great," I say, trying to quickly make my way to the kitchen before I have to hear any more about bohemian books. I wash my hands in the kitchen sink as I always do when I get home from a long day, and when I go to throw away the paper towel I used to dry them, I open the closet and find that the trash can has been replaced with three different bins.

"Desma," I call into the family room. "What happened to my trash can?"

I hear her scurry from the sofa to the kitchen. "I took the liberty of replacing it with these bins. The yellow one is for glass and plastic and metal, the blue one is for paper and cardboard, and the white one is for stuff the city doesn't recycle."

"Desma, I really don't have time to be sorting my trash—"

"Oh. It's easy. I'll label them for you."

I throw the paper towel in the white bin. "Whatever," I say, knowing I'll ditch her system as soon as she heads back to New York or whatever new locale strikes her fancy.

"It won't be a bother at all," Desma says, pulling the paper towel out of the white bin and putting it into the blue one. "And it's well worth it. By recycling we save natural resources and conserve land. And, you know, it takes less energy to make recycled products, and products from recycled materials create less air pollution and water—"

"Okay, okay. I'll try to throw crap in the right bins." Here I go again, just like I did in college, agreeing with Desma and doing things her way just to shut her up. I remember when I first met her. We were assigned to room with each other our freshman year in college. Even back then, she had a wild afro of long curls and, shortly after being introduced to her, I remember thinking that she was really "neat." She had an air of confidence about her and one of those "don't mess with me" auras. She dressed the way she wanted to dress and wore her hair the way she wanted to wear it without regard to fashions or trends. I, on the other hand, was a nervous young woman just out of high school and desperately wanted everyone to like me.

Our first night together, Desma asked me if I wanted to go to a Young Democrats meeting to kick off the new school year. I told her I was a Republican, and she looked at me in horror.

"How can you be a Republican!? Your last name is Peredo. You're Hispanic," she said in an accusatory tone.

"So?"

"You support the party of good ole white boys? The party that constantly tries to deny women the right to our own bodies?"

"Well . . . no," I said. In reality, I didn't know anything about politics. The only reason I considered myself a Republican was because my father was a Republican, and I thought he was a pretty smart guy. "Is that really true?"

"Of course it's true. You need to come to the meeting with me tonight. We've got to make sure George and Barbara are out of the White House in the next election. President Bush and his thousand points of light bullshit. Yeah, I'll give him a thousand points of light . . . right up the ass."

I was a tad shocked by her words. If I had said anything like that about the President of the United States, whether a Democrat or a Republican, my father would have blown a fuse. He was very proud of his American citizenship and didn't stand for anything unpatriotic.

"Will there be any refreshments?" I asked. If there was going to be free food, I might have considered going.

"I'm sure someone will bring some cookies or something."

I eventually agreed to go to the meeting, and it was quite an experience to see Desma in action, getting everyone all riled up. She truly is a gifted speaker and a natural leader. She blasted President Bush and Bob Dole and a bunch of other big time Republicans of the late eighties. She really had a passion for what she was saying. And she was always able to back up everything she said with statistics (some of them more precarious than others). She's very bright and doesn't have a lazy bone in her body. But as I would soon realize, she has a terrible time staying focused on one thing. She feels passionate about so many things—women's rights, racial equality, the environment, disarmament . . . that she's never been able to choose one cause and stick to it. She's also so busy saving the world that she's never really held a job for any significant amount of time, and, at thirty-five, I'd bet two weeks pay that she has a net worth of no more than a few hundred dollars. In fact, we were only roommates for two years, because she decided to drop out of college after our sophomore year to volunteer for Habitat for Humanity. She traveled around the country helping to build houses for the poor for about six months, until she decided she could be more useful working for the National Organization for Women. She stayed with NOW for a few months, but didn't feel like she was doing all she could for the women's rights movement sitting behind a desk. I think she left NOW to do some sort of AIDS education outreach, or maybe that was when she joined the campaign of some Democratic senator or congressman. I stopped trying to keep track of Desma's career transitions a long time ago.

"So are you really planning on hanging around here all evening? Why don't we go out and try to rustle up some trouble?"

"Desma, my days of 'rustling up trouble' are long over."

"When was the last time you went out and had a few drinks?"

I stop and think for a moment. I honestly can't remember. "I don't know . . . a few months ago maybe," I say, about to head upstairs when there's a light tapping at the front door.

"Hey," Claire says as she opens the door before I reach it, and lets herself in. Claire Edwards is my next door neighbor. She's five years younger than me, tall and thin with large breasts (thanks to Dr. Klein at the Virginia Cosmetic Surgery Center), and has beautiful blue eyes and shoulder length blonde hair.

"Hi," I say. I've known Claire for years, but I'm still not used to the way she taps on my door and comes barging in whenever she feels like it.

"Claire, this is Desma, an old friend from college," I say when Claire and I make it back to the family room.

"Nice to meet you, Desma," Claire says and extends her hand.

"Yes. You, too."

"Are you from out of town? Are you just visiting?" Claire asks, and I know what's coming next. "You're not looking to move here, are you? I'm a realtor if you need any help looking for a place to live."

"She's just visiting," I say, wanting to laugh. Desma probably doesn't know where her next meal is coming from, and Claire is trying to sell her a house? "So what's up?"

"Oh nothing. I just thought I'd drop by and say hello . . . although I guess I was wondering if I could ask you a few questions."

"About?"

"Well . . . I was wondering how you say 'oh, baby' in Spanish."

"Baby is '*bebé*.' I'm not really sure what 'oh' is . . . maybe '*ay*,'" I respond the best I can.

"How about 'harder?'"

"*Mas fuerte.*"

"What about 'You're the king?'"

"'*Tú eres el rey,*' I think."

"How about, 'That's it—eat me, baby?'"

"*What!?*"

"'That's it, eat me baby.' Or maybe 'bury it—yeah, bury it in me?'"

"What's this for?" I ask suspiciously as Desma looks on curiously.

"I met this guy, Julio, at salsa lessons the other night, and he's coming over tomorrow. I thought I'd surprise him by speaking Spanish while we get it on."

"You've got to be joking," Desma says in disbelief, which isn't surprising. If I didn't know Claire as well as I do, I'd think she was joking as well.

"No. I think it'll be hot."

"I can tell you the translation, but it's hard to really translate the kind of phrases you're asking about for the purposes you're intending. 'Eat me, baby' is '*comeme, bebé*,' but I'm not sure that it will convey what you have in mind . . . I don't know, maybe."

"Could you check with your mom? She speaks fluent Spanish, doesn't she?"

"Yes, and she's also *seventy-five years old*. I'm not asking her how to translate sex talk. Just stick with '*Ay, Dios mío*.' You can't go wrong with that."

"Fine. I'll just ask the cleaning lady at my office tomorrow."

"You do that." And the scary thing is, Claire will ask the cleaning lady to translate dirty talk for her. Modesty and inhibition are not two of Claire's strong points.

"So what are you two girls up to?" Claire asks.

"I was just trying to convince Jennifer to come out with me and have a few drinks."

"Oh, that sounds like fun. Can I come?"

"There's nowhere to go. I'm staying in. I've got some work to get done, and then I have an appointment with a hot bath and whatever I can find on cable."

"Maybe we can go to Harry's Tap Room over in Clarenden. It's sort of upscale and there tends to be a few eligible men hanging around the bar," Claire suggests, ignoring my comment.

"That sounds fine to me," Desma replies as if the decision has been made that we are going out.

"Good. Then it's settled. I'll go home and give you two some time to get all hooched up and come back about eight. How does that sound?"

"Sure, we'll be ready," Desma says and looks at me for confirmation.

I reluctantly cave and decide that maybe a night out would be fun, even if I am tired. "All right, but I'm only going for an hour or so."

"Sounds good," Claire says. "Oh, by the way, can I drop Koda off here for a couple hours tomorrow? Julio is coming over, and I'm afraid Koda will give him a hard time."

"Who's Koda?" Desma asks.

"Her one-hundred-and-ten-pound German shepherd. She drops him off here when she has . . . um . . . her male friends over."

"Yeah, he gets really nasty around any man other than Ted."

"Who's Ted?" Desma asks.

"My husband," Claire replies as she reaches for the door handle. "See you in a couple of hours."

7

"I'm telling you—good food, good music, and good sex, those are the three things that make life worth living. If we're going to be deprived of any of them, we may as well lie down and die. I'll be damned if I'm going to be deprived of good sex simply because I'm married," Claire says to Desma. They are in the front seat of Desma's car, and I'm in the back, looking out the window, while Claire responds to Desma's question about why she has a man named Julio coming over for "sex in Spanish" when her husband's name is Ted.

"So why don't you divorce Ted?" Desma asks.

"Because I love him. He's really sweet, and I enjoy being with him. He's just terrible in bed."

"What if he finds out about your lover?"

"*Lovers* . . . with an s," I call from the backseat.

"There're only two," Claire says, turning to look at me and rolling her eyes. "At the moment anyway," she adds before returning her gaze to Desma. "He won't find out. He's quite clueless and works all the time. Besides, we have sort of a 'don't ask, don't tell' policy when it comes to my fidelity."

"Yeah. Claire hopes that Ted never asks, and she certainly never plans to tell."

"You hush back there," she says to me. "Just because you hole up in your house and haven't even tried to go on a date since your divorce doesn't mean you need to get on my case."

"I'm not on your case, Claire. You know I'd never judge you. Your . . . um . . . *extracurricular* activities are your business," I respond and think for a moment about what she said about my chronic lack of male companionship. I guess she is right. I really haven't even attempted to get back into the dating scene since Mario and I divorced. I could argue that I don't have time, but that may not be entirely true. I do have every other weekend on my own when Andrew stays with Mario, but I'm just not interested in going out into the freak show of a dating scene. I'm not twenty-five anymore, and, the older you get, the harder it gets out there and the more baggage everyone comes with. I don't even know where to begin to try to meet someone. I'm certainly not going to start frequenting some twenty-something club where teenagers with fake IDs are having beer chugging contests. And then there's the whole Andrew issue. I don't want to bring men into his life who may only be around for a short while. Dating was hard enough ten years ago when I had more time, wasn't divorced, and didn't have a young son. I can't imagine what it would be like now.

I look down at myself as Desma and Claire continue to chat up front. I'm wearing a pair of black slacks and a burgundy knit top. I haven't gotten dressed for a night out with the girls in a long time, and I must say it was fun to get ready for something other than work or a day taking care of Andrew. After I got dressed and took the time to blow out my hair and put on some makeup, I looked in the full length mirror in the hallway and was not completely aghast by the way I looked. I'm about five feet seven inches, and, at one hundred fifty pounds, I could certainly stand to lose a little girth, but my body's in okay shape, and hopefully these black pants I have on are slimming.

"Why so quiet back there?" Desma calls to me while eyeing me in the rearview mirror.

"Who can get a word in edgewise between the two of you?"

Desma laughs, but her demeanor suddenly changes as she continues to look in her mirror. "Shit!" she says.

I turn around and see a cop with his lights flashing behind us.

"What's he want? I'm not speeding," Desma says as she pulls over to the side of the road.

"Look innocent," Claire says as we wait for the cop to approach the car. "Should I unbutton my blouse?"

Desma glares at her as she rolls down the window. "I hope you're joking. Women should never use our sexuality to get what we want—it's positively primitive."

"Hey . . . God gave us all sorts of gifts and tools to help us get what we want. What's the harm in using them?"

Desma's about to respond to Claire but doesn't have time to say anything before the cop reaches the car.

"Good evening, ma'am," a stern-looking police officer says to her in a deep voice. "License and registration, please."

"Is there a problem? I'm certain I wasn't speeding," Desma says as she reaches over Claire's legs and rummages through the glove compartment to find the registration.

"I didn't stop you for speeding, ma'am."

"No?" Desma hands him her driver's license and registration.

"No. I stopped you because of the bumper sticker on the back of your vehicle."

"Oh?"

"Yes. Ma'am, you can't have a bumper sticker on your car that says 'Don't be a . . .'" He stops for moment. "That says 'Don't Be a C-U-N-T, Vote Democrat,'" he says, spelling out the c-word.

"You have that on the back of your car!?" I call from the backseat. "The car that's been sitting in front of my house for the last two days?"

"My understanding is that we have a right to free speech in this country. Or is that yet another civil liberty the Republicans have taken away?"

"This isn't about free speech. This is about having an obscene word displayed where anyone can see it. If you remove it now, I'll let you go with a warning."

"Do as he says," I tell Desma from the backseat, knowing it's highly likely that she won't. She turns and looks at me, and I give her a look that says, "I know you don't have the money to pay whatever fine is associated with this sort of thing, and I'm not paying it for you." She faces forward again and thinks for a moment.

"Fine," she says and starts to get out of the car. "I swear . . . we live in freakin' Nazi Germany."

"You can have 'don't be a jerk' or maybe even 'don't be an ass,' but not a C-U-N-T," we hear the officer tell her as they walk to the back of the car. Claire and I watch through the back window until most of Desma disappears after she squats down to remove the bumper sticker.

"Asshole," she says as she watches the policeman in the rearview mirror when she's back in the car with the door closed.

"He's not an asshole, Desma. You can't have vulgar words displayed on your car. I wouldn't want Andrew seeing a bumper sticker like that."

"Why not? Is it not true? Republicans are—"

"Republicans are *what*?" Claire asks. "I'm a Republican, you know. And proud of it."

"Big surprise there," Desma says, a certain amount of hostility in her voice.

"No discussing politics," I interject. "It puts people in a bad mood. Now, you two play nice."

My words seem to shut them up, and we're mostly silent for the rest of the drive. When we finally arrive at Harry's Tap Room, the place is packed. It's a two-story restaurant in a trendy neighborhood in Arlington, Virginia, just minutes outside Washington, D.C. The crowd at the bar is a mix of ages, ranging from kids in their mid-twenties to people in their thirties and forties. Luckily, one of the coveted tables in the bar area frees up just as we walk in. Claire and I nab it before anyone else has a chance, while Desma goes to get us on the list for a table in the restaurant.

"It's going to be at least an hour," Desma says as she sits down. "Could this place be any whiter?" she adds with a snarl as she looks around. The crowd *is* probably ninety percent white. "And, my God, it's nothing more than a slaughterhouse," she continues as she eyes a little bar menu on the table. "Burgers, steaks, chicken, crab cakes. I guess I'll be having a plain salad once we get a table."

"Oh please, with your figure, you can eat whatever you want," Claire says, not realizing that Desma's concerns about the menu are related to cruelty to animals, not vanity. "Besides, if you're worried about your weight, just do what I do: eat whatever you want, then just vomit it all up afterwards," she adds with a laugh.

"Are you making a *joke* about *bulimia*?" Desma questions, a harsh expression on her face. "Bulimia is a very serious disorder. Do you know how many women die from it every year?"

Claire gives me a "is this chick for real?" kind of look. "Ah . . . well, no," she responds, at a loss for words. "I guess we better get some drinks over here," she adds, probably just as an excuse to get away from the table and Desma's glare. "I'll make a run to the bar. What are we drinking, ladies?"

I'm about to say a Sex on the Beach, but last time I mentioned one of those, Claire made fun of me and said people haven't been drinking Sex on the Beaches since 1985. "Just get me whatever you're having."

"How about pomegranate martinis all around?"

"Sounds good," I say, and Desma nods her head.

We watch Claire sashay toward the bar, and I wonder how long it will take her to come back. Knowing Claire, she'll strike up a conversation with a handsome man, and Desma and I won't see her again for hours.

I look around the bar and inhale the air laced with perfume and cigarette smoke, and it reminds me of all the time I spent in clubs when I was in my early twenties. I'm sure most of the places I used to frequent are closed now. There was a place called The Cellar, a big dance club where I spent many a Saturday night, and Chief Ike's Mambo Room where coworkers and I used to go after work for happy hour, and Heaven and Hell, which had an eighties dance party on Thursday nights. I remember going out three or four nights a week . . . the beer, the rum and cokes, the occasional one-night stand. God, that seems like such a world away. I can hardly imagine a time when I had only one person to worry about—me.

"Jennifer Costas?" I hear from behind me as I'm lost in thoughts of days as a young single woman.

I turn around. "Ben!" I say with recognition. "How are you?" I get up from my chair and hug him.

"Good . . . fine. How funny to run into you."

"Yeah," I say, cognizant of Desma watching us. "Um . . . this is my friend, Desma. We went to college together . . . many moons ago."

"Hi," Desma says and shakes his hand before turning to me. "I've got to run to the restroom." She does this thing with her eyes that says "you go on, girl . . . get you some."

"So what have you been up to?" I ask him. "It's been years."

Ben and I used to work together when I was an HR Generalist for an accounting firm downtown. He had a few troublesome employees in his department, so it seemed like I was always meeting with him to go over human resources issues. We got to know each other pretty well and even went to lunch every now and then, but I lost touch with him after I left the company to take my current job in the personnel department of a national law firm.

"I'm still at good ole Saunders and Kraff . . . managing one of the auditing departments now."

"Oh, a promotion." I touch him on the arm. "That's great!"

"Yeah. I guess," he says with a smile. He looks just as good as when we'd worked together. He's probably just shy of six feet tall, with light hair, blue eyes, and a lean build. I think he's a couple of years younger than me, maybe thirty-two or thirty-three.

"So you're just out with your friend tonight? Leave the husband at home?"

I offer an awkward smile. "Mario and I are . . . well, we're no longer together."

"Oh. I'm sorry to hear that."

"Yeah . . . things happen." Yeah, things like your husband being a frickin' homosexual. "What about you? Are you still seeing . . .

I can't remember her name." And I really can't remember her name. I recall Ben dating someone fairly steadily when we worked together, but I'm not sure how serious it was.

"You're probably thinking of Kate. God, I haven't seen her in more than a year."

"I guess a lot has changed since I left Saunders and Kraff. You got a new position and a new girlfriend."

"New job, yes. New girlfriend, no. I'm single at the moment."

"Really? Are you here by yourself?"

"Sort of. I live right up the street, so I stop in and have a drink every so often. I usually run into someone I know."

"Like tonight for instance."

"Yeah." He pauses. "So, how about you? Are you seeing anyone?"

"Me?" I say as if the idea of me dating anyone is beyond ridiculous. "No, no. I'm so busy with work and my son. Who has time?"

"You've got to make *some* time for yourself." He hesitates for a moment again. "How about you and I go out and have a drink or catch a movie or something sometime?"

I can't explain it, but, as soon as I hear his question, I get this quivering feeling. I feel anxious and excited at the same time. It feels good to get some attention from a man . . . to be asked out on a date. Somehow it makes me feel *alive*, but at the same time I have this lingering apprehension.

"Oh that's so sweet of you to offer, but with my son and work . . . and my mother isn't faring that well these days. I just don't think I have time, Ben."

"Nonsense. How about this weekend?"

"My ex-husband's in a drag show this weekend." If I didn't nix his interest by reminding him that I have kid and telling him that I have a needy parent, I can certainly get rid of him with the drag queen ex-husband thing. He's cute and nice and all, but, honestly, I just don't have the energy to deal with dating right now.

"That sounds like fun. How about I come with?"

What, are you joking me? "Really?" I ask.

"Sure. Why not?"

"You're not curious about why my ex-husband is in a drag show?"

He shrugs his shoulders as if to say, "None of my business."

"If you're really interested, it's at eight o'clock on Saturday night in the basement of the Unitarian Church on 16th Street in the city."

"I can meet you there, and then maybe we can go for a drink afterward or something."

"Okay." I can't help but smile.

"Great. I guess I'll get moving and let you get back to your friends." He eyes Desma and Claire at the bar, who have been looking on the whole time like a couple of schoolgirls.

"Okay. It really was good to see you again, Ben."

"Yeah. You, too."

Ben barely steps away before I see Claire and Desma make a beeline back to the table.

"Who was that? I sensed some serious flirting from the bar," Claire says to me.

"He's just a friend I used to work with."

"I saw the way he was grinning at you," Desma says. "I don't think he was interested in being *friends*."

"Did you give him your number?" Claire asks. "And you better say yes, or I'm going to give him mine. He was *fine*."

"No, I didn't give him my number, but he's going to meet me Saturday night . . . just a *friend*-thing."

"Where are you meeting him?"

"At Mario's drag show."

"You're going to spend a first date with a new guy watching your ex-husband run around dressed like Charo?"

"Apparently," Desma says, before I have a chance to respond.

"It's not a date," I protest, even though I know it is a date. I know that should be a good thing, but the idea of it makes me nervous. Dating takes so much energy, and the chance of any-thing actually working out is quite unlikely. I remember what dating was like before I was married—all the losers and freaks, and that was before things got so complicated—before I had a son, and before I became a "divorcee." I haven't been on a date since Mario and I did the whole courting thing before we got married—and we all know how well that turned out.

8

It's Saturday morning, and a week has passed since my night out with Desma and Claire. Saturdays are generally the only day of the week that Andrew gets up before I do. As with most Saturdays, I awaken to Andrew standing next to my bed staring at me—almost like he's wishing me awake. He never says anything or tries to jostle me. He just stands there and waits until I feel his presence in the room.

"Morning, sweetie," I say, my head still lying on the pillow.

"Can I watch cartoons in your bed?"

"Of course." I watch him climb up in bed with me and reach over and grab the remote control from the nightstand.

He turns the TV on and goes straight for *Jimmy Neutron*, who, quite frankly, gets on my nerves.

"Turn it down a little." If he keeps the volume low, I may have bought another hour or so of sleep. *SpongeBob SquarePants* comes on after *Jimmy Neutron* and that usually holds Andrew's attention. But by the time *The Fairly OddParents* springs into action, he'll be restless and want breakfast. I shut my eyes again and try to block out the sound of the television. I so *love* Saturday mornings. I wouldn't go so far as to say that I get to sleep in, but at least I do get an extra hour or so of snoozing while Andrew watches cartoons next to me.

You'd think he'd tire of cartoons—they're constantly on these days. When I was a kid cartoons were such a delight. With the exception of the occasional holiday specials during prime time, the only opportunity we got to watch cartoons was on Saturday mornings. Now, kids can turn the TV on at any time during the day and watch anything from *Scooby-Doo* to *Pokemon* to *Lilo & Stitch*. Cartoons just aren't special anymore, but that doesn't seem to impede Andrew's enjoyment of them.

The great thing about Saturdays is that we can take things a little bit slower in the morning and mill about in our pajamas for a while instead of rushing to get myself together and then bundling up Andrew for us to head out into the cold. Saturday mornings are when I miss Andrew the most during the weekends he spends with Mario. I do appreciate the peace I have when he's at his father's, but I can't help but miss him lying against the pillows, occasionally giggling as SpongeBob and Squidward go at it.

I'm about to drift into a light sleep, when I hear someone knocking on the front door. I figure it's the postman with a package or something, so I decide to ignore it—he can leave it on the doorstep or come back later. But, whoever it is, they're persistent and keep banging, so I reluctantly lift myself out of bed and trudge down the steps. I look through the peephole and see Claire standing there, which is odd. I don't usually see much of Claire on the weekends. Being a real estate agent, she's generally tied up with clients on Saturdays and Sundays.

"I know you've lost your mind—banging on my door so early on a Saturday," I say after I open the door.

"I'm sorry, but I need your help," she says and steps inside without an invitation to enter. "Can you be one of my white people today?"

"Your what?"

"One of my white people. I'm holding an open house in D.C. . . you know, in one of those *transitional* neighborhoods." She does the air quote thing with her fingers as she says the word "transitional." "I need some white people to just mill about in the neighborhood and pretend they live there. Maybe you and Andrew can just walk up and down the sidewalk for a few hours. I've got a few other friends helping me out, but Sarah and Alan canceled on me. I figure it'll be worth at least ten grand over the asking price if potential buyers think a few WASPs live in the area already."

"You've got to be kidding me."

"No. I could really use the help."

"Well, first of all, aside from the whole thing being deceptive, I'm not exactly white, Claire. I'm Latina." Yes, I know, there are white Latinas, but I don't think I'd qualify as one of them. As the product of my Colombian parents, I inherited my relatively fair skin from my mother, but I have my father's deep brown eyes and his dark brown hair. I also have the full lips that run on his side of the family. With my mix of Colombian genes, people really aren't sure what to make of me. Sometimes people are able to peg me as a Latina, but just as often I've been thought to be Italian or Greek, and I get the occasional person who asks me if I'm Middle Eastern.

"Well, you're white enough for my purposes. And it's not really deceptive. Just because you're walking around the neighborhood doesn't necessarily mean you live there."

I sigh. "I can only do it for an hour or so. Andrew and I have to go to Fredericksburg later and run errands with my mother. What time would we need to be there?"

"If you could get there about twelve-thirty, that would be cool. And don't worry about how the neighborhood looks. It's pretty safe during the day. There haven't been any shootings in months. But I'll show you where to walk . . . if you go too far in one direction, you'll end up by one of the crack houses."

"What!? Forget it, Claire. I'm not walking around a neighborhood like that with my son."

"You don't have to come with Andrew. You can come by yourself."

"Oh, sure. And I'll leave Andrew with my invisible live-in nanny."

"Ugh. Who else can I get?"

"I don't know. Maybe you should have run an ad beforehand: *Needed: A few good WASPs.*"

"Very funny. I'm just trying to earn a living," she says, and turns to leave. "I'll let you know how it goes."

"You want a cup of coffee before you go?" I figure I may as well start the day since I'm already out of bed.

Claire follows me into the kitchen and sits down on a stool as I plug in the coffeemaker and grab a filter from the cabinet.

"Oh! So get this," she says as if she has big news. "Remember that guy I told you about . . . Julio? The one I wanted to talk dirty to in Spanish while he was fucking me?"

I nod my head and pour some water into the coffeemaker and turn it on.

"Well, he comes over, and we get it on, and I'm doing my best to speak Spanish in the sack. I'm all like, *"Chupame,"* and *"Ay, Dios mío,"* and *"Tú eres el rey."* I even tried to roll my r's. And guess what?" She pauses for effect.

"What?"

"He's not *Latino*! He's frickin' Asian!"

"Really?"

"Who ever heard of an *Asian* named Julio?"

"That is unusual, unless he's from the Philippines."

"Yes! That's what he said—that he's from the Philippines and doesn't even speak Spanish. He speaks some language called Tag-A-Long or something."

"Tagolog," I correct her. "Lots of Filipinos have Spanish names. The Philippines were under Spanish rule for years."

"Oh, blah, blah, blah. Spare me the history lesson. I felt like such an idiot when he asked me why I was moaning in Spanish."

I laugh. "I guess that will teach you never to assume anything about people again."

"You're right about that. That Julio proved another one of my assumptions wrong. He was hung like a frickin' telephone pole. I've always avoided Asian men because . . . you know . . . they're supposed to have small wee-wees. But I'm not crossing Asian men off my list anymore."

As I grab a couple mugs from the cabinet and a gallon of milk from the fridge, Claire is silent for a moment before getting started again. "Do you think I should have my anus bleached?" she blurts out all of a sudden.

I just look at her with my brow furrowed.

"Don't look at me that way. It's the latest thing . . . *seriously*. Rumor has it Lara Flynn Boyle does it. There's this salon called Pink Cheeks that has a cream to make things lighter. I saw the whole thing on *Dr. 90210*. The salon's in LA, but you can order the cream over the phone, I think."

"It's in LA? Big surprise there. Why on earth would you want—" I'm about to ask her why she'd want to do such a thing, but she cuts me off.

"I almost forgot! Tonight is your big date at the tranny festival."

"It's not a big date, and it's not a *transsexual* festival either. It's just some guys doing a drag show for charity."

"Seems like a really dumb idea—to take your new boyfriend to your husband's tranny show."

"*Ex*-husband. And, would you stop? Ben is not my new boyfriend. I haven't even been out with him yet."

"Sounds like you don't really want to go out with him at all. If you were really interested, might you have suggested dinner and a movie instead of a RuPaul sing-along?"

"So what if I'm not that interested?"

"What's not to be interested in? I saw him, Jennifer. He's hot. Why wouldn't you be interested?"

"Believe it or not, Claire, some of us are interested in more than what a man looks like."

"Yeah . . . what's that about anyway?"

I let out a quick laugh. "Besides, he might as well know about my screwed-up life from the get-go."

"If you say so, but I think you're playing it all wrong."

"I'm not 'playing' it at all. He's going to meet me at the show, and then maybe we'll go for a drink afterward. That's it."

"Who's staying with the kid?" Remembering Andrew's name

is a bit much for Claire, so she generally just refers to him as "the kid."

"Desma has volunteered to baby-sit."

"Really? Where is she this morning?"

"She left early. There's some sort of pro-life . . . or pro-choice . . . or save the baby whales movement thing she had to go to."

"Is she a lesbo?" Claire blurts out. "I mean, she does seem like quite the Birkenstock-wearer."

"No, Claire. She's not a lesbian. At least not so far as I know . . . she's just crunchy, that's all. Why?"

"Just curious. I haven't had good experiences with lesbians in the past. They're all so 'rah rah girl power' and shit when what they really need is a nice stiff—"

"Shh," I say and put my hand up to Claire and direct my eyes behind her to the sofa in the adjoining family room. She turns, and we both look at Andrew's legs, the only part of him we can see on the sofa. He must have crept downstairs without me noticing. Shit . . . I hope he wasn't listening when Claire was talking about anal bleaching or my date with Ben. Not that my date with Ben should be a big deal. I have every right to go on dates but, when it comes to Andrew, I still don't know how to approach the subject. He was only three when Mario and I split up, so he doesn't really have much memory of us being an intact family, but I know how much he likes to see us together. And I'm quite certain he would be none too pleased to see me with another man, which really hasn't been a problem since I haven't even tried to date since the divorce. At some point, I guess I'm going to have to figure out a way to broach the idea of me dating other men with Andrew, but certainly there's no need to do it right now. I'm meeting Ben for one evening. As far as I know, I may never see him again after tonight. I don't see any reason to trouble Andrew over what might be a single outing with Ben.

Claire turns back around. "Hmmm . . . what to talk about that's G-rated?" She reflects for a moment. "Can I take the rest of this coffee to go?" she asks and gets up from the stool. Apparently, anything G-rated is not worth talking about. "I need to get ready for the open house."

"Okay . . . bring my mug back," I call after her as she exits the kitchen.

"Will do," I hear before she shuts the door behind her.

9

"It's ten dollars," the skinny man with too much gel in his hair says to me after I make my way to the church basement. Gotta love the Unitarians—who else would let a bunch of gay men in women's clothing perform in their building?

I hand the guy a twenty and tell him to keep the change—it's for charity after all.

"Should I put these somewhere?" I ask him, lifting a box of cookies. Mario asked me if I'd bring something for the refreshment table, so I stopped by the Safeway and picked up a box of cookies from the bakery.

"The refreshments are in the far back corner over there." The man points toward the other side of the room.

"Thanks." I walk toward the table, keeping one eye out for my ex-husband in a dress and another out for Ben. Ben looked up my number, and we talked briefly on the phone this morning. He said he'd meet me here before the show started.

"Hello! My name's Diva Longoria. Sour apple, pear, or watermelon?" I hear a voice call to me as I set the cookies down. I turn toward the makeshift bar and see a man in a bad wig and a cheap sequined gown hovering over a display of liquor bottles and martini glasses.

"Uh . . . hi. How about a cosmopolitan?"

"Oh, cosmopolitans are so late-nineties *Sex and the City*. Let me make you one of my pear specialties."

"Okay," I respond, not wanting to argue with a six-foot-tall man in a dress.

As the bartender prepares my drink, I see another man in a dress approach from my left.

"You made it!" It's Mario's voice, but that's almost all I recognize. He's wearing a short black cocktail dress, fishnet stockings, and three-inch heels. He's got a short black wig on his head and piles of makeup on his face.

"Yeah." I try to smile and hide my discomfort as Mario gives me a hug. I know this is just a silly thing he's doing. It's not like he's a full-fledged drag queen or anything—it's all about entertainment. But how can I not be bothered? This man, standing next to me, looking like Liza Minnelli, used to be my husband.

"So what do you think?" he says, after he releases me and spins around. "Nineteen dollars at Payless, forty-three dollars from Ross." He motions from his heels to his dress.

"It looks great," I say, hoping the heat in my face isn't showing. "Can I have the dress when you're done?" I joke, again trying to hide my discomfort. I've gotten used to Mario being gay. I don't like it, and I still have a lot of pain over the whole issue, but I've accepted that he is who he is, and there is nothing I can do about it. I love him, and, even though he essentially deceived me for years, I know he loves me too. And I know he never intended to hurt me. I do blame him for lying to me about his sexuality, but I've realized how complicated things are, and I guess I also blame society in general for all the pain I've endured having been married to a gay man. I've made Mario take responsibility for his actions, but, at the same time, I understand the reasons he did what he did. He grew up being taught that what he was was wrong and deviant, and that he had to hide it. I know he went through so much of his own drama with the whole "being gay" thing, and when we got married, I'm certain he really did think he could suppress it or deny it or whatever. And, at the time of our wedding, I believe that he intended to stay married to me for the rest of his life. But I still can't help but have a certain amount of anger over the whole thing. He came out to me over two years ago, and, like I said, I've accepted the situation and have tried to forgive and forget, but a small part of me still wants to beat him to a pulp with a baseball bat every time I see him.

"I'm so nervous. I'm doing Eartha Kitt first, and then my second number is a Gwen Stefani tribute."

"How fun! I'm sure you'll be great," I say with forced enthusiasm, hoping that one day I'll be more comfortable in situations like this and won't have that tinge of sadness and regret that comes over me whenever I get overt reminders that the man I married is gay. There are days in which I still entertain the idea that it just isn't true—that Mario is just confused and one day he's going to realize that he isn't really a homosexual, and we'll reconcile, and the past two years will be something to never be spoken about again. I know in my heart that such thoughts are crazy, but I miss us being a family so much sometimes. I can't help but think of the all the nights that Mario and I were on the sofa and Andrew had fallen asleep in the chair. On winter evenings, we'd have a fire going in the fireplace, and I'd feel the burst of cold air come in every time Mario would step outside to get more wood. We'd watch TV, snuggled close together, and sometimes Mario would rub my feet. It all made me feel so safe and secure, and simple evenings like that are what I miss the most about my marriage.

As Mario and I continue to chat, I keep looking around the room for Ben. The show's due to start in another five minutes, and he still hasn't arrived. I start to think that maybe he blew me off. And the odd thing about the possibility of him ditching me is that I feel more relieved than anything. Now, if he tries to call me and ask me out again, I can pretend to be mad about him standing me up and be done with the whole deal. I'm just about to give up on him when I see him handing some cash to Mr. Too-Much-Hair-Gel at the entrance.

"Why don't I let you get ready for the big event? I've asked a friend to meet me here, so I better go look for . . . um . . . her." If I'd said "him" it would lead to questions, and it would just be awkward to talk to Mario about a date—a date that's probably going nowhere.

"Okay. Wish me luck."

"Good luck." I give his hand a quick squeeze and scurry in Ben's direction.

"Hi," I say to Ben, trying to stand up straight and smile.

"Hey," he replies, and we stand there and look at each other for a minute, unsure of what the proper physical greeting is. Hug? Kiss on the cheek? Handshake?

"It's good to see you again." He gives my arm a quick brush with his hand.

"Yes. You, too. Shall we sit down? I think the show is about to start."

"Sure," he says and we take a seat in the back. "So is your ex-husband Bubbles Champaign, Dixie Crystal, Lady Dominique, Ivanna Wantaman, Starlita Diamond, or Trixie Delightful?" he asks, looking at the program.

"You know, I don't remember what he calls himself when he does . . . you know . . . this sort of thing." I can't help but be embarrassed by all of this. I know I shouldn't be. It has nothing to do with me, but no matter how I slice it, I'm "the girl who married a homosexual," and, real or imagined, I feel a stigma about it—like I'm branded or something.

"That's great that you and your ex-husband are still friends," Ben says, with no trace of being uncomfortable with the whole men-in-dresses thing, or with the fact that I used to be married to a gay man.

"Yeah . . . well, we have to try for Andrew's sake." Which is true, but I would have wanted to stay friends with Mario regardless of whether or not we had a child together. I love him, I enjoy his company, and I want him to be part of my life. We get along so well. We would have had the perfect marriage if it wasn't for him being gay. I really just wish he . . . oh, hell, there I go again.

"How old is Andrew now?"

I'm about to answer Ben's question when the lights go down

and a small Asian man in drag (at least I assume he's a man, he's so petite and feminine it's hard to tell) welcomes us to the show, does a little banter with the crowd, and introduces the first performer.

Ben and I watch as a beefy man in a high-styled blond wig, a fifties poodle skirt, and saddle shoes does a high-energy routine to "My Boyfriend's Back." The crowd really seems to like him (or should I say "her" in this instance?), and lots of people are giving him one-dollar bills, some of which he shoves in his fake cleavage.

I keep glancing over at Ben to see his reaction to all of this, and he seems to be having a good time. At one point, when Dixie Crystal makes her way down the aisle, Ben actually pulls a couple of singles out of his wallet, hands them to her, and turns his head for him/her to kiss him on the cheek. I'm glad he's relaxed and having fun with this. He always seemed like such a straight-laced guy when we worked together—I thought he might be too uptight for an event like this, but apparently he's not quite as inhibited as I thought.

As the show goes on, Diva Longoria, the drag queen who made my pear martini, comes around with a pitcher of some high-octane concoction and refills my martini glass. I'm not sure what's in it. I taste raspberry, but mostly I taste vodka. It's so strong, I wince as I sip it and watch a new performer take the stage. Her name is Starlita Diamond, and she enters wearing a long cape singing "Ring My Bell." When she gets to the refrain, she throws off her cape, and reveals a dress covered in tiny bells and starts gyrating to make them all ring in unison. The crowd, including Ben and I, have a good laugh, and I even reach for my purse to tip the performer. We watch a few more performances until the host comes out and introduces Bubbles Champaign (my former husband's name for the evening). As she makes the announcement, I motion for Diva Longoria to come over and pour some more gasoline in my glass.

I take a long sip as Mario takes the stage. He's changed clothes since I saw him earlier. He's wearing black leather pants, a sparkling black blouse, and four-inch heels. He's got a long black wig on his head and little cat ears on top of that. To finish off the ensemble, he's wearing a pointy black mask around his eyes. He starts to sway as a high tempo dance song begins to play. I don't recognize it, but as soon as the vocals start, I know it's by none other than Eartha Kitt, who so masterfully played Catwoman in the old *Batman* episodes that I used to watch in reruns after school.

"He's good," Ben says to me, as if I should be proud.

I just smile to affirm his statement. And, actually, probably thanks to Diva Longoria's cocktails, I'm not nearly as uncomfortable as I thought I'd be, watching my ex-husband claw around a church basement in spiked heels, rolling his tongue as if he's a cat in heat. When Mario makes his way down the aisle, I hand him a few dollar bills, smile, and even do a quick dance with him. Who would know how much I'm bothered by all of this? From looking at me, you'd think I was having a great time. And I guess I am having a good time. The show's been fun to watch, and I've had a few laughs. I just wish that Mario . . . oh, never mind.

I guess I'll never get used to Mario showing what I have termed his "gay side." Before he came out, he was very careful to never appear feminine. He watched sports on television and discussed NFL plays and stats with the best of them. He always dressed very conservatively and didn't even like to dance to any upbeat music. He shunned fruity drinks in favor of beer and always tackled the more masculine jobs around the house. But, after he came out, his whole demeanor changed. Aside from this evening's appearance in drag, most of the changes I've noticed in Mario have been very subtle. It's not that he's become a flamer or anything, but he's definitely dropped his guard and seems so much more relaxed these days, which, in a certain way, saddens me. Of course, I'm glad that's he's happy now, but seeing him so relaxed and secure just reminds me of how shackled he must've felt pretending to be straight and being married to me.

We sit through the final numbers—"Shania Twain" in full cowgirl regalia singing to "That Don't Impress Me Much," "Aretha Franklin" in some sort of papier mâché car driving on a "Freeway," and the show closes with a brawny black man in a blond wig and an afternoon-tea sort of hat doing a rendition of Carol Channing's "Hello Dolly."

When the lights come up, I look at Ben, and he smiles at me. "That was a hoot," he says, and we make our way to the aisle and toward the exit.

"Did you want to say good-bye to ah . . . I don't remember his name . . . your ex, I mean former . . ."

"Husband," I say, finishing what was apparently an awkward thing for him to say. No one knows how to talk to me about Mario. Talking to a woman about her gay ex-husband is just something that keeps folks at a loss for words. I know it's not my fault, and I shouldn't feel any shame or embarrassment about it, but that's easier said than done. And it doesn't help that virtually everyone I know approaches the subject with a hush-hush sort of attitude—like I have a husband in jail or a husband who's cheating on me. Sometimes I feel like Kathy Lee Gifford must have felt when her husband was set up and filmed with a sleazy flight attendant in a hotel room. It wasn't Kathy's fault that her husband was a louse, yet everyone expected *her* to be embarrassed, to hang *her* head in shame. Mario being gay has nothing to do with me, but everyone around me seems to act like it does. Although, I guess that it could quite possibly be because I just can't quite shake the feeling that Mario being gay *does* have something to do with me.

"I said hi to him before the show. I think we can head out."

As we make our way up the steps, I flip open my cell phone and check in with Desma.

"How are things going? Is Andrew behaving?" I ask.

"Sure. We're having a blast. We made popcorn, and I read him a story I wrote about global warming. I tried to teach him how to meditate, but he couldn't sit still long enough, so now I'm teaching him all about feng shui."

"Okay," I say, feeling sorry for Andrew. He must feel like he's in school. "Don't let him stay up too late," I add and wrap up our conversation.

"Everything okay at home?" Ben asks when we're out the door.

"Yeah. Fine," I reply, and we stand in place for a few moments to decide what to do next.

"Would you like to go get a drink somewhere?" Ben asks.

I stand there for a moment and try to decide on an answer. I've clearly had enough to drink and perhaps coffee would be a better idea than anymore cocktails. At some point, I still have to drive home. But at the same time, I am enjoying the relaxed feeling I have from the martinis, and, quite honestly, I find myself enjoying the feeling of standing outside with Ben trying to think of someplace to go. It's not something I've done with a man in a long time.

"Sure," I say. "Any ideas?"

"We can walk up to 17th Street and grab a drink in one of the restaurants there. It's only a block over."

"Okay," I say, and we start walking.

"So you enjoyed the show?" he asks.

"Ah . . . yeah, I did. You?"

"I thought it was a riot."

"So you weren't uncomfortable with any of . . . the . . . well, you know, men in dresses and such?"

"Gosh, no. I think you'll find I'm a pretty open-minded guy. I try not to judge people. I don't want them judging me."

"Good to know." I take an extended look at him. Maybe it's the martinis, but he suddenly looks so attractive to me. I take in his eyes and his wavy hair and the hint of stubble starting to appear on his face.

"What can I get for you?" asks a tired-looking bartender after we find our way into a little Mexican restaurant and grab two open stools at the bar.

"Margarita?" Ben asks in my direction.

"Maybe just a cup of coffee for me."

"Two coffees then."

"I've never been here before," Ben says to me as the bartender starts pouring our coffees. The bar is fairly quiet and intimate, and I like the way Ben looks with his face highlighted from the flickering candlelight.

"You look great, you know," he says to me, and as he's speaking his knee ever so slightly touches mine. You wouldn't think such a trivial gesture would get a girl going, but as soon as our knees met, I could feel my heart beating. Believe it or not, this is probably the most intimate contact I've had with a man in more than two years. I freeze my knee in place, not wanting to lose touch with his, but also not wanting to press any more firmly against it. "You haven't changed a bit since you left Saunders and Kraff."

I lower my eyes and smile, afraid he's making me blush. "Time has been kind to you as well," I say and mean it. He's trimmed down since I last saw him, and I think he may have ever-so-slightly changed his haircut.

We sip our coffees and find that conversation comes easily. We talk about former coworkers and what's involved in our careers now. Then we recap the show from earlier in the evening and enjoy a few shared laughs.

"It's funny," he says. "Running into you the other night."

"Really? How so?"

"Oh, I don't know." He puts his hand over my mine. "I wasn't expecting to meet someone . . . well, not *meet* . . . we already know each other . . ."

"I think I know what you mean."

We look at each other, and he smiles and I smile, and then he starts to lean in to give me a kiss. I see his lips moving toward mine, and I'm not sure I can describe the longing I feel for them—the longing I feel for some intimacy with a man. I didn't think I missed it that much. By focusing on my work and my son and my mother, I convinced myself that I didn't have time for a man, and that I could quite nicely get by without one, but, as Ben leans in to kiss me, I feel a yearning for him—to feel him against me—to feel a masculine touch. Yet, when his lips are millimeters from my own, I pull my head back.

"Yeah, I wasn't expecting to run into you either," I blurt out.

Ben looks startled and a bit dejected. He offers a kind smile as if to say, "Okay, I get it, too soon."

And I guess it is too soon. Isn't it? Or maybe it isn't. What the hell do I know? I married a gay man. I don't know why I jerked away from him when I really did want him to kiss me. I guess I feel like the moment I let him kiss me is the moment that this— he and I—becomes something. As long as we only talk and have a drink, it doesn't mean anything. I can still get out of it with no drama. But if I kiss him, then I've started something, and I'm not sure I want to start *something* with him . . . or anyone.

"Would you like another cup?" he asks, looking at my empty coffee mug.

"No . . . thanks," I say. "It's getting late. I guess I should think about heading home. A friend of mine is staying with my son tonight, and I have lots to do tomorrow. Andrew takes up so much of my time." Here I go, laying the groundwork for getting rid of him. I'm telling him how busy I am, so I have an excuse not to go out with him again. And, of course, I reminded him of my son, knowing that a woman with a child can be a big turn-off to many men. Why am I doing this? I ask myself as I continue to talk about all the stuff I have to do tomorrow. I like him. He's nice and good-looking and seems like a decent guy. Why am I putting the brakes on? Why am I so scared?

"It sounds like you're juggling a lot."

"Yeah. I manage though. What else can you do?"

"Fall apart, I guess," he says with a laugh.

"Some days I get pretty close," I say, as if I'm joking, which I'm not.

"Can I walk you to your car?"

"Sure."

I try to contribute to the bill as we settle up with the bartender, but Ben won't hear of it, and it's only a few dollars anyway. On the way back to the car, the conversation turns awkward.

I guess he's reading my cues and can tell that I'm trying to wrap things up.

"I had a nice time tonight," he says when we reach my car.

"Yeah. Me, too."

"Would you like to get together again sometime?"

"Ah . . . maybe. I tell you, it's hard to get away between work and my son . . . and my mother takes a lot of my time, but . . . well, you know."

"Yeah," he says with a defeated smile. "Perhaps you can call me if . . . you know . . . when your schedule calms down."

"Sure. I'll do that."

"Good night, Jennifer," he says, and gives my upper arm a slow squeeze.

"Good night," I say and turn to put my key in the door.

When I get inside the car, I watch Ben walk away in the rearview mirror, and I feel sorry for him. Here we were, having a nice time . . . great conversation, laughing, and then I freak out and try to nix the whole thing. What's wrong with me? Most women would kill for a man like Ben. I think we could be good together, but then I thought Mario and I could be good together. I'm not ready to develop the kind of feelings I had for Mario with another man. I'm not ready for that kind of intensity. I'm not ready to get hurt like that again.

10

I'm feeling a little blue as I walk through the front door of my house. It's after eleven and everything is quiet. Andrew should have been in bed hours ago, but I expected Desma to still be up.

After I close the door behind me, I go to put my coat on the rack behind the door, and it drops to the floor as I realize the coatrack is no longer there. Then I notice that the little table I keep next to the door, the one I use as a place to toss my keys and the mail, is missing as well.

Oh, my God! I've been robbed, I think to myself. "Desma?" I call, my heart starting to race. "Desma!? Andrew!?" I holler again and scurry into the family room. In my haste, I walk right into the sofa, which has been moved from its original position and is now blocking the path to the kitchen.

"Why are you yelling?" Desma says to me when she finally emerges from the basement.

"What's going on? I thought we'd been robbed. The coatrack's missing . . . and the table by the door . . . and the sofa's been moved . . ."

"I told you I was teaching Andrew about feng shui."

I breathe a sigh of relief. "You said you were teaching him about it. You didn't say you were going to ransack my house."

"I hardly ransacked your house." Desma gives me the look I remember getting so often in college. The look that says, "You're so close-minded."

"Where's the coatrack?"

"I put it in the basement. The main entrance of any house is the 'Mouth of Chi,'" she says to me, as if only an idiot wouldn't know this. "It has the strongest influence on how chi flows into your home. You're not going to get any fresh chi in the house if the main entrance is all cluttered."

"Well, unless I can hang my coat or lay my keys on this chi-business, I'm not really interested."

"Andrew thought it was 'neat.' We tried to move the sofa into a proper position as well, but it was too heavy. Do you want to give me a hand moving it now?"

"I'll give you a hand moving it back where it was."

"Jennifer, you really want the sofa placed in clear view of the door. And you don't want it in front of a window. Chi flows from the window—"

"I like the sofa where it was. Now help me move it back."

"You're hopeless," she says to me, and we both squat down and grab an end of the couch and return it to its position in front of the window.

"So, your date didn't go well, did it?" Desma says to me as she plops down on the sofa.

"What makes you say that?"

"I don't know how you can have any good dates with so much clutter around your front door, not to mention all the crap in your *relationship* area."

"My relationship area?"

"Yes. Look at this ba gua I made when I was teaching Andrew about feng shui." She grabs a sketch of my floor plan from the coffee table. "See, your relationship area is in the back corner of the room. And look at all the crap you have stuffed back there . . . Andrew's toys, books, the vacuum. It's like a wet blanket smothering your opportunities for romance."

"Oh, really? Then how do you explain my date going quite well actually."

Desma looks at me . . . more like *through* me and raises her eyebrows.

"Oh, all right. So it didn't go so well. I—" I'm about to tell her the details of my evening when we hear someone banging on the front door. "Who could that be? It's almost midnight."

I get up from the sofa and walk to the door. I look through the peephole and see Claire on the other side.

"Hi. Is everything okay?"

"Sure. I saw you pull up. I just had to know how your first date in ages went."

"Get in here," I respond, rolling my eyes. "Aren't we the busy-body?" I comment as Claire follows me into the family room.

"Oh," I hear Claire say like she swallowed something distasteful as she catches sight of Desma on the sofa. "You're still up. How's it going?"

"Fine," Desma says. "I was just trying to teach Jen about feng shui."

"But Jen wasn't really interested," I say. "You want anything to drink? I think I might make some chamomile tea or something."

"Sure. Tea sounds good."

"You should switch to green tea, Jen," Desma calls to me in the kitchen. "It's much healthier than chamomile."

I pretend not to hear her as I fill up the kettle.

"So, tell us about the date," Claire says as both of them move from the sofa to the counter that divides the kitchen and the family room and sit down on the stools.

"Well, the drag show was actually kind of fun. I didn't really enjoy seeing Mario in a dress and heels and such, but watching the other guys was a hoot."

"She didn't ask about the show. She asked about the date," Desma points out.

"I'm getting to that." I put the kettle on the stove and turn up the flame. "Ben was nice. He seemed to enjoy the show. We went and had a drink . . . coffee actually . . . at a little Mexican place up the street and had some nice conversation, but . . ." I'm not sure how to put into words why I halted the date from getting to a more romantic level.

"But what?" Claire asks.

"Gosh. I don't know. At one point, we were talking and laughing, and he leaned in to kiss me—"

"Now we're getting somewhere," Claire interrupts me.

"But I pulled away and—"

"What? You idiot!"

"I couldn't help it. It was a reflex. Something inside me wouldn't let me take it any further."

"Jennifer, he's a nice-looking guy. You should have gone for it."

"Not if she wasn't ready or was apprehensive," Desma argues on my behalf.

"I even made a conscious effort to mention Andrew to remind him I have a child. And we all know a woman with a child is worse than a woman with gonorrhea to most men."

"That's for sure," Claire says. "At least you can get rid of gonorrhea with a shot . . . albeit, a painful one. Did you know they have to inject that shot right into your muscle? It really hurts . . ." Claire lets her voice tail off. "I mean . . . I've heard."

"What was holding you back?" Desma asks.

"I don't know. I guess I'm just not ready to start a relationship with anyone." I grab three cups from the cabinet and start to put the tea bags in them.

"Who said anything about a *relationship*, Jennifer," Claire says. "Couldn't you look at it as a little fun? What would have been so wrong with having a quick roll in the hay with him? You worry too much about the long term. You need to learn to just 'ride the wave,' sweetie . . . 'ride the wave.'"

"Maybe you're right, but Ben somehow didn't seem like the kind of guy I'd want to have a one-night stand with. He was too . . . oh, I don't know. I guess he's just the kind of guy I want to still respect me in the morning." I sigh and lift the kettle off the stove. As I'm pouring hot water into the cups, I see Andrew emerge from the foyer into the family room.

"What are you doing up, young man?" I can't help but smile. He looks so precious in his Superman pajamas with his hair all sticking up.

"You were yelling, Mommy." Andrew responds with a "duh" sort of tone in his voice.

"Sweetie, you need to get in bed. It's not good for you to be up so late. Things were out of place when I came in. I was concerned." I walk over to him, give him a hug, and pick him up in my arms.

"Can I sleep on the sofa until you go to bed?"

"All right, only for tonight."

I carry him over to the sofa, let him lie down, and put the afghan over him. "Now, go to sleep," I say with a smile and give him a quick peck on the cheek.

"Can you turn the TV on?"

"No." I laugh. "Go to sleep."

"You know what you need?" Claire says when I get back in the kitchen. "A really good-looking man who's kind of a jerk. Someone you can use for sex and then punt to the curb."

"Shh," I say and point my eyes toward the sofa where Andrew is laying.

Claire lowers her voice. "And I know exactly where to find him."

"Where?" Desma asks for me.

"My church."

"*You* go to church?" Desma asks with her brow furrowed.

"Oh, yes. I've found it's one of the best places around to meet men."

"Okay. So a married woman goes to church to meet men. What's wrong with this picture?" Desma asks.

"I don't think I'm interested, Claire," I interject. "I'm not very religious these days."

"Oh, please, Jennifer. No one goes to church for religion anymore. This is one of those mega churches with a stage and fog machines. It's really more of a motivational speaking engagement, and the services are just long enough for you to scope out all the eligible men to zoom in on during the social hour afterwards. We'll go next weekend. Would you like to come, Desma?"

"No," Desma says emphatically. "Not a fan of churches. I've

found that most of them refuse to acknowledge women as equals, advocate for bigotry against gay men and women, and are more concerned with money and power than worshipping the Lord."

"Oh, no, I'm not talking about a *Catholic* Church. This is the Tyson's Bible Church. Although I guess I'm not really sure where they stand on women's equality or gay rights and stuff. I don't really pay attention during the services."

"They're all the same," Desma says.

"I'm with her," I respond, nodding my head in Desma's direction. "Sunday mornings are one of the times I actually get to do nothing, and I'd like to keep it that way. And, honestly, I'm not feeling very spiritual these days."

"Then what's with the little statue of the Virgin Mary on your window over the sink?" Claire says, pointing her eyes toward the statue my mother brought over years ago and insisted I display (Colombians love them some Virgin Mary). "And you have your son in Catholic school."

"Andrew goes to a Catholic school?" Desma asks as if she just learned I imprison him in the basement with a hungry tiger.

"Yes. And I don't want to hear about it."

"How can you put your son in a Catholic school? His father is gay. You're okay with him learning all that stuff that that jerk-Pope says about gay people, and that it's okay to treat women as lesser human beings?"

"What do you want me to do, Desma? The public schools around here suck, and the Catholic schools are the only remotely affordable private options. If I have to put up with a little Catholic nonsense so my son can get a good education, then so be it. And don't you think calling the Pope a jerk is a bit strong?" I can't help but think of what my mother's reaction would be if she heard Desma call the man she always refers to as "His holy father" a jerk.

"No. The Pope *is* a jerk and he—"

"Ladies!" Claire interrupts. "How did we go from trying to get Jennifer laid to talking about the Pope? When did I ever mention religion anyway? I'm just talking about finding you a man for some stress relief. Does Mario have the kid next week-end?"

"Yes."

"Then it's settled. We'll go to services next Sunday."

"Whatever," I say, rolling my eyes. I guess it won't kill me to spend a Sunday at church—at least my mother will be pleased.

11

"I wish you would have gotten here sooner. I'm afraid we'll be late," Mom says to me after I walk through the door of her house, in lieu of, "Thanks for taking the morning off work to drive all the way out to Fredericksburg and take me to my doctor's appointment."

"We have plenty of time, Mom. You look like you're ready to go."

She's sitting on the sofa with her coat, hat, and gloves on— just sitting there without the television on or anything. I was going to ask how long she'd been waiting for me, but I was afraid of her answer. Somehow, I suspect it may have been hours. I don't think she knows what to do with herself anymore. It wouldn't surprise me if she got up at six this morning, got showered and dressed and has been sitting on the sofa waiting for me for the last two hours.

"Why are you wearing jeans, Jennifer? We're going to a *doctor's* office. Couldn't you have dressed more appropriately?"

"I seriously doubt anyone at the doctor's office is going to care what I'm wearing, Mom." I say as we make our way out to the car. "So, how's your week been?"

"Fine. I'm trying to get that upstairs closet cleaned out. So much of your father's old junk is still in there. You know anyone who would want it?"

I'm not sure what "old junk" she's referring to. I went through my father's clothes last year and donated most of them, and he wasn't much of a pack rat. My father, Alberto Peredo, was a much less complicated person than my mother. He believed in working hard and most of his life focus was on being a provider for his family. Because he spoke English when he arrived in America, he was able to obtain reasonable paying employment almost immediately. He started out working for a bank and later landed an entry level position with the telephone company where he rose through the ranks as the company survived all the mergers and takeovers of the telecom industry and stayed there until he retired. When he wasn't working, he was puttering around in the yard, watching sports on television, or taking naps. He always had a kind word for me, but, for the most part, our conversations were superficial, and he left the task of raising his children to my mother. It was always Mom who I fought with about how late I was allowed to stay out, how much makeup I was permitted to wear, or why I couldn't take the car out whenever I wanted after I got my driver's license.

My father's relaxed personality always provided a nice respite from my mother's more rigid nature. While he held his Colombian heritage dear to his heart, he seemed to understand more than Mom that things in America were different, and, sometimes, you had to let go of certain parts of the way of life in South America.

Dad was really the only person who could ever get my mother to lighten up. When I was in high school, my mother and I had one of our blowout fights over the dress I was going to wear to the senior prom. We had spent the afternoon trying on gowns at Spotsylvania Mall and couldn't agree on anything. Basically, she expected me to wear a full nun habit or a Pilgrim dress to the dance. She axed dress after dress that I pulled from the racks. She didn't want me wearing anything with spaghetti straps, and I certainly was not to wear anything off the shoulders. Compared to what high school girls wear today, my selections were positively conservative, but Mom seemed to want me covered from my neck to my feet. After trying on so many dresses, I eventually gave up and let her buy me this hideous bridesmaid-looking thing, knowing full well that I would get a friend to drive me back to the mall and exchange the dress for the one that I wanted, a strapless lavender satin gown. I knew I wouldn't be able to keep my defiance from my mother, but I figured I'd just deal with the fireworks when they happened, which hopefully wouldn't be until she saw my prom photo. I had planned to take the dress, concealed in the garment bag, to a friend's and get ready for the prom there. Unfortunately, Mom found the exchanged dress in my closet a few days before the event. She claimed that she took it out of the garment bag to see if it needed pressing, but of course she was snooping. I came home from school, and she had laid the dress on the sofa, and was sitting next to it with tears in her eyes.

We went through the whole "me not respecting her" routine, and, by the time Dad got home, we weren't speaking to each other. Mom told him what was going on, and he went into the living room and looked at the dress with the two of us following.

"Let her wear the dress. It's not so bad."

"That's not a dress for a proper young lady," Mom protested.

"Let her wear the dress," he said again.

"Fine," Mom said, and I walked over and hugged my dad, amazed at how easily he was able to get her off my case. Mom and I had argued for hours over my dress selections, but all it took was a few words from Dad to calm her down and get her to let things alone. I miss him for many reasons, but more than anything, I miss his ability to handle my mother.

"Like what?" I ask Mom.

"I don't know. His camera and his suitcase . . . stuff like that."

"Why don't you just hang on to them for now?"

"It will just be one more thing you'll have to take care of when I die."

"You're not going to die anytime soon, Mom."

"Well, we'll see what Dr. Hubbard has to say about that."

"You mean Dr. Miller. Dr. Hubbard's been dead for more than a year, and he retired long before that." Dr. Hubbard was my mother's doctor for most of her life until he retired about five years ago.

"Oh, yes. My mind just isn't what it used to be."

"I'd say you're doing all right for a seventy-five-year-old." I look over at her and smile. Her posture is not the best at the moment, and she looks sort of hunched over in the passenger seat. She's extending her neck like a turkey. She often does that when we're in the car as she strains to see outside the window. I notice that she has her Estee Lauder lipstick on, which is comforting. I have this theory that everything is okay with her as long as she remembers to put her lipstick on. She stopped wearing most makeup years ago, but I've yet to see her leave the house without running a tube of lipstick over her lips, and I'm surprised she hasn't gotten on my case this morning for not wearing any myself.

I turn my head back toward the road and try to relax. I'm not sure why I'm anxious, but just being around my mother makes me anxious lately. She's starting to look feeble, and her little mind lapses worry me. I'm not sure how much longer she's going to be able to live on her own without some assistance, and I just don't think it's good for her to be so isolated all the time anyway. When my retirement home idea was met with such staunch resistance, I brought up the subject of her just getting an apartment close to me, so I can check in on her every day, and she can spend more time with Andrew and have dinner with us a few nights a week. But she is adamant about not leaving her house. I can understand her desire to stay there. She's lived there for thirty years and raised two children there, but I know she's lonely, and I think her seclusion might have something to do with the declining sharpness of her mind.

It's sad to see her get old, and I'm not sure it's something I'll ever get used to. She was always such a strong and stubborn woman. It's hard to deal with her losing her independence. I remember the first time I started to realize that my mother was truly getting old. Surprisingly, it had nothing to do with her health or mental acuity. The realization came to me one day when I was shopping for clothes with her at the mall. It was almost ten years ago, before my father died, and we were shopping for dresses for his retirement party. We were at Lord & Taylor, my mother's favorite store, and she was trying on a light blue suit. Of course, I saw my mother all the time, but I guess, as we often do with people with whom we spend a lot of time, I hadn't really *looked* at her in quite a while. But as I watched her, standing opposite the three-way mirror in the dressing area, for the first time in my life, she looked like an old woman to me. We always hear people talking about "this old lady" or "that old lady" and, that day at Lord & Taylor, I realized that such a term could apply to my mother. Her hair had really grayed, her age was showing in her face, and there was something about the suit that made her look elderly—it looked like something Sophia Petrillo would wear on an outing to Wolfie's with the other Golden Girls. I remember being horribly depressed that day. I just didn't want to deal with the fact that my parents were "getting on in years."

When we get to Dr. Miller's office, I fight the urge to sign my mother in myself and let her do it. It would be easier for me to run up there and scrawl her name on the clipboard, but I try to let her do things for herself.

"They've remodeled since we were here last," she says when we sit down.

"No. I think it's pretty much the same."

"No, the carpet was different last time. It was more of shag and the walls were a different color."

"Well, maybe," I say. "They have some of the large print *Reader's Digest*s. Why don't you take a look?"

"I'm fine just sitting here."

I decide to pick up the *Reader's Digest* myself and start flipping through it.

"How's Mario?" Mom asks out of the blue when I'm about halfway through the article I'm reading. I *so* hate when she asks about Mario.

"He's fine. I saw him over the weekend . . . seems to be doing well."

"I just don't know why you couldn't make it work with him. He was a good man, Jennifer."

"I never said he wasn't a good man. Sometimes people just aren't meant for each other." I've never told Mom that Mario is gay. I have no I idea how she'd react to the news, and I'm just not interested in finding out. I've never really heard her say anything one way or another about gay people, but she's very conservative and very Catholic, so I just don't "go there." But I guess the real reason I've never told her about Mario's sexual orientation is that I'm afraid she'll somehow blame me for it. She'll say that I didn't treat him right, or that I emasculated him by having my own career, or maybe if I "had just worn lipstick more often . . ." Telling her about my divorce was one of the hardest things I ever had to do. It wasn't my fault, but I couldn't bear telling her the real reason behind our breakup, so I just told her that Mario and I had problems we were unable to resolve and felt it was best to end our marriage. I explained that I didn't want to elaborate—that it was a personal decision between Mario and me, and, although we tried our best to work things out, in the end, getting divorced was our only option. And for the past two years, that's been my story, and I've stuck to it, despite her repeated pleas for more information.

It's almost funny to me how upset my mother still is over my divorce, considering she was never a fan of my marrying Mario in the first place. She was always pleasant with him when we were dating, but, when I announced my engagement, she was none too happy. Mario was handsome and likable, but Mom was convinced that he'd never make a decent living as a social worker. "Marry him, Jennifer, and you'll have to work the rest of your life," she used to say. She tried to persuade me to call off the engagement, but, by this time, she had mellowed a little with age and knew better than to antagonize me too much. If nothing else, she'd finally learned that I could be just as big a bitch as she could, and, if she had insisted that I break off my engagement with Mario, it would have only fueled my determination to marry him.

Her reaction to my divorce was pretty much what I expected it to be—she was more accusatory than supportive. "Why can't you just work things out? You have a child together. Have you thought about what life is going to be like for Andrew, growing up with divorced parents? There must be something you can do to work things out?" These were just a few of her responses to the news of my divorce, and I've been hearing them over and over again for the past two years. There are times when I almost lose it and tell her that, unless she has any ideas about how I can magically sprout a penis, then "no, there is nothing I can do to work things out."

"Things would be so much better for Andrew if his parents were still together."

"Speaking of Andrew," I say, doing what I always do when Mom brings up Mario—changing the subject. "He learned all about feng shui the other night. Have you heard of it?"

"No, I don't like Chinese food, Jennifer. You know it makes me backfire."

I hear the lady next to me let out a giggle as she keeps her head down toward her magazine.

"No. Feng shui has something to do with how you place your furniture around the house. Desma taught Andrew all about it. You remember Desma. My roommate in college. She's been staying with me for the past couple of weeks."

"Yes. That crazy girl who doesn't eat meat?" Mom will never forget the first time Desma came home with me from college and politely declined her *pechugas de pollo al coco*, a chicken dish with coconut sauce, and ruined the meal by telling everyone about how chickens are electrocuted at slaughterhouses. "Who ever heard of such nonsense?"

"Yeah. She has been driving me sort of crazy." I'm about to tell Mom about Desma rearranging my furniture when a nurse pokes her head out of the doorway.

"Mrs. Peredo?"

"Right here," Mom says, and I get up with her, and we follow the nurse down the hall. I didn't used to go back with Mom when she had her medical appointments. She's a grown woman— why would she need her daughter in the examining room with her? But, over the past year, she's forgotten to tell her doctor about certain things and then forgets to tell me what he's told her. It's just easier for me to hear things at the same time he's telling my mother, and I can also make sure she's telling him everything that's bothering her.

"How are you today, Mrs. Peredo?" the nurse asks, raising her voice.

"I'm blind, dear, not deaf," Mom replies.

"I'm sorry. A lot of our patients are hard of hearing, so I try to speak loudly. How are you feeling?"

"I'm okay. No complaints." I know this isn't true. She's always complaining that her blood pressure medication makes her tired. She's been talking about being dizzy lately and went on for several minutes the other day about how dry her mouth is. I would step in and mention the issues to the nurse, but I figure I'll wait until the doctor comes in. No sense repeating myself.

"Did you color your hair since last time?" Mom asks the nurse.

"I did change the color a bit . . . added a little auburn to it."

"It looks nice," Mom says. "I used to color my hair, but I've gotten too old to keep up with it, and, since I can't see to drive, it's hard to get to the beauty parlor on a regular basis. I was like you when I was younger. I used to try out different shades and colors. I even went blonde once. My *papí* had a fit. He was an old school Colombian and women with dyed hair were of lesser moral values in his eyes."

The nurse does what most people do when my mother starts telling stories. They try to listen patiently, but they always have this look like someone has lassoed them—like they'd love to stay and chat, but something is pulling them away. I'm sure the nurse has a hundred other things to do, and, unfortunately, doesn't have time to listen to Mom go on about her younger days. I see Mom doing this all the time. She starts going on about her childhood or my father or what she watched on television last night to anyone who will listen, whether it be the teller at the bank or the checkout girl at the Safeway. Most of the time people are polite to her as they try to get her on her way. The say things like: "Isn't that a nice story," to wrap things up, or "That's really interesting. I guess I'd better get back to work." I don't blame her for trying to strike up a conversation with random strangers. She spends so much time alone that she must be desperate for companionship. I offered to arrange for her to be taken to the senior center a few miles from her house, so she could have some more social interaction, but she wasn't interested. She has a few friends she stays in touch with over the phone. And, of course, I talk to her daily as well, and see her twice a week, but other than that, and the few spotty calls she receives from my brother in Florida, she doesn't have much social interaction. I think that could explain why her mind seems to be slipping lately—whose mind wouldn't start to go if all you did was stay at home all day and watch *The Golden Girls* and the occasional Colombian *telenovela* on Telemundo.

"I'm sure he was just looking out for his little girl," the nurse responds and puts her hand on the doorknob.

"Yeah. He looked out for all of us. I had two brothers and a sister. Clara's still alive, but Juan had a heart attack three years ago, and Manuel had cancer. He's been dead for more than two years. He died shortly before my husband—"

"Mom. I'm sure the nurse has a lot of other patients she has to tend to."

"Unfortunately, I do," the nurse says. "We'll have to chat more next time, Mrs. Peredo. You can go ahead and put on a gown, and Dr. Miller will be with you shortly," she adds and quickly steps out of the room.

"You know, I saw in the paper that the senior center now has a book club on Tuesday evenings. What do you think about joining that?" I ask as Mom gets undressed.

"You know I don't see well enough to read."

I know this is not true. Her vision certainly has been compromised by her diabetes, but she religiously reads the obituaries in the newspaper and always reports who's died to me. She also sees well enough to read her mail and obsess about every single piece of it. And even though she won't admit it, I know she reads the large print *Reader's Digest*s that I arranged to have mailed to her house.

"They only read large print books, Mom. Your friend Gladys still drives. Maybe you can rope her into joining, and the two of you can go together." I want to add, "Wouldn't that beat trying to socialize with busy nurses," but I don't.

"I don't want to sit around with a bunch of old biddies. All they will want to do is talk about their ailments and how their grandchildren never come to see them."

"Fine." I sigh. I don't know why I bother. She shoots down every idea I have to try to improve her quality of life.

"Speaking of grandchildren, when am I going to see Andrew again?"

I'm about to answer her question when there's a quick tap on the door, and Dr. Miller comes into the examining room.

"Hello, hello, hello!" he says loudly with vigor. "The beautiful and talented Mrs. Ana Peredo! How lovely for you to come to see me today."

"Oh, stop!" Mom says and rolls her eyes. I can see her blushing. Dr. Miller is always very upbeat, vivacious, and full of flattering words. He's probably in his early sixties, with brown hair, kind eyes, and a pretty nice build for a man his age. He specializes in geriatric care, and his waiting room is full of walkers, canes, and blue hair. I figure he's such a "Dr. Sunshine" all the time because it's the only way to survive in his business. When you deal with sick elderly patients all day, it must require constant effort to stay positive.

"How are you? All is well, I hope?"

"I'm not too bad."

"Good, good! Let's give you a listen," Dr. Miller says and adorns his stethoscope before slipping it underneath Mom's gown and listening to her heart. "Whadda ya know . . . it's still beating."

Mom laughs.

When he's done with the stethoscope, he puts it back around his neck and takes a look at her file. "Your blood pressure's good. I'll have Samantha come back in and draw some blood. Are you watching your diet? Keeping your glucose levels in check?"

"Of course," Mom says, and she is pretty good about what she eats. She never really was into sweets, and she's been pretty good about cutting out starchy foods as well.

"Let's take a look at your legs, Ana," Dr. Miller says, squatting down on his knees and taking a tape measure and wrapping it around her calf. "They're still swollen, but at least they haven't gotten worse since you were here last," he says after standing up and looking at her chart.

About a year ago, Mom started getting intense swelling in her legs. Dr. Miller ran some tests and found that Mom's kidneys were not up to par, and that, combined with her heart issues, was probably what was causing the swelling. He did some additional tests and came to the conclusion that the kidney damage had been caused by her diabetes and there wasn't much we could do about it except try to keep her glucose levels as stable as possible and try to keep her blood pressure down. Luckily, although her kidney function is still compromised, it's remained stable over the past year.

"So how are you, really? Anything I need to know about?" Dr. Miller asks in a more serious tone.

"Not that I can think of offhand."

Oh, good grief. "She's been saying that her mouth gets really dry," I interject. "And she's been dizzy here and there lately."

"What can you tell me about that, Ana?"

"Oh, it's nothing. But my mouth does get dry sometimes. And I do get dizzy occasionally, especially when I get out of bed or up from the sofa."

"Let me ask you this: How bothersome is the dry mouth and the dizziness? Are they getting in the way of your daily activities? Are they distracting?"

"I wouldn't say they're getting in the way of my daily activities . . . but . . ."

"The reason I ask is that both symptoms are most likely side effects from your medications . . . probably the Norvasc for your blood pressure or maybe the Lasix for your edema. We can try other medications, but, unfortunately, dry mouth and dizziness are common side effects for most medications."

"Maybe we shouldn't go messing with my drugs."

"Why don't we keep an eye on it for the next few weeks and see how things go?"

"Okay," Mom says.

"Mom, you've been telling me how dry your mouth is for weeks. I think it might be a good idea to try something else. There's no reason for you to run around not feeling your best if we can help it." I say this to her, but I hope my words get through to the doctor as well. Maybe I'm being paranoid, but I get the feeling that he, like a lot of people, is willing to write off her complaints as part of old age—a "you're old, deal with it" sort of attitude. And, granted, there are things about getting old that can't be helped, but I want to make sure that my mother's doctor does his best to keep her feeling well. "I think you should give another medication a shot."

Dr. Miller looks at me and then at Mom. "We can do that. Why don't I write a script for Lisinopril, and you can try it instead of the Norvasc? And we'll see how it goes."

"What do you think?" I ask my mother.

"That's fine. It would be nice for my mouth not to feel so dry all the time. And maybe it will help with the dizziness."

My mother is from that old school of dealing with doctors— you offer them your utmost respect and don't question them. That's another reason I started coming back with her to the examining room. She needs someone to advocate for her and sometimes push the doctor on a thing or two. I'm not an aggressive person, but, when it comes to keeping my mother healthy, I force myself to be more assertive.

"Then it's a plan," Dr. Miller says, whips out his prescription pad, and starts writing. After he hands her the prescription, he looks at me and asks, "Who should I call with the lab results?"

His question makes the hairs on the back of my neck stand up. We've been coming to see Dr. Miller together for quite some time, and this is the first time he's asked such a question. In the past, he's always just called Mom with her lab work. It's just one more reminder of my mother's continuing dependence on me.

"You can call her. They're her lab results," I say with a friendly smile. I want my mother to stay as independent as possible for as long as possible. She's been a little goofy lately, but her mind is certainly still clear enough to understand her lab work. Besides, I'm just not ready to deal with the fact that my mother needs me to take her phone calls. "If I have any questions, I'll call the office."

"Okay. You stay well, Ana. It was positively wonderful to see you," Dr Miller says, offers me a smile, and exits the room.

"So we'll stop by the drugstore on the way home and fill the new prescription, and see if it helps you feel any better. I'll let you get dressed and wait for the nurse to come back," I say and start to step out of the room myself. "I'll be in the waiting room."

On my way down the hall, I see Dr. Miller head into another

examining room and close the door behind him. As I walk by the room, I hear him through the door. "Hello, hello, hello! The beautiful and talented Mrs. Judy Donnelly!" he says, uttering the same words he used with Mom to another patient. "How lovely for you to come to see me today."

12

"Hi, Benita," I say as I enter the human resources department at Currier and Timmons, the nationwide law firm for which I've been working for the past two and a half years. I'm a human resources generalist. I'm involved in recruiting and hiring new employees, analyzing our benefits plans, helping managers deal with troublesome employees and all sorts of other special projects. I also have the unfortunate duty of managing Benita, the receptionist for the human resources department.

"Hi, Jennifer," Benita says to me, as she shoves some sort of glossy magazine in the drawer next to her.

"No magazines at the front desk, Benita," I say in a friendly tone, even though this is the second time I've had to mention it to her, as I breeze past her desk. Currier and Timmons is a prestigious law firm. It's not uncommon for honors law school graduates from the likes of Yale and Harvard to come through the doors, and I don't want them seeing our receptionist all laid up with the latest issue of *Us Weekly*. I hired Benita, against my better judgment, about six months ago, and I'm still regretting the decision. She's nice enough and manages to show up on time most days, but she really seems to struggle with appropriate office behavior. I came in last Tuesday, and she was clipping her toenails at her desk, and she didn't even have her feet over the trash can. I'd hear this *ping* and a piece of toenail would fly into the air and land on the carpet. I've had to talk to her about that just like I've had to talk to her about chewing gum at her desk, the volume of the radio she keeps next to her, and why it's not okay to come to the office of a conservative law firm without wearing a bra. Benita is just . . . hmm . . . how do I say this politely: white trash. Okay, so that wasn't so polite, but I don't know how else to accurately describe her. The position doesn't pay much money, and we needed someone to fill it immediately, so I decided to give her a chance. But if I catch her with a magazine at her desk one more time, I'm going to write her up.

"There are three people waiting in your office," Benita says to me, standing to grab a file off the top of one of the cabinets.

"Who?" I ask.

"Mark Castor from upstairs and two of his employees. I forgot their names."

Yes. It's hard to remember names when you're trying to catch up on the latest Jessica Simpson news. "Benita, I need you to find these things out for me. That's part of your job."

She doesn't respond, at least not verbally. Instead, she gives me what I've come to call her dazed and confused look. She seems to think if she stands there and looks like an idiot without saying anything, I'll leave her alone. And, in actuality, I guess she's right.

I sigh and walk toward my office.

"Hi," I say as I come through the door and see Mark Castor, one of our paralegal supervisors, leaning on the edge of my desk with two women sitting in the chairs opposite him.

"Hi, Jennifer. I'm sorry to bother you, but Lynn insisted that we have a meeting with human resources about her issue, and Benita said you were due in at any moment."

"Okay. What is it?" I take a seat behind my desk.

"Lynn and Taylor are paralegals, and Lynn here," Mark says, gesturing toward a large white lady who appears to be in her early fifties, "has an issue with Taylor," he adds, looking at an African American woman who I'd guess to be about forty.

"Good afternoon, ladies," I say, sensing the tension between them. "Tell me about the problem." A request I've made numerous times during my years in personnel, and I've regretted it every single time.

Lynn gives Taylor a hateful look. "She stole my scissors!"

"I did not take her scissors," Taylor responds, rolling her eyes.

"Oh, yeah?! Then how do you explain them being in the cup on your desk?"

"They're not in the cup on my desk, you loon," Taylor says back to Lynn then looks at me. "She's a complete wack job. She always thinks I'm stealing her stuff."

"I marked my scissors with fingernail polish, so I'd be able to spot them *anywhere*."

"*Who* does that? What kind of loop-de-loop marks their frickin' scissors?"

"Ladies!" I say, afraid the earrings might start to come off at any moment. "Is there a shortage of scissors on the seventh floor? I mean, really, we billed a few million dollars in legal services last year—we'll get you another pair of scissors, Lynn."

"I don't want *another* pair of scissors. I want *my* scissors." These are the words of a fifty-year-old woman.

"Where did you originally get the scissors, Lynn?"

"From the supply closet."

"Okay then. So they never were *your* scissors." I say. "They are the property of Currier and Timmons. I suggest you get another pair from the supply closet, and this matter will be closed."

Lynn exhales a long breath the way Andrew does when I tell him he can't have anymore ice cream. "You better not take my new pair!" she says to Taylor, and gets up from her chair and leaves.

"My God. I'm a kindergarten teacher all of a sudden," I say and look at Mark. "Why did you bother me with this?"

"I didn't have any choice. Lynn demanded a meeting with human resources. You know our policy—once an employee does that, we have no choice but to bring them down here."

"Well, I hope you'll handle things like this on your own from now on. I'm sure Taylor here didn't take her scissors."

"Actually," Taylor interjects, "I sort of did . . . just to mess with her," she adds with a wicked laugh.

I put my head in my hands and give it a little shake. "Okay. I *so* didn't hear that," I say, before Benita pokes her head in my door.

"Jennifer?"

"Yes, Benita."

"Your sister is on line two."

"I don't have a sister."

"She said her name was Greta and that she's calling about your son."

I laugh. "I don't have a sister named Greta." And then it hits me: *Sister. Greta.* Sister Greta is Andrew's school principal. "I need to take this," I say to Mark and Taylor, goose bumps appearing on my forearms as I wave them out of my office.

13

My head is already pounding as I pull into the parking lot of St. Paul's Primary School. Sister Greta felt it best we talk in person, so I had to duck out of work. She said only that they were having a disciplinary problem with Andrew, and that she would elaborate further when I got there. I'm relieved to know that he hasn't physically hurt himself, but I'm still worried about what Andrew did that would warrant me being called to the school.

"Hello. I'm Jennifer Costas, Andrew's mother. Sister Greta asked me to come in to see her," I say to one of the school secretaries.

She picks up the phone and dials. "Ms. Costas is here to see you, Sister," she says, listens for a moment, and then hangs up the phone. "She'll be right with you. I'll go get Andrew," she says to me and gets up from her desk.

"Good day," I hear as the door behind me opens, and I see an elderly nun poke her head out. Only a hint of her white hair is not covered by her habit. She wears thick glasses, a white blouse, a polyester black skirt, and no-nonsense shoes.

"Ah . . . hello," I say, suddenly intimidated by her. I went to a Catholic school myself, and my mother taught me to offer nothing but my respect and absolute obedience to the nuns. Of course, that was back in the seventies and eighties when there actually were nuns in the Catholic schools. At the moment, aside from

Sister Mary Ellen who is even older than Sister Greta and only minds the children during lunch, Sister Greta is the only nun working at the school All the other teachers and support staff are what we Catholics call laypersons.

"Please. Come in," she says, not in a friendly tone, but not exactly unfriendly either.

"Thank you." I'm tensing up, starting to think of all the things that come to mind when I'm around nuns: *She thinks I'm a whore. She thinks my skirt is too short. Does she know I'm divorced?*

"I called you in because we had a problem with Andrew today and have yet to resolve it," she says as we both sit down on opposite sides of the desk.

"Oh?" My God! What could he have done?

"This morning, after prayers, Andrew, of his own volition, turned his desk around and moved it against the wall. His teacher, Mrs. Knox, asked him to move it back, and he refused. He said that the way it had been was not 'fung shui.'"

"Desma," I mumble under my breath and start rubbing my temples.

"He insisted that 'chi' would not flow properly throughout the room unless everyone moved their desks—"

Sister Greta ceases conversation as the door opens, and I see the secretary I spoke with earlier nudge Andrew into the room. His eyes are wide and his shoulders are practically up to his ears. He reminds me of a dog with his tail between his legs who's just had an accident on the carpet.

"Andrew? What's all this I'm hearing about you moving your desk without permission?"

"Aunt Desma said that my desk should face—"

"I don't care what Desma said. When you are at school, you will obey your teachers, young man."

"Apparently this Aunt Desma is full of advice," Sister Greta says.

Oh shit, here we go.

"Yesterday, during the 'Pledge of Allegiance,'" Andrew took

it upon himself to add a few words to the ending." Sister Greta turns to Andrew. "Do you want to tell your mother what you added to a pledge that was written long before any of us were born?"

Andrew looks down and shakes his head.

"He ended with 'with liberty and justice for all," and then added 'unless you're gay.'"

"My daddy's gay," Andrew says, out of the blue, and I see the nun's eyes widen.

"Yes, your father is very happy, Andrew," I say. "Now hush."

"He was in a drag show and wore one of Mommy's dresses."

I laugh awkwardly. "Enough with the stories, Andrew. You stand there and be quiet." I feel Sister Greta's eyes piercing through me. She's judging me. I know she is.

"He said that his Aunt Desma told him that the 'Pledge of Allegiance' is a lie because there isn't liberty and justice for *all*."

I want to say that "that's sort of true," but instead I say, "I will have a talk with Andrew about all of this. And I assure you, it won't be a problem in the future."

"Are there problems at home, Ms. Costas?" Yep, she is judging me.

I'm not a whore! I'm not! "No, no. We're just busy . . . juggling a lot, but I promise Andrew will behave," I say and look at Andrew.

"I should hope so. We are a Catholic school, and subscribe to the traditions of the church. Perhaps, if you're a person of more," she hesitates for a moment, "*liberal* values, you should place Andrew in an appropriate school."

"Oh, no . . . no liberal values here," I lie. Oh, God, I'm lying to a nun. "Andrew and I are going to go home and have a long talk."

"Okay. Thank you for coming in. I'm sure you'll get this resolved," she says with an "and if you don't, your kid's outta here" edge to her tone.

"We will," I say, feeling like a schoolgirl myself, one who's been caught smoking in the bathroom. "Let's go, Andrew."

"That's a lovely picture you have of the Pope," I offer, trying to make nice by commenting on her wall art as I leave the room.

"Aunt Desma says the Pope's a jer—"

"German," I say very quickly over Andrew. "Yes, I do believe the Pope *is* a German," I add abruptly and grab Andrew's hand and pull him from the office.

14

I'm driving home from Andrew's school, eyeing him in the backseat with the rearview mirror. He's been silent since we got in the car, and I have as well. I don't know what to say to him. His behavior was totally out of character. He's usually a mostly agreeable child and has never really challenged authority in any major way. I can't even picture him refusing to move his desk after being asked to do so by his teacher, Mrs. Knox. I've met Mrs. Knox, and she has a strong sense of authority about her. Why would Andrew so brazenly disobey her?

I'm trying not to do it . . . I really am, but I can't help it—every time Andrew acts out or displays any sort of unusual behavior, I blame it on the divorce, and today is no exception. There's a part of me that's afraid to ask him what was behind his behavior today. I have this fear that he's going to say that he acted out because "you and Daddy abandoned me."

"So? Are we going to talk about this, Andrew? Are you going to tell me why you disobeyed your teacher today?" I finally muster the courage to ask.

"Aunt Desma told me that that my desk should be placed—"

"I don't care what Desma told you. You know better than to disobey your teacher. And I don't expect that I'll be hearing that you've done it again.

"Don't you roll your eyes at me," I say, catching him doing just that in the mirror. "What is going on with you, Andrew?'

"Nothing."

"Don't tell me 'nothing,' Andrew. It's not like you to be disrespectful to your teachers. I don't believe you refused to move your desk just because of Aunt Desma's little lesson in feng shui. Why did you do it?"

His eyes meet mine in the mirror. "I don't know. Why don't you ask *Ben*."

My face suddenly flushes with heat. How does he know about Ben? "What are you talking about?"

"You went out with him, and you didn't tell me," he says and quickly folds his arms.

So that's what this is all about. He's mad about my first date since Mario and I split. I was careful not to tell him about it. I didn't see any reason for him to know about my date with Ben, or any dates with anyone, unless I thought it would actually amount to something. But Andrew's always been so quiet and can move around like a Delta Force operative when he wants to eavesdrop. He must have overheard me talking to Desma or Claire.

I'm at a loss for words. What am I supposed to say? I have every right to go out on a date. It's been two years since Mario and I divorced. And I don't think there was anything wrong with me not telling Andrew about it. He's five years old—he doesn't need to know everything that goes on in my life. There was nothing wrong with the way I handled the situation, and it certainly doesn't justify Andrew's behavior at school. I want to tell Andrew all of this: that I'm thirty-five years old, and an adult, and his mother—and I don't owe him explanations for everything I do. But I see him in the backseat with an angry look on his face, and it breaks my heart. He barely knows a time when his mother and father were a couple. He's been passed around between two houses since he was three years old. I can't begin to imagine what that must be like and, of course, there is going to be some trauma involved in hearing about his mother going out with a man who is not his father. I feel like I'm stuck in an impossible situation. Andrew has to be disciplined for behaving badly at school, but how do I balance reprimanding him with understanding what a difficult situation he's in—that we're all in?

I take a slow deep breath. "Andrew, if you had concerns about my outing with Ben, why didn't you ask me about them?"

"Why didn't *you* tell me about him?"

"Because I didn't think it was necessary for you to know about it. Ben is just someone I used to work with, and we went out together for an evening." My God! I feel like I'm back in Sister Greta's office being interrogated. "You know, Andrew, your father and I have been apart now for two years and, occasionally, I may have a date or an outing with someone, but it's nothing for you to worry about. And it's certainly nothing to get upset over."

I see him in the backseat looking out the window as I speak. "I don't even plan to see Ben again. You see, what was the point in my mentioning him to you when I don't even plan to see him again?"

"You're not going to see him anymore?" Andrew asks, and I see a hopeful expression in his face and a relieved look in his eyes.

"I don't plan to, no." I pull into the driveway and stop the car. "Wait just a minute," I say when I hear him click the door handle. I want to say something to him, but I can't put it into words. I want to assure him that no matter who I go out with and what happens with them, he will always be the most important person in my life. "Andrew, if you overhear things . . . things like information about my date with Ben, and you're concerned, you need to tell me, and we'll talk about it. Okay?"

"Okay." He pushes the door open and gets out of the car.

"Not so fast, little man," I say behind him as we walk into the house. "There'll be no television tonight, and I'm going to tell your father . . ." I was about to say that I was going to tell Mario that Andrew had lost his TV privileges for the weekend, but then I'd have to explain the afternoon to Mario and that would include Ben, and I just don't feel like going there. "I won't mention your behavior to Daddy, but when you get back from the weekend with him, there'll be no television for a week. And if I ever hear of you behaving badly at school again the punishment will be a lot worse than no television. Got it?"

Andrew nods.

"You know you're still my number one guy?" God, I'm such a pushover.

He gives me a smile, and we head into the house, so I can get him packed to spend the weekend with Mario.

15

"Who is it?" I hear my mother call from the other side of her front door.

"It's me, Mom."

"Who?"

"Open the door, Mother. What's wrong with you?" I called her this morning and said I would be by this afternoon.

"Jennifer? Is that you?"

"No, it's the tooth fairy, Mother. Who do you think it is?"

I hear the dead bolt click, and she opens the door.

"Hi," she says.

"Hi. Didn't you remember I was coming this afternoon?"

"Is it afternoon already?"

"It's nearly noon." I notice that she is still in her housecoat, and the shades are drawn in the living room. "Are you feeling okay?"

"I suppose so."

"Why aren't you dressed?"

"I guess the morning got away from me. I've been busy working on my scrapbook."

I follow her into the kitchen and watch her sit down at the table, which is covered in old newspapers. She picks up a pair of scissors and a sheet of newspaper and starts cutting, going about her business as if I'm not there. I see an old photo album lying on the table with the clippings and pick it up and start to leaf through it.

"What's this?" I ask. The book is filled with clipped obituaries. "Why are you putting all these obituaries in a photo album?"

"Well, what do you expect me to do with my time? There isn't a damn thing on TV. I figure I might as well make a keepsake of my friends' 'fifteen minutes of fame' in the newspaper."

"What a way to become famous—to drop dead," I say, realizing that most of the obits in her scrapbook are from fairly recent newspapers. She must have clipped more than a hundred from just the past few weeks.

"Mom, you don't know any of these people."

"Of course I do."

"Okay. Who's Elford Monroe?" I inquire, eyeing a page in the album.

"Who?" she asks with a blank expression.

"Elford Monroe. He's in one of the clippings you have in here. Do you know him?"

She lifts her eyes for a moment and thinks. "Hmm . . . I don't suppose I do."

"Betty Jackson? Do you know her?"

"Give me that," she says and snatches the album from my hand without answering my question and picks up the scissors again.

"Mom, we have lots of errands to run today. You said you wanted to go to the bank, and we need to get you some groceries. And we can go by the mall if you want to do some more shopping. Why don't you put the scissors down and go get dressed?"

"The store," she says as if our plans for the day are coming back to her. "Yes. I need bananas and some eggs."

I watch her get up from her chair and walk out of the kitchen toward the steps. It's so unlike her to still be in her housecoat this time of day. She's always been a creature of habit, and every morning since I can remember, she'd get out of bed, come downstairs in her housecoat and have a cup of coffee. Then she'd climb back upstairs to shower and get dressed. And what's the deal with the obituaries? That's just odd.

I feel my body tensing as I process what's happened this afternoon. I've always known that it's not good for her to be alone so much since my father died, but now I'm thinking that we really need to start looking into finding her a place to live closer to me—whether it be a regular apartment or maybe a suite in an assisted living facility. I dread the thought of bringing up the idea with her again. She just about spit fire at me the first time I mentioned the idea of her moving, but I can't have her sitting around the kitchen table clipping strangers' obituaries and not bothering to get dressed in the morning. If she were close by, I could check on her on the way to work and stop by in the afternoon, and she could even spend some evenings and some time on the weekends at the house with Andrew and me (oh, joy . . .).

And, yes, I've given some thought to her moving in with me altogether (brief thought . . . *very* brief), but my jaw locks so tight every time I think about it, it's really only something I'd seriously consider if it became *absolutely* necessary. My mother and I have always been akin to oil and vinegar, and while we love each other, the idea of us living under one roof brings visions of two Chinese fighting fish stuck in the same bowl. I don't think it would be good for either of us, and it certainly wouldn't be good for Andrew.

While mother is upstairs getting showered and changed, I sit down at the kitchen table and sort through the newspapers to see if I can find an article to occupy myself with until she's ready. I can't find anything of interest in the paper, so I just sit there and look around, and it doesn't take long before I'm . . . well . . . sad. The light is dim in the kitchen and, while it's clean, it's a bit dingy from time and use and hasn't had a serious remodeling in more than twenty years. The kitchen used to be the center of life in this house. My entire family spent the majority of our time awake in the house in this room. We, my parents and my brother and me, scarfed down cereal together on weekday mornings and enjoyed more leisurely breakfasts of *pericos* (a Colombian way of preparing scrambled eggs with tomatoes and green onions) and *chorizo* (Colombian sausage) on the weekends in this room. It was the "decompress" room for all of us after school and work. Book bags were laid on the counter, briefcases were tossed on the table, coats were placed over the backs of the kitchen chairs. My brother Tom and I did our homework at the table while Mom fixed dinner and Dad read the paper. It used to be so full of life—like the Grand Central Station of the Peredo home. Even after Tom and I moved out, I know my parents spent the bulk of their time in this room, and it was still the meeting place when visitors came over. My parents always preferred a pot of Colombian coffee around the kitchen table with guests over entertaining in the living or dining rooms.

It's sad to see this room looking so empty and bland when it was once so full of life—I guess it parallels the whole house, which is becoming more and more a ghost of what it once was. The house used to have loads of what Claire calls "curb appeal," but my father is not around anymore to tend to the flower bed out front, and Mom's back isn't really conducive to gardening, so it's now just a pile of empty mulch. A kid in the neighborhood cuts her grass, but he's nowhere near as meticulous as my father was. I've been meaning to try to find someone to paint the trim on the exterior, but it keeps falling to the bottom of my priority list. And, although the inside of the house is neat, it's quite dated. The carpet should have been replaced years ago, and the furniture, while in good condition, hasn't been in style since the eighties. Mom is financially secure—she gets a decent check from Dad's pension fund in addition to her Social Security payment and has savings, but she's paranoid about money and wouldn't think of spending any cash to update the house. I haven't pushed her on it as I'm not sure how much longer she's going to be able to stay here on her own. Maybe, before I come over the next time, I'll pick up some brightly colored pillows or a nice flower arrangement to liven up the place.

I'm about to step into the living room and open the shades to let some light in when Mom comes back downstairs ready to go. The tension I've felt in the back of my neck since I came through the front door lets up a bit when I look at her fully dressed, with her hair combed and some lipstick on. She almost looks like a woman who has it together, unlike the picture I walked in on earlier, but something about her is off. I don't know why, but it takes me a moment to notice what it is.

"Ah, Mom? Your dress is on backwards."

"What? It is not."

"Yes, it is. It zips in the back."

She looks down at her body. "Oh, my. You're right," she says, the embarrassment showing in her face. "I wear my house-coat so much these days and that zips in the front. I guess I just forgot."

"No biggie," I say. "Just go flip it around."

She turns around and starts back up the steps, taking each step slowly, like her legs are heavy and weak, which shouldn't be a surprise considering how much swelling she has had in them lately.

Several minutes later, we pull up in front of the Safeway, and I let Mom out at the curb and go park the car. I turn the ignition off and grab the book I tossed in the backseat before I left home and try to make myself comfortable in the driver's seat. Like I usually do when I take Mom to the grocery store, I occupy myself in the car for at least twenty minutes before I go in the store to catch up with her. I've found it's easier to let her get started and poke around the aisles by herself for a while before I join her and help her find the final items she can't seem to locate and read some of the prices she claims she can't see.

After I've read about thirty pages of my book, I look at the clock and decide it's time to head inside, find Mom, and see if I can't speed her up a little. Our grocery shopping excursions would be much more productive if I was able to do the shopping for my house as well. But since Mom's house is anywhere from an hour to more than two hours away from mine (depending on the traffic on I-95) it doesn't make sense to buy any items that need refrigeration or freezing.

When I find her in the store, she's still in the produce section . . . *still* in the produce section, the first section of the store.

"Hey. How's it going?"

"Melons," she says to me.

I look at her and wait for her to elaborate.

"I can't find the melons."

"They're right over there." I point to the honeydew melons on display.

"No. I don't want that kind."

"Do you want a cantaloupe?"

"No. I want *melons*," she says with irritation in her voice that the situation doesn't warrant.

"What kind of melon?"

"Just a melon," she says, and I see anger starting to stir up in her. "They never have what I want at this store. Never!"

"Okay. Okay. Why don't we look for something else, and we'll check back for the melons later," I suggest, eyeing her cart. She has the top part filled with a couple of tomatoes, potatoes, and apples, none of which she has bothered to put into plastic produce bags.

"Why don't we put these in bags," I say and start ripping some bags off the roll. Why wouldn't she put her selections in plastic bags? She always has in the past.

"What else do you need? Milk? Juice? Paper towels?" I ask after I've bagged the produce and nonchalantly seized control of the cart and walk toward the dairy refrigerators. I have a hundred things to do when I get home, and I need to speed up this little grocery shopping excursion.

"Yeah. I need some milk."

I continue to push the cart around the store with Mom following behind me and insisting I go down aisles that I know don't have anything she wants or needs, and, after nearly an hour, we finally meander toward the registers.

"No. He's slow as molasses in winter," she says and nudges

me away from the line manned by a gawky-looking young man. "There are certain jobs that men were not meant to do, and 'cashier' is one of them. They are always so slow."

Oh, suddenly, you're in a hurry? I think to myself as we move on to the next open register. Somehow we manage to get through the checkout line without incident, push the cart out to the car, and load the groceries in the trunk.

"I think we'll have to save the mall for next time," I say once we're settled in the car and on our way out of the lot. "The day's getting away from me, and I have a lot of stuff to take care of when I get home."

"Okay. I don't really need anything from there anyway."

We're both quiet for a while, and, after a few minutes, I decide now is as good a time as any to bring up the dreaded subject of her moving.

"How is your friend Amelia?" I ask, knowing that Amelia recently moved to an assisted living facility.

"Why do you ask?" Mom replies suspiciously.

Shit. She's on to me. "I thought I heard you mention that she had moved into a senior apartment complex, and I was wondering how it was working out."

"I don't think the place she's in is an apartment complex. I think it's a step or two below a nursing home."

"It is not. New Horizons has some nice communities. You remember, I gave you a brochure about their community in Alexandria last year."

The only response I get from her is a brief sigh, so I continue. "Have you given any more thought to maybe getting a place closer to Andrew and me—not necessarily at a senior's complex, maybe just an apartment or a condo, so you're not so isolated."

"You're not putting me in a nursing home, Jennifer Peredo." She always uses my maiden name when she's annoyed with me. "If you do, I'll change my will and leave everything to your brother."

"Oh, yeah . . . my brother. And the last time you heard from him was?"

"He's very busy, Jennifer. He has a wife and two kids to support."

Oh, and I suppose I just sit around the house eating bonbons all day. "Did I ever even utter the word nursing home, Mother?" I decide to ignore her comment about the will and my brother. "When I came over this afternoon, you were sitting in the dark clipping obituaries of people you don't even know. It's not good for you to spend so much time alone. Wouldn't you rather be close by, so we can see each other more often, and you can spend more time with Andrew?" And I won't have to trek all the way out to frickin' Fredericksburg two times a week.

"I'm not leaving my house, Jennifer. I've lived there for thirty years. I've raised two children in that house. It's my home. I make out okay there. I'm not leaving." She crosses her arms the same way Andrew does when he's being stubborn.

I decide to let the moving conversation go for the time being. She's obviously in a place right now in which she isn't willing to even entertain the idea.

"Fine. We'll discuss it some other time. But can you at least give it some thought and try to have an open mind about it? I can certainly understand you not wanting to leave your home, but give some consideration to the advantages of us living closer together. You wouldn't have to eat all your meals alone, we could run errands more often, if you have a crisis, I'll be nearby . . . just give it some thought. Can you do that?"

"I'm not leaving my house," she says, looking out the window with her arms still crossed.

16

"My God! Are we at a church or the Verizon Center?" I ask as Claire, Desma, and I make our way toward the parking garage of the Tysons Bible Church. Traffic was backed up for several blocks on Route 7 to get onto the church grounds and that was with a police officer providing direction.

"Yeah. It is a bit grandiose, isn't it?" Claire says to me.

"Oh, look, a waterfall," Desma says, pointing to the cascading water along one side of the mammoth building. After much thought, Desma changed her mind and decided to join us this morning, saying she's working on a book about the perils of organized religion—a book, like so many others on which Desma has "worked," that will never materialize. "Isn't that nice? People starving all over the world, and a church is spending thousands of dollars on a waterfall. And look at all these cars," she adds, buzzing her head around in every direction, as we continue our stop-and-go pace into the parking garage. "Mercedes', BMWs, Infinities. Hmmm . . . their Bible must exclude the part about it being easier for a camel to go through the eye of a needle than for a rich man to enter the kingdom of God."

"Or maybe they just didn't get the memo," Claire responds and turns up the radio to drown out any further commentary from Desma as we keep inching along until one of several parking attendants directs us into an empty space.

"Hmm . . . just what I thought," Desma says, stepping out of the car and looking around. "White people, white people, and more white people."

Claire and I ignore her, and the three of us walk over the little causeway that connects the parking garage to the church. When we're inside, Desma and I look around in awe as we follow along behind Claire. I feel like we're inside the lobby of the Kennedy Center. The area we're in must rival the length of a football field. There's some sort of ticket booth at the far end of the room and little information stalls are all along the sides. Each stall has a banner in front of it. One says "Welcome Center," another says "Singles' Ministry," another says "Kids' Christian Corner," and so on and so on.

"Wow. This is sort of one-stop shopping for all your life needs," I say.

"Yeah. Isn't it cool?" Claire says.

"Hardly. I've done my research," Desma interjects. "This church is very hostile toward gays and a woman's right to choose. The pastor is nothing more than a right wing politician, posing as a minister to advance the conservative agenda."

"Well, apparently he's very good at it," Claire says smartly. "Look at this place. It's packed. I think something like ten thousand people attend services here every weekend."

"Did you know the pastor used to be Jewish, and now he insists that all Jews need to be converted to Christianity?"

"Blah, blah, blah," Claire says. "We're not here to talk about Christians or Jews. We're here to get Jennifer laid. Now come on," she adds, bypassing the welcome table and leading us over to the Singles' Ministry.

"Hi," Claire says to the two we-only-come-to-church-to-try-to-find-a-husband looking women standing behind the counter. "My friends here are interested in the Singles' Ministry. I've been to a few events, but I guess we need an updated calendar and such." While Claire's speaking, I notice that somewhere between leaving my house and arriving at the booth her wedding band has disappeared.

"Sure," one of perky ladies says and hands us a flyer. We have a music and teaching session every Thursday night at seven-thirty, and then we have specialized gatherings throughout the week. We have groups for people of different ages and a group for recently single or divorced individuals."

"What about a group for gay people?" Desma inquires.

Miss Perky's smile suddenly fades. "We don't have anything like that," she says flatly.

"Oh. So you have a group for divorced people, but not one for gays, even though divorce is decried in the Bible far more often than homosexuality?"

Miss Perky gives her a blank stare.

"Typical," Desma says and walks away.

"I don't know why she wanted to come if she was just going to be negative," Claire says to me after she thanks the ladies, and we walk away to catch up with Desma and try to keep her out of trouble. When we reach her, she snatches one of the flyers out of my hands and starts giving it a quick read. Thankfully, before she has a chance to complain about whatever it says, the lights in the lobby flash, signaling us that it's time to enter the auditorium for the service.

"It seats almost three thousand people," a handsome gentleman with light hair and a goatee says to me, after noticing the way I'm looking around once I'm through the auditorium doors—the same way a small town girl might look at the skyscrapers on a first trip to New York City.

"Really?"

"Yeah. And, at some services, it gets completely full and people have to use the overflow auditorium downstairs."

"Popular place."

"Yes," he says. "I'm Grant, by the way. I'm an usher for this service."

"Jennifer," I respond, and shake his hand.

"Nice to meet you. Is this your first time here?"

"Yes, I came with my friends." I look around for Claire and

Desma and see that they are already on their way up the steps to some open seats. "Guess I'd better catch up with them," I say, pointing my eyes in their direction.

"Okay. It was nice to meet you. You should come to the newcomers meeting after the service. I'll give you a tour of the church."

"Sure." I'm not really sure what plans Claire has for me after the service, but it would have been impolite to decline his invitation.

I smile at Grant and climb one of the many staircases between the vast rows of seats like I'm at a Cher concert or a Wizards' game.

As soon as I sit down in between Claire and Desma, I hear the middle-aged woman sitting next to Desma say hello to her. She's wearing a purple shirt, a purple hat, and dangling purple earrings.

"Are you a member of the church?" the woman asks Desma.

"Oh, no. I'm just doing research on churches that subjugate women, advocate for discrimination against homosexuals, and allow themselves to be used as tools for the political right."

The woman's smile quickly fades. "Oh . . . um . . . how nice. I'll pray for you, dear."

"Because prayer is *so* effective," Desma says sarcastically. "Can I have cash instead?"

The woman has no reply for Desma's slight—only a bemused expression. Eventually she turns away and feels under her seat for a Bible, pulls it out, and starts flipping through it.

"My God! Do you know this place took in sixteen million dollars last year?" Desma says, looking at the bulletin. "Harvard Business School students should study this place and—"

Desma's about to continue when we spot a group of ten men taking their seats on the stage. They're carrying trumpets and saxophones, and one of them slides behind a grand piano. Then, without warning, they fire up their instruments, and, if I closed my eyes, I'd swear I was at a downtown jazz club.

"This is how they suck you in. With catchy music," Desma

whispers to me as we join the rest of the congregation and stand up. A few moments later a young man with blond highlights and a tailored black shirt walks on stage and starts to sing with a feeling-the-holy-spirit sort of smile on his face. I see his blond highlights and his insane smile even though we're in the far upper seats of the auditorium, because the venue is outfitted with no less than ten huge movie-size projection screens that would not be out of place at Madison Square Garden.

"He's cute," I say to Claire.

"I know him. Joseph Anderson. He's gay."

"I thought Desma said this was an anti-gay church?"

"I think he overlooks that small inconvenience. Where else is he going to get to sing in front of three thousand adoring fans? It's either this or karaoke night at some gay bar."

After the singers finish and take their seats, the music continues and a young woman with only one arm comes to the front of the stage and starts to read what apparently is "her story" set to music. She speaks of an accident that caused her to lose her arm, and how she has since found comfort in the Lord.

"I prayed to God for the strength to deal with my disability, and my prayers have been answered," she says.

"If she believes in prayer so much," Desma leans in and says to me, "why doesn't she pray to get her arm back?"

"Would you hush?" is my only response. I was actually sort of moved by the young woman's story. She's suffered a debilitating blow and seems to be carrying on, and, if a little prayer helps her get through the day, then so be it.

After the young lady leaves the stage, she's replaced by an elderly black man, and I guess it's his turn for musical story time. As he speaks with the saxophones playing lightly in the background, we learn that he was an evacuee from the floods in New Orleans a couple of years ago, and that he's enormously grateful to God for surviving the tragedy and finding a new home in Virginia.

"I pray every day for all the other victims of Hurricane Katrina . . ."

"You mean the victims of Hurricane George Bush," Desma says under her breath.

"That they managed to land on solid ground," the man continues. "I pray that they find saving in the glory of God, and I pray that they find peace and happiness."

"Yeah, because prayer worked so well when he was praying that the levees wouldn't break in the first place."

"Enough, Desma!" I say quietly but sternly, and she leans back in her chair and rolls her eyes.

When the minister finally makes his grand entrance, with some little minion carrying out his podium for him like he's Marie Antoinette at Versailles, he welcomes the congregation and says a prayer while we all (with the exception of Desma) bow our heads. He begins the service, and I settle into my seat and try to relax. Although he is clearly a gifted public speaker, I'm finding him a bit smarmy. I feel like he's trying to sell me something, and the whole service is just too much. Whenever he quotes something from the Bible, the exact verse appears on all the screens overhead, and the lighting behind him keeps changing from clear to violet to soft green. Growing up in the Catholic church with plain wooden pews, a single church organ, and stained glass windows makes all of this seem excessive and maybe even manipulative . . . or maybe I'm just being influenced by Desma's negative reaction to the place.

It wouldn't be any church service without the collection basket coming around; however, here at the Tysons Bible Church, rather than the staid Catholic wicker baskets, they pass around little velvet sacks that look like something from which a magician might pull a rabbit.

"A percentage of today's offering will go toward financing the sanctuary choir's upcoming trip to Russia where they will perform for our sister church in Moscow," Reverend Clarke says from the pulpit.

Desma passes the sack to me without making a donation. "Russia has an out of control mafia, skyrocketing AIDS rates, young girls being sold into prostitution and what they need from a church is a bunch of rich white people from McLean to come over and *sing* to them?"

I chuckle at her comment and pass the sack on to Claire, who, like Desma and me, makes no contribution. The service continues with Desma often rolling her eyes, me fidgeting uncomfortably in my chair, and, when I turn to Claire, I see that she's reviewing some of her real estate listings while the minister preaches.

She sees me eyeing her. "Male pickings are a bit slim today," she says after a brief look around. "We'll have to stop by the cafeteria after service and see if the options are any better out there."

"There's a cafeteria?"

"Oh, yes. And a coffee bar. It's just like Starbucks . . . only it's called Holy Java or something like that."

"You're kidding?"

"No. They make a mean latte."

Desma is going to have a field day with that. I can hear her now: "Millions of people all over the world are living in squalor and these *Christians* (she'll do the air quote thing when she says the word "Christians") are serving lattes at church."

17

When the service finally ends, I'm glad to be out of my seat as we make our way back to the lobby.

"Why don't you two go to the newcomer's orientation, and I'll check in with the after-service social," Claire says to Desma and me. "Maybe by the time you're done, I'll have a few prospects scoped out for you, Jen . . . if I don't snatch them up for myself."

"I'm not really interested in the newcomer orientation. I think I've had about all I can stand of this house of hypocrisy for one day."

"Then why don't you go sit in the car until we're ready to leave," Claire says shortly to Desma.

"Claire!" I reprimand her.

"I'm sorry, but I don't understand why you came," she says to Desma. "All you've done is complain since we got here. We get it. You don't like this place."

"I'm sorry if my observations offend you, but I was only saying what I believe to be true."

"Well, can you just chill for a little while? You've made your points. Now why don't you relax? How about I buy you a cup of coffee in the coffee bar while Jen goes to the orientation," Claire suggests, offering the best apology she can.

Desma softens her stance. "All right, but there'd better not be any holy water in my coffee."

"Do I really need to go to the orientation session? I really don't think I'm interested in joining."

"Thank God!" Desma says. "Sorry," she adds after Claire eyes her.

"Yes. There's bound to be an eligible man or two in there. Just go. It only lasts a few minutes. Meet us downstairs when you're done."

"Okay," I reluctantly agree and make my way to the orientation room.

When I walk in, I'm greeted, once again, by Grant, who chatted with me briefly before the service.

"Hey. Glad you decided to stop by. Jennifer, right?"

"Yes. Thank you."

"Did you enjoy the service?"

"Sure."

"Don't let the size of the place overwhelm you." He puts his hand on the upper part of my arm. "We have so many small group ministries that help you get to know other members and be active in the church."

"Good to know," I say, taking a closer look at him. He's slightly taller than I am with a kind face and a lovely smile. "How long have you been a member?"

"Just a few months. It was all overwhelming to me at first, but now I love it here. The church gives me so much support."

Is it a church or an AA meeting? I want to ask. "Yes, everyone says good things."

"It's like anything—you get out of it what you put into it."

He's about to elaborate when Reverend Clarke makes his grand entrance. He's all smiles and quickly walks around the room shaking hands and introducing himself.

"Welcome," he says to me.

"Thank you," I reply and shake his hand.

"How are you, Grant?" he asks, turning away from me. Grant smiles back at him and says that he's fine.

Grant takes a seat next to me, and Reverend Clarke gets started with the orientation. He tells us a little about how the church started and how it's structured, and hits on a few of the different programs and ministries that the church offers. He says everything in a salesman-like manner and makes a few jokes here and there to keep people at ease. Later he hands out a welcome packet with some brochures, a map of the church's layout, and a little booklet about what the church teaches and believes. After he answers a few questions, we finish up with an overly dramatic prayer about God giving us newcomers the wisdom to "come over" to the Lord.

"Would you like me to give you a quick tour of the place?" Grant asks me as folks start to leave the room.

"I guess that would be helpful, considering you apparently need a map of the building to get around."

"Yeah. It's a big place," he says as we step into the lobby and head toward the main hallway.

"That's the bookstore," Grant offers as we pass a fairly sizeable bookstore. "It has lots of great resources on marriage and family. Are you married?"

"No, but I have a son."

"Oh, great! He'd love the bookstore. It has a great children's section and lots of *Veggie Tales* DVDs."

"*Veggie Tales?*"

"Yeah . . . you know. It's a cartoon about moral and religious tales hosted by Bob the Tomato and Larry the Cucumber."

"Oh. I think Andrew had it on last Saturday," I say, and recall Desma sitting on the sofa behind him, wondering out loud if Susie the Carrot had the right to make decisions about her own body and voicing something to the effect of, "So Bob the Tomato is sort of like the Pope of Veggie Land. I wonder if he worked vigorously to cover up Father Potato molesting the little brussels sprout brothers."

"The kids really enjoy it. It has lots of good lessons. You should bring your son . . . Andrew, you said?"

"Yes."

"How old is he?"

"He's five."

"Oh, then he'd love our Sunday morning kids camp, which he can attend while you're at the service. They have all sorts of great activities."

"Really?" I can't help but wonder if I could drop Andrew at this morning camp and then go to the mall for an hour and a half or maybe take a nap in the car rather than attend the service.

We walk further down the hall into an open area, and I'm gradually hit with the wafting scent of bacon.

"This is our café."

I look around the spacious area and see several tables and chairs and a full service cafeteria line. There's a breakfast buffet with eggs Benedict, pancakes, and all the other usual breakfast items. I smell rich coffee and see a display of fresh donuts at the end of the counter. No wonder a few thousand people come here every weekend. Free child care and a full service buffet— can't beat that.

"And downstairs, we have a gourmet coffee bar called Travels. They have great cappuccinos and lattes and iced coffees . . ."

"That sounds great. Looks like they think of everything here."

"It really is a great support system."

Grant continues to show me around, and I get to see the kids' camp area, a few of the many, many, many community rooms, the gym (yes, a gym . . . with a full size basketball court), and a second auditorium, which apparently holds an additional thousand people when the main auditorium fills up ("the overflow room with all the losers" as I recall Claire referring to it). We finally wrap up the tour at the much anticipated coffee bar.

"Can I buy you a cappuccino or something?"

"Oh, let me get it to thank you for the tour."

"No, no," he says, pulling out a seat for me at one of the tables. "What would you like?"

"Actually, a plain old cup of coffee would hit the spot. Cream, no sugar." I smile, sit down, and watch him go up to the bar. Well, he certainly isn't the kind of guy that you could sleep with and drop to the curb like Claire was hoping I would find at this place, but he is very sweet and cute. He's very "boy next door" and maybe a little *too* into the church, but, just like during my evening with Ben, it's been nice to get some attention from a man.

"Relax," I quietly tell myself, reminding myself not to think too much into this. During my date with Ben I let nerves overtake me and may have given up a good thing. I'll just play it cool with Grant and try not to have any expectations.

"One coffee with cream," he says and sets a cup in front of me.

"Thanks." I take a cautious sip. It's just hot enough and on par with anything I'd get at Starbucks or Caribou.

"So what made you come here today?"

My friends thought I might meet a quick lay. "I don't know. My neighbor comes, and she thought I might like it here."

"I think you would. I know I'd like for you to keep coming. I've really enjoyed meeting you." There he goes with the gorgeous smile again.

"It's been nice to meet you as well," I say, unable to stifle my own grin.

"So, do you stay at home full time with your son?"

"No, I work in human resources for a law firm downtown."

"That's interesting."

"Not really. How about you, what do you do?"

"I'm a project manager for a government contractor. It's one of those 'pays the bills' jobs."

"I hear ya."

"Are you from around here?" he asks and I realize that we've officially started with "first date" conversation: "What do you do? Where are you from originally? Blah, blah, blah."

I answer his questions and ask him a few of my own, and, as we're chatting, I start doing something I haven't done in quite some time—I start imagining what it would be like to have sex with him. Should I be doing this in a church? I wonder.

I notice the hair on his arms while he talks with his hands, and eye the roughness of the skin on his neck, wondering what it would be like to kiss it. While he tells me what brought him to the D.C. area from Upstate New York, I can't help wondering what it would be like to feel him on top of me, to run my hands through his hair and feel his lips on mine. I haven't been with a man since Mario and I divorced, and I've been so busy and tired that I haven't thought about sex that much, but something about Grant is oddly turning me on, and, after a few more minutes, I realize what it is—he has a scent, an understated, strong masculine smell about him. It's the sort of smell you usually notice only when your face is very close to a man, like when you lay your head on his chest. I inhale deeply and, for a moment, I close my eyes and feel a tingle run through my body, right here at the coffee bar at the Tysons Bible Church.

We talk for a few more minutes while I try to stay focused on the conversation and not let my mind wander into the proverbial bedroom.

"Do you have plans for the afternoon? Maybe I can take you to lunch."

I'm about to respond when Desma and Claire show up at the table.

"We've been looking all over for you," Claire says, quickly eyeing Grant.

"Yeah . . . they kicked me out of the antiabortion meeting. I asked if I could drop off all the unwanted babies at their houses to be cared for," Desma says. "They weren't amused."

"Grant, these are my friends, Claire and Desma."

Grant stands and shakes their hands, clearly not sure what to make of Desma's abortion comment.

"Are you ready to go?" Desma asks.

"It looks like Jen might want to hang out for a while," Claire says to Desma and winks at me. "Maybe we can look around the bookstore for a few minutes."

"You three came together?" Grant asks.

"Yeah, and I guess it is about time for us to head home. Thanks for the lunch invitation, but . . ."

"Why don't we all go to lunch? It's always fun to get to know other members of the church."

"Who you callin' a member?" Desma asks, and, once again, Grant isn't sure what to make of her.

"That would be great," Claire answers for all of us. "Why don't we go over to Coastal Flats at the mall? I could use a mojito."

"Sure," Grant says. "I'll drive."

Grant and I toss our empty cups in the trash, and the four of us make our way back to the parking deck.

18

"This is a nice car," Claire says as she and Desma hop into the backseat of Grant's red Jetta.

"Yeah. Very sporty," I say, climbing into the front seat.

"It's okay. I've only had it for a few months."

Grant puts the key in the ignition. He must have had the radio turned up really loud when he parked because Kelly Clarkson is blaring from the speakers as soon as he starts the car.

"Sorry," he says, turning the stereo down.

"Someone was jamming on the way to church," Claire jokes from the backseat.

On the way to the restaurant, the four of us make small talk, and I try to steer the conversation away from the church for fear of any comments Desma might add. It's chilly today, but the sky is blue, and the air is crisp. It feels nice to be in the midst of a relaxing Sunday afternoon among friends and maybe a potential . . . well, not a potential boyfriend, but maybe a . . . oh, I don't know, but whatever it is, it feels nice. It also feels nice to be in the passenger seat of a car with a man at the wheel. It makes me feel feminine. I know it's silly—that something so benign as being driven around by a man can have an effect on me, but I have to be both the man and the woman so often when it comes to life. In more ways than one, I feel like I'm always the one driving the car and, somehow, it's just nice to have a man doing it for a change.

After a short drive from the church, we arrive at the mall and walk to the restaurant.

"That's a nice blouse," Grant says to Desma. She was quiet in the car, so I guess he's trying to break the ice with her.

She thanks him for the compliment and, after we check in with the hostess, we all take a seat at a comfy booth and open up our menus.

"Do you think it's too early in the day for a cocktail?" Grant asks and looks at his watch.

"There's no such thing as 'too early for a cocktail,'" Claire says.

"Well, then, order me a strawberry daiquiri if the waiter comes, will you? I'm going to run to the little boys' room."

"He's nice," Claire says when Grant's out of earshot.

"Yeah," I say, and a smile comes across my face. "I sort of like him. He's very sweet."

"You don't mean 'like him' like him? Do you?"

"Well . . . I don't know. I promised myself I wouldn't over-think it."

"Jen, sweetie, I think this might be one you *do* want to over-think."

"For once, I think I agree with Claire," Desma says.

"What do you mean?"

"Sweetie," Claire says, pursing her lips. "I didn't really notice anything when you introduced us to him at the church, but . . ." She pauses for a moment. "He drives a bright red Jetta. He had Kelly Clarkson blaring on the stereo."

"So?"

"Don't you think . . . you know . . . the way he talks . . ." Desma says. "Doesn't he seem sort of . . ."

"Gay," Claire finishes the sentence for her.

"What?! No."

"Oh come on, Jen. You know I'm not one to make judg-ments about people, but he just has that *quality*. He told Desma he liked her *blouse*. How many straight men do you know who use the word blouse? Next thing you know he'll be complimenting me on my *slacks* or saying something about a pashmina."

"I'm sorry, Jen, but for once, I think I agree with Loosey Goosey over here," Desma chimes in, momentarily looking at Claire. "He wanted us to order him a cocktail. When was the last time you heard a straight guy say *cocktail* . . . and a strawberry daiquiri no less."

I'm quiet for a moment while I take in what they're saying.

"He's probably in the bathroom now washing his vagina," Claire says. "You think he can tell me where to get a good bikini wax?" she adds before quickly stifling her laughter when she sees Grant returning to the table.

I give her a "behave" look as Grant sits down.

"Did the waiter come yet?"

"No," I respond and take a long look at him—no obvious homosexual signs to me, but then again, I married a gay man.

"What is it you said you wanted to drink?" Claire asks him and then gives me a look.

"I was thinking that a daiquiri sounded good."

I see Claire and Desma exchange looks and something about them being in agreement over something really bugs me.

When the waiter finally comes over, we place our drink orders and continue with some lunch conversation.

"So you're in real estate," he says to Claire.

"Yeah. If you or anyone you know is in the market to buy or sell a home, be sure to let me know," she replies, sounding like an ad on the radio.

"I don't think I'm going anywhere soon in this market. Besides, I like where I live."

"Where's that?" I ask. *Please don't say Dupont Circle or Logan Circle,* I think to myself, conjuring up images of two of the gayest neighborhoods in the city.

"I have an apartment off Dupont Circle in the city. I love it there. Lots of great restaurants."

"Among other things," Claire says and doesn't even try to hide the smirk on her face.

"So, you said you work for a government contractor. Are they downtown? Close to your apartment?" Yeah, that's why he lives in Dupont—to be close to work.

"No, actually, they're in Arlington, but it's a quick Metro ride."

"So what do you like to do for fun, Grant?" Desma asks.

"I'm pretty busy with work and the church, but when I have some free time I like to take advantage of some of the cultural activities in the city."

"So, not a big sports fan?" Claire asks, that same smirk still on her face.

"No, not really."

I'm watching him carefully as Claire continues to interrogate him, and I just don't see what they mean about him "seeming gay." What makes a guy seem gay anyway? Yes, he talks with hands, and maybe he doesn't have the deepest voice in the world, but he doesn't seem any gayer or straighter than any other man I know. But, then again, neither did Mario.

While we dine on lobster rolls and grouper fingers and share some banana pudding and a chocolate waffle for dessert, Claire and Desma eventually seem content to let their suspicions go, and the four of us just make pleasant conversation. Grant continues to grow on me, and I think he even makes some inroads with Desma and Claire.

I'm still a little concerned about his dedication to a megachurch, but he has such a likable personality, and there's something comforting about his simple features. He's someone you'd want to take home to meet Mom . . . maybe not my mom, but he's the kind of guy mothers would like for their daughters.

Grant is careful to include Desma and Claire in the conversation, but his interest is clearly in me. He asks about my past, where I grew up, went to college, more about my work. By the time the bill comes, I've almost forgotten about Desma and

Claire's protest, and I'm impressed when he picks up the check for all of us.

When we get back to the church, stuffed from a heavy lunch, I think we're all ready for a long Sunday afternoon nap. And, with Andrew at Mario's until this evening, I may just go home and snooze.

"It really was nice to meet you, Grant," Desma says and starts to get out of the car.

"Yeah. And thanks for lunch. That was sweet," Claire adds before rummaging through her purse and pulling out a business card. "And remember, if you know anyone—"

Grant cuts her off. "I'll definitely refer anyone who's in the real estate market to you," he says and accepts her business card.

"We'll let you two say good-bye," Claire says. "We'll wait for you in the car, Jen," she adds, and she and Desma close the door and go on their way.

"I'd like to see you again sometime," Grant says as soon as we're alone.

"That'd be nice," I respond, apprehensive pangs starting to come back—the same kind of feeling I had at the Mexican restaurant with Ben. *Don't over-think this, Jennifer,* I think to myself. I hear Claire in my head: "Just ride the wave . . . ride the wave."

"Maybe we can get together before next week's service."

"Sure," I say, not sure I intend on coming to next week's service. "Let me give you my number." I grab a slip of paper and a pen from my purse. "I enjoyed lunch."

"Me, too. Enjoy the rest of your Sunday."

"I will." I reach for the door handle and give it a pull. I'm about to get out of the car, but I hesitate. "You know, Grant. Do you mind if I ask you something?"

"No. Of course not."

"This is a weird question. And please don't be offended by it, but my friends seem to think . . . God, I don't know how to ask this." And I really don't know how to ask what I have in mind, but thoughts of all the years married to a gay man and my determination not to go down such a road again trigger me to make the uncomfortable inquiry. "My friends sort of thought you might be . . . well, that you might be gay. I know that's ridiculous, and I don't agree with them, but, for reasons that are too detailed to go into right now, I just had to ask."

He starts laughing before I'm even done talking. "I'm not offended," he says, in between chuckles. "That's funny. Of course I'm not gay," he adds. "At least, not anymore."

19

"Excuse me?" I can feel my eyebrows lifting as I speak. "What do you mean? You're not gay *anymore*?"

"Well, I *used* to be gay, but I'm part of the church's Out of the Darkness program, and now I'm straight."

Oh, dear God! "Really?" I say with a long sigh.

Grant turns his eyes away from me. "I guess I'm not *entirely* straight just yet, but I'm working on it. I'm praying really hard like Reverend Clarke says."

"So this program teaches you to pray yourself to heterosexuality?"

"Prayer's a big part of finding grace away from sexual deviancy, but the group is also giving me a lot of support."

"Like what?'

"We have a men's meeting where we get together and learn how to bond with other men in healthy ways. We learned how to throw footballs last weekend."

Oh, dear God! "And all of this is really making you straight?"

"Sort of. And I do some things on my own as well that seem to be helping."

I look at him, not sure that I want to hear the details.

"I take photos of Brad Pitt's head and put them on Angelina Jolie's body. Or sometimes I'll take Catherine Zeta Jones . . . the straight guys think she's sexy, don't they? And I'll put her head on George Clooney's body and . . . you know, look at the pictures and try to transfer my desire for one sex to the other."

Oh, dear God! "And this is really helping?"

Grant looks down at his lap and then back at me. "Maybe . . . a little. I mean I guess I don't find, you know, women and vaginas as yucky as I used to." I can actually see the sides of his mouth turning downward as the word vagina comes out of it— the same look on his face that Andrew gets when I try to make him eat spinach.

"Grant," I pause for a moment, unsure what to say, although the words "see ya, wouldn't wanna to be ya," are coming to mind. "You do what you have to do. If this ex-gay program is something you feel like you need in your life right now, then that's your business, but, I have to tell you, I'm *so* not interested in being a part of it."

I see a look of sadness and frustration on his face.

"The only reason I had the nerve to ask you if you were gay is because my husband was gay . . . is gay . . . ex-husband . . . my ex-husband is gay. He didn't want to be gay so bad he deceived me and himself and married me. We were married for five years and, guess what? He's still gay. I don't think being gay is something you can pray your way out of. I can pray for the sky to turn purple . . . hell, I could pray for my hair to turn purple, but it just ain't gonna happen."

"I have to try," he says, as if anyone who thinks otherwise is insane. "Reverend Clarke says I can be free of homosexuality if I'm willing to work hard enough for it."

"That's your decision, Grant," I respond and open the car door. "But I can't . . . I just can't," is all I say and get out of the car. "Good luck, Grant," I offer as gently as I can and lightly close the car door. Claire's car is on the other side of the parking garage, and she starts to drive toward me as I walk in her direction.

"Yes, he is gay. And, no, I don't want to talk about it," I say as I climb into the backseat.

"What? He told you?" Claire asks.

I don't answer her. I just look out the car window. "I'm sorry, sweetie," Desma says.

"Yeah, that's a bummer, but be glad you found out now."

"Yeah, we could have gone out for years and then gotten married and had a kid before I realized I was with a gay man. Oh, wait," I say. "I've already done that." I really meant my words to be funny . . . to take the edge off Grant's revelation, but as they fall from my lips, they make me sad. I've only known Grant for a few hours. Why am I so upset about this?

Desma and Claire are silent in the front of the car—that kind of uncomfortable quiet that transpires when something awkward happens to someone and no one knows what to say.

"How could I make the same mistake again? Is this some sort of colossal joke? How could you both see so clearly that he's gay, and I couldn't? Did everyone know that Mario was gay before I married him, too?"

"If it makes you feel any better, I had no idea Mario was gay when you two were married. I didn't get a gay vibe from him at all," Claire, who knew Mario and I for a couple years before we split up, says.

"Really?"

"Yes. Don't beat yourself up over Mario. There were no obvious clues with him. He didn't have that *quality* like Grant has."

"I guess you're right." There probably were no obvious clues that Mario was gay, at least to observers outside our relationship. But there were dozens of warnings to which only I was privy, and I brilliantly chose to ignore all of them. I was so in love with him and in love with the life we had created together that I refused to entertain the notion that he might be gay.

Mario and I dated for almost six months before we had sex. With all my other boyfriends since high school, it was usually a matter of three to five dates before we got into bed together, and it was always because of *me* that we waited *that* long. I was so used to guys eagerly trying to get from first to second to third base as soon as they thought they had a shot, that it was actually quite refreshing when Mario didn't push me. I had been out of college for two years when we met, I was at a point in my life in which I was ready for a long term commitment, and a guy who was interested in more than just sex seemed like a good match. The long waiting period prior to sex also helped Mario and me develop a kind of friendship that I'd never had with another guy. Instead of "getting it on" all night, it wasn't uncommon for us to lie on the living room floor for hours talking and enjoying each other's company. We developed a mental connection that I was convinced was going to make the sex so much better when it finally happened.

During the first couple of months we dated, I waited for Mario to make the first move. There had been a lot of kissing and a lot of "over the sweater" action, but Mario never really pressed for things to go further than that. I had two roommates at the time, and one of them had her share of overnight guests. It wasn't uncommon for Mario and me to still be sitting on the sofa when she and her flavor-of-the-evening male companion made their way to her bedroom. Mario always expressed disapproval and bemusement about her ability to have sex so casually, which helped me rationalize his lack of sexual interest—I chalked it up to him being conservative. He was also three years younger than me, which led me to conclude that he might still be a virgin. He had only recently turned twenty-one when we met, and twenty-one-year-old virgins aren't that uncommon, are they? I figured he was nervous about "performing" for the first time, and his anxiety kept him from aggressively pursuing sex.

I came up with a multitude of reasons to justify Mario's lack of sexual prowess, but his being gay was never a reason I seriously considered. Had I met Mario now, his homosexuality might have come to mind more quickly, but I met him during the early nineties. I know it wasn't *that* long ago, but you just didn't hear much about gay people then. Mario didn't fit any of the stereotypes I had grown up with—he was masculine and preppy and had a deep voice. At the time, the only gay men I was familiar with were Little Richard and Elton John and, I guess, somewhere in the back of my mind, I figured all gay men were flamboyant and feminine. Mario and I dated before Ellen DeGeneres announced she was a lesbian, before *Will & Grace* was on the air, before gay marriage amendments were being debated all over the country, before the Governor of New Jersey came out of the closet . . . I had little reason to think about gay people or gay issues.

Now, sitting in the back of Claire's car, I can't believe I had to sit there and listen to another man, who feigned interest in me, tell me he's gay. You would think having it happen once in a lifetime would be enough. Why have I been singled out as the girl gay men latch on to in hopes of suppressing their sexual orientation?

Much as I try to contain it, my experience in the car with Grant brings back the memory of that horrible day two years ago when Mario finally told me the truth. For weeks afterwards, it was all I could think about, but, at some point, I made a commitment to put it out of my mind. It was too painful a recollection and whenever thoughts of that afternoon would try to weasel their way back into my consciousness, I'd use a thought-stopping technique I learned on *Dr. Phil* or *Oprah* or some other show to push them out of my head. I actually got pretty good at it. But, today, I just don't have the energy to fight it. I can't help but think of Mario sitting on the sofa, and me coming through the front door, convinced that he was going to surprise me with a trip to Hawaii.

When he announced his news—when he told me he was gay, I'm not sure I can put into words the feelings that rushed through my body. At first I was stunned, and, for a brief second, I thought he was joking, or that I was in the middle of a dream, and, in a few minutes, I'd wake up, relieved that what he had just told me was some weird thing my brain had conjured up while I was asleep. But I quickly realized that it wasn't a joke or a dream—it was reality.

The first and only word I voiced after Mario's revelation was, "What!?" I must have heard him wrong.

"I'm gay, Jennifer," he said, visibly shaking. "I'm so sorry, but I just can't pretend any longer."

"You're *what*?!"

"I think you heard me the first two times."

And, of course, I had heard him the first two times, but I couldn't believe that what he was saying was true.

"Again, I'm so sorry to have to tell you this. I love you, Jennifer. I really do. But, I can't love you the way you deserve to be loved."

"What?! What are you talking about?" A woman in denial doesn't give it up too easily.

"I wanted to be straight, Jen. I wanted that so bad, and I figured I'd get there sometime, but now I know it's never going to happen."

At this point I was finally starting to absorb his words, and a form of pain that I have never felt before and hope to never feel again began to seep into my bones. I had no idea what to say to him. What do you say to a man who's deceived you for years— a man with whom you share a child. Oh, God! Andrew! I remember thinking. What does this mean for Andrew?

"What am I supposed to do with this information, Mario?" I finally asked when I was able to speak.

"I don't know, but I had to tell you. I had to get it out there."

I turned away from him and just stared into space.

"I know it hurts—"

"You don't know *anything*!" I shouted back at him. "You bombard me with this revelation, and then have the nerve to act like you know how I feel."

"I didn't mean to imply that I know how you feel, I—"

"Good! Because you don't." I remember getting up from the sofa and pacing the room. "So now what, Mario? Did you have a plan in mind about where to go from here when you decided to share this little tidbit of knowledge with me?"

"We don't need to talk about anything like that right now. Why don't we just get used to the idea—"

"*We*?! What do you mean, *we*? You've had heaven knows how long to get used to . . . used to . . . *this*!"

"Do you want me to leave? Do you want to be alone?"

"Oh, you'd like that, wouldn't you? Just come in here and blow our marriage out of the water and then leave the scene of the crime and take off for . . ." I pause while, out of the blue, thoughts of the tickets to Hawaii come back to me. "Hawaii?" I ask. "You had tickets to Hawaii in your briefcase."

"How'd you know about that?"

"Not *everything* gets by me, Mario," I said, and suddenly, I'm convinced that he never intended to take me to Hawaii. He was going to break this news to me and then run off with some . . . God, I couldn't even think about it.

"I've been thinking about a lot of things lately, and I was at a point a few weeks ago at which I had decided that I'd made a marriage vow and was going to respect that vow. We've been distant lately, Jen. You know that. I booked a trip to Hawaii, thinking that it would be a way for us to reconnect, but the more I thought about it, the more it just felt like a lie. And, marriage vow or no marriage vow, I finally decided that we couldn't go on like this. It's just not right. It's not fair to either of us."

"And what about Andrew?"

"I don't know. We'll work it out. He's the most important thing in the world to me."

I recall sitting back down on the sofa at this point and starting to calm down enough to have a more rational conversation, but we didn't talk much longer. I needed to get away from him. I didn't even want to look at him, so I eventually asked him to leave. Up until that point, despite my sadness and rage, I hadn't cried. But when I closed the door behind Mario, I felt like I was closing the door on so much more. Once the door had clicked shut, I pressed my back against it, slid to the floor, and started bawling—bawling with grief over the loss of something so precious to me . . . my husband, my marriage, my family. In one brief instant it had all gone up in smoke. And, now, two years later, I can still feel the pain of that day like it was only hours ago.

"My friend Larry is gay," Claire says, pulling me back from my thoughts of Mario's day of declaration. "And he says there is only one real way to tell if a man is gay."

"Where was your friend Larry ten years ago when I needed him?"

"He says if a guy won't go down on you, he's definitely gay."

"Really?"

"Yes, he says a lot of gay men can get it up and go through the motions of intercourse with a chick, but don't think you're going to be getting any cunnilingus out of him. Gay men are grossed out by vaginas. All the flaps and folds scare them."

"You think?"

"That's what Larry says."

"Well, then it must be true."

"You tell us, Jen," Claire says with prying eyes as she gives me a look in the rearview mirror. "Did Mario enjoy dining in the Lady Garden?"

"That's none of your business." I have no interest in discussing my sex life (or lack of one) with Mario. To this day, I feel humiliated when I think about it—especially when I think of all the excuses I used to make for Mario to explain what I thought was his low libido. Sometimes I'd tell myself that he was tired, or that he was stressed, or that he was just one of those people with a low sex drive. Other times, I'd wonder if it had something to do with me. Was I lousy in bed? Did he not find me attractive? Had I put on a few too many pounds? I'm still recovering from the damage done to my self-esteem during all those nights that I'd press my body next to his and slip my hand under his shirt or down his boxers, gestures that were, more often than not, greeted with little interest or enthusiasm. I so wanted him to return my touch, but, most of the time, he'd pretend to be asleep or say something about how tired he was. As our marriage progressed, Mario began to stretch his bedtime to later and later hours. He'd always let me go to bed first and not come upstairs until he was quite certain I'd be asleep, which I now know was to avoid sex with me.

He was always more than happy to use my "time of the month" as an excuse to avoid making love. Most of the men I dated before Mario couldn't have cared less if I was on my period or not—they were more than happy to get it on either way. What's so funny is that during the early part of our relationship, I would withhold sex when I was mad at Mario. Can you imagine? I was punishing a gay man by not letting him have sex with me. Little did I know that the joke was on me.

"Oh, come on . . . we're all friends here. You can tell us," Claire insists.

"Well . . . Mario would sort of go down on me, but very rarely."

"What do you mean, 'sort of?' " Desma asks

"He'd go down . . . you know . . . down there, but he always sort of stayed on the outer edges of things, if you know what I mean. Not like some of the guys I was with before Mario who'd get their face all up in my business." I'm starting to blush as I speak. I'm not usually one to talk so openly about my sex life. "In fact," I add, "Now that I think about it, I'm quite certain he used to hold his breath while he was down there and routinely came up for air."

Claire laughs. "I can relate to that. I caught Julio doing the sniff test on me the other day."

"What, pray tell, is the sniff test?" Desma asks.

"You know, when you're making out, and a man works his finger into your vagina and then tries to discreetly lift it to his nose."

"Why would he do that?" I ask.

"Because he wants to make sure your pussy doesn't smell like the seafood department at the Food Lion before he heads south and eats you out."

"You are so *nasty*!" Desma says and laughs.

"I just speak the truth, Desma."

"Where was all this truth when I needed it, before I fell in love with Mario and married him?"

Claire and Desma are quiet. I guess they don't really have an answer to my question.

20

"Hello," I say in a haze after picking up the phone. I arrived home from church about an hour ago and was in the midst of a light sleep when it rang.

"Hi, Jen."

"Tom?"

"Yeah."

"What's going on?" I ask, bypassing any pleasantries while I sit up in bed, and my shoulders quickly lift with tension. I haven't heard from my brother in almost a year, so one can imagine my anxiety when his voice suddenly materializes on the other end of the phone.

"I'm fine. Thanks for asking," he says.

"Sorry. It's just that I haven't heard from you in quite some time. Is everything all right?"

"Things are fine down here. Lindsey and the kids are good. I just wanted to check in with you about Mom."

"Oh?"

"Yeah. Has she seemed strange to you lately?"

"Now that's a leading question," I say and let out a quick laugh.

"I'm serious, Jen. She's been a little loopy on the phone when I've talked to her the past few times."

"She's been loopy on the phone twice in the past six months?" I ask, taking a jibe at Tom about his infrequent contact with Mom.

He ignores my question. "I talked with her this morning, and she asked me how Mona was."

"Mona?"

"My response exactly. When I asked her who Mona was, she said she didn't know and wasn't sure why I brought her up, which of course, I hadn't done. Then she said something about Dad waking her up last night, as if he were still alive."

"She's seventy-five, Tom. She's going to be a little off sometimes. I just saw her yesterday. She's a little forgetful and gets sort of spacey at times, but I don't think it's anything serious. She's just spending too much time alone. I think she falls asleep sometimes during the day and gets her dreams confused with reality."

"How often do you check on her?"

"I see her at least twice a week," I reply, resenting the question. Who is he to be checking up on how often I see Mom? He hasn't seen her in two years.

"Do you think it would be helpful to see her more often?"

"Sure it would. Are you offering?"

"Jen, I live in Florida."

"Lucky you," I say with a sigh. "Listen, Tom. If you're so concerned about Mom, maybe you can help me convince her to move closer to me. Every time I bring up the idea of her getting an apartment in Alexandria or looking into an assisted living facility, she gets crazy-defensive and insists that she's not leaving her home."

"You want to put Mom in a *nursing home*?"

"What part of *apartment* or *assisted living facility* did you not understand, Tomás?" I say, pronouncing his name the way Mom does (the Latino version: Toe-*mhas*). "God, you're just as bad as she is."

"I can understand her not wanting to leave her house."

"I can too, but she spends so much time alone there. If she were closer to me, I could spend more time with her."

"What do you want me to say?"

"I don't know. Maybe mention that Lindsey's parents are

looking into moving into a senior center, and say how much they are looking forward to it. Just put a bug in her ear about it—get her thinking about it in more of a positive light."

"I'll see what I can do," he says. "So you really think she's okay though?"

"I think she's lonely, and I think she has way too much time on her hands. Wouldn't you start to lose it if you were cooped up in the house for days at a time?"

"I guess you're right."

"Any plans to come up for a visit anytime soon? Mom would love to see you. And it would be nice for Andrew to spend some time with his cousins."

"Maybe I can work something out. Things are so busy. Work is kicking my ass, and the kids have so many activities. How is Andrew?"

"He's fine. A few issues at school here and there, and he almost set the house on fire a few weeks ago, but otherwise he's hanging in there."

"Set the house on fire?"

"Yeah . . . it's not as bad as it sounds. I'll tell you about it later," I say, as if I expect to hear from him again sometime soon, which isn't likely.

"Okay. I'll try my best with Mom."

"Thanks, Tom," I reply, and we say our good-byes.

I hang up the phone and look at the clock. It's almost four. Mario should have Andrew back in about an hour. I get up from the bed and head downstairs to the kitchen to see if I have enough ingredients to pull together some sort of meal. If not, I guess we'll order Chinese or a pizza when they get here. The first weekend Andrew spent with Mario after he moved out, I happened to be getting dinner ready when Mario brought him back home. It was a very tense time for Mario and me to say the least, but I guess manners and my desire to hide my disdain from Andrew got the best of me, and I asked Mario to join us for dinner. We did our best to put on a brave face for Andrew and managed to civilly get through the meal together. Ever since then, we have eaten together when Mario brings Andrew back from his weekend visits. It just seems like a good thing to do for Andrew's sake—a way for the three of us to get together on a regular basis as something resembling an intact family. The gatherings became increasingly less tense as time went on, and now they're a relaxed established routine. We mostly focus on Andrew during our meals together, with occasional mentions of family and work. But even now, two years after we split up, neither of us has mentioned anything about our dating lives to each other, which has been easy for me, considering my dating life has been nonexistent since the divorce. I doubt Mario can say the same, but I'm quite certain I'd rather pry off my fingernails one by one than hear about any of his romances with another man.

About an hour after my conversation with Tom, I see Mario and Andrew pulling up in the driveway.

"Mommy, Mommy," I hear after the front door opens. "I pet a sheep and a deer and an elephant."

"An elephant?"

"No, Andrew," Mario says, coming through the door behind him. "There were no elephants at the petting zoo."

Andrew gives Mario a look that says, "So I was trying to jazz up the story a bit . . . sue me."

"You went to a petting zoo? Did you wash your hands?"

Mario laughs. "No. I told him to get his hands nice and dirty for dinner."

I roll my eyes. "Well, go wash your hands again, Andrew," I say before looking at Mario. "And it probably wouldn't be a bad idea for you to do the same."

"You want me to run out and grab us something for dinner?" Mario asks as Andrew runs upstairs with his backpack.

"No. I've got some spaghetti sauce on the stove. I just need to boil some pasta and put some of that frozen garlic bread in the oven."

"Texas Toast?"

I nod.

"Yum," Mario says and follows me into the kitchen. "So how was your weekend?"

"It was quiet . . . just hung out with the girls." I spare him the details of my Tysons Bible Church adventure.

"Is Desma included in 'the girls'?"

"Yeah, why?"

"Oh, Andrew's been telling me all about Aunt Desma over the past few weeks. From what I hear, she has no shortage of opinions."

I laugh. "Shhh. She's downstairs." I'm filling a big pot with water when the phone rings.

"Hello," I say, shutting off the faucet.

"Jennifer?"

"Hi, Mom."

"Jennifer?"

"Yes, Mom. It's me."

"Jennifer. I can't get the oven to turn off!" There's a sound of panic in my mother's voice.

"What do you mean? Just press the off button."

"I did. I've pressed it several times. But the temperature is still reading five hundred degrees."

"Five hundred degrees? Why did you have the oven up that high?"

"I didn't. I haven't had it on all day . . . not intentionally anyway."

I'm quiet for a moment, unsure what to do. I wish there was a neighbor I could call to go over and check on her, but I don't know any of her neighbors anymore. Everyone who lived on the block when I was a kid has moved away, and most of the houses have turned over several times since then.

"Jennifer. I'm afraid to go to bed with the oven on."

It's only five o'clock. She isn't going to bed at five o'clock these days, is she? "Okay, Mom. Just relax. I'll be there as soon as I can."

"What's going on?" Mario asks when I hang up the phone.

"I'm not sure. Mom claims she can't get the oven to shut off. Can you stay with Andrew until I get back?"

"Of course."

"You two can go ahead and have dinner. It will probably be a good three hours by the time I get out there, see what's going on, and get back. The pasta's in the pantry, and the garlic bread's in the freezer"

"Do you just want to stay the night out there? I can stay here with Andrew and get him off to school in the morning."

"Is Daddy staying over?" Andrew asks, reappearing in the kitchen, a hopeful smile on his face.

"I don't know, sweetie. I've got to go out to Grandma's for a little while. You can have dinner with Daddy, and I'll be back as soon as I can."

Andrew's face immediately darkens. "You're always going out to Grandma's."

"I know, sweetie, but she needs a lot of attention right now. I'll be back as soon as I can," I say and rush upstairs to grab my purse so I can get on the road. So much for my relaxing Sunday.

21

"Jennifer? Is that you?"

"Yes, Mom. It's me," I say from the other side of the door.

I hear her clumsily unlatching the deadbolt. Then she pulls on the door to no avail.

"Unlock the lock on the doorknob, Mom."

I hear her relock the dead bolt and then pull on the door again.

"No, Mom. Unlock the dead bolt again, and then unlock the door knob as well."

She fusses some more with the locks and finally opens the door.

"Hi," I say, stepping inside. "The oven still won't turn off?"

"No. It's the damdest thing, and now it's up to six hundred degrees."

"Six hundred degrees?" I walk into the kitchen and open the range door, expecting a burst of heat, but I feel nothing.

"It's not on, Mom. Feel." I wave my hands in front of the open oven.

"Then why is the temperature up to six hundred degrees?"

"I look at the display on the oven panel. Then I shut my eyes in frustration. "That's the *time*, Mother! It's six o'clock, not six hundred degrees."

She furrows her brow and looks confused. "The time?" she asks, a vacant look in her eyes.

"Yes. It's just the clock."

"The clock, you say?" She sits down at the kitchen table, an odd expression on her face, like she's still trying to process what I've just said. "It's just the clock?"

My frustration with coming all the way out to Fredericksburg over the oven clock turns into concern as I look at her at the other end of the kitchen table.

"I don't know why I didn't think about the clock. That doesn't make any sense. I should have known that." She's looking down at the table as she speaks, like she doesn't want me to see her eyes.

I walk behind her and put my hands on her shoulders. "It's not that big of a mistake, Mom."

"Don't get old, Jennifer. Just don't get old."

"It's just one of those things. At seventy-five, you're entitled to a few mind lapses. Hell, I'm only thirty-five, and I have them all the time."

She looks at me with distrust, like I'm patronizing her.

"A few days ago I was at an intersection waiting and waiting for the traffic light to change. It wasn't until someone behind me honked that I realized there was no traffic light, only a stop sign. I was waiting for a nonexistent traffic light to change."

"Really?"

"Yeah. We can't expect to be one hundred percent all the time." I say, taking a seat at the table.

"I guess you're right."

"But you know, Mom. When things like this happen, we could deal with them so much better if you lived closer to Andrew and me."

"Andrew! Where's Andrew? You didn't leave him alone?"

Is she really asking me if I left a five-year-old child alone? "No, of course not. Mario is with him."

"Mario. How is Mario? I don't know why you let him go."

"He's fine," I say and then quickly change the subject. "Tom called me this afternoon. He said he'd spoken with you."

"Yes. He called. It was so nice to hear from him. I talked to the kids for a few minutes, too. I wish he'd bring them up to see me sometime."

Don't hold your breath. "Yeah. That would be nice." I pause briefly. "Tom and I were talking, and he's concerned about you being alone so much as well. Did he mention anything to you?"

"Nothing new. You know how private he is. And he's so busy with his job and the children."

Unlike me, I suppose, who has all the time in the world. "When I talked to him, he mentioned that Lindsey's parents were looking into moving into a senior center. He said they were actually excited about it."

"I don't know why anyone would be excited about moving into a nursing home."

"Oh, dear God! How many times do I have to tell you the difference between an apartment, an assisted living place, and a nursing home." I get up from the table. I'm not really in the mood to get into it with her, and I should really get back home anyway.

"Is everything else okay?" I ask, taking my purse off the counter and putting it over my shoulder.

"Yeah. You're not leaving already? You just got here."

"Andrew's got school tomorrow and I've got laundry . . ." I'm about to come up with any number of additional reasons why I need to leave, but I see a sad look in Mom's face—she clearly doesn't want me to go. And why would she? Who would want to be left alone at night?

"I suppose I can give Mario a call and let him know I'll be a while. If he needs to go, Desma is there. She can stay with Andrew."

"I've got a baked chicken in the refrigerator. I'll pull it out and make us some sandwiches, and maybe we can play a game of cards." She's trying not to show it, but I can tell she's glad I decided to stick around for a while.

While Mom gets to work on the sandwiches, I give Mario a quick call. Then I open the cabinet and see what she's got to add to the dinner. I had planned to eat with Mario and Andrew, and now I'm quite hungry. I grab some potato chips and then take two apples that were sitting on the counter and start to cut them up.

"You want mayonnaise?" she asks me.

"Sure. And maybe some lettuce."

"Mario's going to stay with Andrew?" she asks, getting up and opening the fridge.

"Yeah. He doesn't mind sticking around. He likes to spend time with Andrew."

"Poor Andrew—not having his parents together in the same house."

"Andrew's doing pretty well, actually. He's adjusting well to kindergarten and really likes his teacher." I've become a master at shifting conversations with my mother away from any discussion of Mario.

"That doesn't surprise me. Andrew's had to get used to adjusting to things. He's so young. If you and Mario got back together, he probably would barely remember your time apart." Unfortunately, Mom is just as apt at steering conversations back to Mario.

"Mario took Andrew to the petting zoo in Reston today. Andrew came in this evening claiming he'd pet an elephant."

"An elephant?"

"Yeah. He was just trying to tell a good story. I think he had a good time." I sit down at the table and take my sandwich from her. I put a few chips on her plate, even though she really shouldn't be eating them, and put the sliced apples in the middle of the table.

"How is work going?" she asks.

"It's fine. There's always some sort of crisis, but it keeps things interesting. Claudette, my boss, is retiring in the spring, so I'm trying to position myself to take over her job when she leaves."

"Really? You want all that responsibility? I'll never get used to the American obsession with careers. In Colombia, we believed in hard work, but we worked to live. Here, people live to work. It doesn't make any sense."

"It's not really much more responsibility than I have now. It's just a different kind . . . with more money and a better office."

"A better office? I've never had an office in my life. My workplace was always the home," Mom says and looks up at the ceiling as if she's remembering another time. Perhaps she's thinking of when she and my father first came to America in the sixties, and how different everything was for them—the customs, the food, the language, the faster pace of life in general. When they left for America, they had never seen an automatic dishwasher, and my mother's family still did their laundry by hand—or, I guess I should say, my mother's family's servants did their laundry by hand. My mother's family was not wealthy by any means, but, in Colombia, even people of modest means have maids to do the cleaning. When my mother first came to the U.S., she didn't even know how to make a bed, and she certainly didn't know how to sort laundry or work a dishwasher. But, like most immigrants, she adjusted and got used to doing house work and seemed to enjoy being a stay-at-home wife and mother.

Mom and I sit and eat our sandwiches, and I try to keep the conversation away from anything that might stir up her criticism or entice her to start asking questions about Mario and me. I know she can't stand not knowing exactly why Mario and I broke up, but I can't bear the thought of telling her that Mario's gay. I'm certain she'll find a way to blame me for it.

When we finish the sandwiches, I clear the table, and we wash and dry the few plates we used by hand. Mom has a dishwasher, but she never uses it—never has used it. Last time I checked, she was using it for storage. As a teenager, I'd occasionally use it after I'd baked a cake or something, but, other than that, it always sat idle. I'd always complain when she asked me to dry the dishes while she washed them. Mom would insist that the dishwasher was a waste of electricity, and that, by the time you rinsed off the dishes, loaded the machine, and unloaded it, you may as well do it by hand. If nothing else, it did give us some quality time together to chit-chat about our days, and it always seemed to be a moment of truce between us—a time when we discussed things that wouldn't bring about an argument about why I wasn't old enough to shave my legs or why I would've sullied the family's reputation if I had moved out of the house before I was married. Mom would gossip about some of the other women in the neighborhood or tell me the latest news about the family in Colombia if she'd gotten a letter that day. I'd share benign information about what was going on at school or talk about recent movies or television shows. We seemed to have an unstated agreement that our time after dinner doing the dishes was for pleasant conversation only. I guess that's why some of my fondest memories are of Mom and me standing by the sink, doing the dishes.

When I open the cabinet to put the plates back, I see Mom's pill bottles, which reminds me that we'll need to go for refills next weekend. Or will we? I think to myself, eyeing the little brown plastic containers—seven of them in total: Lasix to help with the fluid buildup in her legs, Lisinopril for her blood pressure, Glucotrol for her diabetes, and so on and so on. They all appear to be about half full. I think for a moment, and try to remember precisely when we refilled her prescriptions last, and I'm certain it was nearly thirty days ago. Then I look at the "date filled" on one of the bottles, which confirms that they should be almost empty.

"Mom?" I ask, opening one of the containers. "Why is your bottle of Lasix almost half full?"

"Hmmm?" she asks, looking up from the table. "My what?"

"Your Lasix . . . all of your medications. They should be almost empty if you've been taking them on schedule."

"I take them as best as I can," she responds, conclusively.

"As best you can?" I ask, perplexed by her response. "You need to take them exactly as they're prescribed, Mother."

"I do. Some days it slips my mind I guess."

I can feel the goose bumps rising on my forearm. Up until

now I've been able to convince myself that, despite a few instances of peculiar behavior, Mom was still managing okay on her own, but if she's not taking her medications . . .

I put the cap back on the bottle, set it back in the cabinet and close the door. I just can't deal with this right now. I just can't.

"Well, the dishes are done. I need to get going. I've got an early day tomorrow."

"You don't want to play a quick game of Gin?"

"No, not tonight," I respond. "I really just need to go." A feeling of dread is coming over me, and I need to get out of the house. "I'll let myself out. You stay here." I give her a quick peck on the cheek. "We'll talk tomorrow." I grab my purse from the counter and scurry out the door.

When I'm in the car, I quickly start it and head out of the driveway. As I travel along the road, I can't get the vision of Mom out of my head—the vision of her at the kitchen table looking up at me, saying, "Some days it slips my mind."

"What am I going to do?" I say out loud. If she's not remembering to take her medications, we're really in trouble. Something has to be done. She's losing it, and I can't ignore it anymore. Tears start to come to my eyes as I continue down the road. There are so many decisions to make and conversations that need to be had. She's so bull-headed—she'll never agree to move out of her house, and I can't force her. I sense a load coming down upon my shoulders, and it feels like it's crushing me. I don't want to deal with this. I've been able to handle the frequent visits to check in on her, the chauffeuring her around, the daily phone calls, but this . . . *this* is too much. Why can't people just stay healthy? I think to myself, afraid and anxious. I'm scared— I'm scared for Mom, and for me and for what lays ahead for both of us—I'm scared that this is the beginning of the end.

22

"So these two Mormon boys came to my door this afternoon."

I hear Claire's voice in the family room as I quietly come through the front door. No one heard me come in, and I'm not really in the mood to face anyone, so I stand in the hallway and listen.

"I guess I shouldn't say *boys*. I mean, they were over eighteen. That's legal, right? And damn were they cute."

"Did you know that the Mormons used to ban blacks from their priesthood?" I hear Desma ask.

"Didn't know. Didn't care," Claire says quickly and conclusively, clearly not interested in Desma elaborating on the subject. "I always invite the Mormon boys in because they're usually so handsome, all young and virile in their little white dress shirts and ties. I never let the Jehovah's Witnesses in though. They're usually old and never as attractive as the Mormons . . . and their message is so gloom and doom. Who wants to hear about the end of the world? What a buzz kill, you know?"

I hear Mario laugh. I wasn't sure he'd still be here. And what's Claire doing here?

"Anyway, I've always had this fantasy of seducing a Mormon twosome . . . you know, make me a little Mormon sandwich. They'd show me their literature, and then I'd show them . . . well . . . a thing or two. But they're always so straight-laced and on-message, and they don't even drink. How's a girl supposed to seduce a reluctant guy if no alcohol's involved? Maybe if I got a sweet red wine, I could convince them it's Hawaiian Punch."

"I think they'd know the difference," Mario says.

"Yeah, probably. What's that about anyway? How do they get anyone to join a religion that bans booze? Without alcohol, you can't have drunk sex, and we all know drunk sex is the best kind."

"Hi," I say, finally entering the family room and letting my presence be known.

"Hey, Jen," Claire says over Mario and Desma's greetings. "I stopped by to say hello, and Mario invited me to stay for dinner."

"How are things at your Mom's?" Desma asks.

"Fine," I lie and drop to the sofa. "Is Andrew in bed?"

"Yeah. He went down about an hour ago," Desma says. "I think I'll do the same. Good night, guys," she says and gets up and heads toward the steps.

"I guess I should get going as well." Claire lifts herself from her chair. "It's getting late. I'll call you tomorrow." She's about to walk out, but stops. "Oh. I almost forgot. *Someone* has a birthday coming up next week. What day is it?"

"Next Friday," I groan. The last thing on my mind right now is my birthday.

"Well, don't make any plans. Desma and I were talking, and we'd like to take you out."

"That's sweet, but I'd really just like to forget all about it and stay—"

"Nonsense. We'll work out the details later. I'll call you," she says and turns to leave before I can protest any further.

"Thanks for staying with Andrew," I say to Mario after I hear the door close behind Claire.

"Please. He's my son. Anytime. Things really okay with Ana?"

I look at him, but don't say a word.

"That bad?"

"Mario, I don't know what I'm going to do. She's been a little off for a while . . . forgetful and illogical at times, but tonight . . . the whole thing with the oven . . . it was just the clock . . . the clock said it was six in the evening, and she thought the oven was running at six hundred degrees. Then, when I was putting some dishes away, I noticed that her prescription bottles had way more medication left in them than they should. She's been forgetting to take her medications."

"Oh?"

"Yeah. I asked her about it, and she casually said that she sometimes forgets, like it's no big deal."

"So what'd you say?"

"I didn't really say anything. I couldn't deal with it. All I wanted to do was get away, so I told her I had to get home and left. I just can't think about it right now. I'll think about it in the morning and figure something out."

Mario can see the anxiety in my eyes. "It'll be all right," he says and leans in and starts rubbing my shoulders.

"I know." I pull away. I don't want him rubbing my shoulders like he did when we were married—it only reminds me of what I've lost.

"There are all sorts of ways to remind people to take their medications. We'll figure something out. I've seen things on TV . . . different timers and dispensers that elderly people use."

"Yeah. I'll look into that, in between the hundred other things I have to do at work tomorrow."

"Would you like me to research it for you?"

"No. Whatever you find, I'll just have to reread. There's no point in us both doing it."

"Well, if there's anything I can do to help, please let me know." He gets up and grabs his jacket from the arm rest.

"Okay. Thanks again for staying with Andrew."

"Sure," he says, then hesitates. "This is probably not the best time, but I need to ask you something."

"What?" I say very quickly, my anxiety getting the best of me. The last conversation he "needed" to have with me dissolved our marriage.

"I know I owe you a child support check this week."

I nod.

"Can you manage, just this month, without it? I promise I'll make up for it later this year."

"Why?" Again, my words are very quick. It's not like I depend on Mario's checks to feed and shelter Andrew, but it does help with the house payment, and the rest I put in a college fund for Andrew.

"You're going to think this is crazy."

"Please tell me you don't need money for a sex change?" I don't know why I asked that.

"Huh?"

"Nothing."

"I decided to go into business with my friend, Ron. We're going to open a restaurant."

"What? A *restaurant*? You're a *social worker*. You don't know anything about running a restaurant."

"No. But Ron does. He's been managing restaurants for years. You've been to Dillingers in Old Town. He's managed that place for three years."

"So what's he need you for?"

"He needs capital, and he needs manpower. He has a great concept."

"Concept?"

"Yes, we're going to call the place Gonads. It's going to be like a gay Hooters—buff men in Speedo's serving the food, show tunes on the jukebox . . ."

"I'm going to bed," I say abruptly and lift myself from the couch. "I'm too tired to deal with this right now . . . assuming you're actually serious, and this isn't some weird joke."

"It's not a joke. It's a great idea, and I think it's going to be really successful."

"Oh? Because you know *so much* about starting a business?"

"You don't think I'm smart enough?"

"It's not about being smart, Mario. We may not be married anymore, but your financial decisions affect our son. Forgive me if I'm concerned about you pouring money into some strip club."

"It's not a strip club. It's just going to be a campy restaurant. I haven't gone into this blindly. I've reviewed Ron's business plan. I've asked him all the right questions. I really want to do this."

I look at him and then lift my eyes to the ceiling.

"Oh, come on, Jen." I hate the way he says that. It's the same way he said it when he was trying to convince me about various things when we were married. "I really think it's going to be a hit. We've got a location off Logan Circle in the city. We're going to cater to gay men and bachelorette parties and such. Another friend of Ron's is an interior designer, and he's already on board to decorate the place."

"Who is this Ron person anyway?" I ask. "Oh, God! He's not your . . . ?"

"No. Of course not. I wouldn't go into business with someone I was romantically involved with."

"Fine, Mario. Whatever," I say, just eager to end this conversation and go to bed. "You can miss this one payment. But you miss any more, and there'll be trouble. I'm not having my son's college fund blown on some restaurant called Testicles."

"Gonads."

"Like it matters."

"Thanks, Jen. You won't be sorry."

"Somehow, I doubt it," I say and walk past him toward the steps. "You and your absurd idea can let yourself out."

23

I'm so tired. I didn't sleep well last night at all. I kept tossing and turning. I had planned to spend the morning surfing the Internet, looking for some ideas about how to deal with my mother's situation, but I forgot that I had an interview scheduled. One of the partners is in desperate need of a new assistant, and insists that I screen any candidates before I send them up to be interviewed by him.

"Please. Have a seat, Monique," I say, sitting down myself. "You found the building okay?"

"Yes, thank you," responds a "rough around the edges" looking young woman. Her hair has clearly seen one too many chemical processes, and she would definitely have to tone down her makeup to work at a conservative law firm.

"Good. Well, we're glad to have you here at Currier and Timmons today. You have a great resume. Six years as a legal secretary?"

"Yes."

"So, can you tell me a little bit about your current position?"

"Sure."

I look at her to elaborate, but she sits there quietly.

"Your duties? What do they entail?"

"Oh they keep me very busy over there. I'm always running around, making copies, scheduling appointments."

"Do you specialize in a particular kind of law?"

"They're particular kinds?"

"You know, criminal law, employment law, estate law . . ."

"Oh, yes, yes. We did a lot of criminal law stuff."

"A lot of criminal law *stuff*?"

"Yes."

"You mentioned copying and scheduling appointments. What about assisting in preparation for trials, gathering statistics, documenting and organizing legal information?"

"What about them?" She looks at me blankly.

"Your resume states that you have experience in all these areas." I lift the resume from my desk and show it to her, wishing I'd bothered to screen her over the phone before inviting her for an interview. She looks at it as if she's never seen it before.

"I do. I've been with Mulvany and Myers for almost two years doing legal secretary work."

"Your resume says you currently proofread legal documents. Tell me about that."

"Lizzy gives me some documents, and I proofread them."

"Lizzy?"

"She's my boss."

"What kind of law does she practice?"

"She's not a lawyer."

"No?"

"No. She assists the lawyers like I do."

"And she's your boss?" So you're an assistant to an assistant? Lovely!

"Yes."

"So you provide assistance to a legal secretary?" And you stole her resume and stuck your name on top of it and sent it to me.

"Technically, yes. But I do a lot of work with the lawyers too."

I hate interviews like this. I can tell in the first few minutes whether I have a viable candidate or not. In this case, I have a big "not," yet I have to proceed with some form of an interview of appropriate length before I can get her the hell out of here.

I continue on with a few more perfunctory questions and feign interest in what Monique has to say. When I finally get rid of her, I lean back in my chair and shut my eyes. For just a moment, I think how nice it would feel to be back at home laying in bed under the covers. I know if I stay like this for much longer I will actually fall asleep, so I open my eyes, put my hands on the keyboard and start researching information on medication management for an elderly parent.

All sorts of things come up on my screen while I'm doing my research, but, more than anything, I seem to be getting hit with ads for home healthcare agencies. And, the more I check out some of their sites, the more I start to think that having a home healthcare aide come into Mom's house might be a good idea. They offer all sorts of helpful services . . . everything from cleaning to cooking to errand running, and, most important, medication management. Eventually, I manage to find a few companies that serve her area and start navigating through their Web sites, soaking up all the posted information.

"Yes," I say to myself as I pick up the phone to call one of the agencies and get some more details about their services. "This might just be the answer I've been looking for."

24

"I don't think there's any reason to be alarmed at the moment. Forgetfulness and such just happens when people get older, but considering some of the events we've talked about, I think it would be a good idea to do some testing," Dr. Miller says to Mom and me from the other side of the desk. I called him yesterday, and we talked briefly about Mom's behavior—her growing paranoia, the oven temperature incident, the moments where she seems to zone out and forget who she's talking to, her problems remembering to take her pills . . . He suggested that we come in and talk about further testing and decide where to go from there.

"You think I'm going senile?" Mom asks.

Dr. Miller laughs. "Of course not, Ana. You're more lucid than I am, but some things Jennifer and I talked about are enough to warrant some concern."

"She thinks I have Alzheimer's."

"I do not," I say defensively, not wanting to have this discussion in front of the doctor. "Mom, you're not remembering to take your medication. We just need to see if there are some things we can do to help you take your pills on schedule. And if, God forbid, something is going on, if we look into it now, we might be able to keep it from getting any worse."

"Jennifer's right, Ana. Alzheimer's is always a concern, but with your history of high blood pressure and diabetes, your memory issues may have more to do with vascular problems. It may just be what we call mild vascular cognitive impairment."

"Vascular impairment?" Mom asks.

"Yes. It simply means that the blood supply to your brain may be compromised from hardening of the arteries, buildup of fat and cholesterol in the carotid arteries in your neck . . . a number of things. The only way we can really know is to run some tests."

"What kind of tests?" Mom asks, annoyance in her voice.

"We'll start with the least invasive ones. When we go back to the exam room, we'll do a more extensive neurological evaluation and a mental status exam. I'll test your motor skills and your memory. Then I think we should get you scheduled for a CT scan and an ultrasound of the carotid arteries. Lisa at the front desk can help you get those scheduled. We already have recent lab work, and, aside from your kidney function not being where we'd like it, your blood work looks okay. Your B-12 and your folate levels, and your thyroid function were all normal. When I get the results from the other tests, we'll have more to go on, and we can take it from there."

"A CT scan? I'm not getting in one of those tubes."

Dr. Miller offers a smile. "That's an MRI. You won't be put in a tube for a CT scan. It's totally painless and only takes a few minutes."

"What if the tests do show a level of vascular impairment or whatever, then what?" I ask.

"It depends. We may be able to effectively treat it with blood thinners, or we may want to talk about a surgical procedure called an endarterectomy to remove plaque from the carotid arteries, or we may want to discuss angioplasty."

Mom's quiet for a moment, and, for the first time, I can see that she's scared. Up until now, aside from a few brief moments of uneasiness immediately after one of her spells, she hasn't seemed overly concerned about her memory problems. I think her innate stubbornness has allowed her to brush off her instances of odd behavior. But sitting here at the doctor's office, talking about CT scans and ultrasounds, must finally be making it real. I've seen my mother express a lot of emotions—I've seen her happy and sad and angry and anxious, but I can't really think of a time that I've seen her frightened. Until now.

25

"You okay? I know it was a lot to digest," I say to Mom as we walk toward the elevator from Dr. Miller's office.

"All these tests, Jennifer," she says. "Do you really think they're necessary?"

"Yes." I shove the paperwork the receptionist gave me into my purse. I'll have to look at it later and make the necessary phone calls to get Mom's tests scheduled. "Dr. Miller is a good doctor. He wouldn't tell you to have them done if he didn't think they were necessary."

Mom looks away from me as we step into the elevator.

"Mom, overall, I think we got some good news today. He didn't seem to think your issues were anything too serious, and he has treatments in mind once we know what we're dealing with."

"You really think so?"

"Of course."

We're silent on the way to the car, and, once we're settled in and have gone through the whole get-the-seat-belt-engaged-around-Mom routine, I decide it's time to bring up the thing I've been dreading talking to her about.

"I talked with a few home health care agencies this week."

"What for?" she replies shortly.

"To check them out. I think I found one that can offer you a little help around the house."

"I don't need any strangers coming into my house."

"The one I liked the best was called Home Healthcare Solutions," I say, ignoring her comment. I decided last night that I was not going to present having an aide come in once a day as an option that she can say yes or no to. Like it or not, if she wants to stay in her home, this is the way it's going to be. "They've been in business for twelve years. They have a great training program for their employees and, of course, they all have extensive background checks."

"I don't care. I won't let them in. Besides, who's going to pay for all of this?"

"You are. They charge twenty dollars an hour, and they'll come for a few hours, five days a week. I'll come the other two."

"Twenty dollars an hour?!" she yells at me as if it were a million dollars. "You think I'm paying someone twenty dollars an hour? You must have lost your mind, Jennifer."

My mother is by no means wealthy, but she has savings and my father's pension, and the cost of a home health-care aide is not going to bankrupt her.

"Mom. This is the deal. Like it or not. I've already made the arrangements and—"

"You hold on just a minute, Jennifer Peredo. Losing my mind or not, I'm still your mother, and you will not talk to me that way."

I turn and look at her. "I'm sorry, Mom, but this is what's best for you. And it's the only way I'm going to let you stay in your house. Your memory problems are only going to get worse if you don't take your medications the way you need to. A home health care worker can help you stay on track with them, and they can even help with some cooking and cleaning or whatever you need."

"I do not keep a dirty house."

"Who said anything about you keeping a dirty house?"

"Why else would you think I need help cleaning the house?"

"I was just saying that they can help you with the cleaning if you want them to. Honestly, Mother, I don't care what they do as long as we keep you on your medications. You, yourself, said that you don't always remember to take them. It's nothing to feel bad about. I'm not sure I could remember to take as many pills as you have to either. You've said over and over again that you don't want to leave your house. Well, this is the deal I'm offering you. If you want to stay in your house, then you need to work with me here. Otherwise, we need to talk about you moving closer to me."

"I don't want a stranger in my house, Jennifer."

"Once you get to know them, they won't be strangers anymore. Would you rather that you keep forgetting to take your prescriptions and have things get worse?"

She looks out the window and then turns her head. "No, I suppose not."

"I've arranged for us to meet the aide the company has assigned to you tomorrow," I say, thinking about how I will have to take more time off work tomorrow to come out here again. "Her name is Tamara. I talked with her on the phone, and she sounded very nice."

"Tamara? I hate that name. It sounds like a prostitute's name."

"What?" I say and laugh, realizing that I may have won this battle. She's moved on from objecting to my home health care idea to criticizing the worker's name. At least it's progress.

26

"Grandma!" Andrew calls when Mom opens her front door. "Can we make hot chocolate?"

"Of course," she says, and I see her face light up like it only does when she's around Andrew.

"Hi, Mom," I say. "How's it going?" I'm curious to hear her answer. Tamara started two days ago, so I bet Mom is full of complaints.

"Fine," is all she says. She takes Andrew's hand, and I follow them into the kitchen.

"What's in there?" she asks, noticing the plastic bag in my hand.

"Just some organizers for your medications. We can talk about them later."

"Or not at all," she says under her breath and opens the cabinet and pulls out a pot.

"I'll get the *molinillo*," Andrew says, voicing one of the few Spanish words he knows. A *molinillo* is a wooden whisk sort of thing Mom uses to make her famous hot chocolate.

"Okay," Mom says, putting the pot on the stove and reaching into the pantry for her stash of Colombian chocolate. Then she retrieves the milk from the refrigerator and pours it in the pot.

"Can I stir it?" Andrew asks, pushing a chair over toward the stove.

"Of course you can, Tomás."

"Andrew, Mom," I correct from the other side of the table as Andrew climbs up on the stool with the *molinillo* in his hand and starts stirring the milk. Mom hovers over him and waits for the milk to get warm enough to add the solid tablets of chocolate. As Andrew raves about Mom's hot chocolate, I think he enjoys the process of making it more than actually drinking it.

"I'm going to see Grimace, Grandma."

"Grimace?" Mom asks.

"You know, that purple creature at McDonalds," I say. "We stopped by there on the way here, and they had a sign up about him being there in a couple of weeks."

"And we're going to go, right, Mommy?" Andrew asks.

"Sure."

"You *promise*?"

"Yes, sweetie, I promise."

While the two of them are occupied, I open one of the cabinets and take out all of Mom's prescription bottles, put them on the table, and pull out the pill organizers I picked up at the drugstore. I saw all sorts of neat medication management things online when I was doing some research a few days ago: complicated boxes, electronic alarms, even automated dispensing machines that actually snatch pills back if they aren't taken within a certain amount of time. But I thought it would be best to start with simple plastic containers with separate compartments for each day of the week.

"What are you doing?"

"I'm just organizing your prescriptions."

"You leave my prescriptions alone."

"Would you just make the hot chocolate with your grandson? We can talk about this when you're done."

Mom just glares at me and adds the chocolate to the milk.

I open all the compartments on the two organizers and start loading them with the appropriate pills. Luckily, I was able to find ones without child proofing, so Mom can open them easily. When I'm finished, I put the pill bottles in my purse and plan to take them home, so Mom won't accidentally take her meds from the bottles instead of the organizers. Then I sit back at the table and watch Frick and Frack finish making the hot chocolate.

"Okay, Tomás. Now roll it through your hands like this," Mom says, taking control of the whisk and rolling it between the palms of her hands.

"Andrew," Andrew corrects her, taking the whisk back and trying to imitate the way she handled it.

"I don't want any cheese in mine," Andrew says when the hot chocolate is finally done, and Mom grabs some mugs out of the cabinet. It's a Colombian tradition to add cheese to hot chocolate, which Mom does to her own mug. But Andrew and I are not fans of such an addition, so Mom doesn't put any in ours.

"Sweetie, why don't you take your mug into the living room and watch TV? Be careful not to spill it, okay? Grandma and I need to talk about a few things."

When Andrew leaves the room, I slide the organizers in Mom's direction. "From now on, all your pills will be in these two organizers. The yellow one has your morning pills, and the blue one has your evening pills."

She looks at me the same way I used to look at her when I was a kid, and she was going over a list of chores she wanted me to do for the day.

"We're going to keep the morning pills in the kitchen cabinet and the evening pills up in your bedroom . . . maybe on your dresser. I'm going to call you every morning to remind you to take the pills in the yellow box, and then I'll call you again in the evening to take the pills in the blue box. Tamara's going to check the containers when she's here to make sure you're staying on track, and I'll check them on the days she doesn't come."

"How much longer is that Tamara going to be coming?" Mom asks, making no comment at all about the pill organizers.

"Indefinitely."

"She's a nice girl, Jennifer. But I don't need her. Yesterday, she just sat around here and did nothing. I'm supposed to pay someone twenty dollars an hour who does nothing?"

"If she's not doing anything, Mom, give her something to do. She can help with the cooking, the cleaning . . . she can do some laundry."

"I can do my own laundry . . . have been doing it since I came to this country, and I don't see any reason to stop now. Besides, Tamara shrank my favorite wool sweater the last time she was here."

"What wool sweater?"

"The blue one that Tomás gave me for Christmas last year."

"Tom sent you flowers for Christmas last year, Mom," I say and then remember something. "Tom gave you a blue wool sweater for Christmas about ten years ago, and *I* was the one who shrank it in the wash."

"No. It was Tamara . . . twenty dollars an hour, and she doesn't know you need to dry clean wool?"

I talked to Tamara yesterday, and I know that she hasn't done any laundry for Mom since she started two days ago. "No, Mom. It was me. Remember when you were sick with the flu a couple of years ago, and I came over and did your laundry—it was *me* who shrank the sweater. I should know, you reminded me of it for months afterwards."

"It was Tamara, I tell you," she insists.

"Okay . . . whatever. But, whether she shrinks sweaters or not, she's going to keep coming by to check on you. Why don't we go into the living room with Andrew? I'm sure he'd love to play a game with you. Do you still have Candy Land in the closet?" I ask as we get up from the kitchen table and walk toward the living room, hoping that I've squelched any more protests about having an aide come to the house.

All things considered, Tamara has been working out okay. I was here on her first day, and Mom was cordial with her even though she clearly resented her presence. Tamara's a large woman with long hair that's seen a few too many bottles of Nice 'n Easy and shows up to work in sweatpants, but she's very personable and friendly. She's a bit of a chatterbox and was already telling Mom about her two failed marriages by the time I left them for the day, but I really think she and Mom could get along well if Mom would only give her a chance, which I really hope she does. Because, if things don't work out with Tamara, I think we're out of options for Mom staying here by herself.

27

It looks nice from the outside, I think to myself, shivering in the chilly air as I approach the New Horizons Senior Living Center on Duke Street in Alexandria. It's a graceful building designed to look like a Victorian mansion with turrets and pastel siding. I remember when I first started seeing these centers sprouting up in the area. At first glance, I would think they were country inns, but then I'd read the sign, scrunch up my nose and think: *Oh, it's an old folks' home.*

Much as Mom complains about her, I think things are working out okay with Tamara. It's really taken a load off my mind to know that someone is checking in on Mom every day. But, just as a backup, I thought it might be a good idea to check out a few assisted living facilities. This one is only a few miles from my house, so I figured I'd start here.

It's February now, and it's exceptionally cold this afternoon, so the warm air is particularly inviting when I step inside the building.

"Hi. I'm here to see Charlie Foster," I say to a plump woman sitting behind the desk in the lobby.

"Your name?"

"Jennifer Costas. I spoke with him on the phone yesterday."

"Okay. I'll let him know you're here," she says and gets up from her desk.

I take a look around while she fetches Mr. Foster.

The lobby actually does have the feel of a boutique hotel—

nice carpeting, floral sofas, a fireplace in the sitting area off the lobby, and, to the left, I see a quaint little dining room with a juice bar. There's even a grand staircase going up to the next level. But something about the place still feels institutional. It takes a moment for me to put my finger on what's taking away from the charming atmosphere and then it hits me—it's all the elderly people milling about. There are two almost-comatose-looking gentlemen in the sitting room—one is asleep, and the other has the hood of his jacket pulled over his head while he stares blankly at the wall. I catch a glimpse of a table of seniors playing dominoes in the dining area, and, as I stand there, a barely mobile woman slowly scoots by with her walker.

"Ms. Costas?" I hear from behind and turn around to see a pleasant-looking man with reddish hair and fair skin. He's not exactly what I'd call attractive, but he has a nice smile and a welcoming look about him.

"Yes. Jennifer, please."

"Charlie Foster. Nice to meet you," he says and extends his hand. And, I'm not certain, but the way he's moving his eyes, leads me to believe he's "checking me out." "We can step in my office. It's just over here."

I follow him down the hall and get a good look at him from behind. He clearly has a tight body. I can see the v-shape of his back through his snug polo shirt, and he's got a cute set of buns. When we reach his office, we both take seats at a small table in the corner.

"Thanks for coming in today. We're always glad to have visitors."

"Sure."

"So, we talked a bit on the phone, but why don't you tell me more about what brings you in," he says to me, and I swear he's looking at me in a *certain* way. Believe me, I'm not the type of girl who thinks every man I come in contact with is flirting with me—that would make me Claire. But between the way his eyes met mine when he introduced himself and the way he's staring at me now, I'm just feeling *something*.

"Unfortunately, the days of my mother being able to live on her own may be numbered. I have an aide checking in on her daily now, but, if that doesn't work out, I may have some tough decisions to make. At the moment, I'm just gathering information, trying to come up with some options. To my knowledge, New Horizons has a pretty good reputation, so I thought I'd come by and see what you have to offer." Suddenly I notice I'm unconsciously sitting up straighter than I usually do. I'm sticking out my chest and sucking in my stomach, trying to look my best, something I rarely bother to do.

"How about I tell you a little bit about us in general terms?"

"Sure."

"New Horizons has been serving seniors for more than twenty years. The goal of its founders was to create a superior approach to senior living with a focus on independence. At this center, we have assisted living floors and then a locked floor for memory impaired residents."

I assume "memory impaired" is a polite way of saying Alzheimer's.

"As you can see, we are designed to be an attractive social setting. We provide three meals a day in our dining room and offer all sorts of activities. We have a shuttle service to the grocery store and Wal-Mart and Target, and can offer rides to doctor's appointments. We have outings to parks and, last month, we took a group to Atlantic City for the day."

"Gosh. Where do I sign up?" I joke.

He smiles. "So tell me about your mother."

"Up until a few months ago she'd been making out okay on her own. I think she gets lonely, but she's so stubborn and doesn't want to leave her house, which I can understand. But lately she's been forgetful and absentminded and hasn't been keeping up with her medications. As it stands now, I just think she needs some light assistance and some medication management. I also think it would be good for her to have more of a social outlet."

"She'd definitely have that here. She would be able to dine with other residents and participate in daily activities. Here," he says and pulls out a slick folder and retrieves a glossy piece of paper from it and hands it to me. "Here's our activity calendar for the month."

I scan it quickly: morning march exercise, baking cookies, fruit social, bingo, Bible study, jewelry making—it looks like a schedule for a Girl Scout troop. The activities sound fine, but I can't help but feel that they reflect an attitude of "Let's keep them occupied while they're waiting to die."

"So what is the housing like? You have apartments, or are they just rooms?"

"We don't have apartments at this location. We have studios and some two room suites. They all have private baths."

"And they have a little kitchenette or something?"

"No. The units do have a small area with cabinetry, a counter, a small refrigerator and a sink, but no stove or oven. Some residents do bring their own microwaves. Why don't we take a look around, and I can show you some of the rooms."

We get up from the table and move out into the hallway.

"So you have different areas of the center for seniors with different needs?"

"Only two. We have the assisted living floors and then, as I mentioned earlier, we have a locked floor for memory-impaired residents."

"Is there a nursing home level if someone needs round-the-clock care?"

"No, we don't provide that level of service. Occasionally, residents are transferred to nursing homes, but, often it's temporary to take advantage of intensive rehabilitation. Usually, they eventually come back to New Horizons. Most residents stay with us until end of life."

End of life? I think to myself. What a polite way of saying "death"... much easier on the ears.

"So this is the dining room," he says as we step inside. "You can see today's features on the board, and we also have a menu of alternatives if residents don't care for the day's selections."

I look at the board: Chef's Best Soup; Prime Rib Au Jus; Baked

Potatoes; Broccoli; Dinner Rolls; Assorted Dessert Tray; Choice of Beverage. I haven't eaten lunch, and my mouth starts watering just looking at the menu.

"As you're making a decision about your mother's future, we'd encourage you to come by with her and have lunch or dinner at the center."

"That sounds like a good idea," I say, having a vision of trying to convince my mother to do such a thing. I can hear her now: "I'm not going to some nursing home to have lunch with a bunch of old biddie invalids."

"If you and your husband . . . or significant other or whatever . . . would like to bring her . . ."

"I'm not married," I say and feel my face starting to flush. Is that just something he mentioned in passing, or was he trying to find out my relationship status?

"Hi, Alma," Charlie says to the elderly woman I saw scooting by with her walker earlier. She ignores him as she approaches the juice bar. "Hi, Alma," he repeats much louder this time, getting her attention.

"Hello," she says. "There aren't any chocolate-frosted, Charlie. You said we'd be getting the chocolate-frosted," she adds, referring to the box of Krispy Kreme doughnuts lying on the juice bar.

"We'll get you chocolate tomorrow, Alma. I promise."

She grunts at him, grabs one of the glazed donuts, places it on the little shelf at the front of her walker and totters on her way.

Charlie and I go on to tour the rest of the building. He shows me the activities room, the library, and the beauty salon prior to taking me into one of the resident rooms.

"So, do you live in the area?" he asks me.

"Yes. Just a few miles from here."

"And your mother?"

"She's out in Fredericksburg."

"That's a bit of a hike."

"Yeah. And I'm having to go out there more and more to help her out."

"You didn't happen to grow up in Fredericksburg, did you?"

"Yeah. Why?"

"I grew up there as well. My family moved there when I was six years old. Where'd you go to school?"

"High school? Oakridge."

"You're kidding! What year did you graduate?"

"Do I have to answer that question?" I ask with a grin.

He laughs. "I graduated in ninety-two."

"Really? I was a few years before that, but we must have been there at the same time. Isn't that funny?"

"My parents still live there, but I don't get out there very often. Traffic on 95 is a killer."

"You're telling me," I respond while he puts his key in the door of one of the rooms.

When we step inside, I can't really say that I'm impressed or unimpressed with the room. It's about the size of a hotel suite. The carpeting could use replacing, but it has lots of windows for good sun exposure. Like Charlie said earlier, there is no kitchen, just what you might call a wet bar area. It's not a bad little place, but it's certainly not a *home*—it's really just a room more or less. I guess the idea is that residents spend most of their time in the common areas, but I think my mother would really need more of an apartment than what's offered here.

"What do you think?" Charlie asks as we look around the room. And, for a moment, I'm not sure if he's talking about what I think about the space, or what I think about him.

"It's nice . . . small, but nice. Seems to be well maintained. Do you have any rooms available at the moment?"

"We actually don't have anything right now. But things are always changing. I think we may have one or two opening up next month, but it's hard to predict."

Does that mean he expects one to two residents to drop dead sometime next month? "Okay. I'll keep that in mind."

"I think that about wraps up our tour. Are there anymore questions I can answer for you?"

"No. I think that's it for now, other than some information about the cost."

"Of course. I'll get you a folder with pricing information on your way out."

"What are we looking at roughly?"

"Private rooms start at a hundred and thirty dollars a day, and then there are further costs depending on any additional levels of assistance needed."

I do some quick calculations in my head. One hundred and thirty dollars a day. That's about four thousand a month . . . about fifty thousand a year. Oh, dear God! Mom's got some savings and Social Security and my father's pension . . . and all the equity in her house, but, at these rates, she could run out of money in a few years.

"All the rooms are private pay?"

"Just about. We do have a couple set-asides for low income residents, but the waiting list is quite lengthy."

"Good to know," I say, and we make our way down the grand staircase that I'm guessing most of the residents are not able to climb.

"Let me get you a folder with some more detailed information. I'll be right back." He leaves me standing there in the lobby, and I take a long look around. It's really not a bad place, and, in some ways, I think Mom could be happy here, or at least better off than she is now. And with her being so much closer to me, I'd be able to see her practically every day, but there's just something I don't like about the idea of her staying here. As nice as it is, it still seems like a place to warehouse old people until they die.

"Here you go," he says and hands me a folder. "It was nice to meet you," he adds, and his eyes linger on mine for a moment longer than the situation calls for.

"You, too."

"I don't usually ask this when people come in for tours," he says just before I walk away. "But would you like to have dinner sometime or something?"

I feel my ears getting hot the way they always do when I'm nervous. I definitely sensed some romantic interest from him, but I wasn't expecting him to ask me out right here and now. I don't get it. In the two years since Mario and I separated, I've had nary a suitor and now, all of a sudden, it seems like I'm getting more than my fair share of interest—first Ben, then Mr. Ex-Gay, and now Charlie. He's put me on the spot, and I don't know what to say. He's not bad-looking, and he's very friendly, but had he not expressed any interest in me, I probably wouldn't have paid him any attention.

"Um . . . sure," I say.

"Great. When's good for you?"

"You know what? A couple friends of mine are taking me out for drinks tomorrow night for my birthday. To Mango Mike's up the street . . . about eight o'clock. Maybe you can join us."

"Sure. Sounds like fun."

I give him a last smile and make my way out of the building. It feels nice to have someone express interest in me, and, surprisingly, my usual apprehension about any type of romance doesn't seem to be rearing its ugly head. For some reason, I'm actually pretty relaxed about the idea of meeting up with Charlie. Maybe all of Claire's advice about just going with the flow is finally sinking in. Or maybe I'm just too tired to get all bent out of shape about dating anymore. Whatever the reason, Charlie will meet us for a few drinks tomorrow night and what happens happens.

28

Jimmy Buffet is playing in the background when Claire, Desma, and I walk into Mango Mike's, a tacky Caribbean-themed restaurant complete with a tiki bar that serves killer piña coladas in real coconut shells.

"What time did you tell him to meet us?" Claire asks as we take our seats at a table in the bar area.

"Eight."

It's seven o'clock now. I told Charlie to meet us at eight, figuring I'd get a little alone time with the girls and a drink or two in my system before he arrives. In retrospect, I'm not sure how good an idea it was to have us meet here with Claire and Desma along for the ride. He caught me off guard when he asked me out, and, I guess at the time, I thought inviting him along to a group outing would be a low-key way to have a first date. But Claire and Desma can be a bit much to take, not to mention I'll be wondering what both of them think of him throughout the evening.

"All I have to say is, 'You go girl!' Picking up an *hombre* while checking out a nursing home for your mother."

"It's not a *nursing home*. It's an assisted living facility. And it was actually quite nice. I wouldn't mind taking a vacation there myself," I say, and I'm not being completely facetious. New Horizons really didn't seem like a bad place to take a holiday. It would almost be like vacationing on a cruise—you have your own suite, gourmet meals in the quaint dining room, and all sorts of fun activities during the day. It would be a great place to go and decompress for a while—the key words being "a while." I'm not so sure it's perceived as such a wonderful place by the elderly people who know that it's their last stop on the highway of life, and that they will never get to go back to their own homes and their old lives.

"He's cute?"

"He is sort of cute, in a boy-next-door way. He has a great body. He clearly works out."

"You said he has red hair?" Desma asks.

"Have you ever slept with a redhead?" Claire inquires before I have a chance to answer Desma's question.

"No, not that I recall."

"Oh, you'd *recall*, believe me. Just be prepared."

"For?"

"For the . . . hmm, how should I put this . . . the *unveiling*. The first time I got it on with a redhead, I was shocked when he took off his pants. I knew he had red hair on his head but, for some reason, I wasn't expecting the 'carpet to match the drapes' if you know what I mean."

"I have no idea what you mean."

"I mean he had this fiery orange bush around his dick. It was like having sex with Ronald McDonald . . . which is fine, but I just wish I had known what to expect."

Desma and I exchange looks.

"I'm just trying to warn you," Claire says.

"Thanks for the heads-up." I grab a drink menu, and a waiter appears at our table.

"Good evening, ladies."

"Who you callin' a lady?" Claire jokes. I hate when we have male waiters—it always means an endless evening of Claire flirting with them.

He smiles. "What can I get for you?"

"How about a few drinks on the house? It's her birthday, you know," Desma, always the frugal one, asks, pointing to me.

"Well, happy birthday! I don't think I can score you any free drinks, but maybe I can scam you a free dessert or something later."

"Sounds yummy." Claire eyes the waiter as if he's the free dessert.

"How about we do three piña coladas?" I suggest.

"And a couple of appetizers," Desma adds. "Let's do the jerk chicken wings and the Havana nachos."

"Sounds like a plan," the waiter says and goes on his way.

"So, the kid's with Mario tonight. Maybe you can make this Charlie guy your love 'em and leave 'em fling we've been encouraging you to have."

"*We?*" Desma says. "You mean *you.*"

"I just met him yesterday. I'm not sleeping with him tonight. Get real."

"You're such a goody-goody."

"Not sleeping with a random stranger makes me a goody-goody?"

"What? Are you implying that I sleep with random strangers?" Desma and I are silent.

Claire's mouth drops. "I'll have you know that I do not sleep with strangers. I can tell you the name of every man I've ever been with."

"Yeah. Their AOL screen names, maybe," Desma says with a laugh.

Claire laughs too. "Stop! I do have *some* standards, you know," she says as the waiter sets our coconut shells down on the table. "Well, when you do decide to sleep with him, I can hook you up if you need a place to do the deed. You know, if the kid's at home," she adds, before eyeing Desma. "Or if random house guests are lurking about."

"What do you mean, 'hook me up with a place'?"

"I can get you access to any of my listings. Of course, the vacant ones are more amenable, but then you'd have to do it on the floor. I can get you into some of the non-vacant ones . . . you know, ones that still have beds, but only at certain times, and you have to be ready to abscond at a moment's notice."

"You've got to be kidding?" Desma says.

"No. I do it all the time . . . well, not *all* the time. But it got to be such a hassle to have men over to my own house. Obviously, there was always the issue of Ted having to be out of the house. And then, of course, I'd have to shuffle the dog over to Jen's place. And last time I had Julio over, he had on so much cologne, I had to open all the windows and turn on a couple of fans to get the scent out of the house before Ted came home."

"So you meet your lovers in the homes of your real estate clients?"

"Sometimes. It sort of simplifies things."

We're all quiet while Desma and I try to digest what Claire has just told us. Just when I think she can't possibly be any more brazen than she already is, Claire never hesitates to surprise me.

"To Jennifer," Desma says, breaking the silence and raising her coconut. "May the next thirty-six years be even better than the first."

"Did you have to mention my age?" I ask as Claire and I raise our drinks to meet hers. "Cheers."

The girls and I continue to chatter, eat our appetizers, and down our drinks. We're on our third round of piña coladas when Charlie makes his debut. I see him looking around the bar and wave him over.

"Hi," I say, standing up to meet him, my nerves pretty well calmed thanks to all the rum. "Glad you could make it."

"Sure," he replies and hands me a small box of Godiva chocolates and a card. "I'm not sure if this is appropriate, but you said it was your birthday, so I thought I should bring something."

"How sweet. Not necessary. But very sweet." I motion for him to sit down. "This is Desma. She was my roommate in college many moons ago. And this is—"

"Claire Edwards. Real Estate Agent," Claire says, quite happy to introduce herself. "If you're ever in the market to buy or sell a home, keep me in mind."

"I'll do that," Charlie says politely.

"We should get you a drink," Claire insists. "The piña coladas are great."

"I think I'll just have a beer." Charlie motions to the waiter. "A Budweiser, please."

"So are you going to share those chocolates?" Claire asks, eyeing my box of Godiva.

"Geesh. I haven't even opened the card yet." I tear open the envelope, a little weirded-out from getting a birthday card from someone I barely know, although, probably no less weirded-out than he was to be invited to a stranger's birthday party. "Thank you, Charlie," I say after reading the predictably generic card.

Desma takes the card from me when I'm done reading it and flips it over and looks at the back. "You know, Charlie. You should really look for cards made on recycled paper."

"Oh?"

"Ignore her. Everyone else does," Claire says. "I guess it's gift time." She reaches down and grabs a gift bag from under the table and hands it to me. There's no card, so I just dive in and lift some sort of plastic contraption from the tissue paper. It's about seven inches long with a circular base that has two plastic rods extending from it.

"What the hell is that?" Desma asks, saving me the trouble.

"It's a Kegel exerciser."

"A what?"

"A Kegel exerciser. You use it to strengthen you vaginal muscles. You insert the two rods in your—"

"Oh, dear God," I say quickly, dropping it back in the bag, embarrassed to have it out in front of Charlie. "Why would you buy me such a thing? Wait! No, I don't want you to answer that.'"

"Forgive me for trying to heighten your sexual pleasure."

I give Claire the eye and smile awkwardly at Charlie. "Moving on to the next gift," I say and take it from Desma's hands. "Thank you, Desma."

The gift is heavy. "Books," I say after I unwrap two hardcover novels, each covered in protective plastic sheeting. "From the Alexandria library," I add after I flip them over and see that they are due back in three weeks.

"You got her *library* books?" Claire asks with the right side of her nose turned up.

"I'm short on cash at the moment. It's the thought that counts, and I put a lot of thought into selecting those titles," Desma says to Claire before directing her eyes to me. "Just be sure to have them back on time. I checked them out on Andrew's card."

"I will. Thank you, Desma. I'm not sure when I'll have time to read them, but I'll try."

"*Library books*. That's the stupidest gift I've ever seen," Claire says.

"Yeah. Almost as stupid as a Kegel exerciser. What the hell is that?"

"Ladies! I like both my gifts. Like Desma said, it's the thought that counts."

I look at Charlie sipping his beer and watching three slightly inebriated women cackle like hens over ridiculous birthday presents. "I'm sorry you had to witness this. We are usually a bit more refined and tasteful."

"Says who?" Claire roars with a laugh. We're all feeling the booze, but I think Claire's petite frame has sucked it up a bit faster than the rest of us.

"Don't be sorry. I'm having fun. It's either this or sitting on my sofa watching TV. And somehow I bet that this show is more entertaining than anything on cable at the moment."

"You might be right." I delicately remove the gifts from the table. The four of us order another round of appetizers and continue to chat, and, as the evening progresses, Charlie and I become involved in our own conversation while Desma and Claire have a private argument about Lord knows what.

"I think Desma and I are about ready to leave. Do you think you can find your way home?" Claire says with a gleam in her eye.

"We came in the same car, Claire."

"I know, but I thought Charlie here might be happy to give you a ride." She winks at Charlie.

"I can certainly give you a lift home, Jennifer. It would be nice to stay and chat for a while."

I look at Claire and then back at Charlie. "Sure. That'd be fine."

"Then it's settled. Come on, Crunchy," she says to Desma. "Let's make tracks."

"Who you callin' crunchy?" Desma says as she gets off the stool, gives Charlie and me a quick wave good-bye and follows Claire.

There's a brief silence at the table after they leave. At this point I'm not sure how many piña coladas I've had, but I feel more relaxed than I have in a long time and, maybe it's a case of "beer goggles," or I guess I should say "piña colada goggles," but Charlie looks awfully good to me from across the table.

29

Okay, so sue me. I'm in the car with a strange man on the way back to his place. We spent another hour chatting at the restaurant after Desma and Claire left. He told me more about his work at New Horizons and empathized when I went on and on about my mother's situation. How can I not fall for a man who's willing to patiently listen to me talk about the great stressor in my life. As the evening turned into late night, we gradually inched closer and closer to each other, and a little hand-holding led to a little kissing. It was amazing how relaxed I was about the whole thing—I guess it was all the coconut rum.

He put his arm around me as we left the restaurant and looked at me and asked, "Should I take you straight home, or would you like to come back to my place for a while?"

I didn't even hesitate. "Your place might be a good idea. Desma's at mine and . . ." I let my voice trail off. I was about to mention something about the house being a mess with Andrew's toys all over the place, but as far as I could remember I hadn't mentioned Andrew to Charlie and, just for tonight, I figured I'd leave it that way. This could be going somewhere, or maybe it's that one-night stand Claire has been insisting I need. Whatever it is, at this point, I see no need to muddy drunken sex with any mention of me being a mother.

"Everything okay over there?" he asks me as we pull up in front of his house. "You're awfully quiet all of a sudden."

"Sure. Not much to say, I guess." And I guess I don't have much to say. Despite my still-present buzz, my nerves are finally starting to make an appearance. I can't believe I'm doing this. I haven't gone home with a man I've just met since long before Mario and I got married, and I can't help but feel sleazy about it. Suddenly, I'm also having concerns about my safety. Although I haven't said a word about it all night, I *am* a mother, and I have more than myself to think about should something happen to me. But, as we walk up the front steps, I reassure myself—it's not like Charlie is some random guy I met at a bar. He's a professional ... the director of an assisted living facility, and he knows that Desma and Claire know his name and where I met him. Surely, there is nothing to worry about.

"Can I get you anything? I think I have a bottle of white wine in the refrigerator," he asks me once we've made our way inside the house and into the living room.

"No. Thanks. I think I've had enough for tonight ... well, maybe just a glass of water."

"Sure."

While he disappears into the kitchen, I take a quick look around. The living room is pretty plain, which is just as well—if the place were too tastefully decorated, I'd be afraid I'd latched on to yet another gay man and, quite frankly, that might push me right over the edge.

"Here you go."

"Thanks." I take a long sip of water, and we sit down on the sofa.

"I'm glad you decided to come over." He starts rubbing my shoulders, which feels really, *really* good. His hands are big and strong. I shut my eyes, lean into him, and just relax for a few minutes while he kneads the area around my neck. I'd almost forgotten how nice the touch of a man is on my body.

Charlie gives my shoulders one more squeeze and then puts his arms around my waist, lifts my hair to the side and starts kissing my neck. I hear a soft sigh escape my lips as I put one hand behind his head and the other on his arm—holding both tightly, melting with the feel of his tongue on my neck. I feel my breath quickening as he slips his hand under my blouse and rubs the naked skin on my back. At first, I suppress the urge to moan, but when he lifts my shirt over my head and gently cups my breasts with his hands, I just let it come out—a long, high-pitched sigh. He wastes no time undoing my bra and releasing my breasts to be massaged by his thick fingers. The vigor of his hands against the softness of my skin makes me writhe with pleasure. When he slowly turns me around, my lips facing his, I lie back on the sofa and pull him close to me. He kisses me, lightly at first, and then with intensity—his mouth pressed against mine and our tongues racing against each other. I feel his hardness against my pelvis, and it sends a long chill through my body. I'm getting that insatiable tingle in my groin that I haven't felt since I saw Daniel Craig walk out of the ocean in the last James Bond movie.

"Do you like that?" he asks, moving from my lips to my neck and down to my chest.

Not one to converse during sex, I offer a pleasant sigh in response to his question.

He takes his tongue to my breast and lightly teases my nipples before bringing his head back up to mine. "So, do you get into anything kinky?" he whispers with a gleam in his eye.

"Hmm?" I ask, even though I heard what he said.

"Nothing too crazy."

"Oh. I don't know." I don't want to be a prude, but I have no idea what he means by kinky.

He kisses my neck. "Are you open to trying new things?"

"Um . . . maybe. What do you have in mind?" I say, my feelings of pleasure and relaxation morphing into tenseness. If he wants me to spank him with a hairbrush or something, I suppose I could suffer through it, but I doubt it's really my thing.

"I'll be right back."

I watch him head down the hall and hear him opening the closet in the other room. I lie topless on the sofa, wondering what he's up to. Part of me is apprehensive and wonders if I should make a run for it while I have the chance, but another part of me—the part of me doused with piña coladas, is curious and not completely against indulging in something a bit outlandish.

I shut my eyes and rest my head on the armrest of the sofa, and, when I open them, I audibly gasp. Charlie is standing over me, completely naked with the exception of a bonnet on his head and some sort of adult diaper covering his nether region. He has his thumb in his mouth and a wide-eyed expression on his face.

"Mommy," he says in a baby voice, his thumb still in his mouth. "I made a boom-boom. Can you change me?"

"No . . ." I say in a soft daze, still not believing the sight before my eyes—a grown man with hair on his chest and a five o'clock shadow on his face dressed in a pair of Depends and a Holly Hobbie bonnet. "No!" I say louder this time, the reality of the situation sinking in. And I'm not just saying no to his question about changing his diaper. I'm saying no to all of it—to him, to one-night stands, to kinky sex. "No . . . no, no, no, no, no," I utter thoughtlessly as I hurriedly get up from the sofa and snatch my bra and my blouse from the floor. "No," I say yet again, my cheeks swelling with unease and my eyes brimming with disgust—and not disgust at him (okay, well maybe sort of at him) but more at myself for getting into this situation. "I need to go. I just need to go."

"I'm sorry. I guess this was too much for the first time?" he asks, taking the bonnet off his head, but not really looking all that remorseful.

I don't answer him. I can't even bear to look at him.

"I just figured you might be into it."

"Why?" I ask, slipping my arms into my blouse, my bra still in my hand.

"I don't know. You came home with me. We'd just met. I thought someone like you would be—"

"Oh, my God! You think I'm some kind of slut. I haven't had sex in over *two* years! Yes, maybe I was looking for a little diversion, but *this*? I'm a mother, for Christ's sake. I have a son," I say as if any of it manners. I made a really bad decision, and now I just need to pick up the pieces and get the hell out of here.

"Let me get dressed and take you home," he says behind me as I walk toward the door.

Shit! I think to myself, realizing that I have no way home other than him. "No, no. I'll call a cab."

"Really. Just give me a minute."

"No!" I say. "I'll call a cab," and I walk down the hallway and out the door. I put my coat over my shoulders and pull my cell phone from my purse. I'm about to dial 411 to get the number for a taxi company, but I call Desma instead. The first time I get through, the phone rings several times before the answering machine picks up. So I call back, and this time, Desma answers.

"Hello," she says, clearly aroused from sleep.

"Desma. It's me. I need you to come pick me up."

"What? Where are you?"

"At Charlie's."

"What happened?"

"Don't ask. Just come get me. The house number says 4780." I walk just past the house and get a look at the street sign. "It's 4780 Lumberton Street. It's not far from the restaurant. Just use MapQuest and get here as soon as you can."

"Are you okay?"

"Yes. I'm fine. I'll be waiting outside."

"Why don't I stay on the phone with you until I get there?"

I look around at the dark night and feel the chill in the air. "Yeah. That would be nice."

"Did he hurt you, Jen?"

"No, no . . . nothing like that."

"Hold on a minute while I get dressed, and I'll be right back."

"Okay," I say, thankful she answered my call. While the phone is quiet, I sit down by the side of the road. I can't believe I'm sitting outside on the curb after midnight, waiting for a friend to pick me up after a sexual encounter gone bad. This is the kind of thing that happens to a sorority girl during college, not a thirty-six-year-old mother of a young son.

"You still there?"

"Yeah," I say. "Hurry, please," I add, just wanting the night to be over.

30

"What happened?" Desma asks as soon I get in the car. "I really don't want to talk about it, Desma."

"He didn't hurt you? You're *sure*?"

"No. I mean yes . . . I'm sure. I told you it wasn't anything like that."

"So what was it then? You seemed to be getting along fine at the restaurant."

"You really want to know what he did, Desma?" I say, raising my voice. "We were making out on the sofa, and he got up for a moment and came back into the living room in nothing but a diaper—"

"A *diaper*?!"

"Yes. He started talking in a baby voice and said something about making a boom-boom and how he wanted me to change him."

"He *did not*!?"

"Oh, he did, all right."

"What did you do?"

"I got out of there as fast as my feet would carry me."

"A *diaper*?"

"Yes, a diaper," I say, and, oddly, I have the urge to laugh, and a little snicker escapes my mouth. "This could only happen to me."

"You don't think he really . . . you know . . . made a boom-boom?"

"God! I hope not." My little snicker grows into full-fledged laughter, which of course is contagious and Desma starts laughing too.

"That is crazy."

"He looked so ridiculous. He had this bonnet on and his thumb in his mouth . . ." I'm laughing so hard now I can barely speak. "Why would he think I'd be into that? What kind of woman gets turned on changing a grown man's diaper?"

"Please. People get into all kinds of freaky shit. Maybe you should hook him up with Claire."

"You're bad," I say. "Even Claire has her limits."

"I guess."

"Thanks for coming to get me," I say, my laughter subsiding. "What did I do so horrible in my past life that so much bad karma keeps coming around to bite me in the ass?"

"You know I'm not one to say I told you so . . ."

"But?"

"Did I not tell you to move that junk out of your relationship area?"

"Oh, please. That's ridiculous. My bum dates have nothing to do with feng shui," I respond with a sigh, turning my head to look out the window.

Desma and I are quiet for the rest of the ride home. During the silence, I can't help but think about Charlie, and how he seemed like a nice normal guy. Who'd have guessed he had a freakin' diaper fetish. My thoughts about Charlie lead to thoughts about Grant, the ex-gay I met at church. And thinking about both of them leads me to Ben, and how stupid I was to blow him off for no logical reason other than my own neurosis. Ben was handsome, patient, intelligent, and we really enjoyed each other's company. What a fool I was to give him the cold shoulder after the drag show three weeks ago.

As Desma and I pull into the driveway, I contemplate what it would be like to call Ben and try to reconnect. But it's been weeks since I saw him. He's probably dating someone else by now. Besides, he's surely written me off as one of those women with too much baggage to be bothered with. And maybe I am one of those women. I'm divorced, I have a son, I'm still hung up on my ex-husband . . . my *gay* ex-husband, my mother is getting needier by the day—not exactly attributes that look great in a personal ad.

By the time we get in the house, I'm exhausted and just want to go to bed and forget that this whole evening ever happened. I'm about to go upstairs and crawl underneath the covers, but, instead, I trudge down to the basement, and grab an empty cardboard box. Then I make my way to the family room and start clearing out my "relationship area."

31

"I think you're in a good position to take over my role when I leave in the spring, Jennifer," my boss, Claudette, says to me. She stopped by my office a few minutes ago to go over some last minute edits to the presentation about proposed benefits changes we are going to be giving senior management later today. "Today will be a good chance to show the partners upstairs what you're made of and really get on their radar."

"I hope everything goes well."

"Of course it will. You've done some great work. I'll let you take the lead this afternoon. After all, you were the one who did all the research."

"Thanks. And a lot of research it was."

I've spent countless hours over the last few months putting together a plan to reduce the firm's benefit costs without sacrificing quality, which is no easy task considering Currier and Timmons employs some of the top lawyers in the country. You can only play with their benefits so much without sending them packing to another firm. I've been all over the Web and on the phone with companies throughout the country, researching our options related to health insurance, dental and optical plans, disability programs, employee assistance programs, etc. Because we're a fairly sizable firm with good utilization statistics, I've been able to secure very competitive quotes that will bring down the firm's benefit costs without changing the richness of the plans we offer. I've also done a lot of research on child and elder care programs that I'm going to present to the partners today. How nice it would be if we had some of those programs in place now. I'd love to be able to pick up the phone and get some assistance with child care issues, and, more importantly, some help in caring for an elderly parent.

"The slides look great. I just made a couple of minor edits to them."

"Do you want to see them again before the meeting?"

"No, just make my changes, and we'll be ready to roll. We can go upstairs together. I'll stop by just before three."

After Claudette leaves my office, and I start to get back to work, I hear a loud knock on my door and look up and see Claire.

"Hey, hey, hey," she says.

"Hi. What are you doing here?"

"I was trying to nab a listing at a condo complex a few blocks away, so I figured I'd stop in and say hello before I meet Julio for lunch."

"Why do I doubt you'll be doing any eating on this lunch date?"

"Oh, I'll be eating all right."

"I shouldn't have said anything." I get up to shut my office door. "Benita's kind of nosy," I say quietly, directing my eyes out into the lobby toward Benita's desk.

"That chick that was tweezing her eyebrows when I came in?"

"Tweezing her eyebrows? I've told her a thousand times, 'No personal grooming at her desk.' And—"

I'm interrupted by Claire's cell phone ringing.

"Sorry, a realtor's work is never done." She flips her phone open. "Claire Edwards," I hear her say into the phone.

Then I just hear silence as her caller speaks.

"Hi, Mrs. Houston. How are you?"

Silence.

"Really? What's wrong?"

Silence.

"What?! Of course not. Why would you ask me that?"

Silence.

"I would never have sex in your house. That would violate my realtor code of ethics or . . . or something." Claire looks at me and shrugs her shoulders.

Silence.

"I am not lying!"

Silence.

"Oh," Claire says, her mouth turning downwards, a guilty-as-charged look coming over her face. "Nanny Cam, you say?"

Silence.

"Hidden in the teddy bear on the dresser?"

Silence.

"No, I guess the camera doesn't lie." Claire seems to be at a loss for words and doesn't say anything for a moment or two. Then she cocks her head and her eyes brighten. "Well, I always made the bed afterward," she says, as if this revelation will fix everything.

"Hello? Hello?" Claire says into the phone, listens for another moment and then flips it shut. "She hung up on me."

"And you're surprised?"

"Oh, well . . . guess I can kiss that listing good-bye. I wasn't getting any movement on her house anyway. It's not in the best neighborhood and needs a lot of work, but it did provide a steady place for Julio and me to meet. Damn," Claire says suddenly. "Julio and I were supposed to meet there today."

"Can't you get in trouble for this? What if she reports you to your agency or whoever you report realtors who have sex in your house to? Or worse, what if she gets in touch with Ted?"

"I don't think she'd do anything like that. I rarely wear my wedding band when I'm not with Ted, so she probably doesn't even know I'm married. If she tries to report me to the Real Estate Board, I will just say she gave me permission to use her house and threaten to sue her for filming me and Julio. Pervert!"

"I hope Julio is worth all this."

"Oh, he is. In fact, I have a picture of him. Want to see?"

"Sure."

Claire pulls a photo out of her purse and hands it to me. My mouth drops open. "This is a picture of a penis . . . an *erect* penis."

Claire nods her head, a certain amount of pride showing in her face as if it were an eight by ten of her newborn baby.

"I can't believe you're running around with a picture of a penis in your purse."

"Well, wouldn't you? Look at that thing. It's huge."

I take a second look at the photo, certain I'm blushing. "How big is it exactly?"

"I haven't measured. But I'm thinking somewhere in the neighborhood of nine inches."

"Here," I say, handing the photo back to her. "Put it away before someone comes in . . . well, wait . . . let me see it one more time."

She gives it back to me. "That's *crazy*," I say, giving it one more look. "I'm getting sore just looking at it."

Claire laughs and takes it back, shoves it in her purse and gets up to leave. "I guess I'd better go. I need to get in touch with Julio and figure out another place to meet."

"Okay. Thanks for stopping by. Next time leave the x-rated pictures at home."

"Don't act like you didn't like seeing it."

I just roll my eyes as she walks out the door.

After she leaves, I start going over Claudette's edits to the presentation and pull up the file on my computer to make the changes. Her edits are the last thing I need to do with it before I present it to the partners. And it is a pretty stellar presentation, if I do say so myself. I've carefully planned out everything I intend to say, and I even bought a new suit to wear today. Things seem to be lining up nicely for my promotion, and this presentation could help cinch the deal. Sliding into Claudette's director position would mean so many great things for me and Andrew.

It would be a significant salary increase, which would come in handy as I may have to support Andrew by myself once Mario's cockamamie restaurant idea goes up in smoke. I would also get an additional week of paid vacation, and, as boss of the department, I'd have more freedom to come and go as necessary.

I've proven my competency and my work ethic over the two and a half years I've been here, and, assuming the partners don't look outside the firm, the only other person who has a shot at the job is Myra Gibbs. She does have a master's degree in Human Resources Management, but she's only been with the firm for a year, and, although she has impressive credentials, she doesn't seem to be much of a problem solver and always comes to Claudette or me for help and advice. And, honestly, she's a bit on the lazy side. Originally, Claudette had tasked both Myra and me to review the firm's benefit structure, but Myra kept letting her assignments slide and doing things half-assed; accordingly, Claudette eventually asked me to do it alone.

By the time three o'clock rolls around, and I'm giving the presentation one final review, my phone rings.

"Jennifer Costas."

"Ms. Costas?"

"Yes."

"This is Tamara, Ana's home health-care aide."

"Yes. Hi, Tamara. Is everything okay?"

"No . . . no, I don't think so. When I got here the kitchen was full of smoke."

"What?!"

"Yes. The fire had already gone out on its own, and as far as I can tell, there isn't any damage, but Ana is in quite a panic."

"Fire?! Is she okay?"

"Yeah. Physically I think she's okay, but she's pretty shaken up."

"What kind of fire? How bad was it? How did it start?"

"She was baking some potatoes, and, for some reason, she wrapped them in newspaper before she put them in the oven."

"Oh, my God! Can you put her on?" As I ask the question, I see Claudette standing in my doorway ready to go to our presentation.

"Just a minute," Tamara says and the phone is quiet for a second.

"Jennifer. I almost set the house on fire! I thought it was foil. I thought it was foil!" I can hear the panic in Mom's voice.

"Foil?"

"I don't know why. I thought the newspaper was foil. I meant to wrap the potatoes in foil." I think she might be crying. In my thirty-six years on the planet, the only times I've seen my mother cry was when she did it on purpose to make someone (usually me) feel guilty—never because she had lost control of her emotions.

"Okay, Mom. Calm down. The fire's out. It's okay."

"The house. I almost set the house on fire!" It's almost like she doesn't hear me. I feel like she isn't even talking to me. She's just speaking out loud to no one in particular.

"Okay, Mom. Try to relax. I'll be there as soon as I can. Can you put Tamara on the phone?"

"Yes," Tamara says to me after Mom gives her the phone.

"I'll try to get there right away, but it will probably take me more than an hour to get out there. Can you stay with her until then?"

"Yes. Of course."

"You have my cell phone number. Call me if you need to reach me."

When I hang up the phone, I look at Claudette and know my shot at impressing the partners has literally gone up in smoke.

"Family crisis?" she asks, having overheard much of the conversation.

"My mother's been having a lot of problems lately. She wrapped some potatoes . . . it's a long story. But the short of it is I have to go out to Fredericksburg."

"*Now?*" Claudette asks me. "You know how important this meeting is."

"Can we possibly reschedule for tomorrow?"

"No. It's so hard to get the partners' schedules coordinated."

I look down at my desk and stop and think for a moment. I could probably call Tamara and ask her to stay longer with Mom, so I can attend the meeting, but Mom sounded so panicked on the phone . . . so unlike herself. I really think I need to get there as soon as possible.

"I'm so sorry, Claudette, but I really do have to go now."

"I understand, Jennifer. Your family has to take priority. I'm familiar with the presentation. I'm sure Myra and I can handle going over the benefits with the partners, but this was really your chance to shine."

I let out a sigh. "I know, I know," I say, shaking my head. "But, unfortunately, I don't have a choice."

"Okay, Jennifer. You do what you have to do. We'll manage here."

"Thanks, Claudette. I saved the presentation to the laptop." I gesture for her to step over so I can show her where I saved it. "I made all your edits, and it should be good to go."

Claudette takes the laptop from my desk. "I'll let them know that you were behind most of the research and put the presentation together."

"I appreciate it. And if you have any questions, I have my cell on." As I start to lock up my desk, I feel a painful sense of defeat as I watch Claudette walk out of my office with my laptop and *my* presentation. I worked so hard on it, and, like she said, it was going to be my moment to shine. But I guess there isn't much I can do about it now. I've got bigger worries than getting face-time with the partners. I've got a mother who almost burned her house down.

32

"Hey. It's me," I say into my cell phone on my way out to Mom's.

"Hi. What's up?" Mario responds.

"Can you pick Andrew up from his after school program and keep him at your place tonight?"

"Sure. Why?"

"I'm on my way out to Mom's. She's having a crisis, and she's got a bunch of tests scheduled tomorrow at the hospital, so I figure I may as well stay the night at her place instead of driving all the way out there again tomorrow morning."

"Is Ana okay?"

"No," I answer honestly, and, out of nowhere, I feel tears start to form in my eyes. "She's losing it, Mario, and I don't know what I'm going to do."

"What happened?"

"Somehow she thought she was wrapping some potatoes in foil before she put them in the oven, but she used newspaper instead, and, of course, they caught on fire." I'm trying to keep it together but my voice is starting to crack. "I guess the fire burned itself out when the newspaper was gone, but when the home health care aide got there, the house was full of smoke, and Mom was panicked."

"Oh gosh . . ."

"She didn't sound like herself on the phone, Mario. She

sounded all spaced out and scared." I'm not even trying to stop crying anymore.

"Jen, I'm so sorry. It'll be all right. I'll help you through this any way I can. Don't worry about Andrew. He'll stay with me as long as necessary."

"Thanks, Mario," I say, appreciating his words. "I'll call you later with an update."

"Is there anything else I can do?"

"No, not right now. Knowing that Andrew is taken care of is a big help. He could stay with Desma, but he doesn't like being left with her. She doesn't let him watch TV, and she's always trying to teach him about global warming and recycling." A small chuckle breaks through my tears, and I start to calm down.

When I hang up with Mario, I turn up the radio and try to focus on my driving, but I just can't shake this overwhelming sense of guilt—the same guilt I felt about leaving the greasy frying pan on the stove when Andrew started a fire last month. What is it with my relatives and setting things on fire?

What if the fire at Mom's kitchen hadn't gone out by itself? What if the house had gone up in flames? It would have been my fault for letting Mom stay there all alone. The more I think about it, the more I realize what denial I've been in. How I've kept convincing myself that her odd behavior was just part of the natural aging process. I think of all her mental lapses—how she's called me by her sister's name, how she was clipping obituaries of people she doesn't even know, the times she seemed to zone out altogether . . .

I remember the evening when I was trying to convince her not to feel bad about thinking the oven was running at six hundred degrees when it wasn't even on. In retrospect, I can see that I was trying to reassure myself as much as her. The more I reflect, the more things come to me that didn't seem like that big of a deal on their own, but when I add them all up, they really should have signaled a much bigger problem. I remember the time she put her dress on backwards, the time she thought we were going to see her old doctor, who died two years ago, all the times she called Andrew by my brother's name . . . What on earth made me think it was okay for her to stay there by herself?

I guess in some ways I shouldn't be that surprised. I'm pretty good at denial. You learn to ignore things that bother you when you've been married to a gay man. Just like the situation with Mom, there were lots of clues to Mario's sexuality when we were married—maybe on their own they were pretty trite, but when I added up all the times I noticed him looking at a handsome waiter, his lack of interest in sex (sex with me, anyway), or the time I caught him leafing through my *Cosmopolitan* issue with the year's sexiest bachelors, I should have realized that only an idiot (or a woman in absolute denial) wouldn't have seen the red flags. I guess one's mind learns to block out things it doesn't want to address. And I certainly never wanted to address my husband's homosexuality, and I still don't want to address the fact that my mother is no longer able to take care of herself.

33

I can still smell charred potatoes when I come into Mom's house, and it's been at least two hours since the fire. After I left the office, I quickly went by my house and grabbed some toiletries and a change of clothes. I had already scheduled tomorrow morning off to take Mom to the hospital for her tests. They're going to do some more blood work, a CT scan, and an ultrasound on her neck. It didn't make sense for me to come out here tonight to try to calm Mom down and then go home just to make the trip out here again tomorrow morning. Besides, I don't think she can be left alone anymore, at least not with an oven in the house.

When I knock on the door, Tamara opens it almost immediately. "Hello."

"How are things?' I ask.

"Better. She's calmed down some. She was a little spacey earlier, but she seems to have her bearings back now."

"Thanks so much for staying with her until I could get here."

"No problem. Do you need me for anything else?"

"No. Thanks."

Tamara grabs her coat from the rack next to the door and leaves. And I head toward the living room where I find Mom sitting on the sofa looking through some old mail.

"Hi," I say.

"Hi. What's in the bag?" she asks immediately.

"Just a few things for me. I figured I may as well stay the night since we have all your appointments tomorrow."

"Really?" she asks. It's been years since I've stayed overnight here, so I'm sure she was surprised to hear of my plans.

"I'll need to put some clean sheets on the bed in the guest bedroom."

"Why? Has someone else been sleeping in there?"

"Those sheets haven't been changed for months. They must be filled with dust."

"I can just bunk here on the sofa." I sit down next to her. "Sounds like you've had quite a day . . . quite a scare with the oven and all."

"Jennifer, it was horrible. The house was filled with smoke, and I just panicked. When I opened the oven, the smoke got worse, and I saw flames. I wasn't sure what to do. I filled a pot with water, and I was about to pour water into the oven but, by then, the flames had gone out, and there was just a bunch of smoke. I had to open all the windows. I was outside when Tamara got here. She's very nice for a girl with a prostitute's name. But it was *horrible*. I thought the house was going to go up in flames."

I sit next to her and listen to her talk. I know she's talking to me, but it feels like she isn't talking to anyone in particular. It reminds me of the way she speaks when she recollects the evening of my father's death—the way she stares off into space and talks of how he had called to her from the bedroom while she was downstairs in the kitchen. And when she reached him, he was already unconscious on the bed. He'd been fine when she saw him a few minutes earlier when he was helping her get dinner together, but when she got upstairs, he wasn't breathing, and, by the time the paramedics arrived, he was gone. She often repeats the whole story about how she found him, how panicked she was waiting for the ambulance, how helpless she felt not knowing what to do for him, and how she wished she had learned CPR. She always recalls that evening without looking at me or to whomever she is speaking.

"Well, it's over now." That's all I say. I really feel like I should use this as a segue for yet another conversation about what we are going to do about her living situation, but I just don't feel like going there right now. I was starting to breathe easier now that Mom had finally agreed to having Tamara come in and check on her every day. I thought having a home health care aid come into the house on the days I can't be here would really buy us a significant amount of time, but, even with daily visits, I don't think Mom can stay here anymore unless there's someone here twenty four/seven . . . or maybe we could get rid of the oven. But so many things can happen beyond fires starting with the oven. If she falls and has trouble lifting herself up, or Lord knows . . . any sort of thing can happen with her mind going the way it is. But, at this point, I'm just glad she's calm, and I don't want to stir things up right now.

"Well, it's only four-thirty. Is there anything you want to do this afternoon? Do you have any errands we should run?"

"No. I think I have everything I need," she says and then she gets an odd look in her eyes. "You know what, Jennifer?" she asks, and her face lights up.

"What?"

"I'd like to go to the market."

"Really? What for?" When Mom says "the market," she isn't referring to the Safeway, which she calls the grocery store. When she speaks of "the market," she's referring to the Latino grocery store. When I was young, we used to go to the Latino market all the time. Back then, we'd have to drive all the way into D.C. to find one, but more and more of them have been opening in the suburbs, and there's one right here in Fredericksburg now. It's been months since I've been there. After my father died, Mom mostly lost interest in cooking up her Colombian recipes. Besides, these days, she can pick up most of what she needs for them in the international food section at the Safeway.

"I'd just like to pick up a few things. It's been so long since we've been there."

"Well, okay. We can go. Why don't you get your coat?"

I watch her slowly lift her elderly frame from the sofa and walk over to the coat closet off the living room and grab a light jacket.

"Why don't you put on your winter coat, Mom? It's pretty cold outside."

"It's upstairs. I don't want to go all the way up there right now."

"*All the way* up there? Aren't we being a bit dramatic? Get the winter coat. The last thing we need is you getting sick."

Mom lets out a sigh and makes her way to the steps. I watch as she grabs hold of the railing and slowly hoists one leg on the first step and the other leg up to the same step. She takes a quick break, and then repeats the process for the next step.

"Mom? Are you having trouble with the stairs?"

"No, I'm fine. It just takes me a little while. I'm old, you know."

I'm quiet as I continue to watch her slowly . . . very slowly climb the steps, taking small breaks after every couple of steps. I don't know what to say. As many times as I've been over here, I think it's been a few weeks since I've seen her climb the stairs. Lately, she's always downstairs when I get here, and when we go about our errands, there's generally no more than a curb or two that she needs to step up on. Now that I think about it, I'm starting to remember a handful of times that she's asked me to run upstairs and get things for her while I'm here. And, last time I was here, on the few occasions that I asked her to go upstairs for various reasons, she's always declined and made up some reason about why she'd rather do it later. She's clearly been hiding this handicap from me for fear of it adding to my efforts to get her to move.

When she finally makes it to the second level of the house, I hop off the sofa and quickly climb the steps behind her.

"Mom? How long have you had trouble climbing the steps?"

"I'm not having trouble. I'm just slow. My legs are a little heavy sometimes," she says and sits down on the bed.

"Let me see something," I say, and squat down next to her

and roll up one of her pant legs. Today the swelling is much more significant than it was the last time we were at the doctor.

"Why aren't you wearing the support hose that Dr. Miller told you to wear?" She just has on a pair of knee-highs. "You should at least have on a pair of thick socks, Mom. It's winter."

"Those support hose are too tight, and they're uncomfortable."

"They're supposed to be tight. I think we're going to have to go back to see Dr. Miller after your tests tomorrow. Your legs look a lot more swollen than when he looked at them a few weeks ago."

"Doctors. Tests. I'm tired of it already."

You and me both, I think to myself but stifle my desire to say it. I try to remind myself that as much as Mom's health concerns are a hassle for me, they are far worse for her.

"Try not to think about it. It will only stress you out," I say.

I open the closet door and reach for her winter coat. "Okay. Let's go. Maybe you can get down the stairs faster than you came up them," I say with a smile, and she follows me out of the bedroom so we can head to the market.

34

When we walk through the doors of the *Nueva Tienda* a few miles from Mom's house, all the sights and smells remind me of being a child. It was when I was very young that we would go to the Latino markets the most. From the time I was very little until I was about ten or so, we went to the Latino market in D.C. about once a month, but, as I got older, it seemed that we went less and less, and that much of the traditional Colombian food my parents used to make was slowly replaced with American staples like hamburgers and roasts and baked chickens. My father was much more into shopping the markets than my mother, and since he died, I've only brought my mother here a handful of times. She makes out okay in this store, but her favorite one, *La Fonda Paisa*, is in Silver Spring, Maryland. This market is owned by Salvadorians, the dominant Latino group in the Washington, D.C., area, but *La Fonda Paisa* is owned by Colombians, and they specialize in Colombian items, and they also have a bakery with all sorts of Colombian staples. But, much as Mom prefers the Colombian market, she manages to find most of what she needs here since it's so much closer to home.

I let Mom wander around on her own while I peruse the aisles myself, taking in all the different coffees with names like *Café Bustello*, *Café Caboclo*, and *Café Pilao*; all the flours and cornmeals with names like *Colombiana Almojábana* and *Colombiana Bunoelina*; all the canned figs, beans, salsas, and peppers.

The candy and sweets aisle really brings back childhood memories. When I was a kid, I was not terribly enamored with Colombian food. More often than not, I turned my nose up at it in favor of Chicken McNuggets or hot dogs, but I always enjoyed picking out a few treats on our outings to the Latino markets. I used to love the peach and pineapple lollipops, the hot and sour Mexican powder, and the coconut candy bars.

Despite the few treats I was allowed to get on our trips to the market, I always hated going there. It seemed to suck up an entire Saturday. We lived all the way in Fredericksburg, and this was long before Latino markets had found their way to the suburbs. We had to trek into the city, and there were always other errands to run while we were downtown. I didn't like most of the Colombian food my parents cooked, and part of me was embarrassed by it. There was a reason there were no Latino markets in Fredericksburg in the seventies—because there were almost no Latinos in Fredericksburg in the seventies. The only reason we moved there was because the phone company transferred my father out there, and I guess the cost of housing being so much cheaper than in the close-in suburbs had something to do with it as well. Our neighborhood and my school were largely white with a smattering of African Americans and the occasional Asian. Colombian food made me feel out of place. By the time I was in fifth grade, I began packing my own lunch, so Mom would stop putting *pandeyucas* and *pandebonos* in my lunch box. Who wants to eat food made with yuca and cassava starch when everyone around you is eating peanut butter and jelly sandwiches and potato chips?

It was very hard to be in touch with your Latino heritage in an outlying suburban community where there weren't any other Latinos to commiserate with. All my friends were white with last names like Conner and Smith and Dunn. They had never heard of foods like *salchichitas*, *deditos de queso*, or *almorjábanas* and, for the most part, seemed to think such things were weird. They hadn't had any exposure to other cultures, and I certainly didn't want to be the one to offer it to them.

I remember when I was in second or third grade, and my dad came in to my class on parents' day and gave a brief talk about working for the telephone company. That afternoon at recess, all my friends asked me why my father "talked funny," and they started making fun of his Colombian accent. Up until that day, I didn't even know he or my mother had an accent, but after my friends brought it to my attention I was keenly aware of it and embarrassed by it for years to come.

It wasn't until I was in high school that I started to get over my issues with my parents' accents and their eccentric food. I grew to love things like fried yuca sticks, the plantains my dad used to make a hundred different ways, and this wonderful soup called *sancocho*, which is sort of like chicken soup but made so much more flavorful with cilantro, garlic, and green onion. I always particularly looked forward to a thick custard dish my mother would make at Christmas called *natilla*.

"Do you see the white cornmeal?" Mom asks, sneaking up behind me. "I need cassava starch and farmer cheese as well."

"I'll get the cheese from the refrigerated section. Why don't you look down there for the cornmeal?" I say and direct her toward one of the aisles I was down earlier. From the ingredients she's looking for, it sounds like she plans to make some *arepas*, little pieces of cornmeal dough mixed with cheese that Mom cooks in butter. They're delicious. Sometimes she makes them stuffed with eggs and other times she adds sugar and some sort of Colombian syrup mixture to the dough for a sweeter version. I love them all.

Mom and I peruse the store for several more minutes, and, by the time we make it to the checkout counter, she has a basket full of items: cornmeal, cheese, dried corn, yuca, cassava starch, garlic bouillon cubes, avocados, cilantro, and the list goes on and on.

"Mom? What are you going to do with all this food?"

"I'm low on all of it."

"Okay," I say, not sure why she's buying so much. She cooks Colombian food so rarely these days it seems odd for her to pick up so many items, but, if she wants them, that's fine with me.

As we take the groceries from the cart and put them on the counter, it hits me that most anything Mom would make with all these ingredients requires the use of an oven. And, after today's debacle, I'm not comfortable with Mom cooking without someone else in the house with her. Maybe until we can make other arrangements, she can prepare what she wants while Tamara or I are in the house with her, and, the rest of the time, the stove will be off limits. Maybe I can flip the switch on the circuit breaker panel, and cut the power to the oven while I'm not there. But then Mom can always find her way down to the basement and reset it if she wants. There really are no good solutions.

Mom and the cashier converse for a moment in Spanish while I look on and make sure Mom doesn't mistakenly mix in a hundred dollar bill in the group of twenties she hands him to pay for the groceries. She seems to enjoy being out of the house and actually made her way through the little market much faster than she does when we go to the regular grocery store. She also managed to find most of what she was looking for without much assistance from me. When we go to the Safeway she always takes her time and never really has an exact idea of what she wants to buy, but today she seemed to know exactly what she wanted and methodically went about picking it up.

I'm still not sure what she plans to do with all this food, but I'll be with her tonight and maybe after her tests are done tomorrow, we'll have a discussion about using the oven. Right now, she seems to be in a relatively good mood, and her anxiety level is pretty low. I don't see any reason to get her all riled up. I may as well enjoy her contentment while it lasts.

35

We've barely gotten back from the Latino market, and Mom is already in the kitchen pulling out bowls and pans while I unpack the bags.

"What are you doing?" I ask.

"We're going to do some Colombian cooking, Jennifer."

"*Now?*"

"You never had any interest in making Colombian food. You can't even make a decent *arepa*."

"That's not true," I lie. She's right. As much as I love eating Colombian food, I'm clueless about how to make most of it.

"We're going to make some *arepas*, and *pandebonos*, and *sancocho*. Any decent Colombian would at least know how to make those three things."

"You want to make all of that *tonight*? You've got to be kidding."

"I'm not kidding, Jennifer. I'm going to teach you how to make these things tonight. All my cookbooks are in Spanish, yet another thing you didn't take any interest in learning. If I don't teach you now, how will you ever learn?"

"Why, all of a sudden, is it so important for me to learn how to make Colombian food? Do we really need to do this right this minute?"

Mom looks at me, and I can see her response in her eyes . . . the urgency. She's not uttering a word, but the expression on her face is saying, "Jennifer, I almost set the house on fire today. How much more time do we have?"

"Okay, okay," I say, a lump forming in my throat. "Where do you want to start?"

"Melt a couple tablespoons of butter in the microwave. Do it on low. I want the butter soft, not melted."

While I do as I'm told, Mom opens the bag of cornmeal. "See this, Jennifer. It's precooked. Make sure you buy the precooked cornmeal . . . it makes everything easier." She measures about a third of a cup of the cornmeal and dumps it into a bowl. Then she gets up and turns the faucet on and keeps playing with the knobs while testing the temperature. "Put your hand under here, Jennifer."

I put my hand under the running water.

"Feel that? That's how warm you want the water to be," she says and puts a measuring cup under the faucet after I move my hand out of the way.

"Pour the water in with the cornmeal and then add the butter."

I follow her directions and then sit down in front of the bowl.

"Now, get your hands in there and mix it up. You'll know you're done when it feels like paste."

I continue to follow her lead, and, after we let the dough rest for a few minutes, she shows me how to knead it. Then we add some farmer cheese to the dough, knead it again, and form the dough into balls, which we place between wax paper and flatten to about a quarter of an inch.

By the time she's hovering over me as I'm frying them in butter, I feel like I've regressed to childhood. And, I must say, it feels good to be under her supervision for a change. It's been so long since she's been the mother and I've been the daughter. I'm actually enjoying her cooking instruction. It just feels right. Usually when I come over, it's to take care of a few things and then rush home. But, since I know I'm staying overnight, I have a more relaxed sense of myself. In retrospect, I wonder why I didn't spend the night here more often over the past few years. I could have brought Andrew with me, and we could have stayed the night and had some less-hurried visits with Mom.

When I'm done frying the *arepas*, I can't help myself and sneak a bite of one before it really has a chance to cool. It burns my tongue, but it's been so long since I've had one, and it tastes so good, that I barely notice. Mom has one too, and, from the look on her face after she's done, I know they came out just the way she likes them.

"Now get out the food processor and grate some more cheese," she says to me as I wipe my hands on a paper towel. "We're going to make the *pandebonos*."

"Okay," I say, any urge to protest this cooking-fest having escaped my body. Mom seems more alive than she has in months, directing me around the kitchen, showing me how to make her favorite dishes.

"See, Jennifer. This is yellow cornmeal. We made the arepas with white, but I make my *pandebonos* with yellow. Oh, I used to love them when I was a kid. I'd have them almost every day after school in—" She cuts herself off. "Please tell me you remember where I'm from, Jennifer . . . where your father and I came from . . . where *you* came from."

"Of course, Mother. Bogotá."

"Oh, you say that like such an American. Bogotá," she says, using the Spanish pronunciation (Bogo*tah*).

"Bogotá," I say, making sure my inflection is on the "ta."

"How are you going to teach Andrew about his Colombian heritage if you can't even pronounce the capital of the country?" Mom asks as she measures her ingredients and dumps them in the container on the food processor. She's always been on my case about how Americanized I am and how little I know about the country she came from. Every time she comes over to my house, she complains about how I don't display the tapestries or the religious figurines that our family has sent from Colombia over the years. "You would never know a Colombian lives here," she always says when she comes into my Crate and Barrel meets Ikea meets Target inspired home. And I guess she's right—aside from a few Carlos Vives and Shakira CDs on the bookcase, there really is no evidence of my Colombian heritage in my house. I'm sorry, but I don't like the Colombian tapestries—they don't go with my stuff, and, much as I'm sure the Virgin Mary was a very nice woman and may well be the mother of our savior, do I really need thirty statues of her displayed around my house?

"I'll do the best I can."

"You have to tell him about his grandfather."

"He knows about Dad. I talk about him all the time."

"Does he know we came to this country with almost nothing? We had to sell most of what we had to buy the visas to come here. It was much easier to get visas back then, but it was still very expensive to have the paperwork done. Restrepo was president when we left, inflation was out of control, and the drug trade was just starting to take off. Luis, Alberto's brother, kept sending letters saying, 'Come to America.' 'Come to America.'"

"I know, Mom. You've told me the story a hundred times." I'm enjoying the look on her face as she speaks about her past. "I'll make sure Andrew hears every word. You and Dad are the classic American success story. Andrew will be very proud of you and what you sacrificed and went through to become Americans." Where the hell did that come from?

"Make sure he knows about the real Colombia, Jennifer . . . that it's about so much more than coffee and drug cartels. Remember those awful Juan Valdez coffee commercials?"

"Are you kidding me?" I say with a laugh. "He was the only Colombian anyone in this country had ever heard of. Whenever I said I was Colombian, people would look behind me for my burro and wonder why I wasn't wearing a poncho and a sombrero."

Mom laughs and her laugh makes me chuckle even more. It's been a while since I've seen her laugh and even longer since we've laughed together. I wish she'd . . . *we'd* do it more often.

"And make sure he knows how to spell Colombia. No one in

this country spells it right. People always put a u where the second o should be."

"I know. I know. I'll make sure," I say, knowing that what Mom says is true. I've even seen it spelled wrong on coffee packaging at the grocery store.

"Andrew should go to Bogotá to learn to speak Spanish. You know, Rolos are known for speaking perfect Spanish," she says. I haven't heard her use the word "Rolos," a term to describe people from Bogotá, in forever. "You will take him to Colombia at some point? Andrew. You will take him when it's not as dangerous as it is now?"

"Of course," I say, and I would like to take Andrew to Colombia, so he can see where his roots come from, but, at the same time, I have concerns about traveling there. Our relatives in Colombia are always talking about Americans being kidnapped on the streets in Bogotá and held for ransom, but it's hard to tell if what they're relaying is hearsay or fact.

I've only been there once myself, right after I graduated college. I did appreciate seeing where my parents came from and spending some time in Colombia helped me understand them, but the poverty I witnessed while I was there is still with me. While the relatives we stayed with enjoyed a reasonable standard of living, and, like most Colombians of any means, had maids to take care of all the household duties, there were a significant number of poor people in Bogotá. The street children in particular were extremely unnerving. It wasn't uncommon to see them roaming the streets in tattered clothes and bare feet. Sometimes you would see them sniffing glue to get high and alleviate their hunger pains. Poor Colombians make poor Americans seem positively wealthy. At least the poor in this country generally have some sort of roof over their head that isn't made of cardboard.

Now don't get me wrong. There are a lot of good things about Colombia. There's beautiful architecture, sunny beaches, scenic mountains, and the food is amazing. In many ways, Bogotá is a very cosmopolitan city—while I was there, my cousins took me to some wonderful restaurants and hot night spots. I got to see some amazing churches dating back to the sixteen hundreds and, one day, we went to *Cerro de Monserrate*, one of the mountain peaks to the east of Bogotá, and took in the breathtaking view of the city—it was like nothing I've ever seen before.

The more I think about it, I guess I would like to take Andrew there, but, when I do, he'll have to be much older and better equipped to deal with the cultural differences and poverty he is sure to see. I've heard that the city is getting safer, and, maybe by the time Andrew is a teenager, I'll feel more secure about visiting again.

As we finish up the *pandebonos* and start on the *sancocho*, Mom continues to talk about Colombia and tests my knowledge of her and my father's coming to America. She stresses certain pieces of information that I "must make sure Andrew knows about." I'm taking pleasure in hearing her stories—not so much for the content—more because it's nice to see her relaxed. At least she's not nagging me about Mario or obsessing over something she received in the mail. She's really enjoying all this cooking, and since I got here late this afternoon, her mind has been pretty clear—she hasn't said anything loopy, or mistaken me for her sister . . . or wrapped potatoes in newspaper and put them in the oven.

By the time we're done cooking and have eaten more than our fair share of the food, I'm feeling stuffed and sleepy. I've gotten a refresher course in Colombian history, and the early days of my parents' time in America, and I make mental notes of all of it.

Shortly after we clean the kitchen, Mom goes to bed, and I curl up on the sofa and turn on the television, but I find myself unable to focus. The urgency that Mom felt about teaching me a few of her Colombian recipes, and the need she obviously felt to share her stories with me is making me anxious. Up until very recently, I think Mom was even more in denial about her slipping mental capacity than I've been. But she must be starting to worry about it herself. She never came out and said it, but I could feel it—I could see it in her eyes . . . hear it in the tone of her voice—she wanted to tell me things . . . to teach me things . . . while she still could.

36

I wake up feeling so much more relaxed than I did yesterday. Last night was one of the best nights Mom and I have had in a long time. It was nice to be able to unwind and not worry about having to rush home. And there was something comforting about sleeping in the house in which I grew up.

Mom really seemed like herself last night. I still have major concerns about her staying here on her own, but I'm feeling hopeful that her mind lapses aren't as serious as I was thinking they might be on my way over here last night.

It's just after seven when I get up. I figure I'll go downstairs and make some coffee before I wake up Mom, so she can get ready for her appointments. It's going to be a long day of sitting around the hospital waiting, reassuring Mom, and trying to relax her. I had ultrasounds when I was pregnant with Andrew, and I know there's nothing to them, although I guess an ultrasound on a pregnant woman's belly is somewhat different than one done on your carotid arteries. The part of the day that makes me nervous is the CT scan. I've never had one, but I've seen them on television and the machine looks sort of futuristic and overwhelming. I'm not sure how Mom is going to react to having one done.

When I get downstairs, I find Mom's *Café Bustello* and start the coffee-making process. I sit down at the table while the coffee brews and try to really wake up. It's so quiet. Other than a faint noise coming from the refrigerator, I don't hear a thing, which is such a contrast to mornings with Andrew running around, making a mess with his breakfast and changing the channels on the television. Some mornings the racket drives me crazy, and I find myself longing for some peace and quiet. But there's something about this morning's peace and quiet that saddens me. I think of Mom sitting here morning after morning in this silence. She raised two children in this house—for so many years this house was full of life and in a general state of busyness. There were always things to be done, places to go, arguments to be had. But now there's just silence. I wonder what it's like to have a house full of noise and conflicts and meals and discussions and then to watch it gradually slip away. First Tom left for college, and I followed shortly thereafter. Later, Tom moved away from the area altogether, rarely to be heard from again. But after my brother and I moved out, Mom still had my father, and she still had her independence. And, although they were mostly homebodies, at least they could drive and run their own errands and talk and laugh together. And most importantly, my father was someone my mother could still take care of. She's the quintessential caretaker, and, much as she would complain about it, she loved taking care of her husband and her children. She loved cooking for us, and I don't think she minded keeping the house and running me and my brother all over town for our various activities. When my father died, she didn't have anyone left to nurture. And when her vision started to fail, and she lost her driving privileges, not only was she alone, but she no longer had the freedom to come and go as she pleased. She became dependent on me for her transportation needs, and slowly became dependent on me for so much more.

I quickly drink my coffee, and, unable to stand the silence any longer, I go back upstairs and knock on the open door to Mom's bedroom.

"Rise and shine."

Mom's lying on her side facing me. She opens her eyes and looks at me in a daze.

"Why don't you get in the shower, and maybe I'll heat up some of those *arepas* we made last night."

"New York? Is your trip to New York today?" she asks me.

"New York? No, we've got to be at the hospital by nine." I chalk up her New York comment to confusion from just waking up.

"Jennifer, I went to the hospital already. I had the most beautiful baby boy. We named him Tomás," she says, still lying on her side. Her voice is quiet and distant.

"No, Mom. You're thinking of a long time ago. Tom is nearly forty."

"Forty? No. Go, Jennifer. Get him from the bassinet, so I can feed him."

My heart is now starting to pound. She's been confused and incoherent before, but never anything like this. "Mom. *No.* Tom is a grown man," I say and walk over to the bed. "Let's get up," I add and nudge her on the arm, my hand shaking while I do it.

"I can't," she says, her words still very soft. "My arm's asleep."

I watch her as she tries to lift herself up but can't seem to gather the strength to do it. So, I clasp her hand and try to give her a lift. Her torso rises but her legs stay in position, and she doesn't move them.

"I need you to work with me here, Mom."

"My leg's not working, Jennifer." When she says this, I notice that the right side of her mouth is drooping.

"Mom! Mom!" I say, my voice quivering. "I need you to move your leg for me . . . just bend it."

I stand there as she tries to move her legs. Her right leg comes up easily as she brings her knee to her chest, but her left leg just lays there quivering, and I notice her left hand hanging limp over her belly.

"Your arm, Mom! Can you move your arm?"

She doesn't answer me, and she doesn't move her arm. She just lays there, listless.

"Okay. Okay. Just stay here. You're going to be all right. Just stay here. I'll be right back."

"Bring me the baby, Jennifer," she says behind me as I hurriedly leave the room and rush downstairs to the kitchen phone and dial 911.

"911 Emergency Services. What's your emergency?"

"My mother! I think my mother's had a stroke. She's upstairs in bed and can't move her leg or her arm, and she's talking nonsense."

"Okay, ma'm. What's your name?"

"Jennifer. Jennifer . . ." I can't remember my last name.

"Okay. The phone number on my screen has you at 2066 Melville Drive?"

"Yes. Yes," I can feel the phone shaking against my ear.

"Okay. Jennifer. We'll dispatch the paramedics right away. They should be there in just a few minutes."

37

"I'm so sorry, Jennifer. Don't worry about things here. We'll get by until you can get back. Take your time," Claudette says to me over the phone. I'm standing outside the hospital on my cell phone.

"Thanks. I'll get back as soon as I can. I'm still waiting to hear exactly what's going on with my mother. Once the doctors have things figured out, I'll know more."

"Like I said, take your time," Claudette says to me and we finish the phone call.

I walk back into the hospital, thankful for the break from standing next to Mom's bedside. She's such a shell of the person she was—just looking at her makes me so scared and hopeless.

When the paramedics showed up at the house, I was in a panic, but Mom couldn't have been calmer. She said "hello" to them as if they were neighbors stopping by for tea when they appeared in the bedroom, and then she started telling them about her trip to Canada last year (she's never been to Canada) while they took her vital signs, put her on oxygen, and started an IV. She didn't even seem to notice when they pricked her finger to check her blood sugar. She was limp and relaxed when they hoisted her onto a stretcher and carefully carried her down the steps. She didn't really seem to have any comprehension of what was going on as I stood there, helpless, and let the paramedics do their job.

I followed the ambulance in my car, and when we got to the hospital, they immediately took her back to a room, and one of the doctors started asking her all sorts of questions: "Can you tell me your name?" "Do you know where you are, Mrs. Peredo?" "How many fingers am I holding up?"

They lifted her nightgown and stuck little pads to her chest and the nurse put a needle in her arm and started drawing blood. Everything seemed to be happening so fast and all at once. All these people were descending on my mother, and she seemed detached from the whole spectacle. I didn't want to be in the way, so I stepped back and answered their questions as best I could as the hospital team assessed her. She looked so frail on the stretcher. She was still in her night gown, and, of course, her hair hadn't been combed and was sticking up all over the place. Looking at her, I couldn't believe that this was a woman, who once took care of me, who came to a foreign country and made a life for herself, who raised two children and looked after her husband. . . .

As soon as I'm through the hospital doors after getting off the phone with Claudette, I remember that there is another phone call I need to make; accordingly, I turn around and go back outside. I didn't think to grab a coat when I left the house with the ambulance, and I'm shaking from the chill in the air as I flip open my cell phone and dial.

"Tom. Hi, it's me, Jennifer."

"Hi."

"I'm at the hospital with Mom."

"What? What happened?"

"Well, it looks like she had a stroke, but they're still doing tests. When she woke up this morning, she was disoriented and talking all sorts of nonsense. Then, when she tried to get out of bed, I realized she didn't have any strength on the left side of her body."

When I pause for a response, there's just silence on the other end of the phone.

"Tom?"

"Yes, I'm here. I'm just trying to get my mind around this."

"She's having a CT scan now. They wouldn't let me in the room while she's having it done, so I figured I'd run outside and make a few phone calls."

"She's going to be okay, right?"

"I have no idea, Tom. She was really out of it. She was talking about you as if you'd just been born. She was telling the paramedics about a trip she'd never taken. She barely seemed to notice when they were poking and prodding all over her in the ER."

"Did she know who you were?"

"Yes. She did seem to always know who I was."

"Well, that's something I guess."

"Yeah. I think you should make arrangements to come up, Tom . . . sooner rather than later."

"Yeah, yeah . . . of course. I'll see what I can do."

"Okay, Tom. I'll call you when I have more details."

"Yes. Please do."

When I get off the phone with him, I make a quick call to Mario and leave him a message with the latest happenings and telling him to pick up Andrew from his after school program. Then I head back into the hospital and make my way up to the radiology department, so I can sit and wait for news of what the CT scan showed and have a better idea of what we're in store for.

38

"I didn't like that machine. It looked like something out of *Star Trek*," Mom says to me in a weak voice. She's finished with her scan, and they've moved her to a hospital bed, and she keeps vacillating between saying things that make sense and uttering words and phrases that seem to be coming out of left field.

"That was the CT scan machine. They were taking some pictures of your brain to see if they can find out where the weakness on your side is coming from."

"There was a nice woman down there. She said she was going to take me for a *licuado* after the test, but then she never did." A *licuado* is a Colombian milkshake.

"I'm sure she didn't say that, Mom."

"She most certainly did."

I decide not to argue the point. And when Mom shuts her eyes, I take a seat in the chair next to the bed and look at her. Aside from the noise of her monitor and the soft chatter of the nurses at the station outside her room, it's eerily quiet. Mom appears frail and older than she ever has, and, in some weird way, she looks more like a *creature* than a human being.

I wonder if I've lost her. Her body is still here, but her mind seems to have about checked out. The crazy things she's talking about now make the little mind lapses she's had over the past few months seem like nothing. I'm thankful she at least knows who I am even if she doesn't seem to remember much else. I wonder if she'll know Tom when he gets here . . . if he gets here.

"Hi," I hear coming from behind me and look up and see Dr. Miller standing in the doorway. It's nice to finally see Mom's regular doctor instead of all the strangers that have been attending to her since she came in through the emergency room.

"Dr. Miller. Hi. Thanks for coming."

"Sure. How's she doing?"

"She's asleep. I'm not sure if they sedated her before they did her scan."

"Well, we have the results back. It appears Ana has indeed had a stroke."

My heart drops as I listen to him. I knew it was likely that she had a stroke, but hearing it confirmed is really having an impact on me.

I'm about to ask Dr. Miller for more details when Mom opens her eyes and seems to recognize him.

"Dr. Hubbard. How are you?" she asks.

"I'm Dr. Miller, Ana. You remember me. I've been taking care of you for years."

She looks at him, wheels spinning behind her eyes. "Yes, yes. I remember. You and Jennifer had the most beautiful wedding. Jennifer looked so pretty in her gown coming down the aisle with Alberto at Sacred Heart."

Dr. Miller looks at me and smiles and moves closer to Mom's bed. "Ana. We got the results of your tests. You're going to need to stay here for a day or two, so we can keep an eye on you. You've had a stroke . . . a pretty significant one."

My mother listens while the doctor talks to her, but his words don't seem to register.

"You wore a beautiful tuxedo with tails and the flowers were gorgeous—as they should have been. They cost Alberto and me a fortune. Lilies. They were lilies, weren't they?"

"Yes, they were," I say, answering her question to Dr. Miller. She seems to be remembering my wedding with Mario. Aside from the groom, she has the details right. The ceremony was at

Sacred Heart, Mario did wear a tux with tails, and we did have lilies on display.

Dr. Miller takes Ana's hand in his. "You just get some rest, Ana. I'll be back to check on you soon."

He motions for me to follow him outside the room.

"For the time being, we'll try to keep her comfortable and see how things progress over the next couple of days."

"Then what?"

"If she remains stable, we'll need to start thinking about rehabilitation, probably at the nursing home . . ."

Dr. Miller continues talking, but everything after the word "nursing home" is a blur. I could feel the hairs on the back of my neck stand up as soon as he mentioned it. Isn't that one of all of our greatest fears—that we'll end up in a nursing home? Time and time again, when I would mention assisted living facilities or senior apartment complexes, Mom would get very defensive and talk about how she wasn't going to "any nursing home where old people sit around wetting themselves in their diapers." How am I going to tell her that she may need to go to a nursing home for rehabilitation, and, if she isn't able to regain her strength, that she may need to stay there. Just thinking about it, makes my whole body tense.

"How long do you think she would need to stay at the nursing home?"

"I can't say at this point. It depends how things go over the next couple of days and how much of her strength she is able to recover. When we have more information you can start to think about long-range plans."

When we have more information? I can *start* thinking about long-range plans when we *have more information*? How am I supposed to think of anything else?

39

"Hi, Sweetie!" I say with surprise when I see Andrew in the family room with Desma. "I thought you were with Daddy."

"Mario stopped by with him earlier and told me the news about Ana," Desma says. "He came by to pick up some clothes for Andrew. He had some meeting about his restaurant to go to. He was going to take Andrew with him, but I told him I'd watch him. I'm sorry to hear about Ana. How's she doing?"

"Not well. She's had a stroke. She has *some* feeling on the left side of her body, but it's very weak and her mind is *really* cloudy . . ." I feel myself starting to tear up as I talk about Mom's condition, so I just stop talking. I don't want Andrew to see his mother crying.

"What's a stroke?" Andrew asks.

"It's when a blood vessel in someone's brain bleeds or gets blocked. Sort of like when you skin your knee and it bleeds. Only this kind of bleeding happens inside the body."

"Grandma's bleeding inside her body?"

"Well, yeah, sort of, but you let Mommy worry about Grandma."

"Is she going to be okay? Is she still going to be able to make hot chocolate?"

I smile. "We'll have to wait and see, Andrew. You just pray for her and hope for the best."

Andrew walks back over to the coffee table and picks up a worn-looking Barbie Doll and starts playing with it.

"What is that?" I ask, wondering where the doll came from.

"It's a Barbie Doll. Normally I'm not a fan of dolls that subjugate women, but Andrew picked it up when I took him to the thrift store with me earlier. He seemed to like it, so I bought it for him. It was only fifty cents. I thought it might be good for him. All he has are these gender specific toys you push on him . . . trucks and fire engines."

"His toys are gender specific because he's a specific gender, Desma. I don't need him playing with Barbie Dolls."

"What's wrong with playing with Barbie Dolls?" Andrew asks, looking up at me with innocent eyes.

"Yeah, Jennifer. What's wrong with playing with Barbie Dolls?"

"Nothing, sweetie," I say to Andrew and then glare at Desma, figuring I'll let Andrew play with the doll until he loses interest in it as he does with most of his toys, and then just get rid of it. I know I should be open minded and let him play with dolls if he wants to, but, when your son's father is a homosexual, I guess you do your best to minimize creating an environment that might make your son gay as well. Not that I believe that gay people are made gay by bad parenting or anything like that, but I don't see any reason to tempt fate. Of course my feelings for Andrew would be the same regardless, but life's hard enough without being a member of a minority group that so many people seem to have a problem with. I never really paid much attention to gay issues before my husband came out of the closet—quite frankly, I could have cared less about them. If gay people could get married, what did I care? If gay people couldn't get married, what did I care? Like most people, if it didn't affect me or the people I care about, it wasn't much of a concern. But now my antennas go up when I hear about gay issues, and the kind of hate that's out there is scary to me. I just don't want Andrew to ever be a victim of that hate. It will be hard enough for him to deal with a father who's the victim of so much prejudice.

"Is there anything I can do, Jen? If you need me to watch Andrew while you deal with this, I'm available anytime."

Of course you are. You don't have a job. "Thanks, Desma. I'm sure Mario will help out as well."

"You know. It's times like these that I wish that I prayed, Jennifer," Desma says to me. "Then at least I could feel like I'm doing *something*. But I'm a Secular Humanist, and I really don't believe in prayer."

"I think Mom's beyond prayer at this point. What she needs is a miracle."

"How long do you think she'll be in the hospital?"

"They don't know. It depends on how things go. If she remains stable, probably only a couple of more days."

"Then what?"

"That's the million dollar question, Desma. They'll send her to the rehabilitation unit at the nursing home, and see if she makes any progress getting her strength back . . . and her mental faculties back. But she was pretty far gone today. Nothing she said made any sense. I'd say there's about a one percent chance that she will be able to go back to her house," I pause for a moment and stand up. "My God, Desma, what am I going to do?"

As I hear my own words, I see Andrew's eyes meet mine with a look of angst. "What are you going to do about what?" he asks, clearly feeling my agitation.

"Oh nothing, sweetie," I say, trying to relax my demeanor. "We're just going to have to make some new arrangements when Grandma gets out of the hospital."

My answer seems to suffice, and Andrew turns his attention back on the doll.

"I wonder if we can turn the half-bath on this level into a full bath. Maybe I can turn the dining room into a bedroom and Mom can stay here. She'll never be able to make it up to the second floor or down to the basement."

"Hmm . . . that's an idea," Desma says. "If you decide to remodel that bath, you should really look into a composting toilet."

"Huh?"

"Composting toilets are great. My friend Varahi, the yoga teacher, has one."

"You've got to be kidding?"

"No. I'm serious. They're very clean, they don't smell, and they turn waste into composting matter . . . you can even use it in your garden."

"My garden? Since when do I have a garden?"

"You'll have to get one once you have all that compost to use," Desma says with a laugh.

I laugh too.

"You'll be doing something for the environment and saving water. And in some areas you can get rebates from the sewer authority."

I realize that Desma really is serious about this and it makes me laugh harder, the kind of laughing that people do when they are so tired that almost anything seems funny.

"What's so funny?"

"I don't know. I'm just picturing the looks on the faces of the members of the homeowner's association if they were to hear of me putting in a composting toilet."

"They'd probably be all backwards and forbid you from installing it. People are so close-minded."

"Well, I don't think I'm going to be installing a crunchy toilet in my house. Sorry," I say with a groan. "Maybe I can install one of those chair lifts that take people up the steps. Lord, I don't know."

I decide to stop thinking about home modifications for awhile and drop back down onto the sofa. I sit there for a moment with my eyes shut, and, when I open them, I see a small bag of potato chips sitting on the coffee table. It occurs to me that I haven't had a thing to eat in more than twenty-four hours. I grabbed a cup of coffee at the hospital while Mom was back having her CT scan, but that's all I've had all day.

"Have you eaten anything?" Desma asks, as if she read my mind.

"Yeah, I grabbed something at the hospital cafeteria," I lie. If I tell her I haven't eaten anything, she'll try to force food on me, and I just don't have an appetite. In fact, if I eat anything, I'm certain I'll throw it up.

I'm about to suggest that Andrew get ready for bed when I hear a quick knock at the front of the house. Before I have a chance to get up, I hear the door open.

"Hello," Claire says from the foyer. "It's me."

"Hey," I call back. "Come on in." I'm too tired to get up from the sofa to greet her.

"Desma told me about your Mom," she says once she's in the family room. "I'm so sorry. Is there anything I can do?"

"No. Thanks. But I do appreciate the offer," I say and think for a moment. "Actually, you know what you can do for me?"

"What?"

"You can take my mind off all this. Tell me about Julio and his big . . ." I cut myself off, realizing that Andrew is still in the room.

"Andrew. It's past your bedtime. Why don't you head upstairs and change into your pajamas, and I'll be up in a few minutes."

"Come on, big guy," Desma says and gets up from her chair and looks at me. "I'll go up with him. You stay here and chat."

"A Barbie Doll!" Claire shrieks, seeing the doll in Andrew's hand. "Can I see?"

Andrew hands it to her, and Claire starts stroking her hair. "Oh. I miss Barbie. How I used to love to play with her when I was a little girl."

"And then you grew up just like her," Desma says with an evil grin. "Only with looser morals."

Claire laughs. "Look, Andrew," she says, lifting up the doll's skirt. "Barbie's a slut. She doesn't have any panties on."

"Claire!" I say as Andrew looks at her with a bewildered expression on his face.

"If that ain't the pot call'n the kettle black," Desma says and swipes the doll from Claire's hand. "Come on," she says to Andrew. "Let's get you to bed."

"Sorry about the slut comment. I'm not used to being around kids. I have to learn to censor myself. I was just trying to lighten the mood," Claire says to me while Desma ushers Andrew out of the room

I smile. "I know you mean well, Claire," I say. "So what's up with you? How are things?"

"Not good."

"Really?"

"No. Julio gave me the clap."

"The what?"

"The clap. Gonorrhea."

"Oh my God! You're kidding?"

"No. I was having some . . . well, you know . . . issues. So I went to the gyno, and he ran some tests."

"Well, at least it's curable."

"Yeah, and at least I didn't have to have that painful shot. He gave me a prescription, but now I have another problem."

I look at her waiting to hear what it is.

"Ted. I've been sleeping with Ted as well . . . I mean, after all, he is my husband," Claire says as if it's not obvious. "I'm afraid I've passed it to him. He hasn't complained of any symptoms, but sometimes people don't have symptoms, and if he doesn't get treated, he'll just pass it back to me."

"Oh, what a tangled web we weave."

"I know."

"You're going to have to tell him, Claire."

"I know. Fuck! I should have been more careful."

"Ah . . . *yeah*," I say, wanting to add that maybe she shouldn't have been messing around with Julio at all, but I restrain myself. "I can't believe you weren't using condoms, Claire. Come on, you know better than that."

"We *tried* to use condoms, but you saw that picture—we couldn't get them on that mammoth thing."

"Well, at least it's nice to hear about someone else's problems. It takes my mind off Mom."

"Glad I could help. My gonorrhea is your gonorrhea."

I chuckle.

"Well, I need to get home and figure out how I'm going to break the news to Ted. I just wanted to stop by and see how you're doing. And really, if I can help in any way, please ask . . . you know, as long as it doesn't involve any manual labor . . . or work outside when it's really cold . . . or hot . . . or raining . . ."

"Thanks, Claire," I say, wishing there was something she could do . . . wishing there was something anyone could do.

40

"I can't believe they're discharging her already," I say to Vicky, the hospital social worker assigned to arrange for Mom's transfer to the nursing home. We're standing outside Mom's room at Mary Washington Hospital. "She hasn't even been here for three full days."

"That's true, Ms. Costas," Vicky says with an empathetic look in her eyes. "But the doctors have done all they can for her here. She's been stable for two days, and now they think it's best to get her into the rehab center at the nursing home, and see how much of her strength she can regain."

"I know."

I already had this conversation with Dr. Miller about an hour ago, but a part of me just wants to delay my mother's transfer to the nursing home as long as possible. Or maybe I'm just trying to delay having to tell her about it, something I can't do much longer. Vicky has arranged for an ambulance to transport Mom to the nursing home in less than two hours. I have no choice but to tell her now.

"Do you want me to hang around while you break the news?"

"No thanks."

"Okay. I'll check back with you in a couple of hours."

I watch Vicky walk away and listen to her heels click on the tile floor. It's not until she turns the corner and is out of sight that I muster my strength and head into the room.

"How's the patient?" I ask, trying to make my voice sound chipper.

"I'm ready to go home. You get on the phone right now, Jennifer Peredo, and you call your father and tell him to come pick me up."

"Mom, Dad's not with us any longer, you know that. He died over two years ago." I'm trying to vocalize my words as gently as possible even though this is probably upwards of the tenth time that I've had to remind her that Dad is dead.

She looks at me curiously, like she's done every other time I've reminded her of my father's passing, and doesn't seem to process my words.

"Well then, you take me home. It's too noisy here, and hospitals are such filthy places."

Most of what she's been saying since she woke up three days ago hasn't made a lot of sense, but she's had enough wits about her to know she doesn't like it here, and that she wants to go home.

"Actually, I have good news, Mom," I say, the same tone in my voice that I used when I tried to convince Andrew that watching cookies bake in the oven was going to be fun.

"You do get to leave today."

"Oh, thank God. You know how Alberto gets when I'm behind on my housework."

"They're not going to send you home just yet though."

Mom looks at me distrustfully. "Oh?"

"We're getting you some rehabilitation to help you regain the full use of your arm and your leg."

"My arm and my leg are fine."

"Oh yeah? Lift your arm for me and make a fist."

Mom lifts her right arm.

"Your *left* arm."

As soon as Mom tries to raise her left arm, I immediately regret my directive. It's heartbreaking to watch her struggle to lift her arm just inches off the bed and try, but fail, to do anything more than slightly bend her fingers.

"See. You need some rehab, Mom. And once you get your strength back, we can see about you going home," I say, hoping God doesn't strike me dead for telling such a lie. Maybe there is some chance that Mom will get some strength back in her left side, and maybe she won't have to stay in the nursing home, but Paris Hilton stands a better chance of getting into a Mensa meeting than Mom has of going back to her home.

"Where is this rehab center?"

"It's not far from here. It's over on Dixie Drive."

"What's it called?"

"I don't remember," I lie. Even with her current mental challenges, she's bound to recognize the name as the name of the nursing home. I'm hoping that we can get her transferred there and into her room before she even realizes where she is. After all, she will be on the rehab unit, not in one of the resident wings. And maybe she will get some of her strength back, and maybe her mind will start to clear, and we will be able to make other arrangements for her, I think, trying to convince myself that her stay in the rehab unit of the nursing home isn't just a brief stopover to becoming a full-time resident there.

"You're sending me to a rehab center, and you don't even know what it's called?"

"I know what it's called. I just can't remember the name right now. Dr. Miller highly recommended it."

"Why can't I do my rehab at home, so I can be with Alberto and Tomás?"

I don't feel like reminding her yet again that Alberto is dead and that Tom is in Florida with his wife and two children, so I just say, "Because Dr. Miller feels this is your best chance for getting better."

Mom doesn't say anything. Maybe she's run out of arguments, or maybe she's just tired. I look at her and see that she's closed her eyes. Ever since she was admitted, she falls asleep at the drop of a hat. I'll be speaking with her sometimes, and she'll close her eyes and go to sleep while I'm talking to her.

I sit down in the chair next to the bed. I picked up a few magazines in the gift shop earlier, but I've found it impossible to concentrate on any of them, so I just alternate between looking out the window and looking at Mom. I can't help but fixate on how much weight she's lost over the past year. She used to be a stout woman, and, like most of us, spent much of her adult life trying to lose weight. But at her last weigh-in at the doctor's office, she was a mere one hundred and seven pounds, about fifty pounds lighter than she was two years ago. Her weight loss and her slumping posture make her look so small, weak, and vulnerable.

It shouldn't be this way. People shouldn't work hard their whole lives, raise families, and pay their taxes only to end up incapacitated in a hospital bed before being carted off to a nursing home to be kept out of the way until they die. Why can't we be healthy our whole lives and then just suddenly drop dead at eighty-five? That's the way it should be, but as I watch Mom drift into a deep sleep, I realize *how it should be* doesn't matter. This is reality, and this is what I have to deal with.

41

This place hasn't changed much in twenty years, I think to myself on my way down the hall at Glenview Nursing and Rehabilitation Center. Before Mom was admitted, I hadn't been here since I was a kid twenty some years ago. My grade school would send a group of students once a week to this same nursing home to sing during one of their daily masses. We'd arrive in groups of ten or so, half-heartedly sing "The King of Glory" or "On Eagles Wings" during the service, and then spend about a half hour visiting with the residents before we went back to school. Even then, I found the place depressing. I remember standing in the corner during the church services and looking around at all the frail attendees, most of them in wheelchairs. I can still picture the woman who sat through the entire service chewing on her tongue and another woman who always had a piece of toilet paper on her head and called it her hat.

There was one patient in particular we all used to rush to visit after the service. Her name was Vivien and, mentally, she had pretty much checked out, but she loved to sing and was always so cheerful. We'd stop by her room, and she'd smile and sing songs for us. Then one day we stopped by her room, and she was confined to the bed with oxygen tubes in her nose and did little more than open her eyes when we came into the room. The next time we came back, her bed was empty. My friend Meagan and I asked one of the nurses where she was, and I remember her response as if it were yesterday: "I'm sorry, girls. She died a few days ago." And that was it. She gave us no further explanation or counsel. She just walked away. I'm sure death was an everyday occurrence to her, but I had never had any real experience with it. My parents were alive and well, and although I knew one of my grandfathers had passed away in Colombia when I was a baby, that knowledge had never really affected me—I had never known him and had always heard him spoken of in the past tense. But that day at the nursing home brought death into my thoughts. I think it was the first time I realized that I was eventually going to die and, sometime, my parents were going to die. I went back to school that day distracted and anxious, trying to put thoughts of death out of my mind. And, now, here I am some twenty years later trying to do the same thing.

I continue to walk down the corridor toward Mom's room, passing elderly patients, some of them sitting idly in their wheelchairs, some walking along slowly with walkers, another resting on a sofa with a doll baby in her lap. I smile briefly at the ones who make eye contact with me but keep moving. When I reach Mom's room, it's empty. The bed is made, and there's no trace of her in the room.

Oh my God! She's dead! Just like Vivien . . . she's dead! I think to myself before I hear my name being called.

"Jennifer!" Mom calls from behind. I turn around and see her in a wheelchair. One of the aides is behind her, pushing her toward me.

"Hi Mom," I say, relieved to see her and glad that she still knows my name. Who would have thought the day would come when I'd be thankful for every day that my mother remembers who I am.

"This place is a hellhole."

"Why don't we go back to your room, Mom," I say, ignoring her comment as I take the chair over from the aide. It isn't exactly the Four Seasons, but as far as nursing homes go, it's not *that* horrible of a place. It's always had a good reputation, and it's clean, and the staff seems to be knowledgeable and helpful. But a place with plain tile floors, vinyl furniture, and handrails along the wall can only be so alluring.

"Jennifer, tell your father to come and get me. They won't leave me alone here. There's always someone poking at me, and there's so much noise."

"Mom, Dad's no longer living."

She looks at me with curious eyes but doesn't say anything.

"We've got to figure some things out and help you recover from your stroke, and then we can see about you leaving this place."

"I have a baby to take care of, Jennifer. I keep asking them to bring him to me, and they won't. I don't know what they're doing to him. Why are they keeping him from me?"

"What baby are you talking about?"

"Tomás. He was just born a few days ago, and the nurses won't bring him to see me."

"Mom, Tom is thirty-eight years old. He's in Florida with his wife and your two grandchildren. How many times do I have to tell you that?"

Again, she looks at me as if what I'm telling her is not registering. Then she reaches down with her good arm and starts trying to take off her shoes, a pair of white tennis shoes we bought together a few months ago.

"Leave your shoes on, Mom."

"They're too tight."

When I look more closely, I can see that they are, indeed, tight. We bought them before the swelling in her legs and feet had gotten so bad. I bend down and take the shoes off to look at the size.

"I'll pick up a new pair for you as soon as I can and bring them when I come back."

"I'd like for you to bring me my black heels."

"Your black heels?"

"Yes, there's a big dance tomorrow night. Alberto and I are going. Yes, I'll need my black heels."

I'm about to remind her, once again, of Dad's death, but instead I just say. "Okay. I'll remember the heels."

She doesn't say anything for a moment. Then she looks at me. "Mario? How's Mario? You two had the most beautiful wedding."

"Mario's fine, Mom."

"You're keeping him happy, aren't you?"

"Yes," I say. "But let's talk about you. How are you, Mom? You seem to be getting stronger."

"I'm fed up with this place, is what I am. I wish they'd stop poking at me and bring me my baby. A baby should be with his mother, Jennifer."

I'm not sure what to say next. I was just about to lie and say that they (whoever "they" are) would be bringing her baby to her soon. I've already indulged her request for her black heels and let her believe that Mario and I are still married and that I'm keeping him "happy." Why not just ease her anxiety and tell her that her baby will be with her soon? But something inside me doesn't let me do it.

"Mom, there is no baby. There's just me and Tom, and Tom is a grown man." A worthless grown man that can't even get up here to see his mother after she's had a stroke, but a grown man none the less.

"Tomás?" she asks, as if she finally understands what I'm saying to her. "Is he coming to visit me?"

"I don't know, Mom. I think so, at some point. But I don't know when."

"He's a good boy, Tomás. He takes good care of me."

He takes good care of her!? He hasn't seen her in more than two years!

"Are you comfortable in the chair? Do you want me to help you into bed?" I ask after I push her into her room.

"No. Why is everyone always trying to get me to lie in the bed? I just had a baby. It's a perfectly natural process."

"Okay, stay in the chair then," I say, and we continue to banter for several more minutes. I stay with her while she eats her dinner, a grilled chicken breast with a side of pasta and a small bowl of sugar-free Jell-O. Most of what she says doesn't make much sense, but occasionally she seems to have a slight grasp on reality. When she's done eating, she pushes away the little table and manages to slightly turn the wheelchair, using her good arm. She picks up the shoes I took off her feet earlier and puts them in her lap and grabs an afghan that I brought from her house off the bed and lays it in her lap as well.

"Jennifer, take that vase off the table, would you. It's too pretty to leave here."

I grab the empty vase off the nightstand and hold it in my hand. I brought it filled with flowers on Mom's first day here, but one of the nurses asked me to take the flowers home because they'd been having a problem with one of the residents eating the blooms off them.

"Okay. I'm ready to go," she says, and struggles to turn her wheelchair around to face the door.

"Go where?"

"Home."

"Mom, I told you, you need to stay here until you're well enough to go home. I'll be back to visit you tomorrow." I bend over and kiss her on the cheek, and she looks the same way Andrew did when it hit him that I wasn't going to be staying with him all day on his first day of kindergarten.

"Don't you leave me here, Jennifer Peredo!"

"Sweetie, I . . ."

"Sweetie, nothing! I'm not staying here."

"Okay, okay," I say, just trying to buy some time until I can get her mind on something else. "I'll stick around a bit longer, and then we'll see about you going home. Why don't I help you out of the chair, and you can lie down and take a nap until we figure things out."

"You'll leave me here as soon as I fall asleep."

Yes, that was the plan, I think to myself. And I can't bring myself to lie and say that I won't, so I grab the handles on her wheelchair, turn her around, and push her away from the doorway. "I have to go home soon, Mom. But I promise I'll be back tomorrow."

"I'm not staying here," she says like a defiant child.

"I have to go. Really," I say and try to hug her, but she pushes me away with her good arm.

"Leave me here to rot!" she calls behind me as I try to walk out the door, but I just can't do it. I turn around, and she looks so scared, so afraid of being abandoned. How can I leave her now?

I sit down on the bed, and she stares at me with pleading eyes. There's no way I can take her home. I wouldn't even be able to get her up the steps to the front door, and I'm not strong enough to help her to the bathroom. Maybe . . . maybe eventually I can make some modifications to the house and hire an aide or something, but right now, I have no choice but to leave her here.

I put my head down, so my eyes no longer meet hers and try to think of a way for me to leave without her screaming behind me. I can't bear the thought of hearing her plead for me not to leave her here as I walk away . . . I simply can not bear it. So, I do something—something I'm sure I'll feel guilty about for the rest of my life.

I lift my head and face her. "Mom, you don't really want to leave do you?" I ask, guilt radiating through my body on account of what I'm about to say. "You don't want to leave the hospital without the baby, do you?"

She looks at me as if what I'm saying is resonating with her.

"The baby needs to stay for a few more days for the doctors to make sure he's healthy."

"Well, no . . . I can't leave the baby."

"Then it's settled," I say, fighting tears from coming to my eyes. *I will not cry!* I think to myself. I will not cry while Mom can still see me. "You'll stay for a few more days. And I'll be back to check in on you tomorrow."

She doesn't respond to my last statement, but she doesn't protest either when I lean in to hug her and say good-bye. She remains silent as I walk out of the room, and as soon as I turn the corner, I pick up the already rapid pace of my gait, desperate to get out of here before my mother changes her mind and comes after me. If I hear her calling behind me, I'll just die. I'll die right here in the nursing home—a building full of people in their eighties and nineties and it will be a thirty-six-year-old woman who died within these walls today. I walk faster and faster, looking straight ahead, feeling a rush of shame and grief building up in me with lightning speed.

"What else could I have done?" I say when I finally make it to the car and take a seat inside. "How else would I have been able to leave?" I ask myself, or God, or whatever higher power I feel is judging me very harshly at this moment. I try to resolve to put the evening out of my head, but I know I will never forget the look in Mom's eyes when I lied to her. She needs so badly to trust someone right now, and I broke that trust in a terrible way. I know there's little chance that she'll remember anything I said tonight when I go to see her tomorrow, but I'll remember—I'll always remember.

42

"Tom, I really think you should get up here as soon as possible. Mom really isn't doing well," I say into my cell phone. I'm sitting in my car in the nursing home parking lot. I was just about to go in when Tom called. I'm trying not to lose patience with him, but I don't understand why he isn't making more of an effort to come to see his mother. And on top of my annoyance with him, I seem to be coming down with a cold. I've got a sore throat and my nose has been running all day, which makes me even less in the mood to listen to Tom's excuses.

"I know, Jen. It's just that I've got this project at work that I need to finish up. I'll try to get it wrapped up in a couple of days, and then I'll book a flight."

"It's your call, Tom. But I'd really make it sooner rather than later." I'm trying to get it through his fat head that Mom may not have that much longer, and he should get his ass up here and see her while he still has a chance, but I guess stubbornness runs in the Peredo family. Mom, Tom, me—all three of us are as stubborn as can be.

"Okay. I'll call and check in with you tomorrow."

"All right. I'll talk to you later."

Tom and I say our good-byes, and I grudgingly get out of the car and walk into the nursing home. I'm not sure I'll ever get used to this place, I think to myself as I come through the doors. Mom's been here for just over a week. She seems to be adjusting better, and only occasionally makes a scene when I leave. But, despite her improving attitude, she seems to be deteriorating overall. I've driven out here every day since she was admitted, and, about half the time, she has been sound asleep when I arrived. I hated to wake her on these visits, but I wanted her to know that I was here, and that I came back like I had promised.

Sometimes she stays in bed, and we chat in between her falling asleep and waking up again. She always knows me, but most of what she says is based in fantasy. I talked with Dr. Miller the other day, and he said her kidney function has gotten worse since the stroke, which may explain her chronic fatigue. He said that if things continue to deteriorate, we'll need to talk about dialysis, something I don't even want to think about. Mom's in no position to make a choice about going on dialysis by herself, and I have no idea what the right decision would be. Is it even humane to start a seventy-five-year-old woman who's had a stroke and has lost much of her cognitive abilities on a brutal treatment that will only extend her life in a nursing home? I just pray that her kidneys will hold out, and I won't have to make that decision.

When I reach her room, Mom's asleep, so I quietly step next to her bed and sit in the chair. Rather than rouse her from sleep, I usually wait until she opens her eyes and sees me sitting here, which doesn't take long today.

"Jennifer," she says after she awakes.

"Hi, Mom. How was your day?" I ask as if she just got home from a long day at the office.

"Elvis. Elvis was here."

I smile. "I don't think Elvis was here, Mom."

"Actually, he was," Connie, one of the aides I've gotten friendly with says, overhearing us as she comes into the room to check on Mom. "Well, not Elvis exactly, but an Elvis impersonator did do a little performance in the community room today. The residents love him."

Connie has been a Godsend since Mom was admitted. On her third day here, Mom was getting all riled up when she sensed I was getting ready to leave. Connie noticed her demanding that I take her home with me, stepped into the room, and talked so sweetly to Mom. She suggested that she and Mom take a walk down to the dining room and get a snack before bed, which was enough to get Mom's mind off me leaving and calm her nerves. Ever since then, Connie senses when I'm about to leave and comes over and helps me make a drama-free exit.

"Really?" I say to Connie and then turn back to Mom. "So you did see Elvis? Did you enjoy his performance?" I hear myself talking, and I hate the fact that I'm speaking to my mother in the same tone I used with Andrew when he got back from the petting zoo.

"He didn't do 'Hound Dog' . . . only 'Love Me Tender.' Alberto wanted him to do 'Hound Dog,' but he said he didn't have time. Alberto left after the show. Is he here now?"

"No. He's not here now, Mom."

She closes her eyes again.

"That Alberto must have been some husband." Connie says. "She talks about him all the time."

"Yeah. He was a good man," I respond. "How's she been today?"

"She's been tired, but she did get out of her room to play bingo today, and, of course, for the Elvis show. She had a great time at both events."

"Bingo?"

"Yeah and tomorrow we have a magician coming in," Connie says and pulls up a chair next to me. "You see, Ms. Costas. It's not such a bad place."

"I never said . . ."

"Of course, you didn't. No one actually comes out and says it, but we can see it in their eyes. But, really, Mrs. Peredo does fine during the day. She's made a couple of friends on the unit and ate lunch in the dining room this afternoon instead of in her room. She kept talking about aribas or something?"

I laugh. "*Arepas*. They're a Colombian corn cake sort of thing. I'll have to make some and bring them for her."

"You'd be surprised, Ms. Costas—"

"Jennifer, please."

"You'd be surprised, Jennifer. Living here's an adjustment, and it's never going to be her home, but many of our residents like it here. We have residents who are able to take care of themselves and could go home, but they don't want to. We can't get rid of them."

"You're kidding?"

"No. They'd be lonely at home. They wouldn't have their meals taken care of. There'd be no bingo, no Elvis impersonators, no on-site beauty salon, no kids coming in from the local schools to visit . . . We keep them busy. They feel safe here."

I sit there for a moment and think about what Connie has said.

"They just want to be treated like human beings. They want to be touched and talked to and treated with respect. They usually find a staff member or two who they latch on to and like to have him or her take care of them. I'm more than happy to be that person for your mother. I've been here for seven years, and I'm quite certain I'm not going anywhere before she does."

"You're very sweet."

"Just doing my job—and I love my job," Connie says, and gets up to leave the room. "I'm here for two more hours. I'll check in on her again before I leave."

"Thank you."

The room is so quiet. It's a double, but no one's been assigned to the other bed, so Mom has had it to herself since she was admitted. She's done some work with the physical therapists, but Dr. Miller has all but said he doesn't expect her to make any real progress, and she'll need to move from the rehab unit to a permanent room soon, which creates a whole new conundrum: Do I let her stay here, a place she is finally starting to adjust to? Or do I move her to a facility closer to my house? I've been coming every day, but I can't keep that up much longer. It's been taking me about an hour and a half to get here and about an hour to get home. I leave work at five, get here about six-thirty, stay about an hour, and it's usually almost nine by the time I get home. By then, Andrew's in bed, and I'm too tired to do anything but crawl under the covers and go to sleep . . . just to get up the next day and do it all over again. Andrew's always either with Desma or Mario, and I feel like I never see him. The house is a mess, I'm late on some bills because I just haven't had the time to sit down and pay them, I don't remember the last time I did laundry . . . I'm not even sure I have clean clothes to wear to work tomorrow.

When I talked with Dr. Miller, he seemed to imply that Mom didn't have much time left. Between her failing heart and her weak kidneys, she might be living on borrowed time. But who can say for sure? She could be with us for a few more days or a few more years. You just never know, and right now, I seem to only be able to think about things in practical terms. If she really doesn't have much time left then it makes sense to let her stay here, but, if not, I should move her to a facility in Alexandria or Arlington. If only I had a crystal ball to predict the future. Although, the way things have been going lately, I may be better off not knowing what's in store for me next.

43

"No, Claire. I'm not getting involved. You made this mess, now you clean it up," I say to her over the phone in my office, happy to be at work, despite the fact that my cold has advanced to full blown bronchitis. Even though my nose and chest are completely congested, and I can't seem to stop coughing, it feels good to be in a suit around other adults who are coherent and not wearing diapers. I know there's a whole nightmare outside these walls that needs my attention, but I'm glad to be at the office and forced to focus on mundane tasks.

"Oh, come on. The doctor said you only need one dose of Cipro to get rid of gonorrhea. I've finagled another prescription, and now I just need to get Ted to take it. All I'm asking is that you crush it up, mix it with some peanut butter, and put it on a sandwich for him."

"Can't you just do that yourself?"

"I can, but I'm afraid he'll notice that it tastes funny and not eat it. But, if you make it for him, he won't want to insult you . . . he doesn't know you well enough for that. If he says anything, I'll say that you're on some kind of health kick and have been putting protein powder in everything."

"Claire, I have to go. I have a meeting." I say in between coughing spells.

"So, you'll do it?"

"No, Claire. This doesn't even sound legal. Forcing a prescription drug on someone? Are you mad?" I don't mean to be short with Claire, but this bronchitis is really kicking my ass, and I'm just not in the mood to deal with her problems.

"Fine," she says in a huff. "I'll just have to think of something else."

I'm about to suggest the truth but decide not to bother. "I've really got to go, Claire."

When I hang up the phone, I catch up on a few e-mails that have piled up since I've been out dealing with Mom. Then I get up from my chair and head to the conference room where I find Claudette and Myra. I take a seat next to them, and we wait for the representatives from a company called Koclar Systems, one of two vendors we've been meeting with about developing a new human resources and accounting system. They're supposed to give us a final demo of their system's capabilities, and then we'll have to make a decision as to which vendor we want to select to develop the final product.

"It's good to have you back, Jen," Myra says to me. "The workload has been crazy around here without you."

"Thanks. It's kind of nice to be back and get my mind off things."

"I'm glad you were able to make it today. You've been spearheading this project. I'm not sure Myra and I would know enough to make an informed decision."

"I'm sure you would have managed just fine without me," I lie. They really do need me here. That's the only reason I came in today. I really should be home in bed, but Claudette hasn't been terribly involved with this project, and she wasn't even here when we met with Koclar's competitors last month. And Myra has had her usual hands-off approach to the project, so she wouldn't have been of much help either.

"Hi," we hear coming from the doorway. "They're here," Benita says and two men follow behind her into the room. Claudette, Myra, and I stand to greet them. One of the gentlemen seems to be well into his fifties, and the other is a nice looking younger man . . . probably about thirty-three or so—his eyes look at me with recognition, and, for some reason, it takes a moment for me to realize who he is.

"Jennifer," he says.

"Ben. Hi," I say, a surprised smile coming over my face.

"You two know each other?" Myra asks.

"Yes. We used to work together at Saunders and Kraff, an accounting firm over on L Street," I say, collecting myself. "Ben, this is Claudette Rhoades and Myra Gibbs."

"It's very nice to meet you," Ben says and shakes their hands and then introduces his associate.

"Please have a seat," Claudette says, and we all sit down at the long table.

"So you're not with Saunders and Kraff anymore I take it?" I ask when Ben sits down next to me, and Claudette and Myra make small talk with the other gentleman.

"No. I resigned a month ago to take this job with Koclar. I'm doing accounting software development now. We have a meeting with your accounting and payroll departments after this."

"Oh . . . well, good. It's great to see you," I say, and I mean it. It is great to see his face, and, on some odd level, his presence in the room is doing something to me. I've got this school girl knot in my stomach. Looking at him is only reminding me of how stupid I was to blow him off the way I did.

"Yeah. I was hoping I'd hear from you, but . . ."

"I'm sorry," I say. "I really meant to get in touch, but life has been beyond crazy and . . ." I let my voice trail off as I realize that the others have wrapped up their conversation.

"Shall we get started?" Claudette asks.

"Sure," the other gentleman, who Ben introduced to us as Alan, says and opens his laptop and hooks it up to the projector in the room. While he's fumbling to get things set up, Ben quietly smiles at me, and I swear if I were ice cream, I'd melt right here and now.

"With Koclar, it really is one-stop shopping. We cover it all. Our system tracks employee demographic data, benefits, payroll, EEO and affirmative action compliance, I-9 documentation . . .

you name it," Alan says as he clicks through the presentation and shows us some features of the system. While he's talking, I keep noticing Ben sneaking looks at me, and I'm not sure what to do. At the moment, I'm pretending that I don't notice, but I'm also biting my lip to keep from smiling. It's very strange. I immediately felt something as soon as he walked in the room—the same sort of feeling I used to get when Mario and I first started dating, that mixture of attraction and angst and anticipation.

"That's great," I say when Alan pauses to see if we have any questions. "I'm sure Claudette and Myra would like to see the online performance appraisal component."

"Yes," Claudette says. "I'd also really like to hear about how employees can log into the system and make their benefit changes, and how their changes synchronize with the codes for deductions and contributions."

"Of course," Alan says and opens another file on his laptop. He continues with the presentation, and we sit there for another hour while he shows us various features and answers our questions. When they finally wrap up the session, Claudette and Myra walk out with Alan, and Ben lingers behind with me.

"So things are busy?"

"Yeah. *Really*, they are," I say, as if he doesn't believe me. "I did enjoy catching up with you, Ben." I want to add that I'd like to see him again, but, before I can get the words out of my mouth, everything that's going on with Mom comes rushing back to me. Between my efforts to pay attention to the presentation, and my shock from seeing Ben again, I had a brief break from the constant barrage of thoughts about Mom being in the nursing home, but now I feel the stress pouring back into my body. "It would be nice to see you again, but things with my mother have gotten really bad, and between her and my son, and this place, I can barely keep my head on straight."

"I'm sorry to hear that."

"Yeah. I swear, Ben," I say in a tone that's probably not appropriate for the office, "I'm really not blowing you off. My mother had a stroke almost three weeks ago, and she's in the nursing home, and I have to drive out to Fredericksburg every day, and I've got this bronchitis thing going on . . . and I'm not sure what I'm going to do when her time in the rehab unit is up." I can feel my voice getting shaky, which is usually a prelude to tears forming in my eyes, so I stop talking before I start sobbing like a baby right here in the conference room.

"Wow. That is a lot to handle," Ben says, I can hear the concern in his voice. "Do you need a hug?" he asks with a soft comforting smile.

I smile meekly back at him and let out a breath. Then I wrap my arms around him and he gives me a squeeze, and my whole body goes limp. I want to stay here in his arms . . . I want to let myself cry into his shoulder. I want someone to take care of *me*. But instead, I keep the hug brief and manage to maintain some semblance of composure.

"Thanks, Ben. You're very sweet," I say as we pull apart.

"You have my number, Jennifer. Please call me if you need a shoulder to lean on." He touches my arm and turns to leave. "You know what?" he says, swinging back around. "Nix that. *I'll* call *you* to see if you need anything."

"That's really not necessary."

"Yeah. I know," he says and passes Benita on his way out the door.

"Hey," I say to Benita.

"Hi. Your sister's on the phone again."

"I told you, Benita. I don't have a—" I cut myself off. "It's not Sister Greta is it?"

"Yeah . . . that's it."

"Oh dear God! What does she want?" I say more to myself than to Benita as I hurry back to my office to take the call.

44

Why do I feel like *I'm* in trouble? I think to myself as, once again, I step into the administrative office at St. Paul's elementary school. And why can't Sister Greta ever frickin' tell me what the problem is over the phone? Just like the last time Andrew was up to no good, all she would tell me was that they were having a disciplinary problem with him, and that we could talk about it when I got there . . . as if I have nothing else to do all day. I've already missed a boatload of work because of Mom, and now I had to leave work again to have a conversation with Sister Greta that I probably could have handled over the phone.

"Ms. Costas?" the secretary asks.

"Yes," I say, my voice starting to get hoarse from all the drainage going down my throat.

She picks up the phone and hits a button. "Ms. Costas is here," she says into the phone as if the CEO of some Fortune 500 company is behind the closed door to the side of her desk.

I hear the door creak open and Sister Greta pokes her head out and motions for me to come in. I do as I'm instructed and take a seat in her office.

"Thank you for coming in today, Ms. Costas."

Like I had a choice. "You're welcome. What's going on? I'm so sorry if Andrew is giving you any problems."

"Are you aware that he brought this to school?" Sister Greta says and holds up the tattered looking Barbie Doll that Desma bought him at the thrift store.

"No, no. My house guest bought that for him. I didn't know he was taking it to school." *Okay, so my son plays with Barbie Dolls—is that a reason to call me into school?*

"He was taking it around the classroom, lifting up the doll's skirt and saying, "Look, Barbie's a slut. She's not wearing any panties."

I just look at her, speechless. Slut is not a word I ever expected to come out of the mouth of an elderly nun.

"Where would Andrew learn of such things? Do you have cable TV, Ms. Costas? Is he watching it unsupervised?"

"No . . . I mean yes . . . well, no . . . I mean, yes, we do have cable TV, but no, he doesn't watch it unsupervised." Most of the time.

"Well, thanks to Andrew, little Alexa Higgins took off her underwear and starting lifting her skirt to the boys in the class, saying "Look, I'm a slut, like Barbie.""

I gasp.

"Do you know how old Alexa Higgins is, Ms. Costas?"

I assume she is going to tell me, and my sore throat hurts when I speak, so I don't answer.

"She's five. A five-year-old lifting her skirt. Can you imagine?" Sister Greta says. "I will rest assured that this doll will not be returning to school with Andrew." She hands the doll to me.

"No. Of course not." I take the doll from her and quickly shove it in my purse. "I'll talk to Andrew about this. He's having a rough time lately. My mother recently had a stroke and tending to her has been taking up most of my time."

I expect at least a look of sympathy from Sister Greta, but all I get is a condescending stare. "And that's not all Andrew has been bringing to school. I don't even know what this is," she says, reaching into one of her desk drawers. But Andrew has been chasing the girls around the playground with it and squeezing it in their faces."

My eyes go wide as Sister Greta pulls out the kegel exerciser that Claire gave me for my birthday. I had tossed it in my dresser drawer and forgotten about it. "Um . . . that's ah . . . that's my . . . my hand exerciser. I've got . . . um, tendonitis, you know. My physical therapist gave it to me. I've been looking for it," I say and snatch if from her hand, wanting it out of sight before she has a chance to figure out what it is.

"I'll trust this is yet another item that will not be making an appearance at St. Paul's again?"

"Yes, yes. Of course," I reply, wondering if we're done here, or if Sister Greta is going to pull out some gay porn and say Andrew brought that to school as well.

"Well, thank you for coming in today and thank you in advance for assuring me that Andrew doesn't bring anymore inappropriate items to school."

"I'll check his backpack before we leave the house," I respond and stand up. "I'm sure he won't be a problem anymore."

"Good day," she says, and I turn to leave.

As I pass the secretary's desk, I see an anxious-looking woman about my age approach. "Hi. I'm Mrs. Higgins. Alexa Higgins' mother. I got a call to come in to see Sister Greta," I hear her say to the secretary as I walk out into the hall.

45

"What am I going to do with you, Andrew? What possessed you to bring that doll to school and lift her skirt to everyone?" I have to stifle a laugh when I ask the question. I know I need to take this more seriously, but the vision I have of him walking around the class, flashing Barbie's private parts just seems funny to me. "How do you even know what a slut is?"

"It's a person who sells houses."

"What?"

"It's what Aunt Desma calls Aunt Claire, and she sells houses."

"Andrew. I know you knew better than to do what you did with that doll. And you certainly know better than to rifle through my drawers and take my things to school. If I ever catch you getting into the drawers in my bedroom again, you'll be in time-out so long you'll forget why you were put there." I try to sound stern, but I don't think he's buying it. My bronchitis has gotten worse, I feel so sick, and I'm so caught up with Mom being in the nursing home, I just don't have the energy to be much of a disciplinarian. "What's going on with you, Andrew?"

"Nothing," he says and folds his arms.

"Don't you tell me 'nothing,' young man. When I ask you a question, I expect an answer."

"You promised to take me to see Grimace! And you didn't.

You *promised*! You never do what you say you're going to do. All you care about is Grandma!"

"Andrew, Grandma is very sick right now. You know what it's like to be sick. Remember when you had a sore throat and a runny nose a few months ago? Remember how you needed me to take care of you?"

He doesn't answer.

"Well, Grandma is much sicker than you've ever been, Andrew, and she needs a lot of attention right now."

"Are you going to see her again tonight?"

"Yes. We need to go by the drugstore, so I can pick up my prescription, and then I'll get you home. Desma is going to stay with you while I go to visit Grandma."

At first, my doctor refused to call in a prescription for me because I hadn't been in to his office in more than two years. But when I almost broke down crying as I explained everything that was going on and why I didn't have time to come in for an examination, he relented and agreed to call in a prescription for me.

"You go to see Grandma every day." Andrew makes a pouting gesture with his lip.

"I know, sweetie. But she's all by herself at the nursing home. You don't want her to think we've forgotten her, do you?"

"I'm tired of staying with Desma. She doesn't let me watch TV when you're not there."

"I'll talk to Desma before I leave and tell her to let you watch a little TV," I say, knowing I should take away Andrew's television privileges to punish him for the doll and the kegel exerciser incident. But I feel so guilty about the time I'm missing with him that I just let it go.

"I don't want to stay with her!"

I fight the urge to say "Tough shit, kiddo," as we get out of the car in front of the CVS. I have an excruciating headache, it hurts to swallow, I can't breathe out of either one of my nostrils, I'm coughing, I have chills, and my body aches. I haven't gotten a decent amount of sleep in days, and my patience is just generally running thin. "It's a tough time for all of us right now, Andrew. I need you to be mature and not complain about staying with Desma."

"I hate Grandma!"

I squat down to his level when we get inside the store. "You don't *hate* Grandma. You're just upset about all the attention she requires at the moment. Things will calm down once she . . ." I don't know how to finish that sentence. Once she dies? Is that what I was going to say?

"Now go sit down over there." I gesture to the chairs by the pharmacy counter when we reach the back of the store.

"Hi. Jennifer Costas. I'm here to pick up a prescription," I say to the clerk while Andrew stomps over toward the chairs with a scowl on his face.

"Okay. Just a moment." She walks away from the counter and starts leafing through the paper bags filed behind her. She looks and looks and eventually comes back empty-handed.

"It's not back there. Did you drop it off or was it called in?"

"It was called in hours ago."

"Let me check with the pharmacist." She disappears again.

"Andrew don't play with the blood pressure machine. It's not a toy," I reprimand while I stand there and wait, my head feeling like it could explode at any moment.

"I'm sorry," the clerk says when she gets back. "He found it. It will be a few minutes while he fills it."

"How long is a *few* minutes?"

"It should be ready in about ten minutes or so."

How long does it take to put some freakin' pills in a bottle? "Fine," I say with a sigh and turn away. "Andrew, let's get a cart. We may as well pick up a few things while we're here."

Andrew and I head to the front of the store and grab a cart. I figure I may as well do some grocery shopping, or the best semblance of grocery shopping one can do at the drugstore, while we're waiting for my medicine.

"Can I sit in the cart?"

"No, Andrew, you're too big for that."

"I am not! I can fit."

Too tired and sick to argue with a five-year-old, I cave. "Fine," I say and lift him into the cart. "Let's see if they have any milk or orange juice back in the refrigerator case."

I push the cart with Andrew in it around the store. He's momentarily content to be making car noises and riding in style around the CVS. We pick up some milk and orange juice and a few other items.

I'm pushing the cart down a long aisle when I hear my name called over the loud speaker: "Jennifer Costas to the pharmacy, please. Jennifer Costas to the pharmacy, please."

"That was fast," I say to Andrew as we approach the back of the store. But, once we reach the counter, I can tell from the look on the clerk's face that the news is not good.

"I'm afraid we don't have your prescription in stock, but we can have it for you tomorrow."

"What? It's *amoxicillin* for crying out loud. Not some recently approved drug from Canada. What do you mean you don't have it in stock?"

"Just that."

With my head pounding and my body aching, I'm about to lose it. "Oh I'm *sorry*," I say sarcastically. "I thought this was a *pharmacy* . . . you know, a place you come to get prescriptions filled."

"I said we can have it for you tomorrow," the clerk repeats, a meek look on her face.

"I don't want it *tomorrow*. I want it now. Why is it so difficult to keep prescriptions in stock? It's not like they're bananas or apples or something and will perish in a few days if you don't sell them." I'm usually very polite and understanding in these situations, but, at the moment, my last nerve is about to go. "Every time I come here, you don't have what I need." Okay, I'm exaggerating, but they do seem to be short of medicines about the half the time I come here to get prescriptions filled.

"I can call another store and see if they have it."

I take a deep breath, which I must do through my mouth since I can't breathe out of either one of my nostrils. "Fine."

I stand there while she places a call to the CVS a couple of miles down the road. From the sound of the conversation, the news from CVS number two is not good either.

"They don't have it either," she says, with an apprehensive look, clearly afraid I might literally bite her head off.

"Just give it back to me, and I'll take it somewhere else."

"We don't have it on paper. It was called in."

I'm almost in tears now. If they won't have it until tomorrow, I won't be able to pick it up until after work, which means a twenty-four hour delay in starting the drugs. And I really don't have time tonight to be running around to different drug stores to get it filled.

"I can't believe that you don't have a common drug like amoxicillin in stock. That's ridiculous."

"Yeah. We kinda suck. I'm really sorry," the girl says back to me, dropping any pretense of being a loyal employee.

I let out a long groan. "You know what. I'll just pick it up tomorrow." I finally say. "Let me just pay for these items and get out of here." I start lifting things from the basket and putting them on the counter.

"I'm sorry. I can only ring up prescriptions at this register. You have to take that stuff to the front."

"Oh, you've got to be kidding?"

She gives me a blank stare.

"You know what. Just keep it. Keep it all!" I say and throw the items back in the cart and start to walk away.

"Ma'm," I hear her call behind me. I ignore her. I'm not interested in anymore of her apologies.

"Ma'm," she calls again.

I stop abruptly, turn around, and, like a lioness protecting her young I yell, "*WHAT!?*" with a snarl that might scare the devil himself.

She timidly looks back at me. "Um . . . your son?" she says, pointing her eyes toward Andrew, still sitting, bewildered in the front of the cart. In my anger and haste to get away, I'd forgotten all about him. I so rarely lose my temper, he probably didn't know what to make of all of this and just sat there quietly as I walked away. I don't say a word to the young lady as I approach the cart. I'm too embarrassed to even look at her.

"I told you, you're too big to sit in the cart." I lift him from the seat, set him down on the ground, and grab his hand. I pull him behind me and make my way out of the store as fast as I can.

46

There is so much rushing through my head on my way out to the nursing home in Fredericksburg—Andrew's acting out at school, all the things I'm behind on at work, how I'm going to have to make a decision about whether or not to transfer Mom to a nursing facility closer to home, and so on and so on. I keep trying to temporarily forget about it all. Attempting to sort it all out just makes me anxious. I turn up the radio and try to focus on the music, but it's no use. All I can think about is my mother stuck in a nursing home, and how there are no good solutions when it comes to how to deal with her situation. Keeping her in a nursing home seems wrong but bringing her to live with Andrew and me doesn't seem like a plausible solution either. She'd need someone in the house with her full time, and that would be very expensive, and I have no idea how much it would cost to revamp the house into a place that would be conducive to having Mom there. At a minimum, we would need to get rid of some furniture to accommodate a wheelchair, install some sort of chair lift so she could get up and down the stairs, and we'd have to make one of the bathrooms handicap accessible.

All these thoughts are running through my mind, and I keep having visions of all the times Mom begged me not to leave her at the home. She barely knows my name or who she is, but she's keen enough to know that she doesn't like it there. And who can blame her?

"Don't you leave me here, Jennifer Peredo," I still hear her saying before I left one day last week. I can't get the visions of her helpless in a wheelchair out of my head, and, by the time I reach the exit that will take me to the nursing home, I know I just can't face her. I just can't face her right now, so I drive right past the exit and continue down Interstate 95 with no idea where I'm going. All I know is that, at this moment, I can't bear the thought of going back to the nursing home. I know I'll have to go later . . . maybe in another hour or two . . . maybe not until tomorrow, but something inside is just telling me that, for now, I don't have the wherewithal to breathe in the smells of the nursing home, to walk on the shiny industrial tiles, to sit on the vinyl furniture that someone has surely peed on earlier in the day, to see my mother decrepit in a wheelchair and listen to her spout gibberish.

A few miles after I pass the off-ramp, my eyes catch sight of those blue destination signs that alert you to the particular restaurants, hotels, and gas stations that are available at certain exits. When I see the Cracker Barrel logo, something inside me just clicks—I suddenly have an insatiable craving for greasy country cooking, so I get off the Interstate and make my way into the Cracker Barrel parking lot.

I haven't been to a Cracker Barrel in years, I think to myself as I walk inside. The last time I was in one was when Mario and I were still married, and he and Andrew and I were coming back from a trip to Myrtle Beach. Things haven't changed at all. The country store outside the dining room is still the same—chock full of knickknacks, and candy, and a few racks of clothing fit for no one under sixty-five. They still sell old-fashioned rockers on the front porch and corn bread mix and apple butter on the store shelves.

I walk up to the hostess and ask for the nonsmoking section, and she leads me to a table by one of the large windows and lays both a breakfast and dinner menu in front of me. Even with my nose completely congested, the smell of grease and old-fashioned comfort food is somehow penetrating my nostrils. I put the breakfast one aside, and open the dinner menu, and scan the contents. My mouth waters as I look over the options: chicken and dumplings, beef stew, fried catfish, pot roast, meatloaf, pork chops—the choices overwhelm me.

"Hi. My name is Marjorie, and I'll be your server today. Can I get you something to drink?" asks a matronly waitress with wide hips and unruly gray hair.

"An iced tea, please."

"Sweetened or unsweetened?"

I'd forgotten that they serve sweet tea here. I haven't had a good glass of sweet tea in years. "Sweetened, please."

Marjorie leaves the table, and I continue to go over edible options for taking my mind off my mother languishing in the nursing home, and finally decide on the pot roast. While I wait for the waitress to return with my drink, I start to fiddle with the little peg game that sits on the table, and I can't help thinking about the last time I was here with Mario and Andrew. It was after our final family vacation together. We had spent a long weekend in Myrtle Beach and were on our way home. We got hungry along the Interstate and figured that Cracker Barrel was a pretty good choice since Andrew was only three years old at the time, and we needed a kid-friendly restaurant, but wanted something with a bit more to offer than McDonald's. We hit the Cracker Barrel at a busy time and had to wait about a half hour for a table, so, like everyone else, we passed the time looking around the adjoining shop. Of course, Andrew wanted everything in the place—the toys, the candy, the children's books. Mario walked around the store with Andrew and kept him from grabbing massive amounts of candy while I perused some of the cookbooks and looked for a gift or two to take back to Mom. It was no so nice to be able to walk around the store by myself and know that Andrew was in good hands. I rarely get opportunities like that anymore. I don't have anyone to tag team with these days, at least not on an impromptu basis. When Andrew is with me at a store or a restaurant or the shopping mall, he's with *me*, and only me. There's no Mario anymore to stay with him at the table if I have to run to the restroom (God, how I miss not having to "hold it" everywhere I go like I do now, so I don't have to take Andrew into the ladies' room with me) or supervise him in the store so I can shop in peace for a few minutes. Parenting is never easy, but it was so much easier with someone to share the responsibilities.

"Would you like some lemon with that?" Marjorie asks me, setting my tea down on the table.

"No. I'm good, thanks." I'm making an effort to be polite, still feeling guilty after my unpleasant incident with the pharmacy clerk at CVS, but my tone comes across as dull and flat.

"Are you ready to order?"

"Yeah. I think I'll have the pot roast."

"And your three sides?"

"Mashed potatoes and gravy, macaroni and cheese, and fried apples." I'm already tasting the food in my mouth. I know it will be sort of institutional, but I haven't eaten like this in forever, and the thought of food made with butter and cheese and gravy is about the only thing that's keeping me from pulling my hair out.

"Biscuits and corn bread?"

"Um . . . sure."

"Okay. I'll have that right out for you," she says and looks at me more closely. "Are you okay?"

I try to smile. "Yeah. I just have a cold."

"Oh. That makes sense. You seem a little down. You want to trade that for some hot tea with honey?" she asks, eyeing my glass of iced tea.

"No . . . but thanks for asking," I say, touched by the offer.

"Okay. Your food will be up shortly."

"No hurry," I reply, uttering words that have never been truer in my life. The longer it takes for the food to come, the longer I have an excuse to sit here and hide from the world.

I sip the sweet tea and half-heartedly continue to play the little peg game, still thinking of Andrew pulling out the pegs with Mario hunched over him, offering tips. It was one of many moments when I'd look at the two of them together and think about how lucky I was to have them in my life—"my boys" I used to call them. I felt blessed that Mario was such a good father and so helpful with Andrew. Okay, so our sex life left a lot to be desired, but we had so much else as a family that seemed to make up for it. The three of us were so good together. I can remember us sitting at a table at this or some other Cracker Barrel (they all look the same) and chatting and laughing, Mario wiping jelly off Andrew's face while I cut up his meat, Andrew charming the patrons at the table next to us with his smile . . . them telling us what a beautiful family we were. If they'd only known the truth . . . if *I'd* only known the truth.

It only takes about ten minutes for Marjorie to return and start clanking plates and bowls down onto the table. I sit there and watch as a white plate, piled with pot roast and mashed potatoes, both covered in gravy, lands before me. This is followed by separate little bowls of macaroni and cheese and fried apples, a small plate topped with one biscuit and one cornbread muffin, and yet another bowl loaded with butter and jelly.

"You need anything else? More tea?" Marjorie asks, and looks at me curiously again. Her eyes meet mine, and there's a kindness in them that I'm not used to seeing. She's got bright blue eyes, fat cheeks, and a double chin. She could easily play Mrs. Claus in any number of Christmas pageants.

"I think I'm good for now."

"Okay."

She's barely left the table before my fork hits the roast and, with no assistance needed by my knife, breaks off a chuck of tender beef. I put it in my mouth, and, for the first time in my life, I really understand why certain foods are called "comfort foods." It's impossible to think of anything else when you're feasting on these kinds of hearty vittles—they really do provide comfort, or at least relief, by making you think about nothing but their taste and smell and texture. And, for a few minutes, while I devour more calories in one setting than I usually eat during an entire day, I am able to forget—I don't think about my mother while I'm scarfing down creamy mashed potatoes, I temporarily forget about my son introducing the word "slut" into the vocabulary of a classroom of five-year-olds while I'm savoring warm fried apples, I have no thoughts of my gay ex-husband as I put a fork full of macaroni and cheese to my lips. The meal is such a wonderful escape but, like most good things, it doesn't last very long.

By the time I'm scraping the bottom of the bowl of fried apples and popping the last bite of corn bread into my mouth, the feeling of fullness in my belly is accompanied by an increasing sense of uneasiness. Marjorie will come back with the check soon, and I'll have to pay the bill and go back out *there*. I'll have to go to the nursing home and visit with Mom and hope that I'm able to leave without her begging that I take her home with me.

While I wait for the check, I decide to make a quick trip to the ladies' room, so I get up from the table and head back toward the store. When I reach the restroom, before going into one of the stalls, I take a look at myself in the mirror and feel a tinge of anger at the woman I see staring back at me. Is it not bad enough that I've confined the woman who gave birth to me to a nursing home, but I also skipped out on visiting her to stuff myself silly with fatty food? Much as I'd love to skip my visit tonight, looking at myself in the mirror, I know I need to do the right thing and go by the home before heading back to my house.

After another moment or two of reflection, I make my way to the stall and when I'm finished using the bathroom, I stand to lift my panties and my slacks and realize that I've gone the entire day with my underwear on backwards. It almost makes me laugh. I've got a son putting his shirts on backwards, a mother putting her dresses on backwards, and now I've joined the club. Realizing that I'm just too tired to deal with the hassle of taking

off my shoes and my pants just to fix the direction of my underwear, I say to hell with it and leave them as is. I've gone the
whole day with them like this, what's a few more hours?

When I get back to the table, Marjorie is standing next to it,
looking perplexed. I hope she didn't think I had skipped out on
the check.

"Hi. I just ran to the ladies' room."

"Oh good. I was worried."

"No. I wasn't trying to dine and dash," I say with a smile,
and sit back down at the table.

"Oh, no. I wasn't worried about that. I thought you might be
getting sick in the restroom or . . . well, I don't know . . . you
seem like maybe you're not yourself, not that I would know
what 'yourself' is. I just met you. Anyway, I have a daughter
about your age, and she gets a similar look on her face . . . like
the one you've had since you came in here, when she's having a
hard time about things."

"I'm fine, really," I say.

"You sure?"

She's staring down at me, and she has the same look in her
eyes that Mom used to get when she was concerned about me. I
want to repeat that I'm fine, but I'm dumbstruck and can't respond at all. I look down at the table, afraid if I open my mouth,
I'll start crying.

"Oh, sweetie, what is it?"

"I'm fine, really," I say, starting to lose control of my face, a
raw lump forming in my throat. "Really, I am."

"I don't think you are," she says and sits down across from
me and puts her hand over mine.

"It's just that my mother had a stroke a few weeks ago, and
now she's in the nursing home, and it's pretty far from my
house, and I've been going to see her every day, and she's not
improving . . ." Tears are starting to come to my eyes while I
look at Marjorie for a response, but she just looks at me quietly.

"Everything is such a mess. I'm so behind at work, and my
son is acting out at school because he's not getting any atten-

tion." The waterworks are really starting to roll at this point. "He took a Barbie to school and lifted her skirt . . . and the mean nun called me in and judged me to be a bad mother." I'm ranting now, like a lunatic. "I just don't know what else can go wrong. I'm dealing with this all on my own. My husband and I divorced because he's a homosexual, and now he's squandering my son's college money on some gay version of Hooters." I don't even think my speech is coherent anymore. I'm just getting words in between fractured breaths. "He was in . . . drag show . . . and . . . crazy houseguest . . . compost toilet . . . I had a date, and he made a boom-boom . . . and another one . . . photos of Angelina Jolie's head on George Clooney's body . . . and my mother . . . potatoes in the oven wrapped in newspaper . . ." Words are spiraling out of my mouth—a few coherent phrases mixed with nonsense. I'm bawling like a baby and still trying to speak and breathe, but unable to do either very well. My breath is so quick and shallow it sounds like I'm hyperventilating. "And my neighbor . . . gonorrhea . . . wanted me to crush a pill in peanut butter. Sister Greta hates me. Andrew wanted to see Grimace and I forgot. I forgot! I yelled at the pharmacy clerk. I don't yell at people . . . that's not me," I say. "And," I add, shaking with release and grief. "My . . ." I can't stop crying long enough to get any words out. "My . . . my . . ." I take a few thin breaths. "My underwear's on backwards, and I'm too tired to care."

With these words, Marjorie gets up from the table, squats down and hugs me as best as she can while I sit in the chair. I hug her back and sob into her shoulder like a lost child.

"Let it out . . . let it all out," she says, stroking my hair.

I do just as I'm told. I let the tears flow, I let my body quiver, I let myself fall into the kindly Cracker Barrel waitress and, when I'm able to begin collecting myself, I realize that this may have been one of the most constructive things I've done in months.

"I'm so sorry," I say as I finally pull away from her and look around at all the people who quickly divert their eyes and pretend not to notice the crazy woman who just had a complete nervous breakdown in the middle of a crowded Cracker Barrel. "I've made a complete spectacle of myself."

"Oh, who cares?" Marjorie says, standing up and offering a comforting smile. "It sounds like God has sent you a few curve-balls lately."

"Yeah . . . I guess." I try to return the smile as best I can before I reach for my napkin and dry my eyes and blow my nose. "I really should get going. You've been very sweet . . . an angel."

"Not at all. I'm a mother, you're a mother. We take care of people. That's what we do."

"That is so true," I say and rifle through my purse and grab my wallet.

"Put your wallet away. This one's on me."

"No. You've been so nice already." I lay a twenty dollar bill on the table. "Thanks for your support, Marjorie."

"Don't mention it," she says, reaching for my hand with both of hers and giving it a firm squeeze. "You drive safe now, ya hear?"

"I will." She releases my hands, and I try to walk out of the restaurant without making eye contact with any of the other customers.

Great, I think to myself. Not only can I never show my face again at the Duke Street CVS, I'll now be forever known as "the nervous breakdown lady" at the Fredericksburg Cracker Barrel.

47

It's almost nine o'clock and here I am, once again, walking down the hall of the nursing home. I'm sure Mom's asleep, and I imagine the staff frowns upon visitors coming this late, but no one has said anything to me.

I'm so tired, I may just spend the night in the vacant bed in Mom's room. My stomach is full from the Cracker Barrel, and I'm still recovering from my earlier meltdown. Cathartic as it was, couldn't I have picked a better place to lose my mind? At least a better restaurant . . . maybe an Olive Garden or an Applebee's.

As expected, Mom is sleeping when I reach her room. Like I've done so many other times now, I don't wake her—I just sit down next to her. And, while I watch her sleep, I suddenly realize that, physically, I feel so much better than I did when I left the house. The congestion in my nose has softened, I no longer feel feverish, and my coughing has subsided. Maybe I didn't need the antibiotics after all—maybe I just needed a plate of greasy food and a plump waitress's shoulder to cry on.

"You're late," Mom says to me when she opens her eyes.

I laugh. "Yeah. I had to make a little detour."

"A detour? Where?"

"Nowhere important. How are you?"

"Fine," she says, her voice weaker than the last time I was here.

"Fine?"

"Yes. I'm fine," she says, and there's a contentment about her that I haven't seen in her in . . . well, I'm not sure I've ever seen it.

"Did they have any activities today?"

"They wanted me to make cookies in the community room, but I was too tired."

"Well . . . that's okay. I'm sure they'll be making cookies again soon."

"Maybe," she says, as if she could care less whether they do or not. "Do you remember when you were little . . . oh, I guess it was about nineteen eighty or so, and Alberto had taken Tomás on a camping trip with the Boy Scouts?"

"I do."

"We decided to make cookies . . . *Christmas* cookies. That's right, it was near the holidays. I wanted to make *tamales*—we always made *tamales* during Christmas in Colombia. But you insisted that we make cookies. Do you remember?"

"Yes." And I do remember. How is it she can't remember that Dad's dead, but she remembers that we made cookies together more than twenty years ago?

"We'd rolled the dough and cut out the shapes—stars, stockings, bells, Christmas trees, and it was time to make the icing. I had divided the vanilla icing into a few different bowls and started adding food coloring to them. Remember?"

"I do . . . I do."

"I wanted to make red, green, and blue icing. But you were Miss Smarty Pants and decided you wanted to mix all the food dyes together in one bowl."

I laugh. "I did."

"I told you that it was going to come out an unsightly brown color and you said, 'No, no, it'll be neat, you'll see.'"

A huge smile is plastered across my face as I listen to her tell the story, making more sense than she has in weeks.

"I kept telling you not to, but, as you often did, you ignored my wishes and made your icing. And, like I predicted, it was brown—a really ugly shade of brown. But you were so stubborn. You refused to admit that you didn't like it, and you went on and decorated your Christmas cookies in brown icing. Even when Alberto and Tomás got back from the camping trip and asked about the brown Christmas cookies, you refused to admit your blunder."

"I did. I'm not sure I'd admit to it now. But you know where I got my stubbornness from, don't you?"

Mom doesn't answer my question. She just looks at me, and out of nowhere she says, "You tell Andrew and Tomás that I love them."

"I will," I say, bemused by her sudden request and shocked that she mentioned Andrew. She hasn't said a word about him since the stroke. It's been like she'd forgotten he exists.

"And I love you too, Jennifer. You're a good girl. You always gave me so much grief, but you're a good girl."

"*What!?*" The word involuntarily comes out. She hasn't told me that she loves me since I was very young.

"I love you," she repeats. The room is dark, and there's a soft glow about her from the trace of light coming in from the hallway.

I feel my face getting hot. "I love you too, Mom," I say, realizing that she's not the only one who hasn't said those words in quite some time.

She reaches for my hand. "You know what else?" she questions. "I've known that Mario's gay for more than a year. What? You think I don't know about gay people?"

"What?! What are you talking about?" I ask, surprised by her apparent lucidity.

"Yes. Mrs. Yates mentioned it to me last year. She thought I knew." Mrs. Yates is the mother of Dina Yates, a friend of mine from high school, who I still occasionally chat with. Mrs. Yates attends the same church that Mom used to go to.

"Then why did you keep asking me about my divorce? Pestering me for a reason?"

"Oh, I don't know. A girl's gotta have a hobby," she says,

quietly chuckles and lets go of my hand. Then she looks at me for a moment before closing her eyes. She lays there with her eyes shut, and I can't help but wonder what just happened. Why, just now, did she seem like a person with intact mental function? It seems to me that I've read something about people with dementia who have brief periods of lucidity, but it's usually right before they're about to—

"Oh my God!" I say out loud and hop up from the chair. "Mom? Mom?!" I call out, but she doesn't wake up. I try to focus on her chest, looking for movement . . . looking for breath, but neither is there. I nudge her with my hand. "Mom?! Mom?!" I call, but she doesn't respond. I reach for her hand, which is limp in my grasp. "Mom?" I say again, more quietly this time. Once again, she doesn't answer, and, unable to do anything else, I keep hold of her hand, tighten my grip, and drop back into the chair. I just sit there and hold her hand to my forehead and close my eyes. I know I should get up and alert one of the nurses, but I can't move, and, even if I could, I can't speak. I can only sit there and hold my mother's hand and try to make this moment last—try to make the final moment with my mother last as long as I can.

48

I had no idea what to do when I left the nursing home. I wasn't ready to face anyone or deliver the news of Mom's passing, so, rather than go home, I came to Mom's house, and now I'm sitting in her kitchen just looking around.

I've only been here once since the morning Mom had the stroke to pick up some things for her and throw out some stuff from the refrigerator. The house is exactly the same as the day she left here in an ambulance. The coffee mug I used that morning is still sitting in the sink. Her reading glasses are in front of me on the table. Her red cardigan sweater is hanging on the back of the chair across from me. It's almost as if she could be upstairs right now, getting ready for me to run her to the bank or the mall.

When I was finally able to pry myself away from her after she stopped breathing, I walked out to the nurses' station in a daze. "Excuse me," I said softly to one of the nurses. "I think my mother has . . ." I couldn't get the words out, but the nurse could tell from the look on my face what I was trying to say. She got up from her chair, grabbed my hand, and led me back to the room. We didn't hurry—no one grabbed a crash cart or yelled "Code Blue." We just walked down the hall. When we got back into her room, the nurse put on her stethoscope and listened for a heartbeat. Then she removed the device from her ears and looked at me.

"I'm sorry," she said and stepped over and hugged me.

I hugged her back, and I felt like I should have been crying, but no tears would come. I was shocked and sad and bewildered, but more than anything, I think I felt relief. How horrible is that? My mother had just died, and my most prevalent emotion was relief. The past few weeks have been so hard on all of us—me, Andrew, and mostly Mom. I can't help but take solace in the fact that the ordeal is over. She doesn't have to stay in the nursing home anymore, I won't have to see her all withered and weak and barely making sense, she won't be looking for her "baby" or her dead husband, I won't have to spend hours in the car everyday to come see her.

"What do we do now?" I asked the nurse.

"We don't need to do anything now. Mrs. Peredo will be taken care of tonight, and we can talk about all the necessary arrangements tomorrow," she said. And then she went on to ask all the things people ask when they have no idea what to do for a person in crisis. "Can I get you a glass of water? Is there anyone I can call for you? Do you need a few minutes alone?"

I answered, "No," to all her questions, and, after saying a final good-bye to Mom, the nurse walked me to my car.

"Are you sure you don't want to call someone to take you home?"

"Yes, I'm sure. You've been very sweet." I said. "I'll be okay."

I pulled out of the nursing home parking lot in a stupor and honestly have no recollection of how I got from there to here at Mom's house. I only remember wanting to be alone and not wanting to talk to anyone. For some reason, this is where I was drawn.

Mom may be dead, but she still exists everywhere in this house. I look at the microwave and remember how she was afraid to use it for the longest time—she was convinced it was going to leak radiation. The food processor components we used when we were making Colombian food the night before her stroke are sitting next to the sink, where we left them to dry.

There's even a little spot of flour dust on the table that we must have missed when we wiped that table before going to bed.

I get up from my chair and walk over to the other side of the table and lift Mom's sweater from the back of the chair. I bring it to my nose, and I can smell her scent, which sends a shudder down my spine. I put the sweater on, grab each side, and embrace myself with it, realizing that I'll be taking it home with me and will probably never wash it.

Clutching the sweater, I take a brief tour of the entire house, going from room to room, just taking everything in. I remember the entire family watching TV in the living room, I remember all the fights Tom and I had in what used to be our playroom, I remember sitting on the steps and pouting every time I was mad about something, I remember the special dinners we had in the dining room . . . This house, so full of memories, is empty now. Everyone has moved on in one way or another. But I guess that's life. The only thing you can count on is change.

I'm tempted to crawl into Mom's bed and spend one last night here, but tomorrow will be a busy day with the phone calls and arrangements that need to be made, so I decide it's best to grab my coat and my purse and drive home. I'm almost out the door when I suddenly have a frightening thought: What if I hadn't been there when Mom died? What if I had left the restaurant and decided to skip my visit with her for one day—something I came very close to doing. What if she had died alone? Such a thought terrifies me.

"But you didn't skip the visit, Jennifer," I tell myself. "And you were there when she died."

Thank God, I think to myself. Thank God I was there.

49

I'm standing just outside the security screening area that leads to the airport gates. According to the monitor, Tom's flight has landed, and he should be walking into the main terminal any moment. He's traveling alone. Apparently, Lindsey couldn't be bothered to come pay her respects. Tom left the kids at home as well, saying that he didn't want them to miss school, which shouldn't surprise me—why should Lindsey or the girls feel any connection to Mom? They've only met her a handful of times over the last ten years. Still. You'd think Lindsey would come to her mother-in-law's funeral and bring her kids to say a final good-bye to their grandmother, even if they barely knew her.

"Hey," I call, waving my hand as I catch sight of Tom. He's gotten a little bigger around the middle, and his hair has thinned since I saw him last.

"Hi," he says when he reaches me and gives me an awkward hug. "How are you doing?"

"I'm holding up okay," I say, not sure if I'm telling the truth. Oddly, I've held it together quite well for the past few days, but I think the reality of Mom's passing has yet to set in. "You?"

"I'm fine. It was a quick flight," Tom responds as if I were asking about his travels. "Are you feeling better? You sounded sick on the phone when we talked before Mom . . . before she . . . you know . . ."

"Yeah. I'm feeling much better." And I am feeling much better, physically anyway. Oddly, my bronchitis seemed to go away on its own, and I never had to go back to the CVS and face the poor pharmacy clerk I yelled at a few days ago. "Is that all you brought?" I ask, looking at Tom's small suitcase. "Do we need to go to baggage claim?"

"No. I didn't check anything. I just tossed a few things in a suitcase. I can pick up anything else I need at the drugstore later."

"Okay. I'm parked in the garage."

Tom follows me to the people movers, which take us to the parking garage. We're quiet all the way to the car. Our contacts have been so few and far between since he got married that we're almost like strangers with only a dead mother in common.

"Thanks for waiting to make funeral arrangements until I got here," he says once we're inside the car and making our way to the highway.

"No problem," I reply as if I had taken him into account when I scheduled the meeting with the funeral home, which I hadn't. It just happens that my appointment with the funeral director isn't until after Tom's flight arrived. "I'm sorry we have to head over there right away. Do you need to stop and get something to eat or anything on the way?"

"No. I had lunch before I got on the plane."

"How's Lindsey and the girls?"

"They're fine. The girls are in a really competitive school, and, if they miss a few days, it would be hard for them to catch up, so I figured it was best that Lindsey just stay home with them."

"Really? Are there Harvard elementary schools these days?" I mean it as a joke, but it comes off sounding crass.

"They really would have liked to have come, Jennifer."

"Oh well . . . they didn't know Mom that well anyway."

"What's that supposed to mean?" Tom asks with an edge to his tone.

"Nothing. I just meant that they never really got to know Mom."

Tom is silent for a few minutes and then tries to make small talk with me, asking about Andrew and Mario and how things are at work, and we somehow manage to keep a conversation going all the way to the funeral home.

"Hi. Ms. Costas?" A woman in a navy blue suit asks me as we're coming through the front door of the Meridian Funeral Home in Fredericksburg.

"Yes. And this is my brother, Tom . . . Tom Peredo."

"Peggy Buscher. Nice to meet you," she says and shakes both our hands. "I'm so sorry for your loss," she adds respectfully.

"Thank you," I say, and we follow her upstairs to her office and have a seat in front of her desk.

"Again, I'm so sorry that you lost your mother. I know this is a really difficult time for both of you. Dealing with the death of a loved one is never easy and losing a mother is often one of the most difficult losses people ever face."

"Thank you," I say again, knowing that she probably repeats some form of these words a few times a day.

"Do you know if your mother had anything in mind for her viewing?"

"She was a devout Catholic," Tom says. "I'm sure she'd want a Catholic service."

"I've made arrangements with Father Hill at St. Johns, Tom. The church service is pretty well taken care of. Now we just need to plan the viewing the night before the funeral."

"We can arrange for the priest to say a few words at the viewing as well, if you'd like," Peggy offers.

"Yeah. That would be nice," Tom responds before I have a chance to say anything.

"You said on the phone that you were interested in traditional arrangements, so I won't go over cremation details."

"That's fine," Tom says.

"Why don't we step into the next room, and you can select a casket. And then we'll come back and talk about her obituary and the flowers and a few other arrangements."

Tom and I follow Peggy through a side door off her office and step into a large room with several caskets on display. I immediately get a chill down my spine just being in the room.

"Are you okay? Do you need a few minutes before we get started?" Peggy asks, noticing my unease.

"No. We're fine," Tom answers once again as if I'm deaf and dumb.

"As you can see, we offer a wide selection . . . everything from metal caskets," Peggy says with an inflection in her voice and an expression on her face that tells us that only trashy people buy metal caskets. "To the finest cherry and mahogany models."

"I definitely want a wooden casket," Tom says as if I have no say in the matter. "I'm not having my mother buried in a metal one."

"Okay. Let me show you some of the different models," Peggy says and steps toward the other side of the room. "These are the hardwood options. Then over there are the oak and pecan caskets. And over there are the cherry and mahogany versions."

"Let's start with oak." Tom says, definitively.

"No, I think we should look at the pecan caskets," I say to Tom. "You remember Mom's bedroom suite? The one Dad bought in North Carolina back in the eighties. It was pecan, and she loved that set."

"How much are the pecan caskets?"

"They range from two to three thousand dollars."

"I guess that's okay," Tom says, as if I need or desire his approval on Mom's casket selection.

"This one's a beautiful piece." Peggy gestures toward one of the caskets like it's a used car at CarMax. "It's solid pecan with a medium oak stain, and it's manufactured in southern Virginia. It has a satin finish, a patented locking system, interchangeable corner options, wood bars, premium antique finish hardware, and end handles. It comes with a white satin taffeta suite complete with a quilted coverlet and pillow and an inscribed nameplate," Peggy continues. She's trying to be sedate and respectful, but I can't help but feel like she's a model on *The Price is Right* and this casket is part of a winning showcase.

Peggy shows us two other pecan caskets and goes through the same song and dance with each one. But, truth be known, I can't tell the difference between any of them. One's supposed to have a better sealing system than the other two, and one has an adjustable mattress or something.

"I think we'll go with the first one you showed us," Tom says.

"Um, excuse me?" I interject. "Can I have some say in the matter?"

"Of course," Tom responds as though he's surprised by my question. "Which one do you want?"

"I guess I'm fine with first one too. I just wanted to be consulted . . . that's all."

"Whatever," Tom says, a hint of shortness in his tone.

With the casket selection behind us, we go back into Peggy's office and return to our seats.

"Did you bring her clothes and a few recent photos? We picked up your mother's body yesterday and would like to begin embalming tomorrow. The photos will help the technician prepare your mother for the viewing."

"Yes." I reach for the shopping bag I brought along with a few of Mom's things in it. "There's a dress in here . . . and her underclothes and some of her jewelry."

"Her jewelry?" Tom asks.

"Yes. Just her wedding band and her pearl necklace."

"Don't you think we should keep the pearl necklace? I'm sure Lindsey or one of the girls would like to have it."

I look at him, speechless for a moment. He thinks the woman or the children who couldn't even be bothered to come to Mom's funeral or visit her when she was alive would like to have her necklace? Is he kidding me? "She has plenty of other jewelry, Tom. Dad gave her the pearl necklace for their twentieth anniversary. I'd like for her to be buried with it."

"Do you really think that's logical, Jennifer? Don't you think she would have wanted her family to enjoy it?"

"Fine, Tom," I say and take the necklace out of the bag and almost throw it at him.

"What dress did you bring?" Tom asks, unaware of my rising frustration with him.

"It's a nice floral dress we bought together a couple of months ago."

"What about the suit she wore to my wedding? The pink one? She looked nice in that."

"Tom, she'd lost more than fifty pounds since your wedding. It'd never fit her," I say to him, and then turn to Peggy. "Here's a few photos of her as well." I hand an envelope to her. "I know we're having a closed casket ceremony, but it would still be nice if they tried to make her up as best they can."

"Closed casket?" Tom asks. "Why?"

"Because I don't want the last image I, or anyone, has of Mom to be of her cadaver in a coffin."

"We like to use the word *casket*," Peggy interjects.

"I think we should have an open casket ceremony. That's what we did for Dad."

"Yes. I hated seeing him like that. All made up. He looked like a clown. I still can't get that vision out of my head."

"That may be, Jen. But I really think we should have an open coffin."

"Casket," Peggy says again.

"Why?" I ask.

"I just think that's what she would have wanted."

He hasn't seen her in two years and, all of a sudden, he's the expert on what she would have wanted? "I seriously doubt Mom would want her dead body to be displayed to the world."

"I don't care, Jennifer. I want the coffin . . . *casket* to be open. I'd like to see her."

"You'd like to *see* her?!" I say, raising my voice. "You had *seventy-five* years to see her, Tom. If you'd cared half as much about seeing her when she was alive as you do now . . ." I can see the hurt in Tom's eyes that my words have caused, and I stop myself from saying anything further.

"Why don't I give you two a minute alone." Peggy says, getting up from the desk as Tom and I stare at each other in silence.

"I'm sorry, Tom. I didn't mean that," I say, even though I meant every word. "We're all under a lot of stress."

"No," he says, turning his gaze away from me and down toward the floor. "*You're* under a lot of stress . . . have been for a long time, and I haven't done anything to help."

Of course, what he's saying is true, but I don't have the heart to ride him any further. "You were a thousand miles away. How much could you have done?"

"I'm so sorry, Jen. I should have been there for her. I should have come up before she died. But, I couldn't. I just *couldn't*. I couldn't handle seeing her like that," he says, and, for the first time in my adult life, I see him starting to cry. "She was my mother. She was so strong. I couldn't stand the idea of seeing her in a wheelchair . . . in a nursing home."

I reach over and put my arm around him. "I know. I know. It's hard," I say. And, with my arm, I can feel the strength of his body—his broad shoulders and his thick neck, but, at the same time, I can feel how weak he is—weak the same way many men are. Physically they are so much stronger than women—they can run faster, throw farther, jump higher, but when it comes to dealing with matters of the heart, they are so feeble it's pathetic. I didn't like seeing Mom fade into a shadow of her former self anymore than he would have if he had been here to witness it, but I sucked it up, and did what needed to be done. It's in situations like these, that I realize the strength of women. I've just lost my mother, the woman who I've been looking after for years—the woman I've been much closer to than Tom. And, here I am, taking care of him.

God! Men are such pussies! I think to myself as I continue to hold it together, so I can comfort Tom.

50

Okay, so I caved. I let Tom have his way. We're at my mother's wake, and her body is lying in the open casket at the front of the room. They put so much makeup on her she looks like Tammy Faye Bakker. I've only been here an hour, but I've already had enough, and I'm ready to go home.

So many people have come to the funeral home to pay their respects, and I've recognized all of about half of them. It's funny how quickly word of one's death travels. Mom wasn't in contact with a huge number of people the past few years, so I only had to make a few phone calls to alert people of her passing. But five times the number of people that I called have shown up for her viewing.

"You're Jennifer, right?" an unknown elderly woman says to me.

"Yes. And this is my brother Tom."

"Hello," Tom says to her.

"I'm Mrs. Beech. Remember me? We used to live next door to each other when you were kids."

"Oh my God! Yes," I say, smiling with recognition. "How good to see you. Thanks for coming."

"Oh, you're welcome. Gladys Wilson phoned me about Ana's death. I hadn't seen Ana in a long time. Mr. Beech has been sick, and it's hard for me to get away. But Ana and I talked on the phone every now and then. I did love her so. She was such a nice woman."

"Yes, she was," I agree.

"You've grown into a beautiful woman," she says and turns to Tom. "And a handsome man you are. You two were just children when we moved away."

Tom and I nod, and she grabs my hand. "She spoke very highly of you, Jennifer. Every time I talked to her she was anticipating one of your visits to take her shopping or to one of her appointments."

"Really?" I ask, surprised by her words.

"Oh yes. I always heard about how you had a busy job and your son to take care of, but you always found time for her."

"Really?" I ask again.

"Yes, *really*," she says. "I'll let you greet the other mourners. It was nice to see you two again. I wish it were under better circumstances."

As she walks away, someone else approaches and starts talking to Tom, and I see Claire make her way though the door.

"Hey," I say when I reach her. "Thanks for coming."

"Sure. Ted sends his regrets. I'm leaving him, so I told him, if he wanted to come, he could come by himself, but that's a story for another day."

"What happened?"

"We can talk about it later. God, Jen . . . it's your mother's wake. Even *I'm* not *that* self-involved."

I laugh. "No, really. What happened? I would love to hear about something that isn't related to death."

"Well . . . as it turns out, Julio didn't give me the clap."

"No?"

"Ted did."

"What?"

"Yes. I'd been banging my head against a wall, trying to figure out a way to tell Ted he needed to get treated, and yesterday he sits me down and tells me *I* need to get treated.

He's been screwing Sue Hamilton, his secretary. How cliché is that?"

"You're kidding?"

"I wish. I'm not so mad about him cheating . . . I mean, who am I to judge? But with *Sue Hamilton*? I've met her many times. She's a pig! Okay, well maybe she's not *enormous,* but she certainly doesn't need directions to Red Lobster if you know what I mean."

I nod my head.

"I went by his office a few months ago, and she was wearing pantyhose with open-toe shoes. Can you believe that!? My husband was cheating on me with an obese woman who wears pantyhose with open-toe shoes. I've never been so horrified in my life. I told him he could just run off with his fashion-faux pas'd fat girl because I was leaving him."

"Thank you, Claire," I say, laughing.

"For what?"

"For taking my mind off my mother's death for the first time in days."

"Anytime," she says and smiles at me. "We'll talk more later. I'm sure you've got lots of other people to speak to. I'll go say hi to Desma. It's fake," she says, gesturing toward the fur collar on her coat. "But I think I'll tell her it's real and watch her get all riled up. It . . . it amuses me so."

"Okay," I say, and after she walks away, I look around the room at all the people seated in the rows of chairs. There must be more than sixty people here—old neighbors, Dad's old co-workers, members of groups my mother used to belong to when she was able to get out more. Their presence should be comforting to me, but I can't help but feel a certain amount of anger toward them. Now that Mom is dead, people have come out in droves, but where were they when she was alive and needed some help around the house, or rides to the grocery store, or just someone to keep her company? Why is it that people who couldn't be bothered to visit her when she was alive, now feel compelled to come to her wake? I guess because it's so noncommittal—a one-time thing. She's not going to pop out of the casket and ask them to rake her leaves or stay and watch television with her. They can get in, get out, and be done with it. Oh well—at least Mom would be happy to know that her viewing room is full, and a nice number of people came to say a final good-bye.

When Father Hill arrives, I say a few words to him. I'm about to make my way to the back of the room where Andrew has been sitting with Mario, when I hear my name being called behind me.

"Jennifer?"

I turn around and Ben is standing there, handsome as ever in a dark wool suit.

"Ben. What a surprise. How sweet of you to come," I say, touched by his presence.

"Not at all. I called your house earlier today to check on you, like I said I would, and your housemate or houseguest or whatever told me about your mother. I'm so sorry."

"Thank you."

"I never know what else to say in these situations, but if there's anything I can do for you, please let me know."

"I will, Ben. Really, it was so nice of you to stop by. I think Father Hill is about to get started so I guess I'd better . . ."

"Oh, of course. You go ahead. I'll just take a seat."

I give him a quick hug and smile at him then walk over to Andrew and Mario.

"Hey there, big guy. How are you doing?" I ask Andrew and lift my head and smile at Mario. "Thanks for keeping an eye on him."

"Can we go home now?" Andrew asks. I'm not sure he's completely grasped the concept of his grandmother being dead yet. I haven't taken him up to the casket, and, as far as I'm concerned, there really isn't any need to do so. I had no idea how to talk to him about Mom's passing, so Mario and I agreed to tell him together. The three of us sat down on the sofa and had a long conversation.

"You know that your grandmother has not been doing well lately," I remember saying to Andrew.

He nodded his head.

"We talked about how she had a stroke and was bleeding on the inside, right?"

"Yeah."

"And you know that Grandma was very old."

He just looked at me waiting for more information.

"Andrew, Grandma's body stopped working. She's not going to be with us any longer."

"She's dead?" Andrew asked, using the word I'd been avoiding.

"Yes, sweetie. She's dead."

"Can she still make hot chocolate?"

"No. She can't," I said. "But she showed me how to do it, so I'll make it with you."

"When someone dies, Andrew, they can't do things like make hot chocolate anymore," Mario said to him. "They don't breathe anymore or talk or eat or anything like that."

"Will I see Grandma again?"

Mario and I looked at each other. "No," I finally said. "We won't see Grandma anymore. She's in heaven." I'm not sure I believe in heaven, but, if it helped me explain Mom's death to Andrew, I figured I'd believe in it for the time being.

"Mrs. Knox says heaven is beautiful," Andrew said, referring to his teacher.

"Yes. I'm sure it is."

Andrew was quiet for a few seconds and then looked up at us. "Can I watch TV now?" he asked.

I laughed. "Yes," I said, feeling a certain amount of relief that the conversation was over. "Go watch TV," I added. And now, looking at Andrew sitting in the chair at the funeral home with Mario, I'm still relieved that he seems to be handling things pretty well.

"Why don't we go take our seats up front? Father Hill is going to say a few words."

Mario lifts Andrew off his lap, and they follow me to the front of the room where we take our seats next to Tom. I chatted with Father Hill for a few minutes earlier today, and I also gave him some notes to help him personalize his words.

"Thanks to everyone for coming tonight to mourn the loss of a lovely woman, Mrs. Ana Peredo," Father Hill says when he reaches the podium. "I've known Ana since I took over as pastor at St. John's four years ago. She attended services whenever she could, and she always had a kind word for me. She was such a nice woman.

"I chatted with her daughter, Jennifer, earlier today, and she shared some details about Ana's life with me. Ana was born and raised in Bogotá, Colombia. She was in her early thirties when she left for America with her husband, Alberto. Can you imagine? Leaving an entire way of life behind after thirty years? How many of us would have had the courage to do that? But Ana Peredo was a special woman. Jennifer explained to me that Ana spoke almost no English when she came to the States, but became fluent in the language in just a few years. What an amazing accomplishment. How many of us can speak another language? I have trouble with English."

I listen to Father Hill's words, and they give me a renewed sense of pride in my mother. Hearing someone else speak of how brave she was to leave her life in Colombia in hopes of finding a better one for herself and her future children, and how she went from knowing no English to speaking it fluently, reminds me of what a remarkable woman she was.

"Ana and her late husband, Alberto, who I had the pleasure of meeting before he passed away just over two years ago, were a triumph. They came to the U.S. with very little and slowly attained the American dream. Only a few years after their arrival, they had a beautiful home, two lovely children, and financial security. They believed in working hard, taking care of each other, and helping the less fortunate. Ana dedicated her life to being a homemaker—taking care of her children, the house, and her husband. She was an independent spirit and the past year, as her health started to decline, was difficult for her. But, by the grace of God, she was able to live on her own for all but the last weeks of her life.

"Ana had many friends in the community, which is obvious by the turnout here this evening. She'd be happy to know that so many friends and family members have come to say a final good-bye to her. We'll miss her, and we'll pray for her, and we'll take solace in the fact that she's now in a better place."

I hear a few people crying behind me as Father Hill finishes his address, and I wonder why I'm not. It was a moving talk, and I thought he did a really nice job for someone who barely knew Mom, but I guess I'm still numb at the moment. I'm still trying to make sense of my emotions. I've been so busy planning the wake and the funeral and the repast. I feel like all I've done is run around since Mom died, which I guess has been a pretty convenient way of coping with her death. If I keep myself busy enough, maybe I won't have to think about it at all.

After Father Hill leads us in a final prayer, everyone gets up and starts to mill about and finally make their way to the exit. I say a few final good-byes to people I haven't seen in ages and may never see again. I expect the funeral tomorrow to have a much lighter attendance with it being held in the morning on a weekday.

"I'll take Andrew home with me tonight . . . unless you want the company?" Mario asks.

"Why doesn't he stay with you tonight? I might appreciate some alone time," I say and bend down to Andrew's level. "You be good for Daddy. Give me a hug."

I grip Andrew tightly. "I love you, sweetie," I say and slowly release my grip. "I'll see you tomorrow."

I give Mario a quick hug as well, and he leads Andrew out the door.

"Why don't I give you two a minute?" Desma says to Tom and me. "I'll wait for you in the car."

For some reason Desma didn't think Tom and I could handle

driving ourselves to the funeral home, so she insisted that she bring us here.

"Okay," I say, as if I have any idea what Tom and I are going to do when we're left alone in the room with Mom's body.

While Desma follows the last of the guests out of the door, Tom walks away from me and gets down on his knees on the little cushioned kneeler next to Mom's casket. He bows his head, closes his eyes, and puts his hands together. My guess is that this is the first prayer Tom has said since he graduated Catholic high school twenty years ago. I watch him as he opens his eyes, stands up, and leans in and kisses Mom on the forehead.

"I'll wait for you outside," he says.

"No! Don't leave me here!" I want to scream at him, but instead I just nod my head.

When he's out of the room, and I'm completely alone, I walk up to the casket and look at Mom. I kneel down and bow my head, not so much to pray—more so I don't have to look at her when she appears so artificial, like a wax figure at Madame Tussaud's.

"I guess this is it, Mom. For once, you don't get to have the last word," I say out loud with a tiny little laugh. "I'll miss you. You were some kind of lady, Ana Peredo. Stubborn, critical, opinionated. But you were also kind, and caring, and always wanted the best for me. Who will I call every day now? Who's going to answer the phone, 'I'm not dead,' instead of 'hello.' What am I going to do with all the free time I'm going to have now that I'm not running you to the CVS to buy a box of Russell Stover chocolates?" I ask her, or myself, or whoever might be listening. "You realize I'm going to have to make that cumbersome hot chocolate for Andrew now that you're not around to do it anymore. You probably got him hooked on it just to aggravate me," I say, and, finally, for the first time since she died, I feel a lump in my throat and my eyes start to water. "I'll make the *arepas*, and *pandebonos*, and *sancocho* just like you taught me. I'll make sure people spell Colombia right,

Mom. I'll even make them change it if they spell it wrong on the board at Starbucks." I'm sobbing like a baby now. "Andrew will know all about you. Maybe I'll enroll him in some sort of Spanish program for kids. You'd like that, I bet." I try to catch my breath and wipe my eyes. "God, you drove me crazy, you know? You spent most of your life driving me crazy. Who's going to drive me crazy now?" I ask, and, as the words are coming out of my mouth, I feel a hand on my shoulder and turn around and see Desma standing there.

I stand up and turn around, and she takes me in her arms.

"Oh my God!" I call out. "Who's going to drive me crazy now? What am I going to do without her?!" I bury my head in Desma's shoulder, and I sob and I sob. She says nothing. She just holds me tightly and lets me cry—and boy do I cry. I cry so hard that my body shakes and my face quivers. The tears keep coming and coming, and it's several minutes before I'm able to collect myself and pull away.

"Wow," I say. "I don't know where that came from," I add, looking around the room for something to wipe my eyes with.

"Um . . . your mother just *died*, Jennifer. That's where that came from."

I laugh as I reach for a tissue from a box on one of the tables.

"Are you ready to go, or do you want some more time?"

"No, no. I'm ready," I say and turn and take a last look at Mom's body in the casket.

"Are you sure?"

"Yeah, I'm fine. Mom would want me to be strong. I can hear her now, 'Oh, Jennifer, for heaven's sake, stop those crocodile-tears. I'm in a better place. Now, about that outfit you're wearing . . .'"

Desma laughs.

"She was so strong," I say to Desma.

"I'm not surprised. You had to get it from somewhere."

I look at Desma and smile, and I can't help but think of my

own strength and that of my mother. As we walk out of the funeral home, suddenly the words of the nice waitress at Cracker Barrel come to mind:

> *I'm a mother, you're a mother. We take care of people.*
> *That's what we do.*

Epilogue

"Mario! The place is fantastic!" I say. Desma and I have just walked into his new restaurant. Thankfully, they dumped the "Gonads" concept and changed the name to Broncos. Instead of the waiters running around in Speedos like Mario had pitched to me when he first mentioned the restaurant several months ago, the staff is dressed in cowboy boots, very tight Levis, and snug suede vests with no shirt on underneath. Of course, they are all men, and they are all gorgeous. Mario says a few of them are actually straight.

The place is buzzing with people, mostly gay men, but I see a smattering of women in the restaurant, and there must be a straight man or two somewhere in the crowd. The bar area is packed, and, if we weren't one of Mario's VIP guests, we would have a long wait for a table in the dining room.

"I'm sorry I doubted you. It looks like the place is a success."

"Thanks, Jen. It's a lot of work, but things are going very well. We're exceeding all our goals."

Obviously they decided to go with a western theme—hardwood floors; dark paneling; rustic tables and chairs; cowboy hats, saddles, spurs, and paintings of the old west on the walls; and, of course, the obligatory mammoth *Brokeback Mountain* poster of Jake Gyllenhaal and Heath Ledger hanging behind the bar. Apparently, after the restaurant clears out, they turn the space into a nightclub, and Mario says the place is packed with gay men line dancing and doing the two-step.

"You don't have any female staff? *At all?*" Desma asks with a frown.

"Um . . . no."

"I think that's the idea, Desma."

"It hardly seems fair to hire only—"

"Not tonight, Desma," I say. "Just let it go."

"Why don't I take you to your table? There's going to be five of you altogether?"

"Yes. Desma and I . . . and Claire is bringing a date, and then a . . . a *friend* of mine is coming . . . Ben."

"Ben?" Mario asks as we follow him into the dining room. "I was wondering when you'd finally mention him to me."

"How did you know about him?"

"We share a son, Jen. Did you think Andrew wouldn't mention the man that you have apparently been spending a lot of time with?"

"I haven't been spending *that* much time with him," I say, and I guess I'm not really lying, but things are going well enough with Ben that I figured it was time to let Andrew meet him a few weeks ago.

"Whatever you say," Mario replies with a devilish grin while he sets some menus in front of Desma and me after we've taken our seats. "I'll check back in with you later. If anything is not absolutely perfect, please let me know," he adds and walks away.

Desma and I start looking over the menu, and before Desma has a chance to complain about the lack of vegetarian options, Claire shows up at the table with a handsome Filipino man.

"Hi," she says. "This is Julio."

I stand up to shake his hand. "Jennifer," I say. "How nice to meet you and match the face with the . . . I mean it's really nice to meet you." I'm trying to keep my eyes from diverting down to his crotch.

"I'm Desma," Desma says and shakes his hand as well. "We've heard a lot about you."

"Good things, I hope."

"Yes . . . well, *one* good thing anyway."

Claire smiles like a proud parent. "This place is hopping, girl," she says to me as they take their seats. "You should make Mario start paying you alimony and get in on some of this success."

"As long as he makes his child support payments, I won't push my luck."

"I believe this gentleman belongs to you." Mario says, reappearing at the table with Ben next to him.

"Ben. Hi," I say and rise from my chair.

"Hey . . . sorry I'm late. I got held up at work." He gives me a quick peck on the cheek with Mario looking on.

While I make the appropriate introductions, Mario scans Ben from head to toe and then looks at me, raises his eyebrows, and smiles as if to say, "You did good for yourself."

I smile back at him before he excuses himself to take care of other customers.

"Nice place," Ben says, sitting down next to me. "A little heavy on the testosterone, but nice."

My firm ended up going with Ben's company to implement a new personnel and accounting system, so Ben has been on-site at my office building about once a week, working out the final details. We went to lunch one day, about a month after Mom died and had a nice meal together, which led to more lunches. But for several weeks, we didn't take our relationship any further. I had so many mixed emotions after Mom's death, not to mention all the practical things to take care of, that I didn't really have the time or energy for anything more intense. But, eventually, we started having dinner together after work, which led to actual weekend dates. And I'm happy to report that things have been going well for us for the past month or so. We've been spending a fair amount of time together and have gotten to know each other on a deeper level. We really enjoy each other's company.

Although Andrew isn't thrilled about his mother dating someone other than his father, I think I've managed to balance the situation fairly well. I've been making sure that Andrew gets the attention he needs, and, thanks to a few outings to Chuck E Cheese's and the Rainforest Café with Ben and me, Andrew is warming up to Ben.

Andrew still asks about Mom on occasion, but he's grasped the fact that he's not going to see her again. I've been spending more time with him lately, particularly on the weekends. We go to movies and make lunch together. We play games and watch TV. Last weekend, the pool opened up for the summer, so I plan to take Andrew there as often as I can.

I got the news regarding my potential promotion at work about a month ago—I didn't get it. The partners ended up bringing in someone from outside the company to take over Claudette's position as Director of Human Resources for the Washington, D.C. office. Of course, I wasn't thrilled with the news, but dealing with my mother's decline and ultimate death has really helped to put things in perspective and made me realize what's really important in life, and I just accepted the news with grace and let it go. So I'll be an HR Generalist for a while longer—there'll be other promotions . . . other opportunities. I'm quite certain my being passed over for the promotion had to do with all the time I was out of the office after Mom had her stroke. If that is the case, so be it. I did what I had to do, and I wouldn't have done it any other way.

It's been three months since Mom passed, and I'm still struggling with the pain and the grief, and I've also been busy getting her estate squared away. She left Tom all her savings and she left me the house, which I really haven't done anything with yet. The mortgage was paid off years ago, so I'm only footing the bill for electricity, property taxes, and insurance. While that still amounts to a significant amount of money every month, I just haven't had the wherewithal to start sorting through her things and getting the place cleared out, so I can put it on the market. I've been back there a handful of times to check on the place, and it still breaks my heart to look at all the reminders of her.

I'm sure I'll have to get moving on clearing out the house sooner rather than later, but, for the time being, I'm just not giving it much thought.

It's still weird to get up on Saturday mornings, and know that there will be no trip to Fredericksburg later in the day to run errands with Mom. What's even stranger, is to know that, once I sell the house, I'll have no connection to the community in which I grew up and, after thirty-six years, no reason to go there anymore.

It's an odd and often sad feeling to no longer have parents . . . to no longer have a mother. I'm not sure I can call myself an orphan, but that's what I feel like. I certainly have a full life and plenty of people who care about me, but there will never be a relationship, tumultuous as it sometimes was, like the one I had with Mom. No one will love me the way she did, no one will nag me the way she did, no one could possibly ever be as stubborn—there will just never be another Ana Peredo—she was one of a kind.

It's June now, and I'm thankful for the warm weather. It was such a cold winter in more ways than one. But as hard as the past few months have been, I know they've made me stronger and that I learned a lot about myself. I was far from perfect in the way I handled my mother's declining health, and I made many mistakes, but I also know that I did the best I could. And I think Mom knew that I did my best before she died. I'll never forget the look on her face when she told me that she loved me, seconds before she stopped breathing—the look in her eyes will forever be emblazoned in my memory. Logically, I know she's dead, but she lives on in so many ways. I feel her presence whenever I put on her red sweater that I took home with me the night she died, I see her in myself and in Andrew. I think of her when I make her Colombian dishes like I promised her I would, and I hear her voice somewhere in the back of my mind as I go to sleep at night. I don't think she'll ever really be gone. Her memory will always be alive, and, one way or another, she'll always be with me.

GREAT BOOKS, GREAT SAVINGS!

When You Visit Our Website:
www.kensingtonbooks.com
You Can Save Money Off The Retail Price
Of Any Book You Purchase!

- **All Your Favorite Kensington Authors**
- **New Releases & Timeless Classics**
- **Overnight Shipping Available**
- **eBooks Available For Many Titles**
- **All Major Credit Cards Accepted**

Visit Us Today To Start Saving!
www.kensingtonbooks.com

All Orders Are Subject To Availability.
Shipping and Handling Charges Apply.
Offers and Prices Subject To Change Without Notice.